Foundation for Three

Montana Promises
Book 2

Vella Day

Dedication

To Carol Adcock-Bezzo. Thank you for letting me share your wonderful family stories.

Chapter One

Detective Thad Dalton didn't expect any trouble driving down Fourth Street at ten in the morning in Rock Hard, Montana. Regardless, he kept his gaze on the sidewalks for any suspicious behavior. The traffic was going at a comfortable speed, and all looked good, but that was when the shit tended to fly.

"Mind pulling into Dunkin' Donuts?" his partner asked as he dragged a fist over his eyes with a bit too much vigor. "If I don't down some caffeine, I'll fall asleep."

Thad shot Jeremy Warner a glare. Crap. Dark circles underlined his eyes. "You tie one on last night?" His partner loved to party. Hell, so did he, but not enough to affect his performance the next day. Their work required constant vigilance.

"A bit." Jeremy winced and slowly lifted his hand to rub his temple, as if a headache had already taken hold.

Thad worried Jeremy might never get his shit together. He was young, but he'd been a good beat cop before joining the Street Crime Unit. Thad valued loyalty and reliability above everything else in his life. He strove for it personally and expected it from his partner, and right now he wasn't a damn bit sure Jeremy could deliver.

Thad turned into the drive-through on Crenshaw and

drummed his fingers on the wheel while he edged the car forward. Once at the window, he ordered a medium-sized black coffee for himself and a jumbo one for his partner. "Douse the second one with cream, will ya? My partner here needs lots of sugar, too." Thad didn't want to think what Jeremy's insides looked like, but as long as he could outrun a criminal and shoot straight, Thad didn't much care.

Back on the road, he finished half his drink and set it in the cup holder just as his radio signaled. "There's a two-eleven in progress," Dispatch sputtered out. "First and Elm. Wilson's Electronics. Suspects are considered armed and dangerous. All available units respond."

"Fuck." His heart hitched as adrenaline raced through him. It was Chuck Wilson's place. Given the rundown area, good chance it was gang related. Since they were only a few blocks away, Thad pressed on the accelerator and shot up Ridgewood.

"Shit!" Jeremy dropped the coffee into the holder on his side and wiped his possibly burnt hand on his pants.

That couldn't have been helped. "Sorry. Hazard of being a cop."

"My fault." Jeremy flipped on the sirens and answered the call, saying they were only a few blocks away.

Thad cursed and blasted past a car going too slow. As he sped down the street, he kept watch at every intersection to make sure a vehicle wasn't pulling out. Every second that went by meant the thieves would be farther away and harder to catch. He skidded around the corner, hanging a left onto First.

"There," Jeremy shouted, pointing to two men running down the street both carrying what looked like pillowcases.

Seriously? Pillowcases? Thad searched the street for a getaway car, but no vehicles were parked nearby. Chuck burst out of his store, spotted them, and waved his arms, pointing at the perpetrators. As soon as the two alleged thieves ran past the bookstore, they ducked down an alley. Thad jerked the cruiser to the left to follow, but had to slam on his brakes when two dumpsters blocked his way.

"Damn it." Jamming the car in park, he and Jeremy both jetted out of the cruiser. "Go back around," Thad shouted. "Cut them off on the other end."

Sirens sounded from a block away, which meant he'd be halfway down the alley by the time the assist arrived. Given the speed of the thieves, Thad couldn't afford to wait for backup.

He drew his weapon, knowing the dangers of going in blind. Thad raced down the alley, stepping over cans, bottles, and a host of other trash. He counted only two men, but there could be others waiting around the corner. Neither man had a weapon in his hand, but that didn't mean they didn't have an arsenal stuffed in their pants. The dispatcher had stated they were armed.

"Stop! Police!"

No surprise they didn't mind his order and kept running. Thad's heart slammed against his ribs and the strain in his legs burned as he chased after them. The alley stunk not only of garbage but also of something he didn't want to identify.

Pumping his arms hard, Thad sprinted toward them, ignoring every ache and pain in his body. Thirty-four hadn't seemed old yesterday, but it sure felt ancient today. One of the men looked back over his shoulder. Shit. He was just a kid. Maybe eighteen or nineteen at most.

The two thieves came to the end of the alley, where it met Morrison Avenue, and slowed. Both men shot right, which meant Thad might not catch them before they ducked in some store and exited out the front.

Footsteps sounded behind him, but he didn't check to see

which uniform had his six. As Thad came closer to the intersection, the second kid dipped his hand in his pants, raised his arm, and took aim at something around the corner. His shot reverberated down the alley. Fuck. That was where Jeremy should be. A second later another shot rang out and the shooter fell.

Jeremy stepped into view, his weapon leveled at the kid, and shouted for the thief to stay down. Thad's pounding heart slowed. He prayed his partner hadn't been hit, but from Jeremy's fierce expression and steady arm, the first shooter had missed.

Ever vigilant in case the second thief came back for his friend, Thad continued up the alley, zigzagging his way. When Officer Nick Rodgers joined him, Thad motioned for Nick to stay to the right.

As soon as they arrived at Morrison, Nick's radio mic sounded. Luke, his partner, told him he'd caught the second thief and that there weren't any others.

Nick's shoulders sagged as he answered the call. "Take him back to the station. I'll catch a ride when I can."

Thad glanced down at the thief in the gray hoodie. The shoulder wound wasn't bleeding much, but the air was tinged with a sweet metallic smell he hated. The young man was cursing up a storm. Thad might have felt sorry for him, but most likely the robbery was for kicks. The kid would live and Chuck would get his stolen property back. As the adrenaline began to ebb, relief washed through him. Thad radioed for an ambulance and gave the necessary details to the dispatcher.

Jeremy had kicked the kid's gun off to the side, but Thad would bet his badge the thief had a few more weapons stashed on his body. Good thing Jeremy kept his gun drawn. If he hadn't, the boy probably would have used his other hand to retrieve another weapon.

Jeremy was visibly shaking, but that was to be expected after shooting someone—especially when it was his first time. Thad's gut churned at the uselessness of it all. After he donned his gloves, he read the kid his rights while he frisked him for weapons. As anticipated, Thad found two knives and a gun that he set off to the side.

"Hey. Careful," the downed boy yelled, his teeth gritted in pain. "It hurts like a motherfucker."

"Shut up, or I'll show you real hurt." The kid had no sense if he thought there wouldn't be any consequences for stealing.

Nick stepped closer. "You want to escort the guy to the hospital or should I?"

"I will." It was Thad's collar and this smacked of a street gang. He wanted to see how much the kid was willing to give up.

"Okay. Jeremy and I'll wait for the Crime Scene Unit to process the scene."

"Thanks."

The stolen merchandise lay sprawled on the sidewalk. Thad couldn't be certain, but it looked like a couple of tablets and some phones. *Jesus.* The perpetrator could have been killed over a measly few items.

After Thad cuffed the kid, he walked over to Jeremy, whose face was still white. It tore at his heart to see his partner go through this.

"Jeremy, remember you'll need to hand over your weapon for processing." His partner made eye contact then huffed out a breath. The resigned look made Thad ache.

"I know."

Thad had been through this routine twice before. To him, counseling was the hardest part.

Thad stepped over to the kid and asked him questions about his identity, the name of his partner, and which gang he belonged to, but the little thief refused to say a word. His tears had dried and he'd donned a belligerent look.

Thad carefully bunched the kid's sleeve over his wound that had begun to bleed again. "Hold your hand here and apply some pressure. The ambulance will arrive shortly."

The young man did as he was asked. "Fuck, man. That hurts." There went his bravado.

"Then you shouldn't have fired at an officer. What were you thinking?"

"Didn't want him catching me." The wounded man's lips pursed as he glared at Jeremy.

About five or so years ago, Thad had come across an innocent bystander shot to death. The gang member claimed he'd murdered the woman because he'd wanted to know what it was like to kill someone. Thad shook his head, pissed right now at society for having failed these kids. He'd give anything to find a solution to solve their need to steal.

Sirens sounded as an ambulance raced up Morrison. "Time to go." Thad reached into his pocket and tossed his cruiser's keys to Nick. "Catch."

Since Nick's partner had taken his vehicle to transport the second kid back to the station, Nick could use Thad's cruiser. They'd be able to leave as soon as the CSU arrived.

Thad stepped over to his partner and patted him on the back. "Good job." He smiled, hoping to blot out Jeremy's guilt over having shot a kid.

Two medical personnel rushed to the scene pushing a gurney.

"Hey," Thad said to Stone Benson, one of the paramedics. He and Cade Carter, a fellow detective at the Rock Hard PD, were now engaged to Amber Delacroix, a nurse at the hospital who Thad had met during an undercover assignment. "Heard congratulations are in order."

"They are indeed. Thanks." Stone nodded to the boy. "What do we have here?"

As Thad uncuffed the kid's hands and secured his uninjured wrist to the gurney, he told Stone what had gone down. The thief grumbled and spewed a long list of rather unimaginative words as Stone checked out the victim, and the EMT hooked the kid up to an IV.

Because the boy was in custody, Thad rode in the back with him. While Stone administered aid, Thad asked a few more questions, but other than finally confessing his name, the boy wasn't talking.

It didn't take long before the ambulance rolled up to the Emergency Room entrance. Thad escorted the thief inside and after calling his parents, he stayed with the injured boy until he was brought into surgery. Just as Thad was about to call someone from the precinct to come pick him up, his cell rang.

It was one of his friends in the Sheriff's Department, and the tension in his shoulders relaxed. "Tom. What's up?"

He doubted the call was about the shooting. The grapevine between the police and sheriff's department wasn't that good. This must be for social reasons. Thad often spent time with Tom and a group of other deputies playing darts and pool at Banner's. He smiled as he pushed open the hospital doors to step outside.

"I called to warn you out about a domestic violence call I had this morning." His tone came out serious, and Thad stopped. He shifted his weight, trying to ease the bit of soreness in his calf.

"Warn me about what?"

"Garrett McDonald beat up your ex-wife and then ran off. We can't find him."

"Shit." Thad didn't need this.

Garrett was now married to Peggy. Thad and she had divorced almost three years ago, and she'd married the loser a month later. Thad had tried to tell her the guy was a piece of crap, that he'd been accused of abuse twice by both of his previous wives, but had Peggy listened? Hell no. She might have cheated on Thad, but that didn't mean he wanted anything bad to happen to her. "She okay?"

"No. She's at the hospital. It's pretty bad, Thad. She asked for you."

He straightened. "Why?" Except for a brief encounter at the Fourth of July parade, he hadn't spoken with her since the divorce.

"I'm guessing she's turning to you because you're safe."

She didn't seem to care about safety when she fucked another man less than five years after they said their vows. Thad turned around and went back inside. As much as he wasn't in the mood to deal with her, he couldn't say no to a woman in need. "I'm here now."

"Peggy's in room 201."

He didn't want to stop by, but he would. "You said it was bad. Do you know the extent of her injuries?"

"I'm not a doctor, but when we tried to question her, it was too painful for her to talk."

A twinge twisted his gut. It was wrong for a man to hit a woman no matter the circumstance. "Thanks for letting me know."

Thad disconnected the call then took the elevator to see what his ex wanted to tell him. He wasn't sure what he'd say to her. That wasn't true. He wanted to tell her to get her act together. Find a job. Build some self-esteem, and leave Garrett McDonald.

Trying to brace himself for the next encounter, he went to her room. As soon as he stepped inside, his gut soured. He'd just seen a young kid gunned down today, but he hadn't been as sick as he was looking at her face. One eye was swollen shut, her lip cut, and her cheek was bruised.

"Peggy?" His voice caught.

She opened her good eye. He thought she tried to smile, but she immediately touched her lips. She leaned over, picked up a white board and a dry erase marker and scribbled on it. She held it up. "*Jaw broken.*"

He feared that might be the case. He pulled up a chair, telling himself he would not get sucked into her siren's call again. Been there done that. "You needed to tell me something?" She had asked for him. He hoped her injuries weren't life threatening. He couldn't handle that.

"*Garrett hit me,*" she wrote in letters that looked like someone three times her age had penned them.

"I'm sorry. Was he drunk?" Damn. He shouldn't have asked, as it was none of his business. "Never mind. Look, I'm sorry. I really am. When the doctors release you, you need to go the women's shelter."

She flinched. "Uh-uh."

Damn. Once the sheriff's department found her husband, Thad suspected she'd be crawling back to the bastard the moment he was released from jail. Her brows pinched, and he bet her lips would have puckered if she'd been able to move them better.

She scribbled more words and held it up. "*Garrett thinks I want to leave him for you. Watch out.*"

Was that what started their fight? Peggy probably just threw that in Garrett's face to piss him off.

"I appreciate the heads up, but I can take care of myself." He stood. "I'll stop by in a few days to see how you're doing." Thad turned back toward the door before she asked for something he couldn't deliver.

Once in the hallway, he'd taken only a few steps then halted. Fuck. Garrett McDonald was coming straight at him. Twenty feet. Now fifteen.

Chapter Two

"**S**top." Thad's hand hovered over his holster, his fingers itching to draw his weapon. "Garrett, you can't be here." A tight band wrapped around Thad's chest.

The man halted. His gaze darted right and left, and his lips curled in apparent disgust. "Fuck you, Dalton." He flexed his right hand, acting as if he was debating whether to go for a weapon that was probably hidden under his coat. He shifted his weight from one side to the other, agitation rolling off him in waves.

Peggy's husband's dark hair was matted to his head, and he hadn't shaved in what looked like days. Thad was too far away to check his eyes, but he wouldn't be surprised if they were bloodshot. With fidgety fingers, Garret lifted his hand closer to his body.

"Don't even think about it." Thad couldn't be positive Garrett was packing, but he had to assume he was. "Peggy's hurt bad. She needs her rest." Thad doubted anything he said would make a difference to this prick.

The door behind Garrett opened, but fortunately he didn't seem to notice or perhaps he didn't care. When Thad saw who it was, his heart stopped. Shit. It was Dr. Zoey Donovan, the woman who'd pretended to be his shrink during the sting operation to bring down the mercy killer. Her red hair flowed wildly about her shoulders, and her gaze was cast downward as she read something from the folder in her hands. He wanted to shout at her to turn around, but he didn't want to draw Garrett's attention her way.

Look up, Zoey. See the danger. Come on, come on.

Garrett jerked his head toward her. Faster than a lizard could capture a fly, he snagged her by the throat and dragged her close. Thad's heart lurched. The folder in her hands fluttered and papers fell from it, scattering onto the ground. She squeaked out a gasp and latched onto Garrett's wrists fighting to get loose. He tightened his hold, and her breaths came out faster. Wide eyed, Zoey whimpered, but she didn't scream.

Good girl. Keep calm.

She caught sight of him, and recognition dawned. When she mouthed, "Help me," her terror stabbed him in the gut.

Thad's training kicked into high gear, and he sifted through his options. Not wanting Garrett to think he had the upper hand, Thad jerked his right shoulder forward and widened his stance.

"Garrett, let her go," Thad stated in a slow, easy manner, not wanting to set him off even more. Thad held up his palms, hoping to make McDonald believe he wouldn't shoot, even though his weapon was clearly visible in his holster.

Halfway between him and Garrett, two doors across the hall from each other opened at the same time. A nurse and a doctor emerged. From the way they were looking straight ahead, they were oblivious to the hostage situation taking place fifteen feet from them. Before Thad could motion them back inside the rooms, Garrett pulled a gun from inside his coat, and propped his arm on Zoey's shoulder for support. Fuck.

Garrett aimed at Thad, and then swung the weapon around, pointing it at the doctor first, and then at the nurse. Thad's pulse skyrocketed as he tried to figure out the best course of action.

"No one moves, or I'll shoot." Garrett slurred the last few words, sounding drunk or possibly high. Either scenario was bad.

Thad wanted to tell Zoey not to move so as not to set Garrett off, but he didn't want to make the situation worse by shouting out commands. What he needed was a clean shot.

Just wait. Garrett would make a mistake. His kind always did.

Two soft clicks reverberated at the end of the hall behind Thad, indicating a door had opened and closed quickly. With any luck, whoever it was would contact security or RHPD—at least he hoped that person would.

Zoey's lips pressed together as she gritted her teeth. "Let go of me." She tried to wrestle out of the man's hold, but he pressed his shooting arm closer against her head, trapping her. Her mouth opened to gulp in air. She must be scared shitless.

Easy, Zoey.

Thad glanced at the two medical personnel who'd innocently entered the fray. Thankfully, both of the staff members had plastered their backs against the wall and remained still, their gazes darting between Garrett and Thad. He prayed neither decided to be a hero.

"What do you want, McDonald?" Thad figured he was here to take back Peggy. If he could keep Garrett talking, it might give security time to arrive.

"I came for my wife, and you can't stop me. I want you to stay away from her. She's mine."

Thad saw no reason to argue with him. "Her jaw's broken. You need to let the doctors fix her first." Garrett stepped forward with Zoey in tow.

In a slow, even motion, Thad raised his left arm away from his body. It might look like he was backing down, but his weapon was more accessible this way. "Let the woman go, and I'll do what you ask." *Or not.*

Peggy's husband's head shifted right then left, his jerky movements implying he was trying to figure out what to do. His jaw hardened a second before he swung the gun toward the nurse on one side and then at the doctor on the other. With Garrett temporarily distracted, Zoey struggled against the constraint. Garrett looked back at her and yanked his arm tighter across her throat. A gurgling sound escaped from her lips.

Thad wished like hell he could charge the asshole and beat the shit out of him, but attacking him with others close by would be stupid.

Zoey opened her mouth, probably to plead with him to do something, and all Thad could do was laser her with a stare to remain still. She narrowed her eyes and firmed her lips, acting as if he'd abandoned her. Her pain sliced him to the core.

The door behind Thad opened and a high-pitched grunt sounded. God damn it. He didn't have to look behind him to know it was Peggy. How she had the strength to get out of bed, he didn't know. From the way she'd held her pen, she was weak from all the drugs.

A slight thud sounded as if she'd hit the wall or worse the ground. In that one second, Garrett appeared to change his focus, and his arm loosened its hold around Zoey's neck.

Thad drew his weapon, cocked the barrel, and took aim. The sharp click was enough to cause Garrett to return his gaze to Thad. Garrett squinted, snarled, and shot. The loud blast from Garrett's gun reverberated off the hospital walls. The ache in Thad's arm didn't register for a long second, but when it did, his vision blurred, and world seemed to stand still. He refused to give in to the injury until he'd taken Garrett down.

"Move, Zoey," Thad shouted.

As if each frame of Thad's life moved in slow motion, Garrett's arm recoiled and his eyes blinked closed. Zoey lifted her foot and kicked the man's shin hard. He gritted his teeth and smashed Zoey in the head with the butt of the gun. She groaned and listed to the side about a foot. That shift gave Thad the window of opportunity he'd been looking for. He blinked to clear his pain-filled eyes and aimed carefully. His left arm shook from the effort, but he ignored the sharp ache.

Garrett swung his arm forward to get off another shot, but before he succeeded, Thad exhaled and pulled the trigger. His heart galloped, and he prayed he hadn't hit her.

Garrett dropped like a dead weight, taking Zoey down with him. Blood covered her side. Oh, shit. Was she hit? When Garrett's arm went slack, Zoey rolled off him. She tried to scramble to her feet, but she slipped on the blood and crashed down on her knees. Thad's heart nearly stopped when she whimpered. Hopefully her cry was from fear and not one of pain.

He wanted to tell her that Garrett wasn't getting up, that she was safe, but the words refused to form.

Seconds later, his brain cleared. "Everyone get out of here," Thad said, waving his uninjured arm. Keeping his gaze on the downed man, Thad's breaths came out fast. Blood gushed out of his wound.

As the others headed for safety, he stumbled toward Garrett and Zoey. Before he reached them, the doors on both ends of the corridor burst open, and a swarm of blue uniforms descended. He needed to make sure Zoey wasn't hurt, but as he turned to find her, several nurses blocked his view.

"Easy, Detective," said one of the male nurses. "Get him on the gurney."

Another nurse held the wheels steady as a third person helped Thad up.

He jumped back down. They could take care of his wound in a minute. "I need to see if Zoey is okay."

Cade Carter suddenly appeared before him. "Thad. It's okay. Let the staff patch you up."

He wasn't hurt bad. Was he? "Is Zoey okay?" If he hit her, he'd never forgive himself.

"Go with these nurses, and I'll find out."

Thad wanted to check on her, but as he tried to get past Cade, three sets of arms held him down and his world turned black.

✧ ✧ ✧

"I'm fine." Zoey Donovan held up her hands to prevent the nurse from fussing with her again. Only then did she notice how much effort it took to keep them steady, so she lowered her palms to her stained pants. "I'm just bloody."

Sarah, her nurse, dabbed Zoey's temple to clean her wound. "You have a contusion."

"I do?" Is that why her head pounded like she had a dozen people smashing her with hammers? Zoey batted the woman's hand away to assess the damage herself and pressed the side of her head. When she lowered her hand, she hadn't expected to see the sticky goo on her fingers. "Oh, my God. What happened? Did a bullet graze my head?"

She remembered that terrible man strangling her and Thad not allowing the creep to go somewhere, but the order of the events were hit and miss. Her stomach tumbled and her heart banged against her ribs at her lack of memory. Fuzzy images flitted across her brain.

"One of the nurses who was there said the man hit you with the butt of his gun. Did you black out?" Sarah pressed a cleansing pad again to the injury.

"I don't think so." There had been a nurse in the corridor? If she had blacked out, that would imply a concussion. Her stomach clenched, only now recalling that terrible man's rancid body odor and foul breath that smelled of alcohol. She wrinkled her nose at the memory. One minute the man was holding her hostage and the next a gun had gone off right next to her head. Her ears still rang from the deafening sound. "I should have dropped to the ground if I'd passed out, right?"

"If he was holding you tight, you might not have fallen."

Zoey rubbed her neck to ease the knot of tension that had gathered at the base of her skull. It was tender and probably bruised from where he'd held her. She searched her mind, but there were too many lapses. Now she understood what her patients who'd been in bad accidents had gone through.

Her mouth was dry from the anxiety. She chewed on her bottom lip and closed her eyes, hoping to recreate the incident. "After the gunshot, I remember the man who held me collapsed and took me down with him." She opened her eyes. "I was alert, though. At least I think I was. It all happened so fast." How many times had she heard that phrase before?

Sarah placed a bandage over the wound then patted her hand. "I'm going to schedule an MRI. I'll be right back." She stepped from the room and the door clicked close.

An MRI? Is it that bad? The air conditioning kicked on, and Zoey shivered. Her damp shirt clung to her. She groaned, partly from pain and the rest from frustration. She wanted to go home, soak in her new jetted tub, and forget this day ever happened.

What if her brain swelled though? If she was home, she might not be able to get help. At the frightening thought, she rubbed her palms over her closed eyes. Who the hell was that man and why had he grabbed her?

She slumped forward and rested her elbows on her knees. Why couldn't she remember everything? It was like someone had cut out part of her memory.

A light knock sounded and the door opened. The chief medical officer, Dr. Hector Sanchez, breezed in, concern filling his face. "Dr. Donovan. I just heard about what happened. Are you all right?" Pain laced his tone.

"Yes. I'm a bit bruised, but I wasn't shot."

He moved in close and tilted her face to the side as if he had X-ray vision and could see through the bandage. "Those bruises on your neck. Where did you get them?"

While he wasn't the head of the hospital, all administrators feared bad publicity. She detailed what had happened the best she could.

Dr. Sanchez shook his head. "If any of the staff here doesn't give you the best care, you let me know, okay?"

The man was so sweet to take time out of his day to come see her. "Thank you."

"Make sure you take off a few days and rest, you hear?"

Then she wouldn't get paid since she wasn't a hospital employee. She only rented the office space at LACE. "I will." However, trying to treat her patients with a head injury wouldn't do them any good.

He firmed his lips, spun on his heels, and left. She'd only seen the man at large hospital events, but he always came off as very sincere and kind.

"Knock, knock."

She looked up and thought Dr. Sanchez had returned, but it was her best friend's fiancé instead. "Cade!" Relief filled her. He might be able to shed some light on what happened after the doctors brought her down here. He was a detective for the Rock Hard Police Department, after all. "How did you get here so quickly?" He couldn't have driven from downtown that fast. Or had more time passed than she realized? "Were you having lunch here with Amber?" His fiancée did work at the hospital.

"You guessed it. Amber had just headed back to work when I got the call about the hostage situation." He studied her injuries. "How are you doing?"

Zoey pulled her soaked shirt away from her body to show him it wasn't stuck to a wound. "It's the other guy's blood."

"Good." Cade stepped closer. "Neck's red."

She struggled to take a full breath. "He had me in some kind of chokehold." She undid her top button to give her more air.

"What about that bandage on your head?"

She'd just told the story to Dr. Sanchez, but she bet she'd be retelling the series of events many more times before this was over. Her fingers shot to the wound to make sure it was real and not a dream. "He hit me with his gun."

Cade pulled out a pad and paper. "I've been asked to take the lead on this case. How about you tell me what you remember?"

She was happy he understood she might have some holes in her story. "I was on my way back to my office from the break room when... Oh, shit."

"What is it?"

Zoey glanced around, hoping she still had the information with her. "I was carrying a folder when the man grabbed me. I must have dropped it. I can't have anyone see those files." A rush of panic raced through her, causing her voice to rise with each word. A prominent doctor's career could be jeopardized if anyone read the contents.

She slipped for the exam table, but Cade held up a finger. He pulled out his phone and made a call. "Ethan, did you collect any papers on the floor next to McDonald? Good. I'm in the ER, room four. Can you bring them here when you get a chance?" He disconnected, looked up, and smiled. "All good."

At the near disaster, she let out a big breath and hopped back up on the table. "Thank you."

"Then what happened?"

"The man was waving his gun around, and when Thad tried to get him to release me, he became more agitated. Then I heard a shot. Or maybe it was two shots. I can't remember."

The nurse returned with a clean pair of scrubs. She halted and glanced between Zoey and Cade. "Oh, I didn't know you had company."

He held up a hand. "I'll catch up with Zoey later."

"Thanks, Cade." Having him here, even if it was to ask questions, helped settle her.

Sarah set the clean scrubs to next to her. "I thought you might want to wash up. These look like they'll fit you."

"They'll be perfect." Zoey tried to unbutton her blouse, but her fingers shook too hard. She disliked asking for help, but she needed to change worse than anything. "Can you help me? I'm sorry. My fingers don't seem to be working. They're cold."

"Sure."

Zoey took off her shirt with Sarah's help, and her mind wandered back to when she'd first met Thad. He'd been covered in stage makeup to look like a dying cancer patient. After the sting operation ended, he'd stopped by to thank her for her role, but he was in and out so fast she hadn't had time to find out much about him. He'd intrigued her, though. She'd hoped he'd call after that, but he never did.

"Zoey?" The nurse held out the wet cloth for her to take.

She'd spaced out. "Sorry."

Zoey wiped her chest and arms the best she could while Sarah cleaned her back. Then she changed into the clean scrubs. Even if Zoey could get the blood out of her clothes, she didn't want to be reminded of this day. Ever. She dumped everything but her shoes in the trash.

After waiting another hour, a technician showed up to escort Zoey to get the MRI. By the time the image was taken, her stomach was growling something fierce. She'd missed lunch, but she still had to wait for the results of the scan before she could leave.

After what seemed like forever, the doctor stopped by. "Good news. The MRI shows no damage."

"Fantastic."

"Physically, you'll recover, but you've suffered quite an emotional trauma. I'm no shrink, but you should consider seeing someone for it."

"I will. Thank you. Am I free to go?"

"Yes, but check back with us in a week."

Finally. "I will." She was a little shaky and a lot achy, but on the whole, she was good. For the sake of closure, she needed to thank Thad. First, though, she needed to go home and change.

As soon as she walked out of her room toward the bank of elevators, she expected the relief to help calm her. Only it didn't. Now that the adrenaline had left her body, reality was seeping in. She could have died.

Zoey pressed the elevator button to go up to her office, but it appeared to be stuck on the fifth floor, so she hit it a few more times.

"There you are," Cade said, striding across the hallway. "Remember anything else?"

"No. I'm still processing." Or else she'd shoved the incident to the back of her mind.

He nodded, looking as if it was commonplace for a person to need time. "That's understandable."

"I'm surprised you're still here."

"I had to check on Thad."

"Check on him? Why?"

"You don't remember? Thad was shot."

Chapter Three

Upon hearing the terrible news, Zoey's stomach tumbled and the blood rushed from her brain. As her knees started to buckle, Cade grabbed her shoulders. "Zoey?" The hard pressure brought her back to awareness.

She inhaled and locked her knees. "I'm okay. I was a little light-headed for a moment." She ran her hands down her thighs to dry her palms. "Thad was really shot? I thought he was wearing a vest."

Why didn't she remember him getting hit? Perhaps having the gun go off so close to her head had splintered her memory. Or else the event had been so traumatic, she'd chosen to block out the horror. She prayed once the adrenaline left her body, everything would come flooding back.

"He was." Cade nodded to the padded bench across from the bank of elevators. "You want to sit down?"

"No, I'm good." She drew on her professional demeanor and straightened her shoulders, but her neck sent out a rebellious ache. "How is he? Will he be okay?" She worked hard to keep her voice even, not wanting to admit she wasn't in the best of shape.

"He should be out of surgery any time now."

Guilt swamped her that he'd taken a bullet for her. "Where

was he hit?"

"About here." Cade placed a hand right below her elbow.

While an arm injury wouldn't be life threatening, it could affect how Thad did his job. If the bullet hit his elbow, though, the recovery time could be long and painful. She prayed he'd heal quickly.

"Let's find a seat in the waiting room." Cade led her down the hall. "How about you rest here, and I'll see if I can find out when Thad will be out of surgery?"

"Okay." Her head pounded and chills raced through her as the images of what happened briefly surfaced.

Before Cade had taken more than a few steps, his partner Ethan, who she'd met once before, rushed toward them, waving something in his hand.

He handed her a folder—her folder—the one she needed back. If it meant Thad would be okay, though, she'd have traded it in a heartbeat.

"Dr. Donovan, I'm sorry I took so long to get this back to you. I was delayed."

"That's okay. Thank you so much for retrieving it." She ran her fingers over the red streaks covering the outside of the Manila folder.

"I tried to clean it up." Ethan looked sheepish, acting as if it was his fault he'd returned it in less than pristine condition.

She shook her head at his guilty response. "It's perfect."

Cade motioned with his head toward the two doors at the end of the hallway. "I'm going to check on Thad's condition."

Ethan stabbed his fingers through his hair as if he, too, was overly worried. "Hartwick just called. I've got to get back. Text me when you know something."

"Will do. I'll see you at the station as soon as I finish up here."

Ethan nodded to her and then took off.

As Cade headed toward the nurses' station, Zoey hugged her folder, more for comfort than anything. Her hands shook and a strong ache squeezed her chest. To keep her mind off poor Thad, she glanced inside to make sure all of her notes were there, but she closed it when it failed to hold her interest. Everything that had happened still hadn't sunk in. Her foot tapped out a beat while she waited for Cade's return.

She still couldn't believe Thad had been shot. She'd never be able to live with herself if he didn't fully recover. When Cade returned a few minutes later, she jumped up and searched his face for some answers. The tension around his eyes appeared to have softened. "How is he?"

"Thad's out of surgery. I spoke with his doctor. He said nothing vital was hit, and that Thad is in recovery now."

She blew out a big breath in relief. "When can I see him?" Zoey hadn't socialized with him outside the hospital, but when they'd talked during his undercover work, she'd seen a good man, a man who cared. She needed to thank him for what he'd done for her. If he hadn't taken down that horrible person, she might have died. Probably would have. Her head throbbed anew at the thought.

"In about half an hour." Cade looked over at the snack machines. "Get you something to drink? I sure could use a coffee."

That was sweet of him to ask. "A diet soda, please?" Even though she was jumpier than a fish out of water, she needed the caffeine.

Zoey was about to grab her purse to find some change to give him when she remembered she'd never made it back to her office to pick up her bag. Cade returned with not only a drink, but a pack of crackers for her. Amber was a lucky woman to have such a nice man.

"Thank you." She glanced at the clock to see how long it had been since Thad's surgery. He'd be groggy for a while, but she wanted to look in on him. After taking only a few sips, Zoey stood too quickly and her temple ached.

Cade jumped up, concern lacing his eyes. "Are you okay?"

Not really. "Yes. I want to bring Thad something." Her fingers worried the hem of her top. "What would he like?"

"I imagine you being there will be enough."

That was nice of him to say, but she wanted to get Thad a thank you gift as a small token of her appreciation. No gift could ever be enough, though. The man had been a hero.

Think. He was a runner, so candy was out of the question. Flowers would probably be dumb. A macho guy wouldn't want them. There had to be something she could find. "I'll go check."

She wanted to visit the store not only for the gift but because she was too nervous to sit. After a quick detour to her office for her wallet, she headed back down to the first floor. For a few minutes, she wandered around before deciding on a stuffed lion. It reminded her of Thad. He acted tough, but inside he was a softy.

As she stepped to the cash register to pay, she spotted an array of balloons. Zoey picked one that just said, "Get Well." It wasn't original, but it represented her wishes.

Armed with her gifts, she returned to the waiting room to find Cade on the phone.

As soon as he spotted her, he ended the call. "I just checked. Thad's out of recovery and in room 609." His lips tightened, as if he debated saying more. He then waved his cell. "Seems I'm needed at the station. Say 'hi' for me."

She was a bit disappointed he wouldn't come with her, but

she understood duty called. "I will."

Zoey made her way up to the surgical floor. Thad's door stood open, so she stepped inside without knocking. His eyes were closed, but his breathing appeared even. An IV stand was next to the bed, and a tube containing saline entered his right arm. Considering he probably had lost a lot of blood, his color looked quite good though she might be comparing him to when he'd worn the stage makeup to create an appearance of looking near death. She debated dropping off her gifts and leaving, but she really wanted to speak with him.

Like she had a month ago when she was his pretend therapist, Zoey pulled up a chair near the bed. "Thad?" She kept her voice soft in case he was asleep.

He cracked open an eye. His lips lifted but not enough to make a smile. "Hey. You're safe." His voice sounded hoarse and a bit weak.

He was worried about her? "You're the one who was shot."

The ventilation clicked on and it sent the balloon bobbing. Only then did she remember she was still holding it, along with the lion. She pushed back her chair and stood.

"I, ah, brought you these." She rushed over to the dresser across from his bed and tied the end of the balloon to the handle. She returned to the nightstand and placed the lion on top.

He glanced at the stuffed animal. "Roar." He smiled and her heart pinged.

She laughed, perhaps a bit too loudly. *Calm down.* Zoey tried to think of him as another patient and not as someone who intrigued her, but she couldn't. He'd been so strong in her time of need that she was drawn to him.

Thad closed his eyes, looking like he was fighting drugs and fatigue. Without the stage makeup, he was a very handsome man. His brown hair was cut military short, and his nose had a cute little bump in it. A one-inch scar sliced across his chin, which gave him a tough boy look that reminded her of Harrison Ford. What she remembered the most about the time she'd spent with him was how much she liked his eyes. They changed color depending on the light—sometimes a sea green and at other times a warm toast.

He wet his lips and his breathing increased.

"Do you want some water?" The pitcher sat on a side table where he couldn't reach it.

He opened his eyes and let out a breath. "That would be nice."

Happy to have something to do, she poured him a glass. His bed was elevated, so he was able to drink without lifting his head. When she held the cup to his lips and tilted the straw, he took it from her, acting like having a nursemaid would be worse than another bullet. He groaned on the first sip even though he'd used his good arm.

Concern rushed through her, and she leaned forward. "Are you in pain? Do you want me to call the nurse?" She removed the cup from his fingers and set it aside.

He studied her injury. "What happened to your head?" He hadn't answered her question, and the avoidance told her a lot.

"It's nothing."

"Garrett hit you. I remember now." His brows pinched then he pressed his lips together as if he was working hard not to let the ache get to him.

"Maybe I should leave. You need to rest."

He grabbed her hand. "No." His response came out quickly.

Okay. He wanted her here. She wanted to be with him, too. "Did the doctor say how long you had to stay in the hospital?"

"Too, ah, long." He winced and blew out a breath.

"You sure you don't want me to call the doctor?" Had his wound reopened? No blood appeared on the bandage.

"No."

She wouldn't do anything against his wishes. Perhaps she brought him comfort. Being alone after the shooting had to be terrible and talking about it might help him heal. *It'll help me heal, too.* "I'd like to hear what really happened in the hall. My memory's a bit fuzzy."

He grunted again, either from pain or for having to relive the moment. "I'm sorry you were caught in the middle. Garrett McDonald is an unstable man."

"The way I look at it, being there was bad karma." She'd often spoken to her patients about how bad things happened to good people. It was the way of the universe.

Then why do I feel that if I'd been less self-absorbed in my work, I would have seen what was going on and been able to react?

He glanced down at their entwined fingers and shook his head. "When I saw you, my heart dropped to my stomach. I could only imagine what went through your mind."

Speaking seemed to require too much effort for him. He probably wanted her to talk, but she wasn't used to being on the patient side. It didn't feel right, but she owed him. "Can I just say that when that McDonald person grabbed me, sheer terror filled every crevice of my body? I couldn't breathe. I mentally raced through every psych book I'd read to come up with what to do, but I blanked."

"You had every right to be scared."

She was happy he didn't dismiss her anxiety. "When I saw you, it was as if the world slowed. I couldn't figure out why you were in this standoff with this man." A tear brimmed on her lid, and she swallowed past the lump in her throat. Her chin trembled as the horror came back in full force, and the skin around her neck tightened at the memory of her captor's callused hands on her throat. "Scared didn't come close to what I felt. Losing that much control petrified me."

Thad released his grip but kept his hand on top of hers. "Being overpowered can give even the strongest person a feeling of helplessness."

Helpless. Powerless. Total fear. He understood. "Yes. I wanted to do something, but the more I struggled, the harder he choked me."

"You were brave, Zoey. You kept your cool. That was what saved you."

He had it all wrong. The words seemed to rush out before she could contain them. "No. You saved me. I was terrified when the shot rang out and felt warm liquid all over my arm and down my back. I thought I was hit."

A small smile appeared but only briefly. "You are something else, Zoey Donovan. Something else, indeed. Most women would have screamed and done something that would have set McDonald off. But not you."

His compliment had her face heating. "Inside, I was anything but cool. Trust me. Having you there gave me hope. I'll never be able to repay you."

"Aw shucks, honey." His eyelids fluttered close and he panted out a few breaths. "Some things are worth fighting for."

Her pulse soared. Did he mean it? She didn't dare ask. When they'd spoken every day for those ten days at the hospital, she'd felt this intense connection, but he'd never followed up, and she chalked it up to wishful thinking.

Zoey closed her eyes for a moment to regain her composure. Her body kept switching from being too hot to being chilled, making it hard to think. She forced herself to don her professional demeanor to keep on an even keel. In that space, she was safe.

She returned her thoughts to his needs. "Is there anything I can do for you? Do you need me to feed your fish while you're here or take your dog for a walk?"

He winced as if there were a lot of things he'd need to take care of but didn't dare ask. "No. Don't have time for animals. My roommate will see to every…"

His lids finally gave up the fight and slid closed. A soft snore escaped, and she had this insane urge to touch his face. But she didn't. She feared he might wake and ask her why she was caressing him. For that, she'd have no answer. So she watched him sleep instead. As much as she probably should go home, being with Thad was helping calm her. For more than half an hour, she stayed while he rested, absorbing his strength.

Finally, she accepted it was time to go. It wasn't because she didn't want him to find her there when he woke, it was because a powerful fear was building inside her. She had no doubt that as soon as she walked out that door, the memory of what happened would come back and strangle her.

Chapter Four

Before Zoey even stood, a tear leaked out. *Zoey Elizabeth Donovan. Do not cry.* She was a grown woman for goodness sake.

As she swiped away the moisture, Thad's hospital door squeaked open, and Zoey smacked a hand on her chest.

A nurse she didn't recognize came in. "Excuse me. I need to check Mr. Dalton's vitals."

Thad opened his eyes, but they didn't appear very focused. "You're still here." Only one side of his mouth lifted.

"Yes, but I need to go. Your nurse has big plans for you." Zoey almost smiled when he grunted. "I'll stop by tomorrow."

When she squeezed his hand, grief welled inside her at seeing him this way. Even when he'd been doing the sting operation, underneath all that makeup, and despite the moaning and groaning he'd been required to do, he'd been vital, strong, in command. Now he was in pain, and it hurt to see him work so hard to deny what happened.

As if chased by demons, Zoey rushed out. Once in the hallway, the walls pressed in on her. She had to get out of the hospital, even if it was only until tomorrow when she returned to work. Her goal right now was to soak in her new tub while drinking a glass of wine, and then cook a feast for one. Without a plan, she'd crumble.

One stroke of luck was that after weeks of having a crew in her house, Banks Construction had promised all the work would be finished by today—work that included a new master bath and a state of the art kitchen.

As she headed home, she repeatedly checked the rearview mirror, praying some cop didn't pull her over for speeding. She slowed a bit, and the image of Garrett McDonald surfaced. Her throat constricted. She'd been scared. Bad. Even after that admission, she didn't feel much better, in part because she still ached for Thad.

Zoey took a corner too fast and the blood-streaked folder she'd been carrying bumped against her leg. It contained her session notes with Kara Molloy, a cardiac surgery physician assistant, whose story had deeply affected her. Too bad Kara's tale made Zoey feel helpless, too—similar to when Garrett McDonald was choking her. That was why she hadn't been paying attention when she walked through the halls this morning. Zoey had been trying to find a way to tell Kara's tale to the hospital authorities. If it didn't violate her therapist's code of ethics, she would have run to HR herself and insist someone investigate her patient's claim of another doctor's misconduct. The dilemma of confidentiality and ethics still tore at her.

Zoey stopped for a light that remained red forever. She tapped her fingers on the wheel. The traffic was bad already, and it wasn't even rush hour yet. "Change, light!" *Christ.* She was never edgy, but the attack and Thad's injury had shaken her.

Kara Molloy had painfully and tearfully told Zoey about the bullying that went on in the operating room. While Zoey had heard rumors, no one else had ever given details.

Someone behind Zoey honked, and when she moved her foot to the accelerator, the car lurched forward with more power than she'd intended. Damn. When the entrance to her neighborhood came into view, she blew out a breath and turned onto her street. Zoey was dirty, tired, and hungry—a bad combination, especially since she'd only eaten those crackers Cade had bought her. No wonder she was at her wit's end.

As soon as she pictured relaxing in her tub, the tension in her shoulders lessened—that was until she spotted the construction truck in her drive. "Are you kidding me? You're supposed to be done! Why can't you people do what you claim?" Her knuckles gripped the wheel so hard her nail beds turned white.

Her outburst almost scared her. She never should have had the kitchen and bathroom done at the same time. The delays had been a nightmare, but that was what she got for buying a really old home.

Be honest. She was distraught over the attack, and merely disappointed the renovation hadn't been done.

After cutting the engine, she grabbed her purse and folder and got out. The key snagged in the front door lock, and she was tempted to just ring the doorbell instead of dealing with it. Just then, the key slid in and she pushed open the door. Instead of hammers pounding and noisy nail guns reverberating off the walls, silence met her. Someone had to be here. That truck in her driveway and her alarm system glowing green confirmed it. "Hello?"

Her plan was to thank the guy and then ask him to leave—politely, of course.

She waited. No answer. A faint humming came from down the hallway, and she edged toward the sound. The person had to be in her master bath—just where she wanted to be.

When Zoey pushed open the door, the sight of a tight ass bent over her newly-installed jetted tub almost took her mind off her troubles. From the length of his legs, the man was tall. At least six feet. He was kneeling, polishing the porcelain bath, and her mind shot to her last two boyfriends, Mark and Dave. Sure as hell, neither one of them had ever cleaned a bathroom.

She'd had a ton of workmen through her house, but she didn't recognize this guy. "Excuse me?" Regardless if he looked fine from the back or not, he had to leave.

The worker wore ear buds, which was probably why he hadn't responded and just kept cleaning. She tapped his shoulder. The man turned his head, removed the buds, and smiled. Her heart stuttered.

He jumped up and wiped his hands on his jeans. "Sorry. I didn't hear you come in. I wanted to have this all cleaned up before you got home, Ms. Donovan."

She had arrived an hour earlier than usual. "You would be?" That came out rude. "I'm sorry. I've had a really bad day." He wouldn't have any idea what had transpired.

"Oh, shit. Sorry." He held out his hand and despite his tanned face, he flushed. "Pete. Pete Banks. Of Banks Construction."

The owner. To her knowledge, he'd never stopped by before. She shook his hand, but as soon as their palms touched, he let go. Perhaps he could tell his hand was still damp.

A bit embarrassed for him, Zoey nodded to the tub. *Stay calm. He'll leave soon.* "It looks wonderful. I can't wait to relax in it." *As in now.*

He stepped back. "Go ahead. I'm done. I just have a few more things to finish up in the kitchen and I'll be out of your hair."

"You're not done in there either?" *Stop it.* It wasn't his fault.

He tossed her a sheepish grin. "I just need to grout the last few feet of the backsplash. That's all." He nodded to the stack of candles still in their wrapper. "I was about to set them around the edge. I wanted it to be a surprise."

It was a surprise. It was nice even. "They're not pink." Her irrational behavior caused tears to drip down her cheeks, and she swallowed back a sob.

"Ms. Donovan. Are you okay?"

"Why wouldn't I be okay?" The tears fell and she wrapped her arms around her waist to keep from throwing up. It was like someone else had invaded her body, and all reason had disappeared. No one cried over beige candles.

Pete grimaced. "Ah, how about you sit down?" He grabbed a towel off the rack, folded it, and placed it on the edge of her new tub.

He guided her over there and helped her ease down. "I'm fine."

On one knee, Pete knelt in front of her. "I beg to differ, ma'am. Your hands are shaking something fierce, your nose is red, you have a bandage on your head, and... I could go on if you like."

She didn't need him to detail what a mess she was. "A man I knew was injured today protecting me." Why did she blurt that out? She didn't know this guy. "And I could have died."

Pete dropped onto his heels. "I'm so sorry. Want to tell me about it?"

A huge sob bubbled out of her, one that was both unexpected and violent. Pete straightened and reached out, almost as if he thought she'd fall.

"I'm good." That was a lie, and he probably could tell that. When she was able to breathe, she told him—in fits and starts—about how she hadn't been paying attention when she was walking down the hospital corridor this morning. "The next thing I knew, this man grabs me." Bile rushed up her throat, and she rubbed her neck.

Pete placed a hand beside her. "Inhale. That's good. You must have been scared shitless."

His soothing tone helped. In the retelling of the event, more memories had surfaced—ones she needed to deal with. "I was. When the two gunshots rang out, the man holding me fell, and I tumbled, too. If I'd been able to get out of his grasp sooner, the cop could have taken him down before being hit." There. She'd said it. She'd been the cause of Thad's injury. Her vision swam, and she rubbed her hands over her slightly bruised knees.

"It's not your fault."

He'd hesitated. He must know it had been. "It was." The tears came in full force now, dripping into her mouth and down her chin. This time she didn't bother to wipe them away. Pete yanked on the toilet paper roll and handed her a wad. She took his offering and dabbed her eyes and chin. "Thanks."

"I have a friend who's a cop," Pete said. "He's told me a lot of stories. Trust me on this. You did nothing wrong." Pete nodded to her face. "Did you bang your head when you fell?"

Her chin trembled as the pain of the horrific memory sliced through her. "No. My captor smashed the end of his gun into my face." The blunt force trauma could have done some serious damage, but she'd been lucky.

Pete rocked back onto his heels, stood, and held out his hand. "Come with me. You should be lying down. I'll get you something to drink."

She liked the drink part. Pete Banks was a kind man. He also had a strength that she appreciated. Between the ache in her head and the grumble in her stomach, she wasn't sure she was a good judge what was best for her anyway. "Okay."

Once in the living room, he placed a few pillows on one end of the sofa and then made her sit down. "Lean back. I'll get you that drink."

"There's diet soda in the fridge." With him taking control, she didn't have to think. Pete returned with two aspirin and her drink. Wine might have been more soothing, but her headache would have accelerated, not to mention mixing drugs with alcohol would have been stupid.

"Thank you."

He placed a dishtowel on the seat across from her and sat down. "Do you happen to know the name of this cop?" Before she could respond, his cell rang. He pulled it out, glanced at the number and stood. "I need to take this. He never calls during work hours."

"Go right ahead."

"What's up, dude? You what? Fuck. Where? How bad?" Pete glanced at her then walked into the kitchen.

✧   ✧   ✧

Pete did not want to leave Zoey Donovan alone, not when she was this highly emotional and hanging on by a thread, but Thad had been shot. Fuck. Pete had been so focused on what Zoey was saying that he hadn't thought to ask if "her" cop had been Thad. Pete's roommate dealt with gangs, not abusive husbands. "You okay, man?"

"It was a scratch. Left arm. Doc said it didn't hit anything vital. I was lucky."

From the way Thad was working hard to have this conversation, it was worse than he was letting on. "How long will you be there?" Perhaps he needed a ride home if the wound was that superficial.

"Two days tops."

Shit. It had been serious. "You want me to come over now?" Pete would go, but he wasn't convinced Zoey didn't need him more. "Zoey Donovan was the woman you were defending, right?"

"How did you know?"

"It's her house I'm renovating."

"She okay?" Thad's words were a bit slurred as if he was on pain pills.

His roommate didn't need to be obsessing over her. "She's good. How's Garrett?"

"Alive."

Visiting hours were over at eight. Unfortunately, he knew that because last year he'd visited Thad after he'd been in a knife fight with a kid. That injury required about ten stitches. Being a cop wasn't easy.

A woman's voice sounded in the background. "Shit. Another fucking nurse," Thad said, his voice a whisper.

Now Thad sounded like his old self. "I'll let you go. I'll take good care of Zoey. See you tomorrow."

Pete needed to let her know that he and Thad were roommates. When he walked back into the living room, her eyes were closed and her breathing raspy. She'd only sipped her drink.

He needed to make sure she was okay first, and then he'd tell her about Thad. "Zoey?" Her eyes sprang open. "Would you like me to fix you something to eat?" Perhaps if she ate, her energy level would improve, though she might not appreciate him cooking in her house. Didn't matter that he'd helped install all the cabinets and put in the new appliances.

She sat up, licked her lips, and then placed a hand on her stomach. "I'm hungry, but I don't feel like eating." She shook her head as if confusion was clouding her vision. "That doesn't make any sense, does it?"

"Sad to say, it does. Would you like to take a soak in the tub while I order some take out?" That way she wouldn't have to worry about him touching her things.

Her jaw slightly dropped as if no one had offered something like that before. "I..."

He waited for her to finish her sentence. "You what?"

"That sounds perfect. How about Chinese?"

He was more of a Mexican taco kind of guy, but he was flexible. "Wang's Chinese Buffet work for you?"

"Sure. Anything."

She implied she'd eat whatever he ordered. From his phone, he looked at the menu and called something in. A return text stated the food would arrive in forty-five minutes. "There'll be here in less than an hour."

"That's great. You look worried," she said. "Was it bad news on the phone?"

Time to tell her.

Chapter Five

Zoey studied Pete's face. Where he'd been in control a moment ago, his cheeks had suddenly paled, and he appeared conflicted.

"That was Thad," Pete said.

Thad wasn't a common name. "Thad Dalton?"

"Yes."

Her stomach cramped. Why would Thad be calling her construction guy? They must be friends, but now wasn't the time to figure out the exact connection. What was important was if something had happened since she left the hospital. "Is he still okay?"

"He told me about being shot."

She drew her knees up to her chest and wrapped her arms around them. "Had I known you two were friends, I would have mentioned his name."

Pete paced in front of her and stabbed a hand through his hair. "You couldn't have known. Actually, we're roommates."

Thad had never mentioned Pete, but Thad's cover was that he was married. "How about I get you something to drink?" Not only did she want to return the favor, she got the sense he didn't plan on staying around to eat with her, and she wanted him to.

He looked to the side as if he didn't know his next move. "Sure."

She stood, and as she headed to the kitchen, he followed. "Beer or soda?"

"I'd love a beer. Thanks." She handed him one from the fridge.

Then, as if it were totally natural, Pete slid onto one of the new high chairs that was positioned on opposite sides of the large center island. "It's just that the damn fool drives me crazy," Pete said. "He takes too many risks in my opinion."

"All policemen seem to take risks, but it wasn't like Thad asked the man who'd grabbed me to shoot him." She slid onto a seat across from him. "What *exactly* did he say?"

"Thad told me that he took a bullet to the arm, and that you were the woman who'd been held hostage."

"How did he sound?" She hoped Thad hadn't had a relapse.

She had yet to wrap her head around the fact that they knew each other. What were the odds? Hell, probably pretty high. It was a fairly small town.

"Tired."

"Did he talk about how he was feeling?"

"No."

His one-word responses weren't helpful. "Was he calling because he needed you to visit him in the hospital?" Thad was his friend. Pete should stop by.

"I'll see him tomorrow." A cute smile filled his face as he looked off to the side. "I'll bug him so much, he'll heal faster just so he can leave."

Those two seemed to have a good bond. "Is there anything I can do?" If she kept busy, the elusive evil ether swirling in her brain might disappear.

"Do?" He pressed his lips together and slightly shook his

head. "I can't think of anything." His cell rang again and he whipped it out of his pocket. Instead of the concern she expected, a bit of frustration flashed across his face. "It's my former partner, Alex. Excuse me." He slipped off his chair. He tapped the button and answered it, then walked into the living room.

He kept his voice too low for her to hear. Because her drink was in the living room, she retrieved another one from the fridge.

He returned a minute later. "Once again, I apologize."

"No need. Do you have to leave or something?"

"No. Alex just needed some information. The drainage system on one of my projects wasn't installed correctly. It's an unexpected expense, and he wanted to know what I wanted him to do about it. I told him to fix it. Something like that can sink a project. Literally." A quick smile appeared then disappeared.

"He's at the office? I thought you said he was your *former* partner."

"It's a long story. And not very interesting." He kicked back his beer.

"I'm a good listener." She thought that would get another smile out of him, but maybe he didn't know what she did for a living.

"You asked." He glanced to the ceiling. "I don't know where to start."

She'd rather hear about him and Thad, but understanding his connection to Alex would be good, too. "How about when you met?"

"That's easy. I met Alex when we were eight. His dad was my father's gardener." He studied her, perhaps to see if she'd react to the fact that his family was well off. She didn't. "My father is a bit, ah, stuck up. You see, Dad's a lawyer. A very successful lawyer. Hired help was *beneath him*."

Ouch. The name registered. "You aren't Russell Banks's son are you?" Of Banks, Emery, Caldwell, and Pearson.

Now his face reddened for real. "The one and only. Just so you know, if you ever run into dear old Dad, my family calls me Parker instead of Pete." He scrunched his nose. "But I go by my first name."

She mentally said his name and almost giggled. "Peter Parker. You're Spider—"

He held up his bottle. "I know. Trust me, I know. But Pete isn't as ostentatious as Parker. If anyone other than my family calls me Parker or Spiderman, well, let's just say he'll be singing in the choir."

She did enjoy his ability to laugh at himself. "Let's go back to your father's actions toward the help. Are you implying your dad was a bigot?"

"Totally. He won't deny it either."

That was a shame. Pete seemed to be the opposite. "How did that make you feel?" As soon as his brows rose, she spotted her mistake. "Sorry. I slipped into shrink mode, didn't I?"

"You're a psychologist?"

"Yes." His foreman knew, but he must not have mentioned it to Pete.

"I'll answer your question. I was pissed and disappointed. But being the eight-year-old brat that I was, I went out of my way to be friends with Alex."

A rebel. Good for him for standing up for what was right. She suspected he got his principles from some adult figure. "I take it your mom approved?"

His eyes slightly widened. "You're perceptive. Mom encouraged me to be with whomever I wanted." He leaned back and cast his gaze to the side. The tension around his eyes disappeared for a moment. "She never judges anyone."

"She sounds like a wonderful person." Zoey meant it. "But I'd like to hear the rest of the story."

"Alex and I became great friends. He worked really hard at soccer and eventually received a scholarship to Montana State. I joined him there. When we graduated, we both worked with a construction firm. I worked with the manager and Alex was an accountant part time and joined the crew when he was needed. After a few years, we both got tired of answering to others, so we came back to Rock Hard and started our own firm. For a twenty-percent ownership in the company, Dad backed us. End of story."

She doubted that was all. "I'm surprised your father would give money to you, seeing that Alex was involved."

He shrugged. "Money is money. Maybe he gave up trying to separate us."

Separate them? Interesting. "When did Alex's status change to *former?*"

"Two years ago, his dad became ill. He needed a lot of money for the chemo, so I bought Alex out. His dad had moved from Rock Hard to Georgia to be with his family, so Alex went to stay with his parents."

That couldn't have been easy to buy out his partner. She wondered if his dad helped with the financial transaction, but it wasn't her place to ask. "When did he come back?"

"Two weeks ago. His father had passed about a month before, and his mom moved in with her widowed sister."

Before she was able to ask any more questions, the doorbell rang. She jumped up to pay, when a strong ache stabbed her eye, and she grabbed the counter.

Pete was by her side in a second. "You okay? Sit back down. I got this."

It was her house. She should pay. Before she could even recall where she'd put her purse, Pete returned with the tantalizing food. She inhaled deeply, and despite being exhausted, the muscles in her neck loosened.

"Let me get my wallet."

Pete placed the two large bags in front of her. "It's on me. For starters, I promised I'd be done today. Would have, too, if my worker hadn't gone AWOL."

So, that was what happened. "It must be tough to have to rely on others to get the job done."

"You got that right."

She nodded to the food. "Then thank you. I'm actually happy you were here instead of your missing worker." The hostage situation and Thad's injury must have cut right through her filter. But it was the truth. Had she come home to an empty house and broken down, no telling how she'd have coped.

"Well, I'm glad I could be here for you, too."

How sweet was that? It felt odd to be on the receiving end of advice, but she'd been pretty needy.

As if Pete had lived here for months, he found two plates and some paper napkins that he stacked in a pile on the table. He drew in an audible breath and his lids fluttered closed. "Smells awesome."

"It does." Feeling stronger, she pushed back her stool. "I'll find some silverware."

"Got chopsticks right here." He waved them.

She was going to say they needed a fork to pile the food on their plate but tipping the container worked for her. "Care to share how you and Thad met?"

"You were the shrink who was with Thad during his sting operation, right?"

She found it interesting that he redirected the attention

away from himself. Once her mind settled, she'd have to find out why. He seemed to know a lot about Thad's cases, but if they roomed together, it made sense. "Guilty."

Pete dumped a little food from each container on his plate. Make that a lot from each container. She didn't mind, as she wasn't a big eater.

"Was that weird?" he asked.

"Was what weird?"

"Talking to someone about shrink stuff when you know it's fake."

Most people would draw that conclusion. "That was the odd thing about it. It was, yet it wasn't." She scooped up some Lo Mein and took a bite. "I was there pretending to be Thad's therapist. We left the door open in case the killer walked by. Though I had to ask questions that were related to death, we actually had some good talks. Thad is a deep person."

"I know." He immediately stuffed so many noodles into his mouth that his cheeks puffed out. He swallowed then grinned, probably because she'd widened her eyes at the amount of food he'd jammed in there.

Too many unanswered questions swam in her head. "So tell me how the owner of his own construction company ended up with a detective for a roommate." She really wanted to know why some woman hadn't snatched up either of them already. Thad was divorced, which meant he was eligible again. Or was she missing something? Men in their mid-thirties who had established careers didn't usually live together unless they were a couple. Were they? *Crap.* And here, she really liked Thad. *Hell, I think Pete is great, too.*

"Well, let's see. About eighteen months ago, I was finishing up the construction of a convenience store on Valley and Third when some thugs came in the middle of the night and broke the windows and sprayed graffiti everywhere. Fuck. It was a mess."

"I bet that broke your heart."

"Yes, and even though insurance paid for it, the lost time to repaint and reinstall those big plate glass windows set me back."

From what Cade had told her, Thad worked for the Street Crime Unit. He was in charge of dealing with the gangs. "Was Thad the lead on the case?"

"You got it. Turns out it was a gang initiation stunt. We'd both grown up here, but our paths didn't cross." He held up his hand. "I knew of him in junior high, but since I was older, we didn't associate with each other back then."

"What about high school?" Age differences didn't mean as much once a student entered ninth or tenth grade.

He waited a beat. "I went to private school."

She smiled. "So did I."

He gave her a high five. "Anyway, after we met again, we hit it off right away. At first we thought we had nothing in common, but after I ran into him at Banner's Bar, we found out that we did. I used to hang out with his cousin."

She'd become friends with people who had similar interests, too. "How did you decide to room together?" Being acquaintances was different from living together, unless they were gay.

"Thad was renting this dump when the landlord decided to sell it. A few years ago, my father announced that the four thousand square foot home my sister and I had been raised in was too small for them." He pressed his lips together. "More proof the guy has his priorities all messed up. So he commissioned me to build him a mansion and paid me by giving me the old homestead."

"Wow. That was generous."

"Yes and no. It meant I couldn't spend time on any other project. In the end, I did come out ahead, but not as much as one would think. Then I wondered, what the hell was I going to do with such a big place?"

She got it. "In walks Thad Dalton, a man who needed a place to live."

He tapped his forehead. "Give the lady a prize."

That probably worked out well. If Thad was anything like Cade Carter, his hours kept him working a lot. "It seems like you two keep busy. Do you ever get to spend time together?"

"When we're both free we like to play darts, ride horses and motorcycles, shoot pool, you name it."

Her sixth sense went into overdrive, and her curiosity could no longer be contained. "May I ask you something personal?"

A brief flash of indecision skated across his face. *Way to go.* She'd shared her fears with him—had been more open with him than with her own family—and foolishly thought he might want to share back. Zoey loved analyzing people and reverted to shrink mode too often.

He leaned back in his seat. "I'm an open book." He upended the bottle and drank his beer.

That was what most people said, but they really weren't. She could ask him something else, but she couldn't help herself. She was obsessive about compartmentalizing people into personality types, but she didn't want to jump to the wrong conclusion. "Are you and Thad a couple?"

He nearly spit out his beer. "Couple? Fuck no. We like to share our women."

Her heart stopped.

Chapter Six

"You told her we shared?" Thad shook his head at Pete. "What the fuck were you thinking? The woman almost died yesterday. Hell, she witnessed two men get shot. One of them being me." Thad tapped his chest.

That was the problem. Pete had just reacted. This might be Rock Hard, Montana where sharing was the norm rather than the exception, but he knew damn well that a woman like Dr. Zoey Donovan wouldn't be into something like that. *Christ.* She was from freaking uptight Connecticut and even went to a prestigious boarding school.

Pete needed to explain. "She asked if you and I were a couple. Can you fucking imagine? I couldn't let her think that was true." *There.* He'd said it. It had taken a while to get over the embarrassment. He didn't have anything against gays. Hell, two of his best workers were together. Pete just didn't want a beautiful woman to think he swung that way.

"She thought we were gay?" Thad laughed so hard he had to grab his arm. "Shit, that hurts. Don't make me laugh again." He swiped his eye. "What made her think that?"

Pete understood why she'd drawn the conclusion. "She asked how you and I met and how we ended up being roommates. I told her about the convenience store defacement and about how the landlord kicked you out of your apartment. It makes sense she might think that."

Thad dropped his head back on the hospital pillow. "So you mentioned sharing because you wanted to fucking prove to her you were straight." It came out as a statement rather than a question.

If Pete was that transparent then why couldn't Zoey see that? "Maybe. Yes. But I was upset and a bit disoriented. It's not every day I have to comfort a woman who's been through something so upsetting." It wasn't totally his fault. "She's intriguing, you know, and quite distracting."

"You know you fucked things up for us?"

His roommate had seemed quite taken with her during the sting. Now, Pete had probably ruined any chance of her ever going out with either of them. "Zoey seems like the type to forgive."

"How do you fucking figure?"

"When I told her about me and Alex, she didn't judge my dad—much." He shook his head. "Shit. I'm grasping at straws, aren't I?"

"Hell, yeah, you are." Thad inhaled deeply, and then blew out a long breath. "Don't worry about it. She's smart and nice. If she thinks about it, she might forgive you."

"Me? What about you?"

"I don't need forgiveness. I'll just tell her you lied about sharing. Then I'll ask her out for myself."

Pete's jaw hardened, and he gripped the seat of the chair. If Thad ever followed through, Pete would throw his sorry ass out on the street.

No he wouldn't. But he'd think about it.

Thad laughed again. "Gotcha!"

"You're a real shit, you know that?"

His roommate waved a hand. "Trying to lighten the mood, that's all."

Pete leaned back. "When she was crying, my heart broke for her. She was scared, man. It messed with my mind."

Thad looked to the side, suddenly sobering. "I know. I watched every range of emotion cross her face during the exchange. That's why I had to take down Garrett. Well, that and the fact he shot me first. But with the way he was waving his gun, he could have shot her just to piss me off." He dragged his good hand down his chin. "I know I scared the crap out of her by taking that shot when she was standing so close to him, but shit, it was my only chance. Didn't need him getting off a second round."

"You shouldn't feel guilty. You did what you had to. It was self-defense and all. She appreciates that. Trust me."

"Little good it will do us now." Thad reached over for his Styrofoam cup and drank from it. "I'm curious. It may be a moot point, but what exactly did Zoey say after you told her we shared?"

"Nothing. That was the problem. She just stared at me with her hands clenched. Everything from despair to what looked like indecision crossed her face. It was like she wanted to talk about it, but wasn't ready to."

"Why didn't you say you were kidding or something? You had to know she couldn't possibly be in the right frame of mind. Hell. We never bring up the topic until we've both taken out the woman a few times."

"I know. I messed up. Ego, maybe. What can I say?" He put his thumb and forefinger a half inch apart. "But the tiniest part of me needed to know if she might be interested. She's a beautiful woman."

"You've never been known for your patience, but Jesus, let's get to know her first."

"You're right." He'd always taken things too fast.

"I know what happened," Thad said.

This was going to be good. "What?"

"When you spotted that long, flaming red hair, you figured I'd want to pursue her. You were just testing the waters for me." Thad smiled.

He knew all about Thad's fiasco with his first wife and how it had been her red hair that had attracted Thad to Peggy in the first place. "I wish I could claim that." Pete chuckled. "In case you have your blinders on, Zoey is the total opposite of Peggy." Pete inhaled. "Zoey likes you, you know."

"As opposed to Peggy?"

"Haven't spoken with her. From the way Zoey was acting so distraught after you called, I'd say she's interested."

"She might have been at one time, but she isn't anymore I bet." Thad closed his eyes for a moment. He then used his good hand to sit up straighter on the bed. "When we first met, we had this connection, but with what happened yesterday, she'll keep her distance for sure. If she does stop by again, it'll be out of guilt and nothing else."

Pete shrugged. "She's out of your league anyway, bozo." He wanted to put the conversation back on a lighter track.

"You think so?"

At his roommate's intense comment, Pete leaned closer. He knew that look. "What are you thinking?"

"I am a detective. Let me do a little investigating. We might be able to find a way to entice her. Find out what makes her tick."

That didn't seem like a good idea. "Are the drugs messing with your head? No woman I've ever met appreciates a man going behind her back to find dirt. She's perceptive. She'll know."

"I didn't say dirt."

Perhaps it was best to wait until Thad was healed before they talked about pursuing Zoey. "You said Jeremy shot someone?"

Thad cocked a brow. "You know you suck at changing the subject?"

"Always worked on you before, dude." Joking with Thad helped take the edge off Pete's mistake.

That brought out a smile on Thad's face, thank God. "The story's the same old one." Thad told him about the robbery and the subsequent shooting.

"How did Jeremy handle it?"

"He was shaken. It was his first time pulling the trigger and hitting someone."

Pete couldn't imagine what that would feel like. Hell. He had to be the only man in all of Montana who hadn't even killed a deer. "Is he okay now?"

"He stopped by earlier. He's a bit stunned. Turns out the thief he shot was Bobby Dench. Jeremy knew his older brother."

"That sucks. Don't recognize the name. He part of a gang?" Pete couldn't keep track of which kids were good and which ones weren't. Thad's main job was to control them. Not that Rock Hard had a lot of gangs, but with any city close to fifty thousand, they had their share.

"Nick Rodgers called me right before you stopped in. He's taken over lead because I got laid up. Dench said robbing the store was part of an initiation into the Blood Rights gang."

"Shit. We didn't have gangs back in our day."

Thad laughed. "You rich boys just didn't know about them,

that's all."

Pete gave Thad the finger. His friend was going to be okay.

✧   ✧   ✧

Zoey moved the tablet on her desk, fingers poised to take notes. "Kara, you said the tension in the operating room is getting worse? Can you be more specific?" This newest development worried her. If what her patient said were true, more than Kara would be affected.

"Dr. Carson keeps checking me out during the procedures."

Dr. Avery Carson was the chief of cardiovascular surgery, and Kara was his assistant, so perhaps he was assessing her abilities, not her physical attributes. Each time Kara had come in for a session, her attention span had been getting shorter. The anxiety was slowly eating away at her. "Could it be that he wants to make sure you're paying attention?"

"No. It's not that kind of look." Her lips pressed together and her fingers clasped the armchair until the vein in her forearms throbbed. "He also seems to find ways to... touch me." The disgust in her tone was raw and real.

Zoey's heart skipped a beat, but as she took notes she blanked her face. "Is he touching your arm to get your attention? Or is it more sexual?" She wanted to understand the true nature of the concern. As her therapist, she couldn't merely take Kara's interpretation of the events.

"Arm mostly, but there's also been a pat on the butt along with a squeeze to my shoulder."

Zoey noted the butt pat in her notes. "Do the other nurses or doctors comment about this behavior?" She wished she could speak with them to get their side, but that would be unethical.

"No. Even if you asked Dr. Carson, he'd tell you he was

trying to include me in the joking that goes on. They're always talking about sex and who got laid last night."

Everyone? She couldn't picture the females participating in this venture. "I thought many of the operations occurred in the operating theater." LACE was a teaching hospital and students were always watching the top doctors perform their specialties.

"Dr. Carson is good when others are there. It's only when no one is looking that he acts up."

"Remember how we talked about not reacting when he touches you?" They'd tried many techniques, but none seemed to have worked. Zoey hoped that without a response, Dr. Carson would cease his aggressive behavior. Kara said she'd even confronted him but to no avail.

Her chin trembled. "I tried laughing and all, but it's hard. His jokes are cruel and his comments sick."

Kara didn't seem to be in the right space to consider other behavioral modifications. "Have you asked for a transfer to a different discipline like we talked about?" That would end Kara's need to interact with Dr. Carson.

Her eyes widened as she shook her head. "I thought about it, but I love heart surgery."

Or did she love Dr. Carson? Kara's time was up. "For the next session, I want you to write down your emotions before and after the next occurrence of any inappropriate behavior. Be honest with yourself. Are you sending him any signals?"

Kara jumped up. "No. I hate him."

This wasn't the reaction Zoey had hoped for. "Try to keep an open mind." The sudden shift in behavior was troublesome, but Zoey's sister, Courtney, had a similar situation. Unfortunately, hers had ended in heartache.

"I'll try." Kara thanked her, but her words came out harsh and on edge.

Damn. Had Zoey pushed too hard? Her own nerves were still quite raw, so perhaps she had. If she hadn't had a lot of patients on her calendar, she would have cancelled the rest of the day and gone home. As soon as Kara left, Zoey checked her office Outlook and noticed her two o'clock was crossed off. As much as she'd needed the break, this one worried her. Zoey called her secretary.

"Rachel, is Mrs. Fletcher okay?" The woman never cancelled.

"Her daughter was ill, so Mrs. Fletcher had to keep her home. She rescheduled for next week. I put it on the calendar."

Zoey should have looked. "Perfect. Thanks." That gave her the needed time to see Thad and then grab a bite.

On her way out, she told Rachel to text her if anything important came up.

As Zoey headed to Thad's room, she didn't want to arrive empty handed. It wasn't in her nature. Having heard patients complain about the coffee the hospital served, she bet he'd welcome a good cup from Starbucks. When he was working undercover, he'd mentioned his need for his caffeine fix each morning.

At the small coffee stand in the lobby she purchased the strongest blend they had. She wasn't sure if he liked sugar or cream, so she grabbed two sugar packets. There weren't any creamer containers visible, so he'd have to do without.

When she arrived, Thad's door was open and the television on. That seemed like a good sign. She popped her head in and knocked. "Hello?" Her palms were a bit moist, but she chalked it up to holding the hot coffee, and not because she might be nervous. She feared the sight of her might remind him of what happened. When he looked up and smiled, the tension in her shoulders faded.

He turned off the television. "Hey. How are you doing?" he asked, looking better than she expected.

She chuckled, allowing relief to wash over her. "Good, thank you." She placed the coffee on the side table. From her purse, she retrieved the sugar packets. "I didn't know how you took it." She was glad to see the IV stand had disappeared.

"Black, but you didn't have to go to all the trouble." He cocked a brow and his lips curled up at the ends. "I'm a cop. What? No donuts?"

She shook her head and grinned. His humor surprised her, but she liked it. She pulled over the chair. "You're too fit to eat donuts. You told me you ran." It was something they both liked to do—only she wasn't as consistent as he was. Also, she was more of a two miler. He did five.

"I'm surprised you remembered."

She tapped her skull. "Just call me elephant brain."

"I like it." They talked a bit more about his rigorous nutrition plan. Not wanting to wear him out, Zoey started to excuse herself, but Thad stopped her. "Can you stay a minute? I'd love the company."

"Sure. I don't have another appointment for a while." If she had to skip lunch, she would. "I met your roommate." She was intrigued by Pete. College educated, owner of his own company, family rebel, and yet he listened and seemed to be a caring person. It was an uncommon combination of traits.

"I heard. Pete stopped by a while ago. I want to apologize for him."

Now Thad had her attention. "For what? Pete did an amazing job renovating the house." While his workers might have done a lot of the actual work, the attention to detail was exceptional. *Plus, he held my hand and took care of me when I needed someone the most.*

"His comment about sharing." Thad's face colored.

Oh, that. "It was nothing." Pete never hinted he was interested in her anyway, so how he conducted his life was his own business. She nodded to Thad's arm. "How's it doing? Are you able to go home soon?" If he did, would she ever see him again?

He lifted his arm that was held in a sling. "Feeling good. Doc says if the wound looks okay tomorrow, I can leave."

"Fantastic. How long before they let you go back to work full time?"

His jaw tightened. "Desk work for at least a week. It sucks. Plus, I gotta get a psych eval for discharging my gun."

"That should be easy. You handled all of my questions well."

"Yes, but that was fake."

Not completely. The cops had given him a background, complete with a pregnant wife and late stage pancreatic cancer. Sure, he was acting, but she could tell he longed for a family of his own. They'd discussed what was important in the ill Thad's life and how much he'd miss seeing his unborn child when he passed away. Zoey had the sense Thad's answers, while made up, contained a lot of truth.

"One of the nurses told me that man you shot is married to your ex-wife."

Thad nodded. "Garrett McDonald. He married Peggy a month after we divorced." His lips thinned as if the topic was still painful.

Way to go, Zoey. His ex-wife remarrying so soon after a divorce had a lot of implications. None of which were good. "How is our nemesis?"

"Recovering."

She couldn't tell if Thad was relieved or upset. So much for her ability to read people today. "How about I buy you dinner Saturday night?" Normally, Zoey didn't ask men out, but she owed Thad her life.

He grinned and his face lit up. "It's a date."

She pulled out her cell. "What's your number? I'll call you and then you'll have mine in your contacts."

He told her the information then took a drink of coffee. "Ah. That hits the spot. I can't tell you how much the hospital's version of coffee and food sucks. I feel better already." He was exaggerating, but that was probably his way of saying thanks.

Even though Thad looked better than yesterday and his attitude was more upbeat, she sensed he was torn up about having to shoot her captor. "Are you mentally doing okay?"

"You mean with shooting someone I knew?"

There she went again. Trying to get into a person's head. "Yes."

His lips hardened as if he was debating what and how much to reveal. "Let's just say shooting a stranger would have been easier."

She was afraid of that. "He shot you first. Still, it must have been hard." *Stop it.* Why was she trying to pick at his wound?

Zoey was a therapist through and through. She couldn't help it.

"It was."

His short response was his way of asking her to mind her own business and she took his cue. Zoey slapped her thighs and stood. "I need to get back, but I do owe you." She didn't want to overstay her visit, though she wouldn't have minded getting to know him better.

"Don't forget our date," he said.

The butterflies in her stomach flew away, and she smiled. "I won't." She was halfway to the door when she turned around.

How thoughtless of her. "Do you need a ride home tomorrow or anything?" She didn't know if Pete would be at work.

"I could use one. I'm kind of out of commission for a while. Can't drive until the doc clears me."

That might be the toughest part of the ordeal—having to depend on someone. "Call me when you're ready to leave. I'm only a few floors away."

"You bet."

His enthusiastic response pleased her. Happy that Thad was in better spirits, she took the elevator to the second floor. Food was calling her name. It was past the lunch rush, so she made it through the line quickly. Finding a seat near the back, she readied for some peace and quiet. She'd eaten only a few bites of her salad when loud chatter caught her attention. She turned back toward the entrance. Oh, shit. Dr. Avery Carson had come in with plastic surgeon Dr. Raymond Thompson. While she'd never been introduced to either man, everyone knew those two. Being in the same room with Carson curbed her appetite.

Don't judge.

Returning to her meal, she delved in, mentally reliving her visit with Thad instead of thinking about what Kara had told her about her boss. Chairs scraped right behind her, and she chanced a glance over her shoulder. What the heck? The cafeteria was half empty, and yet Carson and Thompson had to sit right behind her? Really? She leaned over to pick up her purse when Thompson spoke up.

"Tell me what happened, Avery. I've never seen you so upset."

She sat up again. Was he about to say something about Kara? If so, perhaps Zoey should leave. She would have done so right away, except that it might look a bit obvious if she moved to the other side of the cafeteria with her full tray.

Liar. Her curiosity was piqued.

Chapter Seven

Zoey had recently checked out Dr. Carson because Kara Molloy had alleged the man had not only sexually harassed her, he'd also made fun of the anesthetized patients and broken numerous operating room rules. It sucked Zoey couldn't hear his side of the story. However, all was not lost. She had observed him when he wasn't looking and had very subtly asked around about the man. Everyone said he had an aura about him that exuded confidence and sexuality.

From his good posture, and with the way he was manscaped from head to nails, she bet he believed he could charm any woman he wanted. From what she'd heard in the break room, most women had already fallen under his spell.

Zoey wasn't into egocentric men. The images of Pete bending over the tub as he finished the bathroom remodel and Thad, as he held Garrett McDonald at gunpoint, flashed across her mind's eye.

"I lost a child yesterday," Carson replied. "I'm still reeling."

He'd lost a child? Oh, no. That wasn't what she thought he'd be speaking about. It was rude to eavesdrop, but there wasn't enough noise in the room to block out Carson's booming voice. His words finally registered, and a wave of depression filled her. A young death would break anyone's heart.

"Avery, man, I'm sorry, but stuff like that happens to the best. What happened exactly?" Dr. Thompson sounded sincere.

"That's the thing, I'm not even sure. It should have been a relatively routine operation. It was one I'd done many times. One minute everything's going well, and the next the kid coded."

"Shit. How old was he?"

"Three and change. Had a congenital heart defect. I tried my best, but in the end I was unable to save him."

Her heart went out to the child and his family. Years ago, she'd counseled a teenager who was suicidal. Nothing Zoey said seemed to have an effect on the girl. The teen's classmates had bullied her until she couldn't take it anymore, and despite Zoey's efforts, Janet had taken her life. For weeks afterward, Zoey had grieved. She'd read and reread her notes to see what she could have done better. Her guilt was so strong that she'd consulted with another therapist. Dr. Claire Daniels told her that Zoey couldn't expect to reach everyone, especially those who refused to listen. Though what Claire said made sense, a bit of the pain never quite went away.

"That's got to be tough." Thompson's voice interrupted Zoey's thoughts.

"You ever lose anyone, Ray?" Carson acted like Thompson didn't understand.

"No, I've been lucky. Cardiac arrest after a procedure is always a risk, though." Neither said anything for a moment. "You've lost patients before. Why is this one so bad?"

"He was a *child*." Carson's voice cracked. "The young boy's parents were devastated. I've never seen such grief. I spent a long time with them, but nothing I said seemed to help."

Zoey's eyes watered a bit. Janet's parents had been inconsolable, too.

"That's horrible," Thompson replied. "What was the cause of his death?"

"Stroke."

Zoey couldn't imagine a three-year old having a stroke. She associated that with the elderly.

"How the hell did that happened?"

Carson blew out an exaggerated breath. "I was repairing the hole. It was a bad one. This issue should have been taken care of soon after birth, but the parents waited. Too long in my opinion. I took so much time trying to make sure the sutures would hold together that I didn't notice a blood clot had broken off."

"It's not your fault, man."

"I keep telling myself that, but it's not working. I swear we tried everything to revive him, but couldn't." What sounded like a fist hit the table. "I was in charge of that little boy. I might have been able to save him if I'd been more careful."

Wow. Maybe Zoey had let Kara's comments color her opinion of the man. He seemed truly distraught.

"How did the team react? You had a ton of people assisting you. Didn't any of them claim responsibility?"

Carson huffed out a laugh. "You would ask. Kara actually went ballistic on me. Said I wasn't focused. Shit, man. She's my fucking assistant. She was supposed to pay attention, too." He drew in a deep breath that sounded closer to a sob. "The bitch of it all is that I couldn't even get mad at her. She was right. I fucked up."

Silverware scraped across plates and cups clanked on the table. "Other than her outburst, is she still calling you night and day?"

There was a pause, almost as if Carson wanted to think

about his response. "Yeah. It's fucking pissing me off. I told Kara to stop contacting me, but she refuses. If I thought it would do any good, I'd go to HR myself and tell them she came on to me and that she won't leave me alone."

Zoey was stunned. None of his sentiments matched what Kara had said. It was almost as if he was speaking about another assistant named Kara.

"Harassment doesn't seem to work in the opposite direction, but it will get better," Thompson said. "You remember Belinda, from two years ago?"

"That the nurse in your office?"

"Yes. She tried to ruin me because I didn't want a monogamous relationship. Fuck that. I'm glad she couldn't make anything stick. Women think because I'm a surgeon that I'm fair game."

"She's gone, right?" Carson asked.

"Hell, yeah. That took work. Trust me."

The conversation turned to football and Zoey suddenly needed to leave. Heavy pressure sat on her chest, and confusion swamped her. Dr. Carson truly appeared to be upset over the loss of the boy. Had Kara been harassing her boss instead of the other way around? Did Carson's attempts to turn her down gently make Kara believe he loved her? It wouldn't be the first time one of Zoey's patients had been delusional.

Only one way to find out. Investigate within the confines of her oath.

✧   ✧   ✧

Zoey had told Thad she'd drive him home tomorrow, but she wasn't sure when that would be, so she asked Rachel to reschedule all of her next day's appointments, except for her eight o'clock. She doubted Thad would be released before nine.

After she finished with her last patient, Zoey headed home. All she wanted to do was kick back with a nice glass of white wine, watch some television, and forget all about Dr. Avery Carson and the continuing drama with Kara Molloy. But damn it. Zoey couldn't figure out why he and Dr. Thompson had to sit right behind her and speak so loudly. She'd heard every word they'd said. All she could think of was that Kara must have let it slip that she was seeing Zoey. Even if Kara had told Avery about the sessions, she'd never have mentioned they were about him.

God. Zoey's head pounded. She had no proof that either party was being completely honest, but with everything that had happened in the last two days, her mind couldn't stop spinning. She needed a break.

As soon as her house came into view, she let out a breath. Home sweet home. Once she was inside, she poured a glass of white wine then plopped on the sofa and leaned back her head. Within seconds her pulse slowed, and the tightness around her temples began to ease.

She closed her eyes, picturing the kind of meal she wanted to prepare this Friday. Cooking had always acted as her stress reliever. If she had the energy, she might even invite a few friends over. Then on Saturday, she'd go out with Thad. When she thought about what was coming up, she was really excited.

Just as Zoey stretched out on the sofa and picked up the television remote, her cell rang. Her pulse raced. Was it Pete? Or Thad? She set down her wine and checked her phone. It was Courtney. When her younger sister called, it was usually because something bad had happened to her love life. They only lived five hours away, but there never seemed to be enough time in Courtney's day for a visit.

"Courtney? You okay?"

"Zoey?" The worry in her sister's voice tore at her.

"What's wrong, sweetie?"

"I left Robbie." The desperation and sadness in her sister's tone broke Zoey's heart.

"Tell me what happened. I want to hear everything." Zoey picked up her glass and sipped her drink while she listened to the series of events that led to the breakup.

For over half an hour, she and Courtney discussed Robbie's inappropriate behavior. Zoey agreed with her sister. No man should ever hit a woman.

"I know it's for the best," Courtney said, "but it's hard."

"I know, and I'm sorry, but things will look better tomorrow."

Courtney sniffled. "Maybe. Why do I keep attracting the same type of man—one who's emotionally unavailable? I can't seem to break the pattern."

Zoey was impressed that Courtney seemed to understand the complicated topic of unavailability. "We've talked about these types of toxic men before. Changing one's mindset is never easy."

"Do you think you could give me some ways to tell if he's the violent type from the get go?"

Being needed helped revive Zoey. "I'd be happy to, sweetie."

She and Courtney discussed what things the next man might say, do, or demand from her that would be a red flag.

"You rock, sis. I'll certainly give those a try. But enough about me. What's going on with you? You'll never find happiness if you don't give men a chance."

Zoey smiled. "I think that was some of the advice I gave you." Courtney's chuckle bolstered Zoey's spirits.

"You're lucky."

"How so?" Zoey asked.

"At least you'll be able to spot the bad ones."

That lightened the mood. "Like I did with Rich and Dave?" Zoey had been so sure they were the two perfect men. Boy, had she been wrong.

"We all need practice."

Zoey loved talking with her sister. The pounding in her head had disappeared. "I think you've been listening to me too much." Zoey often preached that Courtney just had to keep looking, and she'd find Mr. Right.

"So, what about you?" Courtney asked.

Clearly, her sister wasn't going to let up. "I met someone."

As was her intention, Courtney squealed. "You went out on a date?"

"Not exactly a date." She explained that Pete was the owner of the construction company she'd hired to do some renovations. "He'd been finishing up on the remodel when I came home early one day." Given Courtney's state of mind, Zoey wouldn't mention the shooting, which was why she didn't tell Courtney about the upcoming date with Thad. "Pete was cleaning the bathtub when I walked in."

"Ooh. He sounds yummy. But he does the labor himself?" Zoey inwardly chuckled at the snobbish tone. It wasn't Courtney's fault. It was how they'd been raised.

"Only when he's needed to fill in. That's what good managers or owners do. He went to college, so back off, sister." Zoey laughed.

"Okay. Tell me more."

She mentioned Pete was from Rock Hard and had a business partner who'd left for a few years but had returned. "We just talked about, I don't know, stuff. I like him. He's nice."

"When is this hot date?"

"Not sure, but I'll let you know when he asks." She still couldn't tell if Pete was even interested. All he'd seen was a woman who'd broken down on him.

"When he does ask you out, try to have some fun. And for God's sake, don't do your psychobabble shit on him."

Psychobabble shit? Ouch. "Don't worry. I know how to act with a man." Not really, but a lecture was the last thing she needed—especially with everything going on in her head.

"Not even close, sis. Oh. One more thing. I know you're old and shit, but this isn't the nineteen forties. Women have been liberated. They vote now. They even ask men out." Zoey would have commented had her sister taken a breath. "You can, and probably should be the aggressor in bed. Men like that. Doormats are passé. Don't slap his hand if he wants some action."

Her mouth opened. If she followed all of Courtney's advice, she might end up like her sister—alone and unhappy. At least Zoey was only alone. "I'm not a prude. Don't forget Mark and Dave."

"Two men do not a party girl make."

Zoey didn't want to be a party girl. "There were others." Just not memorable ones. Zoey wanted to be open-minded. Was Courtney right? Her sister's concern might have merit, but she'd think about it later.

"Hey. Someone's at my door, Zoe." Zoey hadn't heard anyone knock, but Courtney could have been in the bedroom. "Thanks for listening. As always."

"Love you," Zoey said.

"Back at you." Then her sister hung up.

Zoey smiled. Talking with Courtney did her soul good, but it also made her realize how much she missed having someone to confide in.

While Zoey finished off her glass of wine she let her mind drift to what she wanted in life. Was she looking for something permanent? She was only thirty-two, but there were times when she wanted to have someone to dream about and have him dream about her right back. Maybe she did have things backward. Expecting the man to ask her out might be old-fashioned, but she wasn't aggressive by nature. *I asked Thad out. Why not Pete?*

Because she wanted to be certain of the consequences before she acted. For now, she'd pick up Thad tomorrow morning and have no expectations other than to help him with whatever he needed. She wouldn't worry about Saturday night.

Good luck with that, girl.

Chapter Eight

The next morning around eleven, Zoey's cell rang. As soon as she saw it was Thad, her nerves skyrocketed. It was stupid to be nervous. All she was doing was giving a friend a ride home. She inhaled, ran her palms down her thighs, and then answered with as cheery a voice as she could muster. "Donovan's taxi service. How may I help you?" Normally, she didn't do something this spontaneous, but she felt like it this time. Maybe the "incident" had made her see just how fragile life could be.

Thad chuckled and the tension in her muscles released. "It's Thad Dalton." Ooh, he sounded so formal and in control. Healthy now.

He had to know she recognized him by the caller ID and by the way she'd answered. "Are you ready to go home?" *There.* She sounded more like herself, instead of a giddy schoolgirl.

"Yup. All cleared and paperwork done. If I can convince you to give me a lift, I'd appreciate it. I'm downstairs by the front hospital entrance."

"Be right there." After she informed Rachel that her return for the day was questionable, Zoey rushed to the lobby to meet Thad. Other than when she'd been in the ER, she hadn't taken a day off in months. It was rather freeing. Maybe that was what caused her light-hearted behavior. *Stop it.* She wished she didn't always analyze her every thought. Even Zoey knew it wasn't healthy.

As soon as she stepped off the elevator, she caught sight of Thad standing a few feet away from an empty wheelchair. He was quite handsome in his civilian clothes, and his unshaven face gave him a kind of bad boy chic. The bullet hole and bloodstains must have ruined his police uniform shirt, which would explain his different attire. If Pete had brought his clothes, he'd forgotten Thad's boots. He still had on his black laced-up cop shoes, which looked out of place with his worn jeans. *He's still cute.* Thad's arm was in a blue sling, but she bet he wouldn't keep it on for long. He seemed the type to chafe under confinement.

"Hey," she said as she neared. He swung around and smiled. She didn't want to feel that zing of attraction, but it came nonetheless.

He studied her for a moment, looking like he was trying to decide whether to ask her something or not. His weight shifted. "It's close to noon, and I'm hunkering for a big juicy burger worse than anything. Mind if we stop at Red Robin on the way home? My treat." His brows rose.

This isn't a date. It made sense he'd ask her to lunch. He'd mentioned his need for good food, and she was his only way to get it. "Sounds great."

Not only did she need to eat, this would give her a chance to get to know Thad better. Visiting him in a hospital room wasn't the same as sitting across from him at a restaurant. While she spent her days trying to learn what made a person tick, her clients usually came to her voluntarily. It was her job to understand what was bothering them. Thad and she were equals here, which was a concept that excited her.

Her problem was that when she was with the opposite sex, she kept forgetting that men didn't like her to pry into their innermost thoughts. None of them seemed to get that this was her way of expressing interest. "I'm parked out front."

Outside, the day was clear and surprisingly warm. She'd only lived in Montana a few years, but September seemed to be the time of year where it could be warm one day and quite chilly the next, a combination that made planning outdoor activities challenging. She was about to ask if he wanted to wait by the entrance while she picked him up, but he was perfectly capable of walking. Men like Thad wouldn't like the implication that he was less than able.

As she moved to her parking spot, she tilted her face to the sun and let the warmth soak in. Good thing she'd gotten up a few minutes early to clean her car. Not only had she found some dirty hand towels from when she'd come in from a run, she'd tossed a bunch of other junk behind her front seat—like flares, a can of Fix-A-Flat, and an automatic tire inflator. The last three items now sat neatly in the trunk. Breaking down in Montana could be deadly, and Zoey believed in being prepared for the worst emergency.

She was about to open the passenger side door for him when she caught herself. Cops liked control—even injured ones.

She slid into her side, and as soon as Thad joined her, she started the engine. The restaurant was situated diagonally across from the police station, about four miles from the hospital, so the drive would be a short one. After they ate, would he want to stop in the precinct to say "hi" to his coworkers? She could definitely picture him finding something he had to do, leaving her with a free afternoon. That possibility should make her happy, but it didn't.

"Pete said you liked to ride motorcycles." That wasn't what she really wanted to talk about, but he wouldn't appreciate it if she brought up the shooting again or his ex-wife.

"Don't remind me." He lifted his arm.

"Sorry." Courtney was right. Zoey needed to get out more. "I can't imagine what I'd do if I were incapacitated. Are you in much pain?"

"Not much, but if I banged the wound, I'd be cursing up a storm."

She would, too. "Do you like to read?" Did he even have time for hobbies? Her friend Amber said Cade never did.

"I do too much of that at work, though I imagine fiction would be a lot more entertaining than studying police files."

"Tell me about it. Reading about a person's history never made for late night fun for me either." She headed down Arbor Way, and then turned right on Second Street. "Do you like to go to the movies?" She was trying to come up with things he could do while he healed. Hopefully, he didn't think she was asking him out on another date.

He cleared his throat. "Kind of pathetic to go by myself, don't you think?"

Not really. "I guess so." She went by herself quite often. Was he hinting that he wanted to go with her? If he was, then he needed to just say so. Courtney's comment about her asking out a man rang in her head. Zoey might consider that option, but only after she knew for sure he'd say yes. A thank you date didn't count in her opinion.

Zoey pulled into the lot behind the building then undid her seatbelt. As she reached behind her seat to get her purse, her door opened, startling her a little.

"You need help?" Thad asked.

"Just getting my purse." She twisted around and nabbed the

handle. "Got it!"

As she sat back up, she had to think long and hard about the last time someone had opened her car door for her. Maybe it was when Cade, Stone, and Amber had walked her to her vehicle a few weeks ago. *Sad.* Zoey had been alone too long.

The sun had disappeared behind a random cloud so she buttoned up her jacket and eased out of the car. "Thank you."

"Gotta feel useful."

That seemed to be Thad's core personality—being needed.

Inside, the place was quite crowded, mostly with uniformed cops. As soon as they'd been seated at the cozy table, two men came over.

"Ma'am." The man who spoke was the taller of the two. "Sorry to barge in, but it's good to see Thad up and about."

Thad's neck flushed a dull red, but since he hadn't shaved in a few days, it was difficult to be sure.

He faced her. "This rude guy is my partner, Jeremy Warner, and the other ugly dude is Nick Rodgers."

Both were good-looking men. "Nice to meet you."

"When are you coming back, Thad?" Jeremy asked.

Thad glanced at her, smiled, and then returned his attention to his partner. "You appreciating me now that you have to hang out with Nick?"

Jeremy shook his head. "Guy doesn't drink coffee. What kind of cop is that?"

Nick chuckled. "Let's leave him to his lunch. Seems to me, he got the good end of the deal. I'm stuck with you, knucklehead." Nick nodded at her, and then led Jeremy away.

Zoey liked how the men seemed so comfortable around each other. "You appear to have a good relationship with your coworkers."

"Better have when my life is in their hands."

She hadn't thought of it that way. "Do you swap partners often?" She had no idea how the RHPD worked, other than what little information Amber had provided her.

He seemed to work to keep from grinning. Only then did she realize her slip.

"No. Nick's regular partner's father passed away, so he asked if Jeremy could ride with him until Dale returns."

"You don't mind?"

He shrugged. "Different experiences are what keeps a cop sharp. Each detective has his own way of handling danger. Nick will be good for Jeremy."

She liked that Thad was looking out for others. The waitress came by, and they both ordered coffee and a burger. Zoey only wanted hers with lettuce and tomato, but Thad had the works, including fries.

"How do you stay so fit when you eat like that?" she asked.

"You think I eat like this all the time? Hell, no. I'm lucky to slam down a few eggs in the morning, and maybe grab a chicken sandwich at lunch. If I'm home for dinner, I'll cook some fish. When I'm on patrol, I try to eat salads, though I'm not sure with the dressing if that's much better than a juicy burger."

"That must be tough. I love to cook and I, too, try to use only healthy ingredients when I can get them." She'd been about to say she'd cook him a meal, but she refrained.

"That's why I run and work out."

"I bet you'll be able to run in a few days."

"I'm hoping."

The waitress brought their drinks. Zoey dumped in a packet of sugar and some cream, instantly feeling guilty. He really did drink his black. Starting tomorrow, she needed to get back out and run. With all that had happened at work, coupled with the shooting, she'd slacked off.

Thad placed his hands on the cup, as if he enjoyed the warmth. "Tell me how you ended up in Rock Hard, Montana." He leaned back in his seat and kept his gaze focused on her.

Crap. She couldn't say she wanted to move as far away from Connecticut as possible because of a failed relationship. That wouldn't paint her in a very good light, even though it was the truth. That was one reason why she and newcomer, Amber Delacroix, had hit it off. They both came to town after some emotional fiasco. At least Zoey hadn't married her men. In all honesty, her issues with Dave and Mark were just the tip of the iceberg.

"Wow. This must be some story." Thad cocked a brow.

"What do you mean?" He couldn't be that perceptive. She hadn't even said a word.

"With the way you've nearly mangled the napkin and how your eyes are darting around, it's some tale."

"I'm thinking." *What and how much to tell.*

"Pete said you were from Connecticut. Your hometown anywhere near New York City?"

Now she relaxed. She could talk about geography. "Yes. Right outside." Tell him the truth. He won't judge. "I worked on Staten Island. The pace there was rather hectic, and after a rather unsuccessful relationship I had with two men, I applied to several places out west. I started working for a clinic here, but after almost two years, I decided I wanted to go out on my own." That wasn't so hard. Her story seemed similar to Pete's, actually.

She had inwardly winced at saying the part about having been with two men. Now, Thad would think she was fair game. *Would that be so bad?*

"That's a big change to go from Connecticut to Montana.

The weather is harsher and the population of the entire state here can't be more than a fraction the size of New York City."

When he didn't drill her on her failed relationship, she was grateful. "I love it here. While I am a water person and enjoyed fishing and swimming in the Sound, I like the mountains better. In Montana, the people are far friendlier and life flows at a slower pace."

He lifted a brow. "Slower, huh? Come work for the Police Department. I've never worked outside of Montana, but there's a lot going on every day, all day."

Darn. She hadn't meant to imply his job was easy, and that if he'd worked in New York, it would have been more frantic. "I just meant there's less traffic here, less pollution, nicer people."

He smiled as if he enjoyed seeing her squirm. "I've never been to New York. When I have the time and money, I'd love to go sometime."

She held her breath. He drank his coffee, but he didn't seem to be waiting for an invitation for her to be his guide. She exhaled. "It's a magical place, especially around Christmas. You should see Rockefeller Center with the skating rink and all the festive decorations." She'd missed that part of the city. "Then there are the museums and plays." Why bring that up? A macho man like Thad wouldn't be interested.

"Never had the chance to see a live play, but I'm not against it."

That surprised her. Talking about herself wasn't her favorite topic. "Have you always worked in the Street Crime Unit?"

"No." He drank his coffee. She thought he wasn't going to give her any more information, until he drew in a big breath. "After the service, I went to college, and then joined the Force here in Rock Hard. Cade Carter and I were actually partners for a bit."

"I never knew that."

"Many people don't. I'll never forget. One time, Cade and I got called out to this robbery that involved a local gang. After we caught the kid, he spilled everything for a reduced sentence. I can't tell you why I was intrigued by how gangs worked, but I was."

Maybe he wanted to help the kids. Underneath it all, Thad was a caregiver, but she bet he'd never admit it. "You then applied for the Street Crime Unit?"

"Yup. It's hard, but rewarding at the same time."

Before she could ask more, the server delivered their tantalizing food. Zoey hadn't thought she was hungry, but after one bite, she practically inhaled the meal. Thad, too, plowed through his hamburger. When they finished, she looked around and noticed only a handful of cops remained. She hadn't thought they'd been there that long.

"That was awesome." She wiped her mouth. "Great suggestion."

He waved for the check then handed the waitress his credit card. "I really don't feel like heading home just yet. You up for a game of darts?"

Was he kidding? "Darts? Me?"

"Oh, shit. You gotta be back at work? I wasn't even thinking."

"No. I cancelled my appointments for the rest of the afternoon. I didn't know if you'd need me to drive you around."

"You bad or something?"

For cancelling her appointments, offering to drive him around, or at playing darts? She bet it was the latter. "I'm not any good. I'm more of the cerebral type."

His jaw twitched like he was working hard not to give a flip answer. "I like the Rodin type."

She grinned, liking his wit. "Cute." Zoey could hear her weekly get-together girls telling her to take a chance. Hell, she bet Thad could use a diversion. Why not? She wanted to repay him. *Be honest.* It was more than that. She liked him. "Well, if you don't think the bar owners will mind me putting holes in their walls with the dart, I'm game."

His smile reached his eyes. Boy was she in trouble now.

Chapter Nine

Thad appreciated that Zoey had cancelled her appointments for him. It meant she cared. During lunch, he'd expected her to drill him about the shooting, about Peggy, and about his work in general, but she hadn't. Instead, she really seemed interested in learning about him, about who he was beyond his job. Quite a refreshing change from the women he'd been out with lately.

Thad didn't want his time with Zoey to end, so he'd had to come up with something to do with her that wouldn't put a strain on his injury. It was a bummer that his outdoor activities had to be curtailed for now. Whenever he'd had a day off, he'd tool around on his motorcycle or go for a long run. With the arm out of commission, his options were limited. Even shooting pool was out of the question. Didn't matter he'd been shot in his non-dominant arm.

He supposed he could have asked her to watch television, or go to a movie, but that wouldn't have given him the chance to get to know her better—hence, the suggestion of darts. Teaching her would be fun, and hopefully provide an inside view to the intriguing woman.

"Ready to be wowed?" he asked as he held open the door to Banner's Bar.

She laughed. "Ready to be frustrated? I hope I don't embarrass myself."

Thad grinned. "Never. I won't let you fail."

"You don't know how bad I can be."

"Oh, ye of little faith." He placed a palm on her back as he led her inside. Even having that small contact gave him a sense of protective power. Being around Zoey seemed to alter his thinking.

Inside, the place was calm compared to Saturday nights. Except for four occupied tables, and a couple of regulars at the bar, they'd have Banner's to themselves. He liked that.

Adam, the bartender, looked up from the counter then waved to both of them. Thad bet the guy wouldn't have guessed he'd walk in with someone as classy as Dr. Zoey Donovan. She'd mentioned she and her friends came here weekly for happy hour, but Thad must have been working during those hours. He would have remembered her.

"You want a drink?" Thad asked her.

"At two in the afternoon?" She shook her head.

Way to go. Zoey was already rather tentative around him, and now he'd been unclear. "I meant like coffee. Or do you want a soda?" She didn't respond. "Hot tea maybe?"

Her shoulders lowered. "A diet soda would be nice."

Thad stepped up to the bar and gave Adam his order. "And let me have the house darts. Zoey wants to learn how to play." If he'd stopped off at his house first, he would have grabbed his own set.

Adam nodded to the sling. "Heard you took a bullet. You good?"

"I'll be back to normal in a few days."

"Great." Adam nodded to Zoey. "You sure about this? Thad here can be quite deadly with those darts."

She laughed. "I know of a few good nurses who can patch me up if things go south."

Adam smiled as he handed her a set of six. "Give him hell. I'll bring the drinks right over."

Zoey dumped the darts onto Thad's palm as if she feared they'd explode. She was quite adorable. "You take these."

"Adam was kidding. Unless you plan on standing in front of the board, you'll be safe."

"I know." She smiled, and his groin tightened.

The moment they'd entered the bar, her demeanor had changed. She seemed more comfortable here. Either it was because she knew the waitresses, bartender, and possibly some of the customers, or else he was wearing her down. "Ready for your first lesson?"

"Let me watch you first. I want to study the mechanics of your throw."

"You going to analyze the trajectory, speed, and aerodynamics of the dart?" As soon as his smartass words left his mouth, he cursed himself. *I'm an ass.* He'd been temporarily so relaxed around her that he'd forgotten she wasn't one of the guys. "Sorry. I didn't mean to mouth off."

"No. That sounds good. I'll try that."

He had to laugh. Zoey was a refreshing change from other women. No wonder Pete was so taken with her. Put her in a hospital and she acted like a shrink. Once he got her outside her normal area of expertise, the real Zoey Donovan began to emerge. Under the right conditions, he bet she'd really blossom.

Thad escorted her into the separate game area that consisted of two pool tables, one dartboard, a foosball table, and two video consoles. He led her over to the designated area for darts then placed each one of the loaners in his hand. Zoey stepped close, and her linen scent enticed him. That wasn't good. She didn't consider this a date, so he needed to stay cool.

"What are you doing?" Zoey looked from his palm to his face.

"Picking three that are relatively the same weight and design."

"Is the purpose of having them the same so that it will be easier to adjust your throw if you miss?"

Smart lady. "You sure you haven't thrown darts before?"

She shook her head. "I suck at athletics."

He inwardly chuckled. Only a few men he knew would consider darts a sport. "You run."

"Running doesn't require the same amount of fine motor skills as throwing a dart."

"I know a few athletes who would disagree with you, but we don't need to go there. First thing is your stance. You right-handed?"

"Yes."

He placed the edge of his shoe on the toe-line. "Place your right foot perpendicular to this line, like so, and make sure your back foot distributes your weight evenly." He stepped back. "Give it a shot."

Her face slightly colored. She inhaled as if this was some exam. With care, she slid her foot to the mark on the floor, leaned forward, and lifted her back toe. While Thad could have repeated the instructions, he wanted to touch her. He stepped behind her, placed his right hand on her shoulders and straightened her stance. "Stand up." With his toe, he nudged her right leg back. "No, no. Keep your right toe on the line."

Her fists tightened. She was really trying. After some additional adjustment, and possibly a bit more touching than was necessary, her form looked good.

She looked up at him and smiled. "Thanks. This feels right.

I'm more balanced."

He hadn't expected his pulse to speed up. Thad stepped back and drank some of the coffee that had miraculously appeared on the table right behind them. He inhaled. "Step two."

She moved out of the way. He went through how to hold the dart, about the need to keep it level or slightly elevated in relation to the floor, and then showed her the motion for throwing.

"Throw one to show me," she said.

Her gaze on him, he let one fly, but it hit the outer ring. Damn. So much for looking studly. "Stupid sling." He ripped it off and tossed it on the table then lifted his injured arm to stretch it. "Being confined throws off my balance. This is much better. Let me try again." He refused to be embarrassed. His second throw came closer to the center.

Zoey clapped. "You're really good."

Pete, Cade, Stone, Ethan, Tom, and a bunch of his other friends might have disagreed. "You try."

It would be more fun watching her anyway. He retrieved the two darts he'd tossed and handed them to her. "Remember, don't hop, bounce, stand on your toes, or move your head. It's all about being smooth."

She inhaled and moved her forearm back and forth several times before letting go. The dart hit the board but immediately bounced to the floor. "Oh, no." She faced him, looking distraught.

"It's okay, honey. Darts take hours and hours of practice. It's not as easy as some people make it look." He didn't want her to give up.

She nodded and bit her lip, looking so cute. With more concentration than he'd seen anyone possess in a long time, she picked up the next dart, took aim, and let go with a big exhale. The dart stuck, barely clinging for life.

"I did it!" She hugged him. No one was more surprised than he was at the contact, but she moved back before he could decide what to do.

"You sure did."

"I want to try again." She ran up to the board, gathered the dart, and returned. She must have moved her toe four times before she was satisfied with its location.

"Remember, nice and smooth." He held his breath, wanting her to succeed.

As if a patient's life depended on it, she tossed the dart. This time, it stuck well. Arms raised, she did a little dance. Before he could congratulate her, his cell rang. "Mind if I take this? It could be the precinct."

"Sure." With more joy than he'd seen from her, she retrieved her dart, acting as if she wanted to stay all night until she hit a bullseye.

The caller ID said it was his grandmother. "Hey, Nana." She rarely called, but he knew what she wanted. "Don't worry, I didn't forget about the anniversary party on Saturday." *Oh, crap.* Zoey had asked to take him to dinner that night.

"I figured you wouldn't. You did remember to invite Pete, right?"

"Not yet, but I will. Can I bring a guest?" Even if he hadn't agreed to dinner on Saturday, he'd want to bring Zoey. He bet she and Nana would get along well.

She hesitated. "Do I know her?"

The last time he'd brought a woman, the lady had insulted his grandmother's home. Nana lived on a large farm, grew her own food during the summer, and chewed tobacco like a whisky-guzzlin' redneck. "No. I worked with her when I was helping to catch that serial killer. Remember I told you about that?"

"Vaguely. She pretty?"

He wanted to shoot his grandmother's comment back at her about how it was what was inside a person that counted, but Zoey had both traits. She was gorgeous on the outside, and as far as he could tell, sensitive and caring on the inside. "Very." Zoey was looking at him, and he decided not to say too much. "What time?"

"Come around five."

He would have asked if he could bring the dessert or something, but that would have been an insult. His grandmother enjoyed cooking too much. "Will do." He disconnected the call.

He loved his Nana, even if she was a throwback. He always accused her of traveling forward in time from the 1860s but she vehemently denied it.

Zoey was standing by the table with her drink in hand. A brow rose. "Everything okay?"

"That was my grandmother. It's my parents' thirty-fifth wedding anniversary on Saturday and she's throwing a big to-do at the family farm."

"That sounds nice. As much as I love my siblings, our family wasn't much into big gatherings." She shrugged. "It could have something to do with the fact that both my parents were only children."

"I'm sorry. I don't know what I would have done if I hadn't had all my cousins to get into trouble with."

From her enthusiastic response, she didn't act like a farm was beneath her. "Nana said to bring a guest. I forgot about my folks' anniversary when I accepted your dinner invitation for Saturday. Would you be interested in keeping me out of trouble there instead?" When she'd asked him in the first place he'd been so stunned that the special date had flown out of his head. They weren't at that stage of "meet the parents" yet, but he doubted she'd draw unwarranted conclusions. Hell, they hadn't even gone on a formal date. But he liked her. A lot. She was smart, nice, and caring. Being around thugs all day made him jaded. Zoey soothed his soul.

"I'd love to."

Yes! "Pete'll probably be coming, too." Would that bother her to be around both of them? Or did she prefer one over the other? Thad had never worried about such things before, but something about Zoey made him want to be cautious.

"Super. I'm looking forward to it. A farm sounds cool."

Thad probably should warn her what to expect. "Nana's place is about as far from fancy as you can get. We'll have our meal in an old barn, since it's the only place big enough to hold everyone, and the backyard is an old junkyard." He waited for a scowl, but none came.

Her face lit up. "Do you think anyone would mind if I brought a camera? I love taking pictures of old things."

He laughed. "You can do anything you want. When on the Dalton farm, there are no rules. As for old things, that's all there is there."

"I can't wait."

After her fun dart lesson, Zoey drove Thad to the grocery store so he could pick up some supplies. She didn't need anything, but she enjoyed following him around while he loaded up on what looked like a month's worth of food. Nothing fancy. Just chicken breasts, frozen fish, eggs, bread, and lunchmeat. If she'd been with Mark or Dave, they would have tossed in chips, dip, and a few six packs of beer. Nutrition wasn't even in their vocabulary, which was odd given Dave was a dentist.

"Do you buy stuff for Pete, too?" She was curious how two busy men managed.

"Sometimes, but mostly we do our own thing."

To each his own. That was how Dave and Mark worked, too. Thad tossed some apples into the cart and a few other items, but it was always with his uninjured arm. She hoped throwing darts hadn't set him back.

After they checked out, he let her direct where to put the packages in her car, but insisted he place them just so in the trunk. *Men.*

When she pulled in front of his home, she was impressed with its grandeur. Then she remembered this had been Pete's family home. "Nice."

"It's too big actually. It was built for a family, not two bachelors."

She wondered if he liked his single status. *Stop analyzing.* Courtney would be proud of her big sister for not digging any further for the answer. Zoey couldn't wait to tell her that she'd accepted the dart invitation and hadn't even balked when Thad asked her to his grandmother's farm. Part of Zoey's reasoning was that if his parents were anything like hers, they probably had bugged him about getting married again and about giving them grandchildren. And if he were anything like her, he'd be tired of hearing them harp. Asking her to a party would shut them up, at least for a while.

Zoey cut the engine and jumped out. She popped the trunk and lifted two packages, one in each arm.

Thad was by her side in a flash. "You don't have to do that. I got it."

He was doing his macho thing again. "I know, but I want to thank you for the nice time."

"Uh-uh. You think I need help."

She couldn't deny it. "You were shot."

He gently shook his head and grabbed the remaining bag. "Come on, Miss Helper."

Inside, the place was spacious but sparsely decorated. She loved everything about the comfortable looking living room except the flowered wallpaper. She bet Pete's mom had picked it out and now he didn't have the heart to change it.

A long hallway led off the living room to an open concept kitchen that was totally updated, a dining area that had a crystal chandelier in need of dusting, and a den of sorts that had a humongous television, above a fireplace. As for the furniture, it looked like the men had gone to a thrift store and bought whatever suited their fancy. They didn't seem to care that nothing matched.

"We're not home enough to worry about decorating," Thad said, acting as if he could guess her reaction before she said anything.

"You don't need to explain. I get it. I like comfortable."

Once they placed all the packages on the large center island in the kitchen, she helped him unpack. She had no idea what her next step should be. Was he waiting for her to leave or should she hang out for a few hours to help him prepare dinner? Or would Pete be home by then?

Once more, Thad put the items away using his right hand. It was possible he wouldn't have used his left even if his left hadn't been injured.

Zoey inwardly sighed. The girls would be arriving for happy hour soon. Zoey had already called Jamie Henderson, the point person, to let her know she might not make it. She was pleased that Jamie, who was a hospice nurse at the hospital, had returned to her usual activities of organizing the group. It had only been three weeks since Ben, Jamie's former boyfriend, had inadvertently shot Jamie while he was trying to kill Amber. The emotional toll had yet to sink in.

Thad seemed quite settled, so maybe Zoey could leave. *But do I want to?* No, but with all that had happened, she was equally excited to be with her friends and tell them about her day.

When she'd first encountered Thad, Zoey decided she wanted to get to know him better. He was really nice, but she never thought he was that interested in her. After their lunch today, and with the way he touched her during the dart game, just maybe he liked her back.

Zoey seriously needed help reading a man's clues. "I guess I should be going. You seem to have everything under control." She held her breath.

"You're welcome to stay." He lowered his chin and looked up at her, but no tension filled his face. It was as if her decision didn't matter.

Adrenaline rushed through her, but the high was immediately blocked by an intrusion of common sense. She wasn't ready yet. She needed space to think. "What time Saturday?" Being evasive was so passive, but her jumbled nerves would only muck up the great time they'd had together if she stayed any longer.

"How about Pete and I pick you up at four thirty? Dress warm. The barn can be drafty."

"You bet."

Saturday would be yet another adventure. For the last two years, she'd barely dated, and in the span of a week, she'd met two great guys. The problem was that she'd have to pick just one. Or did she?

Chapter Ten

"You played darts with the cop who was just shot?" Jamie asked. Her voice came out a tad loud, and a few people in nearby tables turned their heads.

Zoey leaned forward. "As for being able to throwing darts, Thad has healed quite nicely already. Or else he was pretending the wound didn't hurt. The bullet hit here." Zoey pointed to the fleshy part of her forearm.

Jamie winced. It was understandable she'd be sensitive around the topic of a shooting after her own gunshot wound. The worst part of the whole ordeal was that Jamie had no idea her boyfriend had been guilty of all the mercy killings in the hospital. So far, she'd been remarkably resilient, but there were a lot of issues they still needed to work out in therapy.

Melissa Williams, an OB-GYN nurse, set down her drink, her eyes looking wistful. "He was a real hero to protect you like that."

Zoey sipped her refreshing wine. "I completely agree. I've never met a man that brave. He brought down my captor after being shot." The group oohed and aahed.

Melissa snagged a handful of chips. "I wish I could meet someone like that."

Except for Jamie, who'd thought she'd found her Prince Charming when she'd met Benny, and Amber Delacroix who'd recently landed her two perfect men, all of the women at the table had expressed that sentiment at one time—including Zoey.

Amber dipped the pita bread into the hummus. "All I can say is that I'd have been scared shitless if someone grabbed me around the throat like that."

"Trust me, I was petrified." Zoey was about to say Amber should know the feeling, but then thought better of it. Her friend had a gun pointed at her by Jamie's boyfriend, which would be a hell of a lot worse in Zoey's opinion.

Melissa wiped her hands on her napkin. "We've never had any of our patients come in with gunshots wounds, but wouldn't any kind of surgery leave him woozy for days?"

"I would have thought so, too, but he's tough."

"And hot," Amber added. If her good friend wasn't engaged to two hunky men, Zoey might have told her to back off.

Becky Andrews, another nurse at LACE hospital, sipped her margarita. "You need to start from the beginning. I must have been spacing out because I didn't even know this went down." She waved her glass. "Where was I?"

Zoey could see the girls wouldn't leave her alone until she gave them enough details. "I'll give the short version for Becky here. I was walking down the hall intently reading my notes, when this guy grabs me." While Zoey told them how she thought she might die, she left out a lot of the details—like nearly peeing in her pants. "After I got out of the ER and made sure Thad was okay, I went home." She inhaled. All four of her friends seemed glued to her story. "I was shaken, but I was holding it together."

Jamie's lips were pressed together. "You sure you weren't in denial? I know I would have been."

They'd spoken about that in their session. "At the time, I was just mad and upset, mostly because of Thad. I had a mean headache from the gun butt, some of that man's blood on me, and was hungry and tired."

"Sounds just like PMS to me," Melissa said with humor in her voice.

The crowd chuckled. "Trust me. It was worse. Remember I told you I was having my kitchen and bath redone?" The girls nodded. "They were supposed to be finished that day, but when I got there, the owner was in my bathroom cleaning the tub."

"No way," Becky said. "I'd have been pissed. When I'm upset, I want to be left alone."

"I was a bit peeved. Having Pete—a stranger to me—where I wanted to be the most set me off. I lost it. I'm not proud of my reaction, but it's what happened." She told them how she'd cried and how Pete had held her hand, brought her something to drink, and listened to her tale.

"Aw," Becky said, her frustration from a moment ago having all but disappeared. "He sounds so nice." Becky was the dreamer of the group who yearned for love in the worst way.

"He was. He even ordered me Chinese food." Everyone knew Zoey's penchant for the stuff.

Becky placed both hands over her mouth. "Why can't I meet someone like him?"

"You sound like Melissa. Don't worry. When the time's right, he'll walk into your life."

"I can't wait." Becky drew her glass to her lips. "You find a man willing to risk his life for you, and then meet a second man who's equally wonderful in the same day. I should be so lucky."

"She's greedy," Melissa chimed in.

Zoey shook her head. "It wasn't like I planned it."

Melissa leaned forward. "What are you going to do about being one woman with two men? Willing to pass one off?" Her brows rose.

"Not going to happen, lady." Zoey sobered then finished her glass of wine. "That's one of the reasons I needed to come. I'm torn."

Amber smiled. "We're all ears. But let me say that Thad's a great guy. He worked with Cade once, who had nothing but good things to say about him. You can't go wrong with a hero."

"I know, but Pete was there for me, too." Zoey stomach tightened at where this conversation was headed.

Jamie cracked open a peanut. "Seems to me like you have a real dilemma."

Melissa waved her glass. "No kidding. Thad is this hunky cop who saved your life. You cancelled your entire day of appointments so you could drive him home. But you're in turmoil because Pete was there for you in your most trying time."

Melissa had nailed it. "You are so right. I like both of them."

A twinkle shone in Amber's eyes. "I remember when I barged into the room where you were consoling a pretend-to-be-sick Thad, and you and he were totally engrossed in what each of you were saying."

That was what made it so hard. "We were. He's deep. He seemed to understand me, too."

Melissa chortled and Becky grinned. Melissa made the shape of a circle with her hands. "My magic ball says you'll be boffing Thad within the week."

Everyone but Zoey laughed. Her face heated instead. "Pete told me they shared." She'd shone the light on the elephant in the room.

Amber grabbed her hand. "I'm so happy for you."

"I am, too. Sort of. Here's the problem. Pete hasn't asked me out. What if he doesn't? You don't think it's going to be awkward being at Thad's house if Pete shows up?"

Jamie shook her head. "You know, for a self-confident shrink, you sure are one confused woman when it comes to men."

Zoey laughed. "You got that right."

Amber looked from one girl to the next. "I'll play shrink here. It's not that Pete won't ask Zoey out, it's that when he does, she'll have to deal with both."

Jamie leaned forward on her elbows and lasered a gaze right at Zoey. "I seem to recall that when Amber mentioned how she liked Cade and Stone that you warned her about ménage relationships. I believed you said they were doomed to failure."

Zoey had said that. "That was before I could see how good Stone and Cade were with Amber. Since then, I've been reevaluating my opinion."

"Amen," Amber said.

Melissa picked up her glass and drained it. "If Pete asks you out, what will you say?"

"Let's not be making any wedding plans for me yet. On Saturday, I'll be going with Thad to his parents' anniversary party. Pete's invited, too."

All the girls grinned. They acted as if her fate was sealed. She so hoped she was ready to delve into the world of ménage again.

❖   ❖   ❖

After a fun evening with her friends, Zoey headed home. She was two streets away from her house when her cell rang. A quick glance showed the number, but not the person's name.

Thinking it might be a distraught patient using a friend's phone, she answered. "Hello?"

"It's Pete Banks. Hope you don't mind that I called. Thad gave me your cell number."

Her right hand loosened her grip on the wheel. "Mind? No." He sounded upbeat, so she assumed nothing bad had happened to Thad.

Was he asking her out or checking on whether she was happy with the renovations? *Stop guessing. Just listen.*

"I wanted to touch base with you to see if you were okay, but it sounds as if you're in a car."

A bit of disappointment ran through her. It was a check-up call. The whine from the wheels on the pavement was rather loud. "I'm just returning from happy hour."

"I won't keep you then, but I was wondering if you might be up for a horseback ride at my parents' ranch after work tomorrow. You mentioned how much you missed your horse from back home."

He was too sweet. Zoey hadn't ridden in such a long time. Growing up, she'd taken Scout, her Paint, out almost every day. "I'd love to. My last patient leaves at three. Does that work?" Normally, she had someone at four on Friday, but she'd cancelled.

"Perfect. How about I pick you up at your house at, say, four?"

She slowed as she neared the turn to her street. First Thad and now Pete. Her social calendar had gone from nothing to being filled up fast. "I'll be ready."

"See you then."

She pressed the off button and smiled until she realized that Pete had just complicated her life, but hopefully in a good way.

✧　✧　✧

Even though Zoey had back-to-back patients to help pass the time the next day, getting through all of Friday had been excruciating. When the last of her patients had walked out of the office, she was finally able to leave. Not only was she excited about riding again, she was thrilled to have the chance to see Pete Banks without tears blurring her vision.

During her short lunch hour, she'd given some serious thought to both Thad and Pete. The dynamics between all three of them were quite unique. It was a help-and-be-helped kind of thing. Thad had saved her by shooting Garrett, and then Pete had been there for her as she'd tried to cope with the nightmare. Two days later, she'd helped Thad when he needed a ride home, though by no means what she did for him equaled what he'd done for her. The only missing ingredient was her helping Pete.

As soon as she entered her house, she headed straight to the bedroom. Knowing there would be little time to decide what to wear, she'd laid out her clothes last night. She wanted to be comfortable, but also look nice. The problem was that nothing fit the bill, but she didn't have time to shop. They'd be outside, so her jacket would cover her less than sexy shirt. Just as she yanked on her boots, the doorbell rang. Yikes, he was here.

Zoey rushed to the door and opened it. *Wow*. Pete was wearing a sexy black shirt, jeans that flowed over his hips like molten steel, and well-worn boots. Through all her tears, she must not have noticed what a great-looking guy he was. "Hey, come in."

"Ready?"

She smiled. "Just need to grab my purse." After she set the alarm, Pete helped her into his truck then jogged to the other side and jumped in.

"Sorry about the mess." He picked up a hammer and tossed

it behind his seat. "I rarely go any place with a lady. Should have vacuumed it at least."

Zoey wasn't sure if that was a come-on or not, but she liked the sentiment. "I have no problem being in a work vehicle."

He smiled. "You don't mind getting a little mud on you then?"

Somehow this seemed like a trap. "Are we going to cross a muddy river?"

He smiled. "No telling where Dad's beasts will take us, but I was referring to contractor's mud. We use it to cover the cracks where the wallboard abuts." He tapped a stain on the seat.

"Ah." She had a lot to learn.

In no time, they arrived at his parents' spread. Pete's folks only lived about six miles from her house, on the northeast corner of Rock Hard, but she wasn't sure if they technically were within the town limits. "How many acres do they own?" She didn't see many homes nearby.

"Only four hundred, but there aren't any roads between Dad's house and the mountains, so no one lives back there. Someday it might happen."

"It's beautiful." The rustic grandeur of Montana never failed to amaze her.

He stopped the truck and helped her out. "Just leave your purse here, unless you think you'll need something."

"I'm good." Pete led her to a barn that was located to the west of the Banks' mansion. The house had to be close to ten thousand square feet. "What do your parents do with all that space?"

He laughed. "Trust me, I asked them the same thing. Maybe now you can see why receiving their old home as payment might not have been the best deal for me."

"Your dad didn't give you any cash to cover the costs of

labor and materials?"

"He did." Pete placed a hand on her lower back and escorted her inside the barn.

From the way his jaw had tightened, talking about his father wasn't his favorite subject. She wondered if after they rode she'd get to meet Mr. or Mrs. Banks. For now, she'd enjoy Pete—or rather Parker Banks.

The rich smell of hay reminded her so much of her high school days and stirred something deep inside her. At the sight of the five beautiful horses, she groaned.

"Bring back memories?" Pete escorted her over to a mare that was already saddled.

"Yes."

"This here is Snow Cone."

Snow Cone. "Cute name." The top of her head was white, and from her eyes down she was the color of a waffle cone. "Hey, there." The horse whinnied. "How nice that the hands saddled her." That way they wouldn't waste daylight.

"Hands? No. I came out before I picked you up and got the horses ready."

Pete was amazing. "Thank you."

"You're welcome." He led Snow Cone out of her stall. "You need help up?"

"I'm good." As if she was sixteen again, she mounted. Pete did the same. "What's your horse's name?"

"Winter Run." He nodded to the outside. "Let's get a move on it, cowgirl. I got a nice place I want to show you, and it gets dark soon in these here parts." She loved his fake cowboy accent.

Side by side they walked their horses for a bit. Going slow allowed her to enjoy the scenery, as well as the scent of sage that was mixed with pine. Mountain vistas never ceased to amaze her. The big expanse took her breath away. When a gust of wind blew across the plains, it cut through her jacket, but the sun warmed her up in seconds.

By taking their time, Zoey got the feel back for riding. She was quite happy that her body had remembered how to sit and how to ride. But after all that had happened this past week, she wanted the adrenaline to pump through her veins, to make her feel alive again.

Time seemed to stand still. "Want to race?" she asked, hoping she wouldn't fall off if he agreed.

He grinned. "Want to lose?"

"You are so going down, cowboy."

Pete tugged on Winter Run's reins and looked around. "Let me see. How about we stop fifteen feet in front of that large boulder?" He pointed to an outcropping of rocks about three hundred yards away.

She petted Snow Cone's flank. "Ready, girl, to beat this old man?"

He laughed. "Old, huh? On the count of three. One, two—"

While Zoey was usually a stickler for rules, the urge to break one this minute seemed right. She nudged Snow Cone before he said three, and the horse took off. It was as if the animal sensed the competitive tone in Pete's voice. A few seconds later, he was by Zoey's side, his horse kicking up dirt. He looked over and waved. Damn him. Determined to win this bet, she leaned forward and urged on her steed.

Pete toyed with her, pulling ahead for a few lengths, and then falling behind. As they neared their destination, his horse charged and crossed the imaginary line first. Damn. By the time she pulled up, she was laughing hard.

Pete jumped off his horse, came over to her, and helped her

down. "Nice riding there."

His hands on her caused tingles to charge up her spine. "Thanks. I see I'll need more practice if I'm going to win next time." The excitement and thrill of the race was fantastic.

"Not a problem. Coming out here soothes the wild beast inside me, too." He pounded his chest, but thankfully didn't give a Tarzan yell. Pete's eyes darkened as he moved close and wrapped his arms around her waist. "How about a kiss for the winner?" He tilted his head and tapped his cheek.

"Why not?" He'd earned it. Zoey leaned in and gave him a quick peck. She caught a slight hesitation on his part as if he was debating whether to go further. At the thought that he might, heat raced up her face.

He slid his hand to hers. "Come on. There's something I want to show you." He nodded toward a path that wove its way between the rocks. "You good with a quick climb?"

"Sure." Now more than ever she wished she hadn't let her running routine fall to the wayside.

Since the path was steep, Pete led. Every few steps, he'd stop and check to see if she was okay. His protective side appealed to her. In less than ten minutes, the trail ended.

"Come take a look at this." He helped her over some boulders at the top.

She was a little out of breath when she stepped next to him. The wind at this altitude was strong and the space to stand meager, but the trip was so worth it. "It's amazing." The tip of peak, far in the distance, had a dusting of snow on top, foreshadowing the coming of winter.

Pete moved behind and wrapped his arms around her. "Don't want the wind to carry you away." As if to prove his point, a strong gust buffeted them, and his grasp tightened.

His warmth seeped through her, and the peace she'd been

looking for finally arrived. He rested his chin on the top of her head. Without a word, they absorbed nature's beauty.

Pete pointed to the peak in the distance. "That's Ch-Paa-qn peak."

"It's magnificent." The brown range below gracefully led up to the base of the rugged mountain. If there had been a good place to sit and chat, she would have suggested it, but there didn't seem to be anywhere up here but against a steeply slanted rock.

"Now you see why Dad wanted to move here."

"Totally."

"Let's head down. There's a small cove inside the tree line that will offer some shelter." He took her hand and together they picked their way down the trail.

The soles of her boots were rather slippery on the pebbles, and the few times she slid, Pete managed to keep her upright. When they reached the bottom, the horses were still there, nibbling on tuffs of grass.

Pete grabbed the reins of both horses and led them a hundred feet to the trees. "Just in case they get any ideas, I better tie them."

Once the horses were secured, he grabbed a blanket and a thermos from his saddlebag. He then led her along a level path into the woods where the fresh smell of pine boosted her spirits. Less than a half mile later, the sound of rushing water greeted her. As soon as they passed a large bolder, a small stream appeared.

"This is awesome."

"It's one of my favorite spots on Dad's ranch." He spread out the blanket and guided her to the ground. He then held up the thermos. "Hot chocolate?"

"Sure." She unscrewed the top, poured half a cup, and returned it to him. The intense smell of chocolate brought back good memories of when her friends would build a campfire and roast marshmallows.

He tipped the bottle to his lips and took a draw. "When I told my mom I was coming out here today, she said Dad wanted to meet you. Are you okay with that?"

She chuckled. "Sure. What do they know about me? Did you tell them about the shooting and my breakdown? I don't want to say something about Thad and have your mom be shocked."

He rubbed her arm. "Relax. I told her I was remodeling your home and had just met you. Nothing about the incident or the aftermath."

The aftermath. That sounded much better than a breakdown.

For the next few minutes, they just listened to the gurgling stream, the leaves rustling in the wind, and the birds singing. It was peaceful and natural. As much as she liked communing with nature, she wanted to learn more about him. "What was the toughest part about growing up as the son of Randal Banks?"

He glanced over at her and raised a brow. "Your shrink side is showing." He worked his mouth as if he was trying not to smile.

"Well, I am a shrink. You asked me out. There are bound to be consequences." She swallowed a laugh.

"Consequences?"

When he sobered, she shrugged. "I like to dig. It's part of who I am."

He grinned. "I'm good with a little unearthing. As I said once before, I have nothing to hide. The ladies I've always attracted seem to want to talk about themselves, but not you."

"I can't learn anything when I'm speaking."

Pete stared out at the water, the trees, and then the sky.

"You want to know about me?" His voice had softened, almost as if it was laced with pain.

"I do."

"Okay, then. Here goes."

Chapter Eleven

Pete couldn't believe it. Zoey was even more fascinating than when he'd first met her. That initial encounter would be something he'd never forget. When he'd turned around in her bathroom, it was like she was holding out an emotional life ring meant just for him. It was an offering. A plea to connect. A gift really, and while it was laced with pain and confusion, it also held immense strength. He bet she had no idea that when she'd told him about her fear of dying and looked at him with both hope and despair over how she'd put another man's life in jeopardy, that a frozen piece of his heart had cracked.

Now, she was giving him another opportunity. Not only did Pete want to know her better, he was thrilled that she wanted to learn something about him. Him! Broken Pete Banks. For the last ten years, he'd put a lot of sweat equity into building his business. Stayed on the job site for long hours and earned a lot of money. He tried to tell himself it was for his future, but deep inside he knew it was to earn his father's love.

Pete had sacrificed a lot to get where he was, which meant he hadn't focused on searching for what he really wanted out of life—a woman he couldn't wait to get home to each night, and a couple of kids he could dote on.

The never-ending doubt refused to stop. Was he good enough? Maybe he didn't deserve his father's love. Or a woman's for that matter. Could Pete's own actions have been the reason he hadn't found what he wanted most? Or did his father have a fatal flaw? Fuck if he knew. Maybe that was why he hadn't tried hard enough to find someone to love.

Thad had chastised him several times saying that just as a woman started to mean something to them both, Pete pushed her away. His roommate claimed it was fear of rejection. Did he truly believe Pete would fucking crumble if someone else he loved didn't return the affection? He was better than that. Or so he hoped.

"Pete?" Zoey placed a hand on his. The worry on her face told him he'd gone inward again, and he prayed he hadn't scared her off.

She'd asked him a question. "Yes, what was it like being me? Hmm." He shook his head, unsure of where to begin. Should he talk about how his father didn't seem to notice he existed when he was growing up? He inhaled, hoping he could do this without looking like a cold bastard—or a pathetic victim. "When we talked before, I mentioned I was pissed about my father's treatment of the help."

"You did."

He felt bad not explaining himself more fully, but at the time, Zoey needed her world to settle first. "I was embarrassed every time he dismissed one of the workers or was rude to them. I still have this image of my father stomping on a freshly planted patch of flowers because he thought they looked cheap."

"That's terrible. I can see why you sought Alex to be your friend. You were very noble."

"Noble? As an eight-year-old, I'm not sure I knew the word.

Sure I liked the kid, but I think I did it more to piss off the old man. My mom taught me it was wrong to judge people who didn't have as much as we did, but I felt helpless to stop my father from acting the way he did. My only weapon was to embarrass him right back." He could see now that tactic hadn't brought them closer as a family. Pete had wanted to show his father that acting superior had its consequences. Too bad he failed to get his point across.

Crossing her legs, Zoey faced him. "Deny it all you want, but your friendship with Alex says a lot about who you were as a young man. Also, I'm impressed at your insight about your dad's faults."

He had barely scratched the surface. It hurt every time Pete had asked his dad to come to one of his games, and his father never showed. "Thanks." A strong ache still resided from those days. Looking back, he wasn't easy to live with. He might only have been ten or so, but he knew what his father disliked. Pete had purposefully been a bad student, given his lunch money to Alex—in large part because Alex needed it—and even locked his bedroom door as soon as he came home from school so he wouldn't have to talk to his dad. That juvenile behavior only caused a bigger chasm between him and the rest of the family, one that was now too wide to cross—at least for his dad. "I'm still trying to figure out why my dad never acted the way a father should."

"How should a father be?" Her tone held no censure.

"Like Alex's dad. His father gave him hugs, praised him all the time, went to his soccer games, and encouraged him. The only real affection I saw from my dad was directed at my younger sister, Dina. Looking back, it was easy to see why. She was pretty much perfect." Two blue jays squawked in the trees above them, but as soon as a squirrel scurried after them, they flew away. What Pete wouldn't give to be able to take flight at the first sign of trouble. *Then I'd be a coward.*

"You really think Dina being well behaved was the reason for your dad's affection?"

"Perhaps. My transgressions seemed to highlight her perfection."

"Have you ever asked him about the disparity in treatment?" She wove her fingers together, almost as if she wanted to tell him how much of his issues were actually his fault. Fuck. Maybe they were. The ache in his belly increased.

"Not directly, but I sure as hell made enough comments to hint at it. He never seemed to take my concerns seriously." Jesus. He sounded like a whiner.

"I'd be pissed, too. It sucks when parents aren't always there for you."

He liked that she got where he was coming from. "Don't get me wrong. My mom was great. She came to my games and supported me with whatever I wanted to do."

"She was always there for you. That's so important. Neither of my parents are as extreme as yours, but they fall closer to your dad than your mom."

He sat up, not liking that she might have experienced a similar situation. It was tough on a boy, but he bet it would be tougher on a girl. "What do you mean?"

"Both of my parents are a bit distant emotionally. My dad worked so much he didn't have time to give us his undivided attention, and Mom didn't know how to cope with having five kids, a husband, and a job."

Even with that baggage, Zoey seemed to have come through life unscathed. Or was she holding back, too? They might have more in common than even he realized. "That had to be rough."

She looked away, and a quick flash of pain sliced right through him. He wished to hell he knew what to say. Zoey picked up his hand and ran a finger down a crease in his palm, almost as if she wanted to pretend as if everything were normal. Her touch was almost too much to bear.

"Tell me something about Dina. Does she live around here?"

"I thought you were going to read my palm." *And look into my soul.*

She smiled. "I wish I had the knowhow." She let go of his hand. *Dumb, Pete, dumb.*

"Dina, huh?" He was happy she'd changed the subject to something a bit less emotional. Acid had dug a nice little ditch in his gut just discussing the tidbit of history about his dad. "She owns a dress boutique in town appropriately called Dina's. Like my dad, my sister has a good work ethic. Unlike my father, she's non-judgmental."

"You have a good work ethic, too." Her brows rose slightly as if she didn't think he was giving himself enough credit.

He was willing to admit that once he'd graduated from high school, he'd always tried his best. "Thanks. I'll brag and say I have a positive cash flow and happy employees." Zoey worked for herself. While she didn't have any employees, she'd understand it wasn't easy to hire good help, order supplies, deal with subcontractors, and be nice when working with the client. "My father isn't the easiest person to know, but he did teach me the value of hard work. Mom is big into volunteering. She works hard, too—sometimes too hard."

Zoey plucked a blade of grass from next to the blanket and twirled it in her fingers, not looking like a woman with all the answers. "Back to your youth," she said, flicking the blade away. "What was the most fun thing you ever did as a kid?" She seemed to have thought about what he said before coming up with her question. He really liked that about her.

"That's a tough one." His parents had taken him and Dina to Disneyland for weeklong trips, but Zoey probably meant what he'd done without his folks. "When I was about eleven, me and my friend Joe ran away once. We lasted about six hours before we realized we didn't have enough money to pay for things and came home." He leaned back on his elbows, remembering that time fondly and smiled. "But during those six hours, we rode buses and pretended we were adventurers who could do anything we liked. The freedom was addicting."

"I never had the courage to do something like that."

"Girls needed to be cautious."

"What else?" She smiled, and an excitement grew deep within him.

"Stole a car once. The rush was unparalleled." Her eyes widened and she covered her mouth, looking adorable. He chuckled. "Don't worry. Nothing was harmed—neither car nor person—in the making of this tale."

Zoey lowered her hand slowly, exposing a grin. "Tell me about it."

"Let me preface this by saying I was thirteen and stupid. Joe, who was a year older, was my accomplice. If he were here, he'd say it was my idea, but since he's not, I'll blame him." He smiled, wishing he were thirteen again, not having to worry about the consequences of his actions.

"You've led a colorful life, I see. So, you *borrowed* a car. Then what?" From the way her eyes sparkled, she seemed to be enjoying this, which had been his desire from the start.

"It was during the summer between eighth grade and ninth. On day, I rode my bike about ten miles to his place."

"One of your parents couldn't have brought you?"

"Mom was at some charity event, and I didn't want to ask dad. Joe's father owned a repair shop."

"Ah, yes. Russell Banks's son shouldn't socialize with a garage mechanic's son."

He cracked up at her stern delivery and was delighted she was on his side. "You got it. If Dad had seen the place, and put himself in my shoes, he might have understood. The shop was so cool. Mr. Dalton had every tool imaginable."

"You loved cars, then?"

"I did. If majoring in construction hadn't worked out, I might have chosen to design or fix cars for a living." Building seemed to be in his blood, and the appreciation from the homeowners helped make up for some of the slights growing up.

"I can tell you like working with your hands."

"I do." But that was getting off the subject. "There were these twin freshmen girls, Stella and Stacey Crumpfield. I'll spare you the details, but suffice it say both Joe and I liked them for reasons other than for their smarts." Zoey laughed, clearly understanding what he was referring to.

She rolled onto her stomach and propped herself up on her elbows. He was thrilled that she seemed comfortable being with him.

"You know," she said, picking some dirt off the blanket, "where I used to live in Connecticut, freshmen girls didn't even give middle school boys the time of day."

Pete ran his hand over the wool blanket near her fingers and enjoyed the rough texture of the material. Touching natural things like wood, stone, and fabrics helped to ground him. "Joe was a freshman, so it was cool. We thought one way to impress them was to have a car. That's when Joe suggested we *borrow* one from his dad's shop and take the girls for a spin. Snow them how cool we were."

"You weren't old enough to drive."

Pete tucked his tongue in his cheek. "Your practical nature is showing. A teenager will do a lot of stupid things in the name of love."

"Love?" She laughed and placed a hand rather dramatically over her chest. "I can see where this is headed."

"In Joe's defense, he'd just finished a driver's education class and thought he was ready for the Daytona 500." He shook his head, knowing she was going to be surprised by what happened. "I can still remember both the joy and the fear coursing through me. The joy was having the girls willing to come with us, and the fear was because Joe's old man had a display case full of guns. He'd have used one on us if he'd caught us."

"But you did it anyway?"

Pete loved her incredulity. Zoey was refreshing, open, and a total delight. "Remember, we were kids. It was fun taking chances, and then believing consequences were for others. We assumed we weren't going to get caught. The adrenaline rush was intense."

She encouraged him with smile. "Go on."

Chapter Twelve

Pete loved seeing Zoey respond to his childhood tale. "We drove to the girls' house. Or rather Joe drove. He did an okay job staying on the road, too." Zoey shook her head, looking just like Dina had when he'd told her what they'd done. "Once we got there, we needed to let them know we were outside without tipping off their parents."

"How did you do that?" She sat back up and crossed her legs again. Only now, she was closer—much closer.

Pete cleared his dry throat, not sure if he should brag, but then decided to go for it. "Being the athletic one, I climbed the tree to the porch overhang and walked along the roof until I found their room and tapped on the window." He unscrewed the thermos and offered to refresh her drink. Zoey held up her cup, and he filled the hot chocolate near to the top. He then took a hit and recapped it. That simple act of sharing seemed so natural, so right.

"Weren't the girls scared to have some guy's face suddenly appear in their room window? I would have been," she said, lifting the cup to her lips.

That was because she was a good girl, and the Crumpfield sisters most definitely were not.

"If they were, they didn't show it. Stella was ecstatic as soon as I showed her that Joe had a car. Long story short, as soon as I helped the girls out of the house, they practically ran to the Ford."

Zoey rolled her eyes, looking like a teenager herself. "You can skip the part about the sex." She drank more from her cup.

Pete couldn't believe how much credit she was giving him. "I wish. We never got far enough for that. You see, smart guy Joe took us out to what we both thought was a deserted country road. He then got the bright idea to see how fast he could drive."

Her mouth parted. "That's dangerous. Had he even driven by himself before?"

It was such a high to have someone respond so easily to everything he said. "When Joe was about ten, his father would let him pull the cars into and out of the garage. He had more practice during the class, but was he good? Hell, no, but Joe thought he was the coolest dude on earth. That was until the cop stopped us."

Her eyes shone with delight. "Oh, no. What happened?"

"At the time I thought my life as I'd known it was about to end, but apparently Officer Phelps was a friend of Joe's dad." He'd almost shit when he saw those lights flashing.

"How did your dad react when he found out?" She pressed her lips together, probably to keep from laughing.

"Find out? He never did. Shit, if he'd learned we were almost arrested and thrown in jail, he would have yanked me out of private school and sent me to some last opportunity school for juveniles. Then I never would have seen the inside of a college classroom."

"So the cop let you off?"

"Hardly." Pete always wondered where he'd be today if Officer Phelps had acted differently. If Pete had been ticketed, would that have gotten his dad's attention? "Let's just say that for a price, the officer promised not to tell either of our dads or the girls' father."

"Price?"

Pete took another drink of the hot chocolate, deciding to let Zoey guess what that might be. When she didn't offer any suggestions, he continued. "Because Officer Phelps was friends with Mr. Dalton, he must have heard him complain about how there wasn't enough time in the day to finish all the chores he needed to do—like paint the fence that rimmed the entire ten acres of his property."

"Don't tell me Officer Phelps said he'd keep quiet if you two volunteered to paint said fence?" She looked like she was about to laugh.

"You guessed it. From that day forward until school started, I rode my bike over there and painted that damned fence side by side with Joe."

"That's a touching story." As she inhaled, she scrunched up her nose. "I was afraid to do anything wrong." Her lips turned into a pout, and he squelched the urge to do something to erase it.

Instead, Pete placed a hand on her arm wanting to let her know that he understood. "I bet you just didn't want to disappoint your parents. Or be a poor role model."

Her smile returned, but it looked a little forced. "Something like that."

Zoey Donovan had totally grown on him. He'd never met anyone who he'd connected with so well. Not only was she a great listener, she seemed interested in what he had to say. Pete didn't want their adventure to end, but he had promised his mom he'd bring Zoey back to meet her.

"Since you'll be meeting Joe tomorrow at the anniversary

party, let me give you the 411."

"Awesome."

"He's Thad's older cousin. He's fun loving, daring, and a bit crazy. He only calmed down after he took over his father's repair shop business."

She blinked in surprise. "I didn't realize you and Thad's family went back that far."

"We do. Joe and I were a year apart in school. He was the cousin I spoke of. Thad was two years younger, so I can't say I *knew* Thad other than as Joe's little cousin. In ninth grade, I was shipped off to boarding school in Denver." The abrupt send-off still stuck in his craw. In his opinion, the C in history wasn't enough of a reason to have yanked him away from his friends. Pete received a great education, but a few parental visits would have been nice.

"I look forward to meeting him."

"You'll like him. It's getting dark. We should go." The two of them had such a good time that he prayed his dad didn't say something to mess it up.

Once they reached the horses, Pete helped Zoey onto the saddle. She probably didn't need his aid, but he wanted to touch her, get close to her, know more about her.

"You set the pace, Zoey." He wagged a finger at her. "But no racing." As well as she rode, she'd held on for dear life coming here. Heaven help him if she fell.

"Okay."

This time they merely trotted home, arriving as the sun set. Before he had a chance to help her down, she dismounted. "Need assistance with the saddle?" he asked. It was heavy, and he worried she might strain her back if she lifted it.

"That would be nice." She glanced around. "Got a brush?"

He pointed to the shelf along the far wall, wanting her to

enjoy sharing their time together. "Help yourself."

Pete lifted off Snow Cone's saddle and carried it into the tack room. He then did the same for Winter Run. When he returned, she was brushing her horse, talking to her newfound friend like they'd known each other forever. Her strokes were gentle yet firm, and he liked that she seemed to love animals like he did.

Pete spent time brushing down his steed, too. Today had made him realize he needed to come out here more often. Riding had given him a clarity he'd been missing for a while— or had it been Zoey who'd helped him see some things better?

Not wanting to keep his mom or Zoey waiting, he finished quickly and put away the rest of the gear. "Ready?" He needed to warn her. "You probably think my dad's a monster. He's not. To guests, he'll be charming."

"Forewarned is forearmed, right?" He laughed at her comment and held her hand as they strolled up to the main house. Zoey looked up at him. "Any topics off limit? Like politics, religion, or the death penalty?"

He rubbed his chin trying to figure out if he wanted to answer her seriously or goof with her a little. He chose the latter. "Those are good. Just don't ask him about Harold Feinway."

"Who's he?"

"The man my dad murdered." Her eyes grew big again, and he got a kick out of her reaction. He couldn't help but continue. "Whatever you do, don't ask my mother why she robbed a convenience store when I was six and Dina was three."

"No way."

Teasing her was fun, but it also helped him forget some of his issues. "She said she had to pay for medicine for us since we were so sick."

Zoey stared at him for a moment, firmed her lips then punched him in the arm. He was thrilled to see the tension he'd sensed earlier disappear. "Funny, funny. I meant like your car thieving days, Alex, or your dad's dislike of the hired help."

"You are something else. Ask anything you want. I'd love for you to hold my dad's feet to the fire." This could be interesting to see if she could get his father to remain focused on a topic that wasn't about him.

Pete escorted her to the house, knocked on the side door, and entered. The rich smell of baking made his stomach grumble. "Anyone home?" He hoped to run into his mom first.

"Russell, Parker's home," his mom sang out from the kitchen. Footsteps sounded and she rounded the corner wiping her hands on a towel. "There you are!"

"Hey, Mom." Her blonde hair was pulled back in a bun, as was always the case when she worked in the kitchen, but she had on more makeup than usual. Perhaps she was trying to impress Zoey. His mom didn't have to go to the trouble. At fifty-nine, she was still a regal beauty even without cosmetics.

She gave him a hug then quickly stepped back. "You must be Zoey."

"Yes, ma'am."

They shook hands. "Call me Isabelle, please." His mom turned back to him and placed the dishtowel over her shoulder, looking younger than usual. "Dad's in the den. Why don't you two join him? I'll be there in a moment."

As soon as they were out of earshot, Pete leaned close. "You want to come up with a signal to let me know when you've had enough of the old man?"

Zoey laughed at his antics. "I can handle your dad. I think our fathers are rather similar."

"For your sake, I hope not." He led her down the hallway

into the den. "Dad?" Jesus, the room was filled with the sweet smell of tobacco. "Can you put the pipe out?" A thin, white haze surrounded his dad's face.

He set down the offensive pipe, stood then held out his hand. "I'm Russell Banks."

"Zoey Donovan."

"She's the psychologist I told you about who works out of LACE hospital." His father responded well to educated people.

"Well, well." Pete was tempted to ask his father the reason for the surprise in his voice, but that might embarrass Zoey. His dad motioned for them to sit on the sofa before returning to his leather chair. "Have a seat so we can chat. Parker never brings anyone home to meet us." *I wonder why.* His dad leaned forward and placed his elbows on his knees. "I think he's embarrassed by us."

Angry would be a more descriptive word, but mostly it was because Pete didn't want his dad to pepper his date with questions about her plans with Pete. "I wanted to show Zoey the vista from on top of the rocks."

"My favorite spot. So, you're a psychologist? What kind of people do you treat?"

So much for discussing their common love of the view.

"Everyday people. Most of them just need some help navigating the rough waters of life."

"Have you dealt with any criminals?"

Here we go.

"A few."

"Well, I know all about criminals. Dealt with every kind from the serial killer to the petty thief. In fact I've put over eighty-percent of those I prosecute in jail."

Zoey let go of Pete's hand and leaned forward. "Sounds like an exciting career. Did you ever want Parker to go into law?"

"Not everyone's cut out to be a lawyer. We need people to build homes, you know."

She leaned back, looking as if she was enjoying the repartee. "Parker said you helped him get his start."

Oh no, Zoey. Now you've stepped in it.

"I did, but he's paid me back in full, plus interest. Guess he couldn't wait to get me out of his hair." His dad laughed, as if it was some big joke.

"I didn't realize you worked alongside of him, helping him run the company. What was that like?"

His father's mouth opened. *Go Zoey.* His heart zinged. Zoey Donovan had his back all along.

Chapter Thirteen

When Pete pulled into Zoey's drive after their fantastic date, she didn't want their time to end. Pete was fantastic and so was Thad. While she didn't know for sure how the two acted together, from the way they treated her, the three of them would get along just fine. She couldn't wait for the images of her last fiasco with a ménage relationship to fade and never resurface.

For the last few years, she'd spent her days helping others, never taking the time to think about what she needed. Having both Pete and Thad there for her when she'd broken down had given her some idea what she'd been missing—a lot. Life was give and take, but she'd been refusing the *take* half for a long time.

Pete and Thad were both good men, but different in an intriguing way. Pete was bright, adventurous, and caring—a people oriented guy. Thad understood both the criminal and regular mind, but he seemed more cautious about what he said and how he acted.

Pete cut the engine. "Here we are." He eased out and walked her to the door, his hand pressed against her back. "Tomorrow you'll get to meet Thad's family. I know you'll love them. My mom would fit in perfectly with his relatives, but my dad definitely would not."

"I liked your dad okay."

He halted for a second. "I could tell he liked you. He usually doesn't try to get to know a person."

The man had only asked her one question. "Are you saying your dad is self-centered?" It was what she believed. Russell Banks appeared to be unwilling or unable to connect to his son. It was a shame.

Pete laughed. "Is that a trick question?"

"No. Out of curiosity, do you spend a lot of time talking with him about what you do?"

"I have dinner at the house at least twice a month. Every time I mention what I'm working on, he has this incredible knack of turning around what I've said and telling me about one of his clients. You evidenced that."

"True. Men like your dad are hard to get close to."

He blew out a breath. "Ever get them to change?" The hope in his voice seemed to come from deep within.

She had to think about how to word it. "People only change when they want to."

"There's no motivation for my dad to be any different, but if you can think of a way, let me know. I'll be forever in your debt."

Now probably wasn't the time to discuss the rest of his father's issues. It was a bit chilly outside, but if she invited Pete in, she might be tempted to do more than give him counsel. Before she said goodbye, she wanted to add one more thought. "Here's the thing. I've worked with a lot of people—many very successful—who don't like who they are deep inside. By keeping everyone at a distance, it prevents others from finding out who they really are. Family members are no exception."

Pete whistled. "Now that's some deep shit. I need to chew

on that for a while."

She chuckled. "I didn't mean to get on my soapbox." She leaned over and kissed his cheek. "Thank you again for the horse ride and for showing me the incredible view."

"My pleasure." The shroud of his bitterness seemed to disappear as he moved closer. She wanted to taste him more fully, so she held still, understanding that Pete would want to make the first move. He seemed to need the control right now. He dragged a knuckle down her cheek. "We'll have to do it again."

Before she could say yes, he slanted his lips across her mouth, and her insides nearly melted. He'd opened himself up to her today, and with the barrier temporarily down, she didn't want to let him go. Wrapping her arms around his neck, she returned the kiss, loving every intimate second of his warmth and tenderness. His shoulders tightened, and he stepped back.

"Better go before I act like that stupid fourteen-year-old again."

Would that be so bad? "Tomorrow then."

He nodded toward her door. "I'll wait here until you're safely inside."

How considerate of him. As soon as she unlocked her door and stepped in, footsteps sounded on the porch, almost as if he didn't trust himself if he lingered. The temptation to run after him was strong, but his emotions seemed too raw. Zoey deactivated the alarm and looked out the window to make sure he left okay.

"You are screwed, Zoey Elizabeth Donovan."

She leaned her head back against the wall and sighed. Pete Banks was a good man It was too bad he didn't recognize it.

✧   ✧   ✧

The next morning Zoey stopped at Zelda's General Store to pick up something for Thad's grandmother, since Zoey never liked to go anywhere empty-handed. Just from the few things Thad had told her about the older woman, Zoey liked her already.

Because Nana grew her own food and loved to can her jams and pickles, Zoey looked for something unique, something his grandmother might not have. After a half hour search, Zoey found the perfect gift. Thad said because the house couldn't hold everyone, the party would be in a big barn. That meant Nana would be preparing the food in one place and transporting it to another.

The chalkboard canning jar caddy would be practical, yet whimsical. The carryall would fit three one-quart jars of Nana's homemade food, and the front had a chalkboard strip where she could write what was in each container. Wanting to have a nice presentation for the gift, Zoey purchased a small wicker basket and a blue and white-checkered napkin to line it with. Some blue satin ribbon that she had at home would make a great finishing touch. Happy to have something Thad's grandmother might enjoy, Zoey headed home to prepare for the evening's festivities.

She had six hours to get ready. Even so, that didn't seem like enough time. It wasn't just figuring out what to wear, it was deciding how to act. This would be the first time she'd see Thad and Pete together. *Just be myself.* She was comfortable around Thad and totally at ease with Pete, so what was her problem? Being with both should be doubly good, right?

Not wanting to dwell on something out of her control, she went to her bedroom to pick out something to wear. If she planned on climbing on old rusted vehicles, she had to dress casually.

Courtney's voice nudged her brain. *Go sexy.*

Sexy. Right. Zoey had already searched her closet for something to wear when she and Pete went riding and had failed. She didn't own much other than practical clothing befitting a therapist. Lydia Sayers, the owner of Naughty Desires, had come to happy hour a few times because she was a good friend of Melissa's. Zoey remembered Lydia saying she could make any sized woman look great. Perhaps it was time to stop over for a visit.

Pushing aside the undergarment issue, Zoey tried on a possible outfit. When she stepped in front of the mirror to see if she looked okay, she groaned. Not even close. She bet Nana would look sexier. That needed to change, but how? Zoey would look funny wearing a silk blouse to a barn, so all dressy options were out.

Jamie had good fashion sense, even if her style was a little more bohemian than Zoey's. It might be what she needed though. She called her friend, hoping Jamie would be free to shop.

"Hey. What's up?" Jamie sounded in good spirits.

"I need a clothing intervention."

"For real?"

Zoey didn't have time to analyze the reason behind Jamie's excitement. Zoey didn't dress that poorly. "Yes."

"It's about time. Is it for your big date tonight?"

When Thad had asked her to the party, it was because he'd cancelled the dinner Zoey had asked him to. But after being with Pete yesterday, she got the sense tonight would be a test to see if all three of them got along. "Yes. When I tried on my casual clothes, I looked more like Farmer Brown's mother than a thirty-two year old, sexy lady."

"You want sexy?"

Zoey told her about climbing on top of rusty cars. "It has to be practical, too."

"Practical but sexy. Got it. I'll be happy to help but I get the final say in what you wear."

That was tough. *To give up control or not.* "Deal."

✧   ✧   ✧

Zoey paced her living room waiting for Thad and Pete to arrive. It was hard not to look out the window, but she didn't want them to pull around the corner and see her peering out. No man wanted an overanxious woman.

She inhaled and checked her outfit one more time. Not wanting to embarrass Thad, Zoey snapped up another button on her form-fitting plaid shirt. The push-up bra Jamie made her buy was comfortable, but it revealed too much of Zoey's large breasts. She didn't want his Nana to freak. First impressions were important. It was bad enough her flaming red hair was untamable, but add in a revealing top and too-tight jeans, and his parents might tell Thad to take her home. Their son was a cop and should be with a conservative woman.

I'm conservative. True, but she sure didn't look that way tonight.

Before she could make any more adjustments, the doorbell rang. A rush of anticipation spiked every nerve in her body. Christ. She needed to relax and enjoy herself.

Making sure her palms were dry, she opened the door. "Come in." They sure did present a formative wall of man.

Pete looked even better than he did yesterday. He was like one of the hot cowboys her friends kept putting up on their Facebook pages with his faded, threadbare jeans that left little to the imagination, and a shirt that accentuated his beautifully developed pectorals. *Yum.* Thad was dressed in a white cable knit sweater, black jeans, and polished boots. He looked more GQ than Pete, but both would turn every woman's head in Rock Hard.

Thad smiled. "Mind if I take a look at Pete's handiwork before we head out?"

"Sure." She appreciated that he wanted to see what his roommate had done. She loved both her kitchen and bath, but if she'd known he'd want a tour, she would have cleaned up a bit more. "Pete, you want to show Thad?" Pete would be better at explaining all of the details.

"Sure. Go right past the dining room, Thad." As soon as his roommate's back was turned, Pete leaned over and gave her a kiss that was more a greeting than one of passion. "Hi." He grinned.

Her brain stopped functioning for a moment. "Hi back."

She followed Pete and Thad into the kitchen. With pride in his voice, Pete showed Thad the custom items he'd installed, from the induction stovetop to the refrigerator drawers in the center island.

Thad kept nodding. "Not bad. I'm liking it. The backsplash is better than what's in our place."

"I can't account for my mother's taste." Pete nodded for Thad to go back the way they'd come. "Zoey's bath is even better than the kitchen."

Zoey waited at the en suite entrance while Pete showed Thad what he'd done. "Over here is the switch for the towel warmer."

She didn't know that. "Seriously? That's so cool."

He winced. "This was what you ordered."

"I know, but I couldn't figure out how to turn it on, so I thought you hadn't installed it."

A shot of guilt crossed his face. "I normally go through all

of the features when I do the reveal, but I was a little distracted."

She'd been a sobbing mess. "I forgive you."

He showed Thad the double showerhead, a hidden storage
closet, and her favorite—the touch faucets.

Thad tapped the faucet and grinned like a little kid when it
turned on. "Sweet. We need some of these features at our
place."

Pete laughed. "You paying?"

"That would be a no." Thad faced her. "You ready to meet
the crazy Dalton family?"

"I am." Being surrounded by a lot of people was just what
she needed to keep her nervousness at bay.

Put her in front of a group of psychologists, and she could
talk for hours without a nervous bone in her body, but when
she was with two hot men, she fell apart.

On her way out, she slipped on her sweater jacket then
picked up the present for his grandmother.

Thad nodded to what was in her hands. "What's that?"

"Just a little something for your Nana."

"You didn't have to do that."

Yes I did. "I know, but I wanted to."

"I'm sure she'll love it." His eyes softened for a second, but
he quickly glanced away.

Pete had brought the truck, and Thad helped her into the
front seat where she was sandwiched between them. The floor
mats appeared to be freshly cleaned, and Pete had washed off
the contractor's mud. That was thoughtful of him.

Thad yanked his seatbelt over his shoulder and clicked the
end into the slot. She had to lean left to find hers, and when she
did, her shoulder bumped Pete's. "Sorry."

"Sure you are." He winked.

"I should warn you about some of my relatives," Thad said, as if he had no idea about the intimate exchange with Pete.

Zoey twisted in the seat to better look at Thad. "I'd love the lowdown."

"Pete said he told you about my cousin Joe."

"He did." She liked that they didn't hide anything from each other.

Pete turned south onto Arbor Way. "Tell her about Joe's brother."

Thad stretched out his legs. "Ah, yes, Tony. He won't be coming, I'm afraid. He's on a cruise to Alaska."

Pete moaned. "I like Tony. He's adventurous and pure of heart."

Thad laughed. "He is that."

Zoey was intrigued. "What's so special about Tony?"

"Tony is as scruffy as they come. Long beard that needs a trim bad, a big pot belly that's as hard as a rock, and let's just say, he's not a big believer in oral hygiene."

She laughed. "He doesn't seem like the cruise type." While she'd never been on one, she pictured the trip goers as either retired people or those with families.

"None of us do. He was a poor, uneducated kid who struck it rich. He's enjoying life to the fullest now."

That sounded fascinating. "How did he make his money?"

"He started making wine from frozen canned fruit. Got real good at it, too. People from far and wide would buy from him. Then he got the bright idea to make Vodka. Within a year, the guy was richer than sin, but you'd never know it, other than it spawned his love of travel."

"Someday I'd like to meet him." She had no colorful people in her extended family, outside of two cousins she hadn't seen in ten years.

Pete turned west onto River Rock, a road that ran parallel to the Harmes River. She'd never driven out this way before. "It's lovely out here." Both Thad and Pete nodded.

Ten minutes later, Pete pulled down a long gravel drive toward a modest home that possibly hadn't been painted in thirty years. About fifteen vehicles were parked haphazardly on the lawn. These were not the junk vehicles. She suspected those were in the back. The narrow twenty-foot-long front porch had a swing, four chairs, a covered grill, and what looked like large speakers all crammed together. Off to the side of the house was a rusted cistern hoisted on stilts fifteen feet off the ground.

Thad sighed. "Home sweet home."

"You grew up here?" She thought this was his grandmother's home.

"No, but I spent more time here than at my own house. So did my cousins. Once the trees lose their leaves, you can see where I grew up." He pointed to the west. "Over there is where Joe lives. His shop is attached to his house."

A barn-like structure next to the end of a rectangular building had a repair shop sign above the door. In front sat about six cars. Thad pushed open his door, picked up her present for his grandmother, and helped Zoey out.

"I'll take that," she said. It was better if one used both hands. So far, he hadn't used his left arm, and she worried his injury might be bothering him.

He handed it to back to her. "Warning. Be prepared for lots of hugging. It's what the Daltons do."

Oh, my. Thad hadn't shown his hugging side—at least not toward her. This was going to be a culture shock for sure. Her family never touched.

They walked up the steps single file, and then had to maneuver around the grill to reach the front stoop. Thad wiped his feet and pulled open the door. "Hey, Nana?"

The foyer was a small mudroom. One wall contained pegs for hanging coats, and the other had cubbyholes for purses and such. All the hangers were taken, but there was a little space on the end of one bench for her things. She'd had to bring a bag big enough to hold her camera.

"Minute," someone called from far inside the house.

All the tension in Thad's face seemed to disappear. Pete lifted the present from her hands. "Why don't you take off your sweater?"

The aroma of bread baking, mixed with something like chicken noodle soup, permeated the air. "It smells divine in here."

"Wait until you taste it," Thad said. "Nana's an amazing cook. She grows all of her own vegetables, so everything is fresh."

Zoey slipped the sweater coat off her shoulders and placed it on the bench. Pete's gaze lingered on her chest, forcing her to look down. Shit. A snap had come undone exposing her breasts. Stupid Jamie.

"There you are!" An older woman with short, no-nonsense gray hair waddled toward them, wiping her hands on her apron. She was big-boned and looked strong, probably from all the gardening and farm work. Her jeans, rubber boots, and loose-fitting shirt had seen better days, but every piece looked well cared for. Her eyes shone with love and happiness.

She gave Thad a hug. He winced when her arms wrapped around his forearm, but he said nothing. He must want the love more than avoiding the pain.

"Ahem," Pete said with a big grin. "No love for me?" He set Zoey's present on top of the coats.

Nana smiled and waved a hand. Two of her bottom teeth

were missing, but the glint in her eyes made her a beauty. "Come here, you." Nana seemed to hug him harder. She then stepped back and her gaze shot straight to Zoey. "Is this your girl, boys? My, my, but she's a beauty." Nana leaned closer to Thad. "She's not some kind of princess, is she?"

"Nana. Watch yourself," Thad said with love in his voice.

Then Nana grinned. "Just checkin'. Don't find pretty and nice in one package very often."

That made Zoey laugh. Pete handed her the gift she'd purchased for Thad's grandmother and Zoey held it out. "This is for you."

Nana's eyes widened. "Whatever for? It's not my anniversary or birthday."

"It's a thank you for inviting me."

"Well, don't that beat all." She took the present. "My, my, not a princess at all." She grinned.

Thad introduced her as Zoey. She was pleased he didn't add the doctor part. Too often when people found out what she did for a living, they kept quiet for fear she'd try to get inside their head and analyze them.

"You three come on into the kitchen so I can see what I got." Nana placed the gift on her hip like it was a child and wrapped an arm around Thad's shoulder. She hugged him close. "You can say 'hi' to the rest of the crowd in a minute. I want you all to myself for a bit." She looked back at Zoey. "I don't get to see my grandson enough. He's too busy saving the fine citizens of Rock Hard from those crazy kids to come visit."

"Nana, I stopped by last week."

"Only for a minute. I want us to sit at my table and talk, like we used to."

"The last time I spent all day here was when I was twelve."

"My point exactly."

When Nana's back was turned, Thad looked over his shoulder at Zoey and slightly shook his head. Nonsense. Nana was adorable.

They passed through the living room where it reminded her of her grandmother's house, and a wave of nostalgia flowed through her. Flocked wallpaper, a scarred table in the corner cluttered with framed family photos that were proudly displayed on a doily, an upright piano against the wall that looked well used, and several flowered sofas filled the neat space. There were enough sofas and chairs to hold fifteen or more people. The large number of photos covering the walls added to the homey touch.

On the other side of the dining room wall was the kitchen. It reminded her of those 1950s family television shows. The floor was faded linoleum, and the curtains over the sink were made from chintz. In the middle of the kitchen resided a big wooden table where she could picture loud family gatherings. She inwardly sighed. Her family ate in a formal dining room.

Thad pulled out a chair for her to sit. The kitchen counters were crammed with food prep, and it appeared as if their arrival had interrupted his grandmother's meal making. Zoey wanted to ask if Nana needed help, but as Zoey started to stand, Thad motioned she remain seated.

Nana had placed the gift on the table. She washed her hands at the sink and returned. "Let's see what this pretty thing is." She pulled on the blue bow and the cloth opened wide. When she lifted the canning caddy, her eyes shone. "Why, I'll be damned. This here is the nicest present I've ever gotten. Thank you, dear." She set the present on the table, pulled Zoey to her feet, and embraced her. Heat infused Zoey's face at the unexpected hug.

Zoey cleared her throat. "I thought it might come in handy

if you need to bring some of your homemade goods from the kitchen to the barn."

"You are so thoughtful. Boys, I can see why you wanted me to meet her."

Thad didn't bring her specifically to meet his family, but she was glad she was here now.

Feet thumped outside the kitchen, saving her from further embarrassment. Two men and a woman rushed in. "Thad!" one of the men exclaimed. The man in front clapped him on the back.

The pretty woman rushed over to Pete. "Long time no see." When she leaned over and gave him a hug, jealousy streaked through Zoey. *Whoa*. Then she remembered Pete had known at least some of the Daltons for over twenty years.

The second man, who looked younger, stood off to the side, saying nothing.

All three were dressed in jeans. The blond, shaggy haired man who'd just hugged Thad wore a T-shirt with the name Dalton's Garage blazoned on the front. He was a beefy guy with thick arms full of tattoos. He might be Joe. The other two were dressed more sensibly in long-sleeved flannel shirts. Both were thin, but looked to be in good shape.

The tattooed man stepped over to Pete who pushed back his chair and stood. the two hugged. "Comrade."

"It's been too long, Joe."

Seemed she'd guessed right.

"Tell me about it." Joe came over to her and held out his hand. "Name's Joe."

"Zoey." Did the comrade refer to their car-stealing escapade perhaps?

Joe nodded to the other man. "This is our cousin, Sam, from my mother's side." Joe looked at the bouncy brunette.

"And this pipsqueak is my older sister Erin. Her husband and three kids are running around somewhere."

Zoey let out a mental breath and leaned back to enjoy the chatter. "Nice to meet you all."

Erin, Joe, and Sam pulled up chairs, and Pete sat back down. Joe glanced at Thad then back at her. "Don't know what you're doing with my cousin here. He's the black sheep of the family."

She knew that wasn't true. "Care to tell me why you call him that?"

She loved that Thad groaned and Pete chuckled. Joe looked over at Nana. He held up a finger. "Can I get a beer?"

"You know where it is."

"Thad, Pete, Zoey? You guys want one?"

They all nodded.

Joe retrieved the beers from the fridge and passed them around. "Why is Thad the bad one? I'll tell you. Thad, you see, was a thief."

Chapter Fourteen

"Joe Dalton, you should be ashamed of yourself," Nana chided.

Her grandson shot the group a mischievous grin. Everyone's affection for the older woman was endearing. Being in her kitchen with her brood made Zoey feel totally at home— or at least what she'd always dreamed an ideal home would be like.

With a stubborn set to his jaw, Joe faced Nana, clearly trying to incite her. "Thad was a little thief, and you know it."

Nana broke apart some lettuce leaves and dumped them in a huge bowl. She lowered her chin and wagged a finger at Joe. "He was eight. You, mister, were eleven, old enough to have known better."

Thad just glanced to the ceiling and blew out a breath, acting as if no matter how many times anyone retold the story, his grandmother would always defend him.

Zoey laughed. "I need details, Joe. The tale sounds adorable." She'd already heard about his later exploits with Pete.

"Not going to happen," Thad chimed in. "You need to hear the *accurate* version. Joe will only exaggerate and make me look bad." Thad looked over at her and winked. She liked how he treated her with such respect.

Joe's mouth dropped open, and he tapped his chest. "Who, me?"

Thad lifted his bottle and tipped back some of the contents. "Here's what really happened." He narrowed his eyes at Joe, and then Thad turned toward her. "Joe and I were running around outside one summer, like little kids do, when we realized we were hungry. We were on the far side of Nana's property, so we didn't feel like coming all the way back to her kitchen for a snack."

Joe picked up his bottle. "I'll admit that I was the one who suggested we pull a carrot or two from old man Rochester's house." He faced Zoey. "He lives behind Nana. Thad was innocent—at least at first."

Thad shook his head. "It's my story. Let me tell it." From the way his cheeks dimpled, he loved the repartee with his cousin. "I didn't want to get caught stealing, so I suggested we pull a row of carrots, cut off the tops, and stick the leaves back in the ground."

"I love it," she said. "So it's only stealing if you get caught?"

"Watch it, wise guy. I was eight. My ethics hadn't been honed to the fine point they are today."

Joe tapped his chest again. "Don't forget to mention that your method had one flaw. The tops wouldn't stay upright." Joe's gaze shot to her. "I had the brilliant idea to clip Mrs. Rochester's clothespins to the green tops, and then plant the wooden pieces so the greens stood up straight."

Zoey pictured it in her mind and couldn't stop smiling. "That was brilliant." Joe preened. "Did Mr. Rochester ever figure out who'd masterminded the prank?" He'd know the carrots had been tampered with at some point.

Nana washed then dried her hands before walking over to the table. "I'll tell you what the hell happened. Poor Jacob came over to my house one day, nearly in tears."

Both Thad and Joe looked at her with disbelief. "Nana," Thad said.

"Okay, he was a little upset. Or he might have just been a wee bit curious. Said he couldn't for the life of him figure out why the tops of his carrots were dying. Since I have a green thumb, he wanted my advice."

Zoey finally let out a laugh. "That's priceless."

Thad slowly shook his head. "The following day, Mr. Rochester's *curiosity* got the best of him, and he pulled up the damn things. After making an educated guess as to the culprit or culprits, he walked right through the back door waving a carrot top with the clothespin attached. I was the unlucky one to be in this kitchen when he arrived."

"What did he do?" This time she didn't try to contain her laugh. Thad had been noble even back then.

"*He* didn't do anything. It was Nana who tanned my hide."

The group all laughed, acting like it had happened yesterday.

Just then a tall woman rounded the corner into the kitchen. "Mom?" she said. "We're all waiting in the barn. Is there a probl—?" Her gaze shot from Nana to Thad. "Oh! You're here. No wonder the production has slowed."

"Hey, Mom." Thad got out of his chair and hugged her.

"Me next," Pete said and followed suit.

Thad nodded to Zoey. "This is my friend Zoey. We were regaling her with the crazy stuff we did as kids."

Zoey pushed back her chair, closed the space between them, and held out her hand. "Nice to meet you, Mrs. Dalton. Happy anniversary." While she'd not met Mr. Dalton yet, she could see the family resemblance between Thad and his mom. Same brown hair, same warm eyes, and identical charming smile.

"Thank you, dear, but please call me Sharon. It's about time my son brought someone over to meet us." Zoey inwardly groaned as Sharon speared her son with an affectionately lethal stare for a brief moment. "Zoey, what do you do?"

Thad exhaled loudly. "Mom. Can we leave the grilling until after dinner? Dr. Donovan just got here."

Her brows rose, just as Thad probably had intended. "Okay." She walked over to her mother-in-law, and placed a hand on her back. "Mom, can I help with anything?"

"How about cutting these tomatoes?"

Zoey had taken up enough of everyone's time. "Let me help, too. I love to cook."

Nana smiled. "She's a keeper, boys."

Zoey hoped the men didn't respond. Being with them both was still so new.

Between Thad's mom, Joe's sister, Erin, and herself, they finished with the prep in less than ten minutes. Zoey's stomach never stopped grumbling as the rich aroma of basil and garlic had her mouth watering.

Like a drill sergeant, Nana directed the men to carry the ham, chicken, and other heavy items into the barn while the women were left with the lighter dishes.

Thad balanced his tray on his right forearm and kept it steady with his left hand, but no one mentioned his odd method of transportation. If Zoey had to guess, he hadn't told his family about the shooting. Just like she hadn't mentioned being taken hostage for a few minutes to her folks or siblings either.

Zoey was tasked with carrying a bowl of beans. She debated asking Thad if he wanted to switch with her, but knowing how proud he was, he'd construe it as her thinking him weak.

"Don't say a word about this," he said, nodding to his forearm. He stole a glance at his mom.

She'd guessed it. "My lips are sealed." A trail of people carried food across the back yard. Now she saw the full extent of the junkyard. Over a hundred cars were jammed close to each other, all at different angles. Some of them appeared to be from fifty years ago, and others were much newer, but all were in various stages of disrepair. Most of the cars had rust clinging to the sides, and her fingers itched to take photos.

"Watch your step," Pete called out.

At the last moment, Zoey looked where she was going. Her pulse jackknifed for a second. She'd nearly tripped over a tire. "Thanks." *Stop rubbernecking.*

The barn was a huge structure, two stories tall, with an open hayloft in the middle of the second floor. Straw spilled out of the upper window, implying the barn might have other uses besides holding large gatherings. The sides were made of slatted wood, but rarely did two adjacent pieces touch.

Loud chatter greeted them even before they stepped inside. She followed Pete into the interior and looked around. "This is amazing."

Never would she have guessed a barn could look so festive. Sure, stored junk, like lawnmowers, stacked chairs, old ladders, and even a Model T that looked to be in pristine condition, were jammed off to the side, but it was the string of lights hanging from the ceiling and the vases full of flowers on the tables along the side that made the place cozy.

Someone had set up about ten six-foot-long tables in a U-shape that opened to a stage along the back wall. The place mats were burlap and the dishes paper. She loved it. About twenty people were seated, drinking bottled beer and chatting. How cool was this?

Erin nudged her and nodded to the large wooden platform. "That was where I was married. The ceremony was incredibly romantic."

"I bet. It's so unpretentious." Zoey had always imagined getting married in a big church, but after seeing this barn, she could totally see why Erin would love it. A quick smile stole across Zoey's face. Her friend Amber had been looking at large venues for her upcoming wedding. "Do the Daltons ever rent the place out?"

"All the time. There are always professional photographers who want to bring people here to take pictures in front of the barn, sitting in the Model T, and at the junkyard."

"I can see why. It's charming."

Zoey would have to take a few pictures to show Amber how neat this place was. Inwardly, she chuckled at what Amber's mom's reaction to the place would be. While Zoey had only met Mrs. Delacroix once, the surgeon would probably be quite horrified to have her daughter married in a place this earthy. Amber, however, would think it was perfect.

There was one glitch with Zoey's plan. Amber's wedding would have to be soon or in the spring, because the barn would be too chilly during the winter.

Thad's mom slipped the container of beans from Zoey's fingers. "Let me introduce you to Thad's dad. Ignore his blustery ways. He can be a bit outspoken."

Zoey could guess where Mr. Dalton got that trait from. Being raised by Nana would have been quite the experience. Zoey's chest tightened as she remembered her grandmother's loving ways. Once Zoey shared this meal with all these wonderful people, she might never be the same again.

✧　✧　✧

Throughout dinner, if someone started to recount a Dalton tale, the group would suddenly go quiet. Some stories were laugh out loud funny, while others were poignant. They all had one thing in common. The tales were colorful, charming, and full of love. By the end of the meal, the Dalton family had definitely won her heart.

Sam, the quiet cousin she'd met in the kitchen, had told Zoey's favorite story. Apparently, one Christmas a whole bunch of the older kids had grabbed the leftover dinner rolls and rushed outside. Sam, being five, followed. They'd reached a tree in the backyard and helped him climb up to the first branch. The older kids, being brats, pummeled Sam with the rolls then ran away, leaving him to figure out how to get down. He said he'd cried and cried, not because it hurt being hit, or that he was afraid to jump to the hard ground, but because he didn't have any rolls to throw back at them. When Zoey had asked who'd saved him, Sam said Thad had come back and helped him down. Even as a kid, Thad had been a hero.

When she, Pete, and Thad finished eating, he pushed back his chair. "If you want to get in some picture taking, we should go now. The light won't last but for another hour."

A few of the women had started cleaning up. "Shouldn't we help?"

"Nah. The Dalton family has it down to a science. The kids even have their assigned chores. They'll be finished in no time."

Thad did seem anxious to show her around. "Great."

In the middle of the meal, she'd used the bathroom in the main house and had snagged her camera on the return.

As soon as the three of them stepped outside, Pete clasped her hand. "Let me show you my favorite truck."

She enjoyed his warm, reassuring touch. "You actually have a favorite?" Given how he used to hang out here as a kid, it almost made sense.

"You will, too, once you check them out." They picked

their way past about thirty cars. "Here it is," he said. "Is this awesome or what?"

It was a rusted truck with a smattering of red on the side door. The windows were long gone, but something about this Ford's bones made it a classic. "I love it. Let me take your picture next to it."

"Come on, Thad. Let's give the lady what she wants." In one leap, Pete jumped onto the hood then climbed up on the roof.

"Be careful," she called out, fearful the thing might collapse. Pete waved away her concern.

Thad crossed his arms and leaned against where the driver's side front fender used to be. It was next to impossible to walk around to find the best view, so she shot from where she stood. Wanting a unique angle, she crouched and aimed upward, creating a slight silhouette of the men. "Great." *Click, click.*

Before she could ask them to stay put for a moment longer, Pete hopped down and yanked open the squeaky driver's side door. He slid in, gripped the bent steering wheel, then leaned out the window and waved. All he needed were overalls, a cowboy hat, and a long piece of straw to chew on to make her believe it was fifty years ago.

When Pete grinned, she moved in close to take his picture. After a few frames, she focused on Thad, who'd sprawled out on the roof, one arm behind his head, his injured arm resting on his stomach. Her heart sped up at his handsome image. She put the camera on multiple exposures and pumped off three shots in a row, hoping to catch the perfect picture.

Pete piled out of the car. "Let me take one of you and Thad."

Zoey appreciated the men were willing to indulge in one of her hobbies. "I'd love that." She was having so much fun that she didn't want to think about anything other than the moment. She set the camera on automatic so all Pete had to do was point and shoot.

"Just push this button." She handed him the camera then stepped close to the car, debating the best method for getting on top.

Before she could decide, Pete's hands clasped her waist. "I'll give you a boost." He twisted her around and lifted her up as if she weighed nothing. In a flash, she was on the hood of the truck close to Thad's knees.

With his good hand, Thad dragged her back a bit, and then stretched his legs on either side of her. When he leaned her back, her breath whooshed out and butterflies lodged in her belly. Pete liked her, and despite the closeness she and Thad had shared playing darts, she wasn't positive about his interest.

Thad leaned over. "Relax. I don't bite."

Pete snapped several pictures in a row. Forcing herself to stop worrying, she decided to test Thad's intentions. She leaned her head back and looked up at him, daring him to do something wild. Would he be as forward as Pete? Or would he be more reserved? Thad pressed his cheek against hers and the camera sprang to life as Pete snapped the pictures.

Without considering the consequences, she rotated her face a half inch from his. His skin smelled of soap and hay, and she kissed his cheek just like she had Pete's. When the shutter didn't snap, she groaned. "Pete. You missed the shot!"

"Then kiss him again."

Pretending not to make a big deal of it, she puckered her lips and placed the kiss on Thad's cheek again while she eyed the camera. *Click, click, click.*

"Perfect," Pete said. "Thad, let me sit with Zoey and I'll make sure to give you an award-winning pose."

Knowing Pete, he'd give her another toe tingling kiss, and her body heated at the possibility. Thad grinned, jumped down, and switched places with Pete. Only instead of having Pete straddling her like Thad had, he got on his knees, leaned over, and kissed her like a man on a mission.

Chapter Fifteen

When Pete broke the kiss, Zoey didn't move— couldn't move. Her lips tingled and desire bubbled to the surface. She held her breath, hoping Thad was okay with this blatant display of affection. It would kill any chance of being with both men if this bothered him. It was one thing to hold hands with Pete, but to kiss him in front of Thad was another.

Pete ran the pad of his thumb across her lips and her body lit up. "Mmm. You tasted good," he said. "Like chicken and sweet potatoes with a hint of tangy beer."

Thad stepped in front of her. "That's not fair, Pete. I just got a kiss on the cheek." The teasing tone in Thad's voice was a relief.

When she glanced his way, his smile erased all of her worries. "You're right," she said. "I wasn't fair to you, and I always like to keep things even. Come here."

Thad's hazel eyes darkened as he wrapped his good arm around her waist and guided her to the ground. Instead of letting her be the initiator as she expected, he leaned forward and kissed her fully and passionately. His tenderness told her a lot about the man. The contact didn't last long, but it sure had her heart pumping.

Thad leaned back with a satisfied look. "There. All even."

Happiness soared through her, but it was time to take this to another level. "Yes. Even. Just the way it should be."

The sun was about to set and the shadows across the yard were growing long, which meant it was about time to leave. The photo shoot had been wonderful and enlightening. Clearly, the men were best friends. Easy going, fun, and adorable, yet seemingly competitive when it came to her. She couldn't have asked for more.

Pete's behavior hadn't surprised her as much as Thad's had. Being with his family seemed to have relaxed him. From the moment he'd entered Nana's house, he'd seemed like a different person from when he'd faced that madman or even when he'd shown her how to throw darts.

Just as she was about to suggest they head back to her place, the barn doors creaked open wide. Three adults and two kids making lots of noise ambled out. Thad's parents, who were holding hands, followed. Nana was next, carrying the caddy Zoey had given her. That was so sweet of Thad's grandmother to use it so soon.

"We should see if Nana needs help." Zoey should have insisted all three of them stay behind and clean up, but Thad had claimed all was good.

"Everything's taken care of. Nana only leaves when the place has emptied out," Thad said. "You ready to head home?"

From the cute way his lips lifted, he might have making love on his mind, too. "Yes." A blast of cold air blew between the house and the barn, and she shivered.

Pete slid his hand around her waist and pulled her close. "Once we get in the car, I'll put the heat on for you."

She wasn't used to men who were so aware of her needs and desires. With them, hints no longer seemed necessary. All of this newness thrilled her.

Joe, Sam, Erin, Erin's husband, and their three kids rushed out of the house carrying something in their hands. "There you guys are," Joe said. "Ready for the annual horseshoe competition? I installed lights on the side of the barn for the occasion."

Thad looked over at her then back at Joe. "We've made other plans. Rain check?"

"Sure," Joe said, looking a bit disappointed.

Thad's action surprised her. Never would she have guessed he'd break with tradition, but she wasn't going to complain. After she expressed her congratulations to Thad's parents again, and thanked Nana once more, the three of them left. Besides engaging in the pleasures of the flesh, Zoey looked forward to downloading the numerous photos they'd taken. No doubt the best shots would be the portraits of Thad and Pete.

Once seated in the truck, Zoey leaned her head back, and she couldn't help but let a small smile tug at her lips. She'd never been with men like these two before. While Thad had to be careful how he moved about, he'd always found a way to have fun. Pete laughed easily, and when prompted, Thad had been spontaneous, too. Together, they had this amazing synergy, seemingly better together than apart.

Today had been a real eye-opener for her about what she'd been missing in her life. She was the oldest of five kids, and had spent most of her teen years trying to keep her siblings and parents happy. Thad's family was different. They were giving and loving all on their own, and probably never needed someone to mediate their family squabbles.

There was one other big difference. While her parents were nice people, they had a hard time expressing affection. They never hugged.

A short while later, Pete pulled into her drive and cut the

engine. Thad slipped out and lent her a hand. As soon as she reached her porch, she faced them. Yes, she was nervous, but she wanted them. From the warm vibes she was getting, they seemed to want her, too. The only thing that might prevent Thad from agreeing was his injury. "Can I convince you both to come in?"

Pete glanced over at his roommate and shrugged one shoulder. "It wouldn't be nice to turn down a beautiful woman, now would it?"

Her heart skipped a beat. Zoey looked over at Thad.

He grinned. "No, it would not."

Yes! While she'd basically orchestrated this potential seduction, this was what she wanted. With trembling fingers, she got the key in the lock on the second try, opened the door, and punched in the security code.

Just as she reached up to take off her sweater jacket, Pete slipped behind her. He slowly eased the wool down her arms, and she shivered, not because it was cold, but because of what his nearness did to her.

"Just helping you, sugar. That's all."

The nickname rolled off his tongue in that soft cowboy way of his. "Thank you." She slid her hands out of the coat and turned around. Damn, but he was a good-looking man. Except where his father was concerned, he seemed to have his act together.

Now that they were all here, she wasn't sure how to go about seducing them. "Anyone want some decaf?" That would help clear her head.

"Sounds good," Pete said.

Zoey rushed to the kitchen, popped the coffee containers into the machine and returned. She didn't want to miss being with them for another minute.

"That was fast," Thad said as he placed a hand on her back. "Let's sit on the sofa."

This was going quite well. Thad at least seemed to have picked up on her subtle and not so subtle hints. He patted the seat beside him and let his gaze drag down her body, his eyes smoldering with desire—or at least that was what she wanted to believe.

Talk to him. Should she ask about his injury? Or more about his family?

Just spit it out. She needed to tell them that she wanted to have sex with them both.

✧　　✧　　✧

The coffeemaker dinged a few minutes later, and Pete jumped up. "I'll get it. You two keep talking."

Thad was telling her about one of his cases and Zoey sounded enthralled, asking questions at all the right places. Pete didn't want the coffee being ready to break their connection. That was another thing he liked about her—Zoey was interested in everything they said and did.

"You need help?" Zoey called from the living room.

He opened a few cabinets and found what he was looking for on the third try. "No. I'm good."

He filled three cups with the delicious smelling hot brew. Zoey liked her drink with sugar and cream while he and Thad preferred it black. After he located the sugar bowl and found the container of cream in the fridge, he carried Zoey's drink out, along with the sugar bowl. "Be right back."

One trip later, Pete had served them all. He probably should have suggested Thad and Zoey come into the kitchen and fix their coffee in there, but talking wasn't really on his mind. Neither was drinking coffee.

Zoey ripped open the sugar packets and poured in the cream with slightly shaking fingers. Why would she be nervous? She seemed to have had a great time at the party, and she certainly had been at ease when they'd gone riding. She'd also responded to his kiss.

While the three of them sipped their hot drinks, Zoey kept running her finger around the top of the cup, her touch light and soft. Was she doing that motion on purpose to drive Pete crazy? Or was she unaware of her actions?

She looked up at them. "Anyone want to look at the pictures I took? I'll have to download them onto my computer first though."

Photography seemed to be a passion of hers, and Pete wanted to view the evening through her eyes. He'd assumed downloading would be the first step, though huddling around the small camera display worked for him as well. "Sure. It'll be fun to see what we have."

"My desktop's in the bedroom. Do you mind going in there?"

As much as he wanted to make love with her, he probably should ask if she was okay being with both him and Thad. This was a big step for anyone. "Not at all."

With coffee cup in hand, she picked up her camera bag, and both he and Thad followed her into her bedroom. From the death grip she had on her cup, she was nervous. Damn. Had she planned on seducing them and was now getting cold feet? Or had his people reading skills vanished?

Once in her room, the air had that sweet linen scent that was so her. Pete had passed through her bedroom to work on the master bath, but he'd never carefully checked it out before. The soft pastels on the bed fit her personality—tailored yet feminine. It was quite homey. One thing was sure, she really liked the color pink. He should have paid closer attention and bought those pink candles instead of the beige ones.

Zoey sat at her computer desk that butted up against the wall across from the bathroom. "Give me a sec to boot this up." She faced Pete. "You want to snag two chairs from the dining room so we can all sit next to each other?"

"You got it." So far so good. In a flash, he was back, careful not to bump the legs against the walls. As soon as he placed one on each side of her, Thad joined them. By the time they were settled, Zoey had the first picture up.

It was the one of him on the truck roof with Thad leaning against the fender. "Two handsome men, I'd say." Pete wanted to keep it light to help her feel more at ease.

Zoey laughed, as had been his hope. The next photos were of Zoey and Thad hamming it up.

Thad leaned closer. "That's a beautiful shot of you, Zoey."

She smiled and looked more beautiful than ever. "Thanks."

Pete waited for the one of him and Zoey kissing. She clicked the next one. There it was. "Can you enlarge it?" he asked.

Her face turned a slight pink, but she made the photo bigger. He'd forgotten that her right hand had been clasping his thigh. She was leaning close, touching his cheek with her left hand, her lips pressed against his.

"Hmm," Zoey said. "I do like it, but the shot lacks... passion."

Was she kidding? "I know I was enjoying it."

She glanced between the two of them then back at Pete. "What do you say we try again, and let Thad be the judge of the level of *passion*?"

Pete was glad he'd finished his coffee, because if he'd any in his mouth, it would have been all over the keyboard.

✧　✧　✧

Pete's eyes widened, but Zoey was tired of second guessing herself. She wanted these men and they seemed to want her. There was no need to be nervous. Zoey leaned forward, cupped the back of his head, and nipped his bottom lip to test the waters. She wanted to delve into his sweetness and take all of him, but timing was everything.

Pete must have wanted her bad, because he took full possession of what she had to offer, his kiss transporting her to the wonderful moment they'd shared at the family gathering. She then ran her tongue along the seam of his lips to tantalize him, and the second their tongues touched, her body heated. As they kissed, she tasted the hint of coffee and smelled the fresh outdoors on his skin. As much as she wanted to explore every inch of Pete, she didn't want Thad to be left out. With much dismay, she broke the kiss, her breath coming out faster than she ever expected.

"Okay then." Drawing on her professional demeanor she faced Thad. "Score?"

He stroked his chin in a deliberate manner and drew in a deep breath. "I'd give it a seven point five out of ten."

Pete laughed. "Let's see you do better."

Thad didn't wait for her assent. He drew her close, and when their lips touched, fire filled her veins and her heart slammed against the ribs. Yes, they'd kissed before, but this seemed more real, more personal. Definitely more intense.

She pulled back, realizing it was the time to tell them, the time to warn them about her lack of experience.

"Another seven point five for sure," she said, a bit out of breath. Giving Thad a different score would only cause bickering. For there to be any chance of them being together, she needed to be upfront with them. "Can I be honest for a moment?"

Thad clasped her hand. "You can tell us anything." All hint of joking disappeared.

She loved how he could sense her every mood. "I told you I'd been with two men, but maybe not in the way you think." Lies between parties only caused problems. She didn't need a degree in psychology to know that.

As Thad ran his hand down her shoulder, his callused fingertips left a trail of sensuality on her warm skin. "What do you mean?"

"The two men I was with weren't into anal sex." Pete's brows rose and Thad's pinched. Shit. While she'd never taken a poll, her friend Amber said she and her men loved it. How many others did, too?

"Did the three of you share a bed?" Pete asked. His voice held no judgment.

"Sometimes, but they worked a lot, so I had sex with whoever came over." That made her seem cheap even though it wasn't like that.

Compassion filled Pete's face. "We don't just want to have sex with you."

Blood rushed fast through her veins. "What do you want?"

"We want to make love with you. We want you happy. Mechanics don't matter as long as we can experience you." Pete's eyes darkened, or else the computer screen had dimmed. "Have you been hankering for two cocks at once?" Pete asked.

It was time to be honest. "No."

Pete smiled. "Then we're in agreement. I'm a pussy man and so is Thad."

"Thank you." With that out of the way, the tightness in her chest released. Since she was going to have sex, she didn't want to have streaks of rust on her hands and face. "Mind if I take a shower first?"

Pete's grin reached his eyes. It was as if she'd just told him he'd won the lottery. Without a word, he stood, drew her to his chest, and gazed deep into her eyes. The gold flecks in his eyes danced amidst the blues and greens, causing her pulse to soar and funny sensations to zip through her. If her mind hadn't blanked, she'd have given the tingling and pulsing a name.

Thad stepped behind her and wrapped his good arm around her waist. Surrounding her. Tempting her. Making her want them badly. "How about the three of us get clean together?" he said as he nuzzled her neck. Heat rushed over her skin. "It'll save water."

She smiled as she looked over her shoulder. "Save water?"

Thad chuckled. "If I had said that I wanted to see you naked, touch your luscious breasts as the liquid cascaded down your soft skin, and devour your lips, you wouldn't have freaked?"

No. It's what I want. "How about you do that and let's see how I react?"

Both men cracked up. Pete tilted her chin toward him. "You are a true treasure."

Zoey wasn't sure what had come over her to say something so suggestive, but now that she had, she was glad. Aggression was not in her genes, but she was enjoying every minute with these men so much that she didn't want it to end. They were smart, noble, sexy, and kind. She'd been wrong in her belief that being with two men would automatically end in disaster.

She ran a finger down Pete's chest. "Now what?" Should she take off her clothes or try to strip them of theirs?

Pete pulled the lapels of her shirt apart, and the snaps popped one at a time. When her blouse fell open, his blue eyes shimmered. "Holy fuck. Thad, look at her. She's perfect."

They were probably trying to set her at ease. Thad twisted her toward him. "Let me see." He whistled. "You've been holding out on us."

At his sincerity, a smile tugged at her lips. Thad twisted her back to face Pete, and then slid her blouse down her shoulders. Thad's lips pressed against her bare neck, and electric pulses shimmied down her body.

"Shouldn't we get clean first?" That way, she could touch them all over.

"Shh." Thad nuzzled her neck again then moved close to her ear. "How about we decide? We'll do whatever feels best at the moment, okay?"

Anything either of them wanted to do was fine by her. "Sure." Her blouse floated to the ground, and the cool air kissed her shoulders. "Do you want me just to stand here?" Having them undress her would be a high.

Pete placed his hands on her breasts and rubbed his thumbs over her bra. "What do you want to do?"

Touch you, feel your skin under my fingertips. Kiss you both.
Show them.

She latched onto Pete's big belt buckle and yanked it open. He smiled. Encouraged, she undid the top button of his jeans, and then unzipped his pants, one notch at a time. When she managed to get the tab to the bottom, she whipped open the two sides. Her breath caught. "Oh shit. Where's your underwear?"

Pete cracked up. "I like to go natural."

Dampness spread between her legs then something heavy clunked behind her. As much as she wanted to check out Pete's cock, she looked back at Thad. Standing on one foot, he tore off his second boot.

She tossed him her best frown. "I was hoping to take off

your clothes." Slowly. With lots of touching.

"With the speed you two were getting naked, it'll be morning before you get to me. I've waited a long time for this, Zoey Donovan, and now that making love with you is near, I can't wait anymore."

She wasn't sure she'd heard Thad say that much at one time before. And for him to express an emotion like that floored her. Not wanting to delay the adventure anymore, she reached out and slipped her hands under Pete's shirt to hurry the process. His warm skin nearly burned her fingers, and she itched to take in more. But Thad was right. She needed to strip Pete naked now.

"You are so beautiful," Pete said. "I can't wait to taste you." When he ran a tongue over his lips, she froze. Her whole body caught on fire as her breath lodged in her throat. Good thing he pulled back or she might have dismissed the shower. "Thad's right. This is taking too long. Don't move. I want to finish undressing you as soon as I get naked." Pete stepped back, shucked his boots, socks, pants, and shirt in record time.

Her gaze zeroed in on his big cock, and then she raised her eyes upward to his flat abs, past his spectacular pecs, and up to his massive shoulders. All the wallboard lifting, hammering, and demolition sure had made his body hard. "Wow."

Pete smiled. "Now, it's your turn—or rather, our turn to get you undressed."

She swallowed. They both wanted to help? *Yes!*

From behind, Thad's hand slipped around to the front and undid the button on her jeans. His touch made her senses swirl. The zipper followed next. Instead of tugging her pants lower, he slipped a hand down her belly over her yellow lace panties. She sucked in a big breath as the thrill of being one with him—with them—made her a little dizzy.

"Nice," Thad whispered. As if he were playing the piano at the apex of her thighs, he leaned his naked chest against her back. When his cock pressed against her rear, a big breath escaped.

Using his injured hand, Thad lifted her hair out of the way and sucked on her earlobe. She let a low moan escape. Hoarse, needy, wanting.

"She likes that, Thad." Pete slipped his hands under her bra and pushed the confining material on top of her breasts. "Incredible." He leaned over and ran his tongue lightly around one nipple. His touch made her lightheaded and hot.

"Did you forget about the shower?" She was barely able to get the words out through the thick haze of lust blocking her brain.

She didn't want to stop them from what they were doing, but at some point none of them would be able to keep from making love. When they sniffed the rust and sweat lightly coating parts of her body, they might be sorry.

Pete laughed. "I don't forget anything you say or want."

How sweet was that? Thad's hands clasped her hips. "I'm naked. I say we get clean." As if he was finished with teasing her, he dragged the right side of her jeans down and then her left, using his right hand both times.

His injury must be bothering him, but if it hurt him too bad, surely he'd stop. "Let me take off my shoes," she said. *And then my bra.* Removing them might be tough for a man with only one good hand.

"I have a better idea," Pete said. A second later, he scooped her up and placed her on the edge of the bed.

Without a word, both men dropped to their knees and removed her shoes and socks. Zoey leaned back on her elbows to make it easier for them. Pete nodded, and both of them slipped off her pants. They acted like a well-honed military unit on a mission, complete with hand signals and head motions.

The bra hiked up over her breasts couldn't possibly look sexy. Since neither man seemed to have this need to remove it, they must think it looked fine, which was all that mattered.

"Thad, you go ahead and finish unwrapping the present," Pete said, "but after we're clean, we go slow. Real slow. I want to hear Zoey beg for mercy."

She'd never begged in her life, but with these men, she just might.

Chapter Sixteen

oth men climbed on the bed like predatory animals. Pete slipped a hand behind Zoey's back and smoothly unclasped the bra hook as if he'd done it hundreds of times. With care, he slipped the strap down first one arm and then the other before tossing the bra to the top of the bed. "Better?"

Zoey's pulse soared. "Uh-huh."

Pete tapped her nose. "I'll get things ready." He slipped off the bed and ducked into the bathroom.

Get things ready? All he had to do was turn on the water. As soon as Thad stretched out next to her, Zoey's focus shifted to him.

He lifted onto his elbow. "You know what got me through those long hours lying in that hospital bed when I was under-cover?"

His soft words caressed her skin. Or else it was his finger brushing against the tip of her nipple. "What?" Shivers of delight flowed down the sides of her breast.

"Waiting for you to come talk with me."

Her heart rate increased. "Seriously?" *Tell him.* "They asked me to visit once or twice to make it appear legit, but once I met you, I was so intrigued that I couldn't stay away." When she wasn't with a patient, she'd stopped in to see him.

"Oh, yeah?"

She rolled onto her back and placed her hands behind her head, as if being almost naked with this man was an everyday occurrence. He leaned over her and caressed her belly with his lips before moving lower. Her breath caught. "Yeah."

"Why's that?" He looked up at her, his eyes sparkling.

Thad was fishing for a compliment, but she didn't mind. She wanted to tell him how much she liked him. "You were focused and determined to do whatever it took to help catch the serial killer, even if it meant putting your life in danger."

"You think I was some kind of hero?" Thad puffed out his chest.

"I don't think it. I know it."

His chin lifted. "I am, aren't I?" She loved the glint in his eyes.

The bathroom door opened. Pete stopped then clapped his hands. "Dude, she's not even naked. What's wrong with you?" He rushed toward the bed, acting as if Thad had committed a crime.

Zoey laughed at Pete's ridiculous tone. Not wanting Thad to hurt himself by having to take off her panties, she slipped them off herself. Only then did she remember not all men liked a waxed pussy. Brazilians were her one vice. Not nails. Not pedicures. Not even haircuts. Just being free of the frizz made her feel more feminine.

Neither man said anything. She looked up at Pete first who blew out a small breath. "You keep getting better and better." Pleasure raced through her.

Thad rubbed a thumb over her pussy lips and electric sparks shot everywhere. "Smooth."

Pete held out his hand. "Come on. I can't wait to touch you

all over, sugar."

She let him pull her to her feet. As she stood, she looked behind her to make sure Thad was okay, that he wasn't favoring his arm.

As Pete led her to the bathroom, he held her hand. When he pushed open the door, she halted. All of the lights were off, except for the one in the shower. Ten beige candles flickered, encasing the room in a warm and romantic bliss. "It's awesome." She was glad he'd found the matches.

"I wish I'd thought to buy pink candles."

He remembered how the beige ones had triggered her breakdown. Zoey stood on her tiptoes and kissed him. "No. These are perfect. Thank you."

"Nice," Thad said, coming in behind them.

"I thought so, too." Pete opened a drawer and picked out the remote. A few buttons later, the shower shot to life.

She'd seen the gadget, but hadn't had the time to figure it out. "That is so cool."

Pete smiled. "It's one of my favorites."

Thad stepped next to him. "Lemme see that." Pete handed it to Thad, who seemed fascinated with it. "You can set each side's temperature?"

"Yup. Nothing but the best for Zoey."

She stared at him. "Did I order that?" Her mind must be playing tricks on her.

Pete shrugged. "No. I wanted to throw in something extra as a thank you for using Banks Construction."

No wonder he was a success. "You didn't have to do that. Your work alone speaks for itself."

Pete leaned over and kissed her this time. "Well, thank you, sugar. But enough talk. It's time to get you clean." When he dragged a finger down her throat, and then around her breast, her nipple puckered. She heard him chuckle, despite the noise from the running water.

Pete pulled open the shower door for her, and she stepped to the side with the more powerful showerhead. When she didn't need to wash her hair, she preferred the side with the Rainshower head. She held out her hand to test the temperature. It was perfect.

Pete entered, and as soon as Thad removed his bandage, he joined them. Staples punctuated his wound, but the injury didn't look too bad.

She looked between the two men. "Can I wash you guys first?" It would help settle her nerves to touch them.

Thad looked at Pete then back at her. "How about you clean Pete's back while I clean yours?"

She was a big believer in equality. "Kind of like a train. I like it. After we do one side, we should turn around and wash the other." That way she could touch them everywhere.

Thad tucked a tongue in his cheek. "Yeah. Then we turn around." She liked this lighthearted side of him.

Hold it. Thad's sexy look registered. "You aren't thinking of having sex in the shower, are you?" She wasn't innocent, but none of the man she'd dated had ever wanted to do that.

"Not us," Pete said with a grin.

She wasn't sure she believed him, but she'd wait and judge if they asked.

"Dunk your head under the water," Thad said. "You need to get wet, so I can wash your back. Then I'll do the same."

As soon as she finished, Thad took her place. The water sluiced over his corded muscles and heated her from the inside out. While Thad stood under the warm flow, she checked out Pete, who seemed to be enjoying the gentle shower.

She grabbed the liquid soap, dumped a handful in her palm,

and then tapped Pete on the shoulder. "Can you step back? I don't want the water to wash away the soap."

"Yes, ma'am. One step back." Pete was such an agreeable guy.

"Hmm. Where to begin?"

He chuckled. It was his fault for her indecisiveness. There were too many wonderful areas to clean. The shoulders seemed the easiest place to start. No sooner had she rubbed her slick fingers over his smooth skin than Thad's slippery palms cupped her breasts from behind. She gasped at the erotic contact.

"Don't mind me. Keep doing what you're doing," Thad said as he pressed his chest against her back. She might have been able to ignore him if he hadn't nestled his cock between her legs.

Pete dunked his head under the water and a blast of spray bounced off his neck and pummeled her. "Hey," she said.

He turned around and grinned. "Sorry. I thought you were facing Thad because you weren't touching me anymore."

That was because Thad's cock was wreaking all sorts of havoc with her libido. "Thad distracted me."

As if to prove her point, Thad twirled her nipples between his fingers, sending a spark of pleasure through her. "Don't blame me, darlin'."

Pete snagged the body wash. "Thad, help me wash her." Pete guided her to the side of the large stall where he plastered her back against the cooler tiles. "Thad, you take her left side. I got her right." Pete nodded to her. "Hands over your head, please."

Zoey obeyed, but instantly realized the vulnerable position she now was in. Sure, she could lower her arms, but she wanted to see what they would do next.

Thad nudged her left leg toward him while Pete drew her

right in his direction, opening her legs wide.

Pete grinned and lowered his gaze to her pussy. "Now for the best part. Just so you know, I'm not trying to excite you, merely getting you clean, so don't think any wicked thoughts."

"Right." She wished she had such control.

"Close your eyes, darlin'," Thad said. "It'll make the experience a lot nicer. We'll be good. You can trust us."

Trust them? With their hard throbbing cocks inches from her open pussy? Strangely, she did, so she obeyed. Using slow circular movements, Thad rubbed her shoulders then ran his hand up to her wrist, keeping the pressure hard so as not to tickle.

"So smooth." His growl made her smile. Thad dripped soap over her belly and began to rub it in.

Pete must have dropped to his knees, because his hands clasped her left ankle. Using an up and down motion, he rubbed and rubbed, making his way up past her knees. All she could think of was what would he do when he reached the top? The soap Thad had rubbed onto her belly finally dripped down her pussy, sending a hard throbbing signal to her brain. Her body yearned for something to fill her, to pound into her.

Just as her imagination ran wild, Thad dragged a soapy hand over her breast. As much as she liked his touch, she wanted to feel his rough skin on hers. It was time to hurry things along. "My arms are getting tired."

Thad reached up and lowered one of her arms. She thought he'd let go but instead guided it to his cock. "It needs washing. Want to help?"

"Yes." She would have soaped her hand first had he not leaned in and kissed her. Or should she say possessed her? As he captured her mouth, liquid heat ripped up her body. When Pete plunged a finger into her opening, her mind froze. She was so consumed with the lust and passion running rampant in her body that she forgot all about rubbing Thad's cock. The kiss intensified and suddenly it became hard to breathe, hard to remain standing.

"Give her air," Pete said. "Keep your eyes closed, Zoey, while I rinse you."

A warm spray of water cascaded down her body. Pete opened her folds and rinsed, but he didn't touch her sweetest place. His goal must have been to drive her crazy.

When she was free of soap, she opened her eyes, and enjoyed how their magnificent bodies shimmered as they rinsed themselves.

The water stopped. "Come with me." Thad led her onto the cushy bathmat, and then both men snatched towels off the rack.

Pete held the terrycloth in front of her. "Now for one of my favorite things to do. Thad, how about you make sure her back is dry, especially between her legs, and I'll concentrate on her front."

"You got it," Thad replied.

While Pete ran the material over her breasts, giving her nipples an extra polish, Thad dragged the cloth down her back before gently drying between her legs. Her excitement heightened with each swipe. By the time the men finished drying her, her whole lower body was throbbing with desire.

A big problem was that her long hair kept dripping where they'd dried. "Let me do something with this mop." After she wrung out the excess water, she dragged a comb through the tangles. In less than a minute, she'd done all she could.

"Gorgeous." Pete picked her up and grinned. "A princess deserves the best treatment."

She wanted to reiterate that just because she went to private school and came from a wealthy family, it didn't mean she was a princess. Even Thad's grandmother agreed with that.

Pete carried her into the room and placed her on the bed. "Ready for a ride?"

"Only if you go easy on me." From the size of their cocks, she wasn't sure she could handle one after the other, but she was willing to try.

"You can count on it." Pete grinned, and as he crawled between her legs and spread them wide, shivers of anticipation crawled up her body. His grip spoke of a skilled lover.

Thad stretched out along her side and propped up his head with his good arm. His luscious lips were within striking distance, and she took advantage of him being near. When she brushed her lips against his, he lingered there for a long moment.

Pete's tongue swiped across her opening and she had to pull away from Thad to catch her breath.

"Don't be that way," Thad said.

Before she could explain that she was overwhelmed, Thad abandoned her mouth to capture her left breast. Between the two men it was like lava had broken loose inside her. Red hot heat bubbled to the surface and she lost control.

"Ah, ah, ah." Her breath whooshed out as the torrent of pleasure slammed into her. The initial tingling turned into high voltage power, setting off a climax so strong, her breath nearly stopped. She grabbed the sheets and balled them up. Why was she so weak?

When the intense rush slowly ebbed, she opened her eyes. Even though both men were smiling, embarrassment skated up her face. "I'm sorry."

Pete laughed. "It's okay, sugar. We're glad you got the first climax out of the way. Wait until the second one. It'll be a lot better." He tapped her hip. "How about getting on your elbows and knees to see if you can excite our wounded cop here?"

Yes! Quicker than they could say her name, she was in position, ready for whatever they could dole out. Her pussy throbbed and her slick walls were ready, in dire need of something big and hard to drive into her. She couldn't wait to see if she could crack Thad's powerful control.

He knelt in front of her, and she cupped his hard sac with one hand and grabbed his throbbing shaft with the other. Just as she ran her tongue from his balls up to the head, Thad reached under her and pinched her nipples hard. The quick shot of pain sent her spiraling out of control again. The delirious sensation then morphed into pleasure.

Behind her, foil tore and a condom snapped over Pete's cock. While she'd wanted to tease Thad without distraction, it seemed Pete had other ideas. The moment his cock pressed against her opening, her mind splintered. With both Pete and Thad touching her, there was no way she'd last.

"I can't wait any longer." Pete grunted and slid his cock into her, stretching her wide. Her pulse soared and her inner walls spasmed. His cock was huge.

As soon as she opened her mouth to let in more air, Thad pressed on her head to remind her he needed her. To hell with teasing. She went for the full frontal assault. Drawing him into her mouth, she slid her lips downward, keeping the pressure tight. When the tip of Thad's cock banged against the back of her throat, she swallowed, allowing his dick to slide in deeper. She didn't know when she'd learned to ignore her gag reflex, but she prided herself on her ability to capture a lot more than half a cock.

"Jesus, Zoey." Thad palmed her scalp.

Pete pulled out and plowed in again. "You are so fucking tight, sugar." His throaty moans and grunts thrilled her.

On his next thrust, her vision blurred and blood pounded in her ears. The faster she pumped her fist up and down on Thad's cock, the more powerfully Pete drove into her. Thad's fingers were going wild on her breasts, and her body kept craving more. How was it possible that these men knew every sensitive spot on her body?

With Pete's next deep plunge, she lost it again. Her second climax swooped in and slammed into her hard, taking her someplace high and far away. As if the men had signaled to each other, Thad's cock exploded a second later, his hot seed shooting down her throat. She pulled her mouth off his cock and swallowed his tangy brew just as Pete detonated. Eyes closed, she let his climax sweep her away again.

What seemed like a lifetime later, Pete draped his body over her back and ran his hand down her damp hair. "That was... 'spectacular' seems inadequate."

She would have laughed at his desperation if she'd had the strength. Pete rolled to the side and tugged her on top of him, kissing her softly. "I like you a lot, Zoey. Damn, girl. Not only are you hot, you're everything a man could want."

His words warmed her to the core. In a matter of minutes, these men had erased years of hurt and self-doubt. For that she'd be forever thankful. A relationship wasn't just about sex, but when three people were able to forget the outside world, it sure helped.

Thad eased off the bed, and then returned with a cloth to wash her, but as soon as he cleaned her, she yawned. "I'm sorry. It's been a long day, but one I'll never forget."

Pete kissed her again and held her close. "You need to get some rest. Go ahead and fall asleep. I'll hold you." These men were both wonderful and considerate.

Thad slid behind her and nipped her shoulder, bringing

another round of throbbing deep and low. "I'm hoping we can convince you to join us tomorrow for breakfast. We like to go to the Valley Café on Sunday mornings."

What a wonderful tradition. "I'd love to." No sooner had they told her the time than her cell rang from the living room. "Ugh."

"You should answer it," Pete said. "It might be a needy patient."

"I hope not. Maybe it's one of my sisters calling." But at ten on a Saturday night? Doubtful.

"I'll get it," Pete slipped off the bed.

Gloriously naked, he jogged out of the room and returned with her purse a moment later with the cell still ringing. Zoey dug her hand in the side pocket, fished out her phone, and then checked the display. "Damn. It's the hospital."

"Answer it." Thad sounded like his cop persona.

She dragged a thumb across the screen. "Dr. Donovan."

"This is Terrance Aldrich. I'm one of the ER nurses at LACE. I'm very sorry to disturb you, but one of your patients, Kayla Perkins, was in an automobile wreck this evening."

Zoey sat up, her throat constricting at the terrible news. "Kayla? Is she okay? Is the baby alive?" Kayla was close to full term.

"Yes. They're both okay for now, but she's hysterical and we can't calm her down enough to treat her contusions. Her rising blood pressure is jeopardizing the fetus. Is there any way you can come in and talk with her?"

She glanced at the men. Their worried faces assured her they'd understand if she had to leave. "Absolutely. Tell her I'll be right there." She disconnected and dropped back on the bed.

Thad cupped her shoulder. "What is it?"

"One of my patients was in a car wreck and is having a

panic attack. I'm afraid I have to speak with her. I know the timing sucks."

"Go," Thad urged.

In silence all three of them dressed. Within five minutes, they'd escorted her out of the house where Thad pulled open her car door. "You won't forget about breakfast with us tomorrow morning, right?"

"No. Nine sharp at the Valley Café."

"Yes." First Thad kissed her then Pete. "Tomorrow then."

She couldn't wait.

Chapter Seventeen

Even though the late night traffic into downtown Rock Hard was light, Zoey had to work hard to keep her focus on the road. She wished she was still cuddled against her two amazing men, but Kayla and her unborn child needed her.

Within ten minutes, Zoey was at the nurse's station. "I'm Dr. Donovan. I'm here about Kayla—"

She didn't need to finish asking the woman's whereabouts because Kayla's scream and then her whimper led Zoey to the curtained room. Zoey rushed in. "Kayla. I'm here." The woman's sobs slowed, but she continued to hyperventilate.

"Dr. Donovan? What are you doing here?" Kayla's words came out on short breaths.

Zoey gently squeezed her shoulder. "I need you to listen to me," Zoey said in her softest voice. "You need to settle down. For you. For your baby." Except for Kayla's bruised face, she appeared to be all right, at least on the outside.

"I didn't mean to hit the other car." Kayla's agitation increased. She looked up at Zoey with tear stained red eyes. "I didn't even see it. Are they dead?"

Zoey hadn't been given any information. "I don't know, but let's worry about getting you and your baby help." She held

Kayla's hand, and the warmth must have triggered something inside her patient, for she calmed a little. Zoey looked up at the nurse. "Has her husband been contacted?"

The man nodded. "He's out of town, but he said he'd catch the first plane here."

"Good."

After fifteen more minutes of reassuring Kayla that she needed to think of her baby, her breaths finally slowed. Because of her pregnancy, she'd had to stop her anxiety medication. Going cold turkey had helped fuel her hysteria. Finally Kayla let the nurse take care of her.

Close to eleven, Zoey hugged Kayla goodbye. "Make sure to schedule another appointment," Zoey said. "We need to talk about what happened, okay?" The anxiety-ridden woman didn't need any more guilt.

"I will. And thank you, Dr. Donovan."

As long as Zoey was at the hospital, she might as well pick up a few files from her office. She'd read them tomorrow after enjoying a nice breakfast with her men. *My men.* It had a nice ring to it. She had to smile at her good fortune. Who would have guessed coming close to death would have united her with two fantastic men?

From the ER, Zoey passed through the big double doors that led to an inner corridor. Ever since the incident with Garrett McDonald a few days ago, she'd been vigilant when walking these halls. She now listened for strange noises, watched out for someone waving a gun—okay that she didn't expect to see—and sniffed for out-of-place smells. To her right were some administrative offices. As she neared the bank of elevators at the end of the corridor, she came to the Family Room where the doctors brought people to discuss organ donation and their loved one's condition. A strange moaning sound emanated from inside. Zoey stopped to listen. Was someone injured and trying to call for help? Heart beating a bit too fast, she strained to hear if perhaps she'd made a mistake. More groans reached her.

Needing to check it out, she eased open the doors to the darkened room. "Hello?"

No one appeared to be inside. *Curious.* Except for the glow of the emergency lights and the outside street lamps casting the room in eerie shadows, she couldn't see much. As she ran her hand along the wall to find the light switch, a woman's voice cried out from the far end of the room.

"Please. Please."

Zoey's senses sharpened. It was coming from the bathroom where light leaked from under the door. Was it a cry for help? Zoey flicked on the overhead light, rushed across the room, and pulled open the door.

"Fuck," Gloria Sanchez shouted.

Zoey's muscles froze. Ten times earth's gravity encased her body and glued her feet to the floor. Not one signal she sent to her brain to get out of the Family Room was obeyed. What the hell was the chief medical officer's wife doing in the bathroom with Dr. Avery Carson? Naked.

"Just get the fuck out of here," the woman shouted, her face contorted with rage.

Dr. Carson wrapped his arms Gloria, whose nude body was plastered against the far wall, her legs around his waist. With his back to Zoey, her view of the woman was already blocked.

Heart pounding, Zoey finally was able to break free of her cement tomb and step back. Had he not been so protective of his boss's wife, Zoey might have feared for Gloria's life. "Sorry. I thought—" Neither would care the reason why she was there.

As quickly as she could, Zoey closed the door and blindly

ran toward the exit. In her haste, her thigh caught the edge of a table, sending pain straight up her leg. "Fuck." She massaged the wounded area as she reached for the exit door and stepped into the well-ventilated, lit hallway. She plastered her back against the cold cement. *Did that really happen?* Of all the people in the hospital to catch doing *that*, why did it have to be Dr. Avery Carson?

After overhearing his story about losing that little boy on the table, she'd begun to question Kara's story. The irony wasn't lost on her.

Christ. Zoey had just witnessed the chief medical officer's wife having sex with the chief cardiovascular surgeon—her husband's top man. Now the woman's begging words made sense. Zoey placed a hand on her chest in an attempt to quell her rapid heart.

Two doctors waltzed through the ER doorway she'd inno-cently stepped through moments before. They glanced her way then returned their attention to each other. She needed to get out of there. The files in her office could wait. Attempting to appear calm, she kept her steps slow and even and her gaze straight ahead. It did nothing to lower her pulse, which was beating a rapid tattoo against her chest.

Sure, she'd heard stories of doctors doing it in the OR, in stairwells, and even in the chapel, but she never expected to walk in on someone actually having sex. What had they been thinking? If nothing else, Dr. Carson should have locked the damned door.

Once outside, Zoey dragged the cold air into her lungs, but that did little to settle her nerves. A siren sounded, followed by flashing lights coming toward the Emergency Room entrance. Zoey scooted out of the way of the oncoming ambulance and dashed to her car. Once she found her keys, she clicked the remote, but nothing happened. Damn. The battery was dead. What else would go wrong today? After a few fumbling attempts in the darkened lot to open her door, she succeeded and slid in. Thankfully, the engine started on the first try.

What had Mrs. Sanchez been thinking? Did her husband know she was on the first floor screwing around with a person he probably considered a friend?

It's none of my business. It might not be, but that wouldn't keep the image of Avery Carson's pasty white ass from being forever burned in her brain.

Right now she needed a nice glass of wine and some sleep. Hopefully, tomorrow would bring some insight into what she'd witnessed.

✧   ✧   ✧

At nine the next morning, when Zoey walked into the Valley Café. Thad didn't like her washed out appearance. She looked fidgety and distracted. He hoped the pregnant woman Zoey had treated had made it.

Both he and Pete pushed back their chairs as she approached, and Thad held one out for her.

"Am I late?" she asked, her voice tight.

Thad appreciated how she was always concerned about not inconveniencing them, but he didn't like that her worry seemed to add to her dismay. "No. We got here early. You okay?"

"Yes. Why?" She hesitated. Something was up.

"Because you look worn-out. Didn't you get any rest after your hospital call?" He hated to think she'd been up all night.

She smiled, and the light in her eyes returned to almost normal. "I arrived home a little after midnight, but if you must know, my insomnia was because I spent the night reliving the shower experience, and then the *aftermath*." She winked. "My sleep pattern was interrupted a bit, but it was for a wonderful cause." She grinned and Thad relaxed, even though he suspected she wasn't being totally honest.

Pete placed a hand on hers and smiled. "You lost sleep thinking about us, huh?"

"Well, you two are exceptional men."

Leave it to Pete to ask, though his roommate had never been concerned before about getting some mythical ten ranking from a woman. With Zoey, it had been different. Pete had talked non-stop about her all last night and again this morning. Thad couldn't remember a time when they'd both connected with the same woman, which was why he didn't want to get his hopes up that Zoey might be the woman for them. If things turned sour, the pain would be debilitating.

Claire, their waitress, came over. "Hey, Zoey. What can I get you?"

"Um."

"Need a minute?"

Zoey shook her head. "Have you two ordered?"

"Just our coffees," Thad answered, "but go ahead if you know what you want."

"I'll have coffee, too. And two eggs scrambled, whole wheat toast, and orange juice."

"You got it." Claire looked over at Thad. "Your usual, detective?"

"You bet."

"Make it two," Pete said.

The bell over the door rang and to his surprise, Cade Carter rolled in with Stone Benson and Amber Delacroix. Thad motioned to Zoey. "Look what the cat dragged in." His comment wasn't far from the truth. Cade hadn't shaven and his shirt was rumpled like he'd slept in it. Amber appeared withdrawn, too. Only Stone seemed fresh.

Zoey looked over at them and waved. "Hey, guys."

They tossed their coats on a nearby booth seat and came over, but their somber mood had his gut tightening. When Cade's gaze zeroed in on Zoey, the color drained from her face.

"What's wrong?" she asked.

Cade's lips thinned. "Someone was murdered at the hospital last night. I've just come from there."

Oh, shit. Since last month's serial killings at LACE, there hadn't been another homicide—until now. Zoey reached out to Amber and clasped her hand. "Who was it?" Zoey's voice shook.

Cade had mentioned that Amber had gone to Zoey a few times after the mercy killer had struck the hospital. Amber had lost her brother to this killer and Cade feared his fiancée might be affected by any subsequent murders. Thad studied Amber for her reaction, but to her credit, she seemed to be holding up well.

"It was Gloria Sanchez," Amber said.

A strangled cry erupted from Zoey's throat, and she clasped a hand over her heart. "Oh, my God. I saw her last night."

Thad cupped her shoulder. "Who's Gloria Sanchez?" From the trembling in Zoey's voice, she appeared to be a friend.

"She was the chief medical officer's wife. She volunteered at the hospital all the time, and even ran the Christmas party for the sick children." Zoey's voice shook. "She'll be missed."

Thad noted Zoey hadn't said that she'd personally miss Gloria. He could only hope they were just acquaintances.

"We need to talk," Cade said as he dragged a neighboring table over to theirs. Stone retrieved their coats from the empty booth then brought over three chairs. All three of them sat. Cade pulled out a small pad of paper and a pen. "Do you remember what time last night you saw her?"

Zoey pressed her lips together. "A little after eleven."

"Where?"

She bit her lip. "I'd rather not say."

Cade let out a breath. "Zoey, this is a murder investigation. There is no patient confidentiality here." Thad had known Cade a long time. When he was in his detective mode, he didn't have a lot of patience.

"I wasn't her therapist."

Claire came over with their drinks and halted. "Oh. More people."

Cade looked up at her. "We'll order in a minute."

"Sure." Claire set the coffees on the table and left in a hurry, as if she'd understood she'd come at a bad time.

Zoey clutched her hot drink. "I was called in to help calm one of my patients who'd been in a car wreck."

Thad nodded. "We were both with Zoey when the hospital notified her. It was a little after ten."

Zoey picked up the paper napkin and wiped her palm. "After I helped Kayla relax a bit, I wanted to stop by my office for some files. As I was passing the Family Room, I heard a moan." She took a deep breath then squeezed her eyes shut for a moment.

Cade sat up straighter. "Go on." He jotted more notes.

Thad placed a hand over Zoey's. It hurt him to see her struggle like this. "You can tell us."

"I went in, saw a light under the bathroom door and heard a woman pleading with someone. I pulled it open thinking she was in trouble." She shook her head. "I wish to hell I'd minded my own business."

"Who was in the bathroom with her, Zoey?" Cade's voice turned hard, probably because Zoey seemed to have regained her control.

"Gloria Sanchez was with Dr. Avery Carson."

Amber sucked in an audible breath. "Both were there?"

"I'm afraid so." She detailed their naked positions. "Gloria screamed for me to get out while Avery tried to shield her body from my view." Zoey glanced to the ceiling. "I truly could have lived the rest of my life without seeing that."

Thad leaned back in his seat, relieved she hadn't come across a dead body or watched Gloria bleed to death. That would have shaken anyone for life. If Zoey had witnessed a murder, he would have hoped she would have called him or Pete right away.

"What was the cause of death?" Thad asked Cade.

His coworker inhaled. "The coroner's report will be more precise, but someone sliced her carotid artery. The cut looked very clean and precise. I'm guessing she didn't last long after that."

"Time of death?" Thad's job might not entail murder investigations, but he was still a cop.

"The coroner's preliminary time of death was at half past eleven, but we all know he can be off by half an hour or so. Dr. Avery Carson might have been the last person to see her alive."

Shit. Thad's mind swirled. "It's possible he was the one who killed her." He couldn't help but add what everyone must be thinking.

Cade speared him with a glare. "I deal only in facts."

"Then you need to find some." As long as it didn't involve Zoey, Thad would be fine.

Chapter Eighteen

A fter an unsettling breakfast, Zoey hugged Amber goodbye. "I guess I'll see you at Gloria's service," Zoey said.

"I'll be there."

Cade wrapped an arm around his fiancée's waist. "All three of us will be there."

Amber looked up at him with a mixture of indecision and love. "You don't need to come. I'll be fine."

Zoey thought about Cade's reasoning, and a shiver snaked up her spine. "Do you think the killer will be there?"

He glanced down at Amber then to Zoey. "Not to bring up bad memories, but the man who killed Amber's brother gave the fucking eulogy, so yeah, it's possible."

Acid bubbled in Zoey's stomach. Chris's death, along with several others, had rocked the entire hospital, as well as the town. Zoey would always mourn those who'd died.

Cade never came out and said a person with medical knowledge had killed Gloria Sanchez, but given how her throat had been slit across a main artery, it seemed likely. Zoey might have even passed this murderer in the halls. A chill slid up her spine. She couldn't help but wonder if Dr. Avery Carson had made love to Gloria then killed her. At the horrendous thought, pressure built in Zoey's chest.

Too bad HR would never grant her access to hospital personnel files. If they would, she'd spend every waking moment trying to see who was sick enough to want Gloria dead.

Thad moved closer and placed a hand on Zoey's back. "Pete and I will be escorting Zoey, too."

She loved that they wanted to protect her, but as much as she appreciated their support, they didn't need to disrupt their day to go to a wake. "You don't have to bother. Even if the killer is there, he has no reason to target me. I've already outed Avery Carson. Besides, Cade and Stone will be there to make sure nothing bad happens."

Thad looked at Cade. "I trust when you excused yourself a little while ago, you called the precinct and asked for Carson to be brought in for questioning, right?"

"You got it. Given the sensitivity of the case, Hartwick said he wanted to conduct the interview. And just so you know, before we came to breakfast, I spoke with Gloria's husband, who claimed he was home all night."

From what Amber had told Zoey, Cade wouldn't make any assumptions until he had proof, but Zoey hoped he found nothing to incriminate Dr. Sanchez. He was such a nice man. She'd never forget how after her episode with Garrett McDonald, Dr. Sanchez had checked up on her when he didn't have to.

Zoey ran a palm down Thad's chest, absorbing his strength. "Are you coming to the wake because you think Dr. Carson will be so upset at having been brought down to the station that he'll verbally abuse me?" She refused to think Carson would harm her.

"I don't know the man, so I can't say what he's capable of. What I do know is that we can't be too careful." Thad leaned over and kissed her forehead. "You know the old saying. It's better to be safe than sorry."

She loved his protective nature. Truthfully, she'd feel more relaxed having them close by. "Then thank you."

Amber nudged Cade. "It's a shame your boss is interviewing Dr. Carson instead of you. You'd have gotten the truth out of him." Zoey actually chuckled at Amber's attitude.

Cade looked down at her with a lot of love. "Like I did to you?"

Amber smiled. "I had nothing to hide if you remember."

"He might not either."

After Zoey hugged her friend goodbye again, all six of them left the Valley Café. Once Zoey's friends left, she was in too big of a funk to sit at home and think about how one minute Gloria Sanchez was making wild, passionate love, and the next she was dead. "You know what saddens me, besides a vital woman being murdered?"

"What?" the men asked in unison. She almost smiled at how both seemed to want to know what she thought. In her line of work, that didn't happen often.

"To know I work in a place where something like this could happen."

Pete stepped up next to her and twisted a long strand of her hair in his finger. "Bad things sometimes happen for no reason."

Zoey had made the same comment after the Garrett McDonald incident "I appreciate you trying to sugarcoat the terrible event, but I'm betting there a reason for this woman's death. If she was found in a room that wasn't being used, the killer must have thought the body wouldn't be found for a while."

"I can ask Cade, but the killer should have suspected the cleaning staff would be through there."

"I bet you're right. My mind is fried." The men escorted her toward the parking lot located behind the Valley Café. "Here's something else I'd like to know. Was Gloria's death premeditated or one of passion?"

Pete tugged her close. "Ah, yes. The sixty-four thousand dollar question."

Thad guided her around a car oddly parked in the lot. "I'm surprised Cade didn't ask if you had any idea who might have killed Mrs. Sanchez."

"I didn't know her very well. Other than the obvious suspects of the lover and the husband, I have no idea. Amber might have a better idea as she hears more than I do. I'm betting she told Cade her suspicions."

Pete shielded his eyes against the bright sun. "Dwelling on Gloria's death isn't going to do any of us any good. What do you say we shelve the topic for a while? Anyone up for an outing?"

Thank you, Pete, for trying to cheer me up. "That sounds great," Zoey said. "What do you have in mind?" She glanced between the men.

Pete nodded to Thad. "Got any limitations?"

He hadn't worn his sling this morning so he must be feeling better. "Other than rock climbing or driving a motorcycle, I'm good with whatever you two want. I have an appointment tomorrow with the doctor, and I'm expecting him to clear me for duty. If I pass my psych eval, which should be easy, I'll be back on the streets by tomorrow afternoon."

She was thrilled for him. "Watch out, gang members."

They both laughed. "Whatever we decide," Pete said, "do you mind if we first stop by the women's home I'm building? I want to check that the drainage pipe was installed properly this time."

"It's Sunday," she said. "Are your guys even working to-day?" Not that she minded, but everyone needed some down time—even Pete.

"No, but the days of the week aren't all that important to me when I have a project. This is for my mom, and I want to make sure everything is perfect."

She rubbed his arm. "You're a good son." If Zoey had to guess, the project was actually more to impress his dad than to help his mother. Zoey had learned long ago that some people would never change, and she got the feeling that Russell Banks was one of them.

"I try to be."

"Do you normally work seven days a week?" A "no" came from Pete and a "yes" from Thad. She raised her brows. "You do know the old saying about all work and no play makes Jack a dull boy?"

Pete's face brightened. "I'll show you dull."

He tickled her and she let out a shriek then stepped back. Her breath whooshed out, but she wasn't fooled by his behavior. His sudden change was his way of avoiding something painful—like the reason for being a workaholic.

"You want me to follow you?" she asked. They had driven separately. It might give her time to mull over his need to check on the building.

Thad grabbed her hand. "You're not getting away that easily."

He brought back some sanity to the whole dynamics. "Who says I want to get away?" Having someone to watch out for her was a nice change.

"Come on." He led her to Pete's truck. "We can pick up your car later."

Charity work was up there with running into a burning

building and saving a child, so Zoey wanted to support Pete. "When you finish this shelter project, will you get to meet the women who will move in?" Their happy faces would be wonderful to see. It also would help Pete realize what a good guy he was.

"Probably not. There can't be any fanfare since we don't want their abusers to know where they'll be living."

"That makes sense." Without a lot of thanks, his contribution was even more impressive.

The new digs were about fifteen minutes northwest of town. When they arrived, the area looked like an ordinary construction site. The only sign belonged to Banks Construction. Nothing else indicated its future use. The unfinished building was two stories tall, but no style was evident yet since the outside was wrapped in Tyvek. A large dumpster filled with scraps of building material sat on the east side, next to a white van. Near the front entrance was a stack of planks. No landscaping had been done yet, but she bet the half-acre would look like a park when Pete was done.

"Alex is here." From the surprise in Pete's voice, he hadn't expected him.

Cool. Zoey was excited to meet his friend and learn more about Pete, especially from someone who'd known him since he was eight. "I didn't realize you demanded such dedication from all of your employees."

He glanced over at her, but from his serious demeanor, she'd touched on a sensitive topic. Damn. She'd been trying for a more casual tone.

"If he's here, it might mean there's trouble. Let's hope he's just double checking something for me." Pete slammed the truck into park and swung out.

She and Thad followed, but as soon as she stepped onto the

thick dirt, she sank down a few inches.

Thad immediately cupped her elbow. "Watch your step." His care meant the world to her.

The inside was framed out, but no one had installed wallboard yet. A man at the end of the building stood and waved. Alex.

"Hey." With a smoothness to his step, he hustled toward them.

His dirty blond hair was a bit shaggy, but except for the difference in hairstyle, he kind of looked like Pete—broad shouldered and fit.

The man stepped over to her and stuck out his hand. "I'm Alex Hendrix. In case my former partner here failed to mention me, my role in life is to keep Banks Construction's finances in order and to keep Pete from working himself to death."

"Good for you." She liked Alex. He seemed to care very much for Pete. "Zoey Donovan." She'd love to get some one-on-one time with him.

Pete dragged a hand over his head. "There trouble?"

"Not anymore. Sanders was out here yesterday. Before I call the inspector to sign off on the installation, I wanted to check that he's finished the job."

That might have been what the phone call from Alex to Pete had been about when he was at her house the first time.

Pete's shoulders sagged as he hooked his thumbs in his jeans pockets, looking like a huge weight had been lifted. "Appreciate it. That's why I stopped by, but I also wanted to show Thad and Zoey the progress."

Alex shifted his gaze from Pete to her. "Try to keep him away from this project. He can't be everything to everybody." He looked back at Pete. "Ian was sick for the last two days, which was why things fell by the wayside. He'll be back tomorrow, so you can concentrate on the two projects that bring in money."

She liked Alex. He seemed to have a good work ethic and wanted the company to be a success like Pete did.

Pete saluted. "Yes, sir."

Alex slapped his friend on the shoulder. "Gotta go. See you tomorrow." He turned to Zoey. "Nice meeting you, and make sure he has some fun."

"You, too, and will do."

As soon as Alex left, Pete faced her. "Want to take a tour?"

Of what? It looked like a big empty warehouse with two-by-fours everywhere. Pete claimed his dad never took any interest in what he did, so the last thing she needed was for him to think she didn't care, especially when she did. "Sure."

For the next fifteen minutes, Pete would step into a space that looked like the previous one, and paint a picture for her of where the kitchen, bedrooms, living room, and hallways would be. She closed her eyes and imagined a finished apartment. It would be a dream come true for a woman, especially one who had nothing.

Pete Banks might have some anger issues regarding his father, but he'd channeled it for a good cause by pouring his heart and soul into building things. She admired his passion and direction, but sometimes a single focus in life could undo even the best of intentions.

Zoey crossed her arms. "Didn't you two promise me some fun?" Her goal was to sound enthusiastic. She didn't want them to think she was complaining.

"You bet." Pete immediately transformed from workaholic to carefree man. To be able to change on a dime like that was an enviable trait.

They both escorted her out of the building. "You ever ice

skate?" Thad asked.

She chuckled. "Not in a long, long time. Besides, there's no frozen pond around here." It was only September.

"You've never been to The Rink?" Pete asked, acting like she was the most sheltered Rock Hard citizen to ever live.

It made sense that the town would have an indoor facility. "No."

Pete held open the truck door for her. "You game for a little adventure, then?"

She hadn't skated in years. "If you both make sure I don't fall, I'm willing to give it a try." This certainly would test their patience. She'd do her best not to slip, but they might give up when she had to grip their arms real tight. She considered suggesting a movie, but she couldn't get to know them if they weren't able to talk.

The skating rink was on the east side of town, and the parking lot was quite full when they arrived. "This must be the happening place," she said.

Thad nodded. "I remember when my parents would drop me and the cousins off every Sunday at noon and not return for hours. Looking back, I think my parents used the rink as a cheap babysitter. We didn't care. We loved it." That meant he'd be a good skater. Darn.

"What about you, Pete? Do you skate?"

Pete found a parking spot close to the street, shut off the engine, and faced her. "When I was sixteen, Dina decided she wanted to be an Olympic ice skater."

Zoey smiled. "That was every girl's dream. I always wanted to be able to do spins and jumps, but since I wasn't willing to practice often enough, I barely learned to skate in a circle. Books were more my style."

Pete chuckled and shook his head as if her comment didn't

come as a surprise. "I drove my sister here from school twice a week for over a year. They let me practice off to the side. Got fairly good, too."

She loved his self-confidence and thought it said a lot about him that he'd do that for his sister. "Oh, come on. You probably just came to watch all the girls in tights and short skirts."

Pete laughed. "Caught me."

What she wanted to ask was whether Russell Banks ever showed up to watch Dina practice. The answer would shed a lot of light on the family dynamics, but today was about fun, not psychoanalysis.

As soon as Thad pulled open the worn-looking entry doors, the booming music hurt her ears, but the tune was wonderfully upbeat. The rink was full of both old and young people. Most were traveling around the perimeter, but a few of the more adventuresome were in the center executing spins and doing fancy footwork. That was one place she'd never venture. She wasn't the take-a-chance type of girl.

Since Zoey had left her purse locked in Pete's truck, she didn't need a locker. After the three of them were fitted with skates, she walked on rather weak ankles toward the ice.

Thad stepped into the rink first. He faced her and held out his hand. "I'll make sure you don't fall." He always seemed to have her safety in mind.

Pete hooked his arm around her waist and guided her be-hind a group of kids. With both men there to help, she didn't even need to move her legs. But she wouldn't get any better if she let them pull her around. Gaining confidence with each glide, she pushed off on her own and was surprised when her ankles didn't buckle.

After one time around the rink, Thad darted backwards to

skate face-to-face again. He took both of her hands and pulled her around the rink at an increasing speed. While she was a bit scared, the joy she felt more than made up for it, and seeing Thad's wide smile made her happy. When they returned to the starting point, Pete's hands clamped onto her waist. Cool air blew in her face, but fortunately, she wasn't chilly. With the men's guidance, she was slowly becoming accustomed to being back on the ice.

Pete moved away and skated on one leg, clearly showing off. "Still got it, right?"

"You're really good." She meant it.

Thad let go of her hands. "Watch this." He moved more toward the middle of the rink where there was some empty space and spun once.

She wasn't surprised that Pete tried to impress her, but she hadn't thought Thad would. He wasn't the type to seek acceptance. "Be careful," she called out as he did a small jump. She worried he'd fall and land on his bad arm.

If she hadn't needed her hands for balance, she would have clapped at his completed spin. Once more Pete slipped an arm around her waist and increased her speed. "Whoa. This is fast." Too fast.

"You're doing great," Pete said.

If he was trying to bolster her confidence through flattery, it wasn't going to work. After a few more loops around the rink, the men began to one-up each other. When they seemed tired of that challenge, Pete flipped her around and had her skate backwards. It was scary not being able to see where she was going, but she trusted Pete. Then Thad skated behind her and placed a hand on her waist, making her gain control once more. The exhilaration gave her a glimpse of what things could be like with these men.

With each completed circle, they pushed her limits farther. After about a half hour, her legs began to tire. "I need to rest, guys." She needed to be more consistent about running.

Pete and Thad led her off the ice where they all removed their skates. She'd had so much fun today. "What do you all think of stopping by the store to pick up a few things and have lunch at my place? I haven't had much time to even use my new kitchen."

Should they end up in bed again, that would be a bonus.

Chapter Nineteen

Zoey loved to cook, but shopping wasn't high on her list of things to do—it was merely a necessity. If Thad and Pete ever volunteered to go with her again, she'd look forward to the chore. Grocery shopping with those two still had her laughing. Pete had been a real goof. One time he picked up a jar of peanut butter along with some grape jelly and pretended they were battling to get in the cart. As much as she wanted to give in to him, eating a PB&J sandwich wouldn't have made for much of a cooking experience.

Thad had been serious about which foods he ate. He'd insisted on checking every ingredient on the can or box to make sure she bought only the healthiest products. How they ended up with anything in the cart, she didn't know. After a bit of friendly discussion, she convinced them to go with vegetable soup and grilled cheese sandwiches with tomato slices.

On the way back from the store, she picked up her car from the Valley Café. Having them with her had helped banish the horror of Gloria's death.

Zoey glanced in the rearview mirror and smiled. *Thad and Pete. Wow.* She couldn't name one person who treated her so well—let alone two at the same time. How had she gotten so lucky? She did worry what would happen after the "honeymoon" ended. A construction project would need Pete's immediate attention and he'd have to cancel a date, or Thad would get a call about a rash of gang-related thefts, requiring him to spend long hours on the job. That was why having two men would be so nice.

Pete pulled in behind her in her drive. Wanting to help with the groceries, she rushed to the back of his truck. Thad picked up both bags.

"I'll get those. They're too heavy for you." Pete said, holding out his hands.

"Fuck you, man. I'm good. I'll be released to full duty in less than a day."

While Pete did seem overly cautious, she loved how they cared for each other's well-being. Thad carried the groceries without Pete saying another word.

Thank goodness he winked at her as they followed Thad up the porch steps. "Appeal to his macho side," Pete whispered, "and you can get Thad to do anything." His laugh confirmed there were many sides to Pete Banks.

She opened the door and turned off the alarm. "Put the bags on the counter."

Like a well-oiled machine, the three of them emptied the groceries. "Why don't you boys sit at the counter while I cook?" Zoey wanted to do something nice for them for a change.

She had the vegetable soup recipe memorized, so it wouldn't take her long to prepare the meal.

"I can cook, you know." Thad sounded a bit defensive.

"I'm sure you can, but I want to do this for you."

Pete stood. "Mind if I grab a beer for Thad and me?"

That much she'd let them do. "Sure. Help yourself."

"You want one?"

"I'm good."

Pete pulled open the fridge and nabbed two beers. Zoey washed the vegetables and placed them on a cutting board. Since she wanted to be with her men, she brought everything to the center island.

Pete tipped back his beer. "Was your mom a big cook?"

"Hardly. With five kids, she either didn't have the time to cook after she came home from work, or she didn't want to hear any complaints if she picked out a meal everyone didn't like. So Mom went with simple—like hamburgers, hot dogs, spaghetti, or easy casseroles."

Pete ran his thumb down the beer bottle label. "When I was little, I liked to watch my mom cook. She was a whiz."

Zoey sliced the carrots, onions, and zucchini then diced the potatoes. "I would have enjoyed working side by side with her, at least during the holidays, but times like Christmas and Easter were super busy for her."

Thad pushed back his chair, walked to the end of the counter, and wrapped his arms around her waist. He kissed her neck. "I'm sorry. Having family traditions are important. I think some of my fondest moments are being with Nana while she prepared meals." He stepped to the side. "She never let me sit, though. She always put me to work."

"Fine. If you want to butter both sides of the bread for the grilled cheese sandwiches, you can do that."

"Whoopee."

Thad did have a need to be useful. Zoey heated the oil in the pan while she finished chopping the Swiss chard. "Pete, how about you open these two cans of Northern Beans for me? I have a hard time using the hand can opener."

"I'll be happy to."

Once all of the ingredients were simmering in the pot, she set out cheese and tomatoes for the grilled cheese sandwiches.

"Now we wait." She put the coffee container in the machine and turned it on. Once seated, she wanted to learn what her men had been up to. "Thad, what have you been doing at work?" She knew he'd been tied to a desk.

"Not a whole hell of a lot. On Friday, one of the fire inspectors brought me photos of some small fires that had been set not far from Pete's new building. Some of the structures were still standing and had graffiti on the side. Max, the inspector, thought they might be gang related and asked if I'd compare the lettering and style to the different gangs."

"I bet being able to lend a hand to another department was rewarding."

"It was."

A few minutes later, the timer dinged, signifying the soup was done. "Now for the grilled cheese sandwiches."

Pete jumped up. "I'll get the dishes, if that's okay."

"My house is your house." She wasn't referring to the fact Bank Construction had gutted and built her a new kitchen.

"I appreciate that, sugar." Pete walked to the cabinet that held her dishes and pulled out three bowls and three plates. After he placed them on the island, he finished setting the table.

In no time, the sandwiches were finished cooking. After she served the soup and placed the grilled cheese sandwiches on the counter, the men dug in. After expending all that energy skating, the food tasted especially good.

"Mmm," Pete said. "This is fantastic."

Thad waved his soupspoon. "Nana couldn't have done any better."

"Thanks, guys. I can see I'll have to treat you to more meals."

Pete grinned, but Thad continued to focus on wolfing down the rest of the food. When they were done, Zoey insisted they leave the dishes for later.

"We can help," Pete said.

"Let's relax first." Zoey had plans. First they'd rest in the living room and then hopefully move to the bedroom.

Thad pushed back his chair. "I hate to do this, Zoey, but I drew the short straw at work."

She groaned. "You have to go in?"

Thad stepped close and kissed her quick. "Afraid so. Got the three-to-eleven shift. I'm covering for Nick. He was the cop who helped me out while I was in the hospital. Crime, unfortunately, still occurs even on Sunday."

"But you can't go in the field yet." This was so unfair.

He lifted one shoulder. "I can still be useful at the station." He drew her to his chest and kissed her. "Skating was wonderful and lunch fantastic."

Pete, too, would have to leave, since he and Thad had driven together. "I hope everything goes well for you tomorrow, and that you get full clearance. Thanks for helping me at The Rink, too." She'd had a great time.

Thad hugged her. "You were a natural." He cupped her face. "You are a special woman, Zoey."

Her pulse soared. "So are you. A special man, I mean."

He laughed. As Thad leaned in for another kiss, she wrapped her arms around his neck. Thankfully, these men seemed to understand the concept of waiting their turn. After Thad broke away, Pete bestowed a heart-stopping kiss on her. Damn. She wanted what they'd shared last night, but perhaps it was for the best. Her body could use the rest. "If I don't see you beforehand, don't forget the funeral on Thursday." She'd look for any reason to be with them.

"We'll be there," Thad said.

Zoey waited by the window and watched as they drove

away.

As soon as the truck disappeared, the depression the men had been able to keep from crashing down on her descended. She still found it hard to believe Gloria Sanchez was really dead. Would someone else be next?

Gloria's viewing was at Larson-Seigel Funeral Home from four to seven on Thursday. Cade's comment about the killer possibly appearing set Zoey's nerves on edge, enough so that she'd purposefully arrived early to study the people as they came in. While she didn't expect someone to rush in and wave the scalpel that killed Gloria Sanchez, Zoey wanted to watch the mourners to see how he or she interacted with Dr. Sanchez. To her relief, an RHPD officer was stationed in plain sight. She wouldn't be surprised if Cade had been instrumental in requesting the additional security.

Zoey sat in the back row of chairs, waiting for Thad and Pete to arrive. The department chairs who worked directly for Dr. Hector Sanchez surrounded their boss, presenting a cohesive front. Conspicuously absent was Dr. Avery Carson, but Zoey had no doubt he'd come. It was still early, and he could be in surgery. Not showing up at all might harm his relationship with his boss, or worse, cast further suspicion on him.

Zoey wouldn't be surprised if Dr. Carson had already sent his resume to other hospitals. Sanchez would eventually find out, if he hadn't already, that Avery Carson was with Gloria right before she died.

While Zoey didn't suspect Gloria's husband of murder, she studied his interaction with the well-wishers. It was possible one of the department chairs wanted retaliation against his boss, but so far Zoey hadn't witnessed any evidence of ill will.

Dr. Sanchez's shoulders were slightly hunched, and even though his eyes appeared dry, her heart went out to him. Once the case came to trial, he'd hear the sordid details of his wife's last hour. Recovering from that kind of betrayal would test the strongest of men.

Zoey's plan was to wait until Thad and Pete arrived, and then give her condolences to Dr. Sanchez. Just as she began to worry her men might be delayed, they appeared at the door. Zoey couldn't take her eyes off them. Both were dressed in suits and ties, and looked amazing. Pete's hair was shorter, too, as if he'd had it cut just for the occasion. She went over to them and kissed each one on the cheek. "You guys clean up good," she said as she added a hug. They smiled and her day brightened.

Thad nodded to the cop positioned at the rear. Both Thad and Pete placed a hand on her back and led her to one of the rows of chairs. Now that her men were here, she expected all of her anxiety to disappear, but unfortunately it didn't. She wished she could figure out why. Did she fear she'd see something and be unsure what to do? Or would Dr. Carson say something to her and set her ill at ease?

Thad leaned in close. "How about you point out who's who?"

Her stomach turned queasy. "You aren't on the case." He didn't need to take any chances because of her.

Before she could offer another reason why that might not be a good idea, Dr. Avery Carson walked in with his friend, Dr. Thompson, and blood pounded in her ears. Thad lifted a lock of hair from her neck and twirled it around his finger. His tender caress helped ease the tension rushing through her. If she didn't calm down soon, she might need to leave. It would look bad for a therapist to make a fool of herself.

"I'm not officially on the case," Thad said, as he ran his fingers up to her neck. Delightful shivers raced over her body. "But if I can be another set of eyes for the department, so much the better."

His argument made sense. "Okay." She pointed out Dr. Sanchez as well as the department chairs, all of whom stood close to Gloria's coffin.

"The man on the left walking toward Dr. Sanchez is Dr. Avery Carson. He's with his good friend Dr. Thompson, a fellow surgeon."

As if Carson knew she was talking about him, when he reached the end of the aisle, he turned toward her and shot her a lethal glare. Acid burned in her belly. Hating to get caught doing anything she shouldn't, Zoey shifted her gaze and chuckled, pretending as if one of her men had told a joke.

Pete must have seen the exchange and lifted her hand to his lips. With the slightest tug, he turned her body toward him. "Don't worry," he said, murmuring against her hand. "The philanderer turned back around."

Zoey inhaled. She would get through this. "I'm okay." She straightened in her seat. "Continuing with our who's who, the hospital's CEO, Dr. Hunter Jackson, is the one leaning over the coffin. He's wearing a black suit and has silver hair. The tall, thin blonde on his arm is Mrs. Jackson. They married last year." Zoey didn't mention the woman used to be his secretary.

Because Zoey had an independent practice and didn't mix with a lot of doctors, she was unable to name many of the remaining attendees. Just as she believed she could relax, Kara Molloy walked in more timid than Zoey had ever seen her. Her hands were clasped in front and her head was slightly bowed. Dressed in a neat, black suit, she looked somber. People expected a medical professional to appear cool and calm, and she looked the part today, but her behavior was quite different from when Kara was in Zoey's office.

"That woman, Kara Molloy, is Dr. Avery Carson's assistant." Kara wasn't nearly as attractive as Gloria Sanchez, but others might disagree. "When I was at lunch last week, I overheard Dr. Carson mention to the man standing next to him that his assistant was harassing him, calling him constantly. Carson told her to stop, but she didn't listen."

Thad faced her. "What do you know about her?"

Due to confidentiality, Zoey had to be very careful. "I've heard neither is married."

"That helps," Thad said, moving his gaze around the room

Zoey wiped her hands down her dress. "I feel a bit conspicuous sitting here. I should mingle." Her men stood. She needed to speak with Kara but not with the men around. "Alone, please?"

She caught Pete's fist tighten and a tic form around Thad's eye. They sat back down, but she was certain they would keep an eye on her. A large group was congregated off to the side near the front of the room. As she approached Kara, Dr. Carson zeroed in on Zoey. Her blood pressure skyrocketed. He wouldn't dare do anything with everyone present, would he? *Stop fretting. He probably just wants to apologize for being in the bathroom with Gloria.*

Carson moved too close, forcing Zoey to take a half step back. Before she could get farther from him, he stayed her with a hand on her arm. It wasn't a hard grip, but the warning was clear.

"We need to talk," Carson said, his fingers switching from clasping her arm to hand rubbing. His touch was soft like a caress, but the implication was anything but. Goose bumps rippled over her body as a shot of anxiety coursed through her veins.

Fear similar to that of being taken captive by Garrett McDonald overtook her. Carson's musky cologne had her gag reflex in overdrive. Normally, the scent wouldn't have bothered her, but right now being near him made it hard to breathe. "What do you want?" At least her voice hadn't cracked.

"I thought the employees of LACE were a family. If I go down, the scandal will rock this hospital so hard, you'll go right down with me."

Her mind reeled. "I had no choice. My boyfriend's a cop. Only after I heard about Gloria's death did I mention seeing you with her."

"Did you know they accused me of murdering the woman I loved?" A ball of spit landed on her cheek, but she didn't dare wipe it away, not wanting him to see her trepidation. "Who else did you blab my affair to?"

He loved Gloria? "No one." She relaxed a bit after understanding his concern. "If they released you, they must have nothing on you."

He lowered his arm. Good thing, too, because out of the corner of her eye, she spotted Thad and Pete circling, ready to pounce. Though she doubted they'd make a scene, having them approach wouldn't be good either.

"I see your men are ready to protect you. A word of advice. If you decide to tell Sanchez about our affair, you might lose your place at the hospital. One more scandal and things could go south."

Her vision blurred. "You should have thought of that when you had sex with your boss's wife under his nose."

"You could never understand." Carson gritted his teeth, spun on his heels, and headed toward Dr. Sanchez, almost as if the two were in cahoots. He better not claim she was the last one with Gloria. Zoey ran her hands down her hips again.

Before she could regroup and join her men, Zoey wanted to speak with Kara, who was standing off to the side, looking lost. "Kara?"

"Oh, hi, Dr. Donovan."

Zoey clasped one of Kara's hands in hers. Being Avery's assistant, Kara had attended get-togethers hosted by Dr. Sanchez and had known his wife quite well. "I'm sorry for your loss." She let go.

"It's so terrible. Who would want to kill Mrs. Sanchez? Gloria did so much for the hospital."

"I know. The police are working on the case."

Kara pulled out a tissue and wiped her eyes. "I'm not sure I want to stay at LACE anymore. What about that pharmaceutical tech who murdered all those people? Is he still in jail?"

"Yes, Ben Ford is behind bars. He had nothing to do with this death."

Kara nodded. Two other women rushed to Kara's side, and Zoey excused herself. She met the men halfway down the aisle. "I'd like to offer my condolences to Dr. Sanchez. Then I'll be ready to leave."

"We won't be far behind," Pete said, clasping then releasing her hand. The supportive move gave her the strength to keep her head high as she approached the grieving husband. It was uncomfortable having Carson standing next to Gloria's husband, but Zoey refused to let Dr. Carson intimidate her. If the light in the somber room had been brighter, she might have been able to tell if the glimmer in Avery's eyes was due to tears or from fear she'd say something.

"Dr. Sanchez." Zoey held out her hand. He turned and gave her a sincere smile. She tried to judge his level of grief but couldn't. Was he even aware of his wife's indiscretion? "I'm very sorry for your loss."

"Thank you." His gaze went to her forehead. "I'm glad to see you've healed."

Automatically, she lifted a hand to the spot where McDonald had hit her. The bruise was almost completely gone, but the painful memory remained. "Yes."

Dr. Jackson came up and drew Sanchez's attention away. It was time to go. As Zoey headed toward the back where Thad and Pete were waiting, she studied the rest of the mourners, trying to decide if one of them could be guilty of murder.

Chapter Twenty

As soon as Zoey stepped outside the funeral home, she inhaled the clean air to clear her mind. The therapist in her wanted to stay around and witness the interaction between Kara Molloy and Dr. Carson to figure out which of the two was telling the truth regarding who was harassing whom, but Zoey's stomach wasn't up to the task. She decided it would be better if she left and worried about them later.

Pete and Thad escorted her to her car that was parked at the front of the lot. Thad slapped a palm on top of her car's roof, blocking her way. "How about telling me what Dr. Carson said? From the way your face paled, it wasn't good. Did he accuse you of tattling to the police?" His jaw tightened.

Those were a lot of questions all at once. She couldn't keep anything from them. "He knew I was the one who said something to the cops."

"And?" Thad's defensive side intensified.

"He wanted to know if I also told Dr. Sanchez about what I saw, and I assured him I had not. He said if I mentioned his affair with Gloria to anyone else, it might damage the hospital's reputation."

Thad shook his head. "That's rich. Regardless of who is guilty, all of this information will come out at the trial."

Crap. A tight knot formed in her chest. "Will I need to testify?"

"Most likely." Thad's fist clenched. "Let's not worry about that today. I'm just pissed that he spoke to you like that."

"I think he was scared. The career he'd spent years building is crumbling all around him, and since I was the one who alerted the police to his indiscretion, it makes sense he'd blame me."

"Don't make excuses for him. Even if Dr. Carson didn't kill Mrs. Sanchez, he's a cheating bastard. And with his own boss's wife. Jesus. The man deserves what is thrown his way."

"You're right." She'd let her emotion cloud her logic.

Pete wrapped an arm around her waist. "I'm driving you home." His sternness almost frightened her.

"I'm fine. Besides, who'll drive Thad?"

Thad waved his arm. "I drove here. Remember, we spoke on Monday and I told you I was cleared?"

The stress was getting to her. "Maybe I'm more upset about Gloria's death than I realized." Or else it had been the interaction with Avery Carson.

Pete held out his hand for her keys. She fished them out of her purse and handed them over. Just as she was getting into her car, Amber, Jamie, Cade, and Stone drove up.

"Let me tell them I'm leaving." Zoey went over to her friends and gave them a hug, seeing no reason to mention anything about Carson's bad attitude. Zoey placed a hand on Jamie's arm. "Pete and Thad are waiting for me, but we have a lot to talk about."

Jamie looked over at the men and smiled. "I say we do. Next week at our get-together for sure if not sooner." With the funeral, they'd cancelled tonight's happy hour.

"It's a date."

After a second round of hugs, Zoey returned and slipped into the passenger's seat.

"The girls are good?"

He must have seen Jamie look over at them. "Yes. I can tell she wants the lowdown on us, but she'll have to wait."

Pete smiled. As he made a right out of the funeral home parking lot, Zoey glanced in the side view mirror to make sure Thad was behind them. He was.

"You hungry?" Pete asked.

It wasn't even five, and while her stomach was anything but settled, she wanted to have some normalcy back in her life. "Sure."

"How about texting Thad and telling him I'm taking you to the Steerhouse?"

The Steerhouse was only the most expensive place in town. "Pizza is good." While she'd offered to pay for her meals, the men seemed to have an issue with that.

"Text him."

Zoey had no energy to argue. "Fine." She did as Pete asked, but told Thad not to text her back. She was merely giving him a heads up. Knowing his penchant for red meat, he'd not complain.

They battled rush hour traffic but somehow managed to find a place less than a block from the Steerhouse. They waited for Thad to park before heading to the restaurant.

"How are you holding up?" Thad asked as he joined them.

"I'm actually doing okay." He probably feared that once she thought about the implication of Carson's words, she'd fall apart.

Thad wrapped a comforting arm around her waist and escorted her inside where they were seated right away. She slid into the booth first, and Thad moved in next to her. Pete sat across from them.

The waiter came over right away and asked what they'd like to drink. "I'll have a Chardonnay," she said.

"Ale," Pete added, while Thad ordered coffee.

Thad placed a hand on her leg. "If I seem a bit distracted during dinner, forgive me. I'm trying to process everything you've told me."

"It's not your case, you know."

"But it involves you, and I want to be sure you stay safe."

Zoey leaned over and kissed his cheek. "You are a good man, Thad Dalton."

Pete cleared his throat. He didn't act embarrassed. Rather he seemed to be trying to lighten the mood. He then stretched an arm across the back of the seat. Just looking at his pose made the recent incident fade.

"The whole time we've been together," Pete said, "you've been able to get us to spill the beans about how we grew up, but I don't know a lot about you."

"I'm not used to talking about myself. Besides, my life isn't very exciting."

"It is to us," Thad chimed in.

"You want the lowdown on Zoey Elizabeth Donovan?"

Thad leaned close. "Elizabeth huh? I like it. We want it all—the whole *naked* truth. The good, bad, the ugly."

That made her laugh. Thank goodness the men were willing to put Gloria Sanchez to rest, at least for tonight. "There's plenty of ugly in there, though not much bad, thankfully." How did one sum up her life without boring them to death? "I have four siblings. Courtney, twenty-nine, works at a craft store in Billings. She's the emotional one in the family. She's made some bad decisions when it comes to men, but she has a heart of gold."

Pete lowered his arm and leaned his elbows on the table. "I think we've all made some poor choices along the way."

Zoey was guilty of that, too. "Yes, but Courtney seems to find men who believe violence is the way to settle disputes."

Thad winced. "If a guy harmed any one of my relatives, I'd level a shotgun at his chest."

Whether he meant to cheer her up or not, he did. "That's not violent how?"

Pete grinned. "She's gotcha there, Thad."

Thad's grip on the silverware lightened. "Point taken. Go on."

The server delivered their drinks. "Are you ready to order or do you need a minute?" the young man asked.

"Give us a few." Thad lifted his steaming cup to his lips and the delicious aroma of beans made her stomach grumble, but she was happy for the wine. "You've accounted for one of the four siblings," he said. "What about the rest?"

Thad was good about paying attention. "Tom is twenty-seven and an investment banker. He's too focused on work and never goes out. He lives in Connecticut and commutes an hour or more each day into New York City." The image of her youngest sister, Kenna, surfaced and she smiled. "Kenna is twenty-five. She's a happily married housewife, with two adorable kids. Hubby's a lawyer, but just like my brother, Dan works too much. Kenna might be a stay-at-home mom, but she gets frazzled easily. Last but not least is Jack. He's twenty and attends Yale. Says he wants to be an actor, but who knows."

Zoey's heart ached talking about them. As crazy as her brothers and sisters made her when she was growing up, she loved and missed them all. She sipped her wine and the smooth blend went down easy.

Pete's cheer had ebbed. "Tell us about your folks. You said

your dad was like mine. Did your family get along? Were they happy, comfortable, dysfunctional, or what?"

A quick bubble of laughter escaped. "Now who's the shrink?"

Thad pressed his shoulder to hers. "He gets this way sometimes. Humor him."

What way? Serious, introverted, interested? The man was more complex than his usual easy-going exterior implied, but if they had any chance of a relationship, she wanted to be honest. "My parents loved all of us, but I always sensed that because they struggled to keep themselves on track, we kids came second. I know that's a terrible thing to say, but after my mom's car wreck, things weren't the same."

"Car wreck?" Thad's voice came out strangled. It was almost as if he was imagining his own mother injured.

"Yes. A drunk driver hit her. She broke a leg, an arm, and a few ribs. She was in the hospital for weeks."

"How old were you?"

"Thirteen." Zoey painfully remembered how her father had crumbled after the accident. It was the first and only time she'd seen him cry. "We found out later that Mom was pregnant with Jack."

"What did you do?" Pete drank his ale, but kept his gaze on her.

"Those days were a blur. My grandmother flew down from Maine to help out, but I was central command. It was the first time my brother and sisters treated me like I mattered."

Thad twisted toward her. "You became the caregiver. Do you think that was the impetus for you pursuing a degree in psychology?"

She shrugged. "I've always wondered if it was, but it gets back to the old nurture versus nature argument. I think I was born to help people, but being in charge of a family of six when I was thirteen certainly helped shape who I am today."

"It makes sense," Pete said, "why you never did anything bad. Your family counted on you too much."

"That's true."

Both Thad and Pete picked up their menus and she did the same. By the time the server returned, they'd all chosen their meal. She went with a light fish, while Pete and Thad both ordered the filet mignon.

All three brought their drinks to their lips as if they were waiting for someone to start a new topic. Thad's question about what made her choose psychology had her thinking. While she bet Thad's family thought the world of him, he was a bit of an enigma. "Tell me what made you decide to work with gangs?"

It was always possible some distant family member was in a gang or had been accosted by a gang member. Personal experiences were often driving forces for what one did in life.

"I can't even say it was one incident or one day, but there's a particular image that will remain in my brain for life. I was new to the force, but had worked with some very experienced cops. This one time I was with Cade, and we found a young woman with a bullet through her forehead."

She winced. "How did that make you feel?" Zoey couldn't help jumping into shrink mode. She wanted to understand him.

"Pissed. Disgusted. And determined to do something so another innocent victim wouldn't be killed."

Zoey shifted in her seat so she could face him better, her knee comfortably bumping his. She didn't want to think about what went through that poor woman's mind seconds before she was shot. "I've heard cops have to develop thick skins to survive. Do you ever get used to seeing a dead person?" She kept her voice low.

"Haven't seen that many, but after a while, you learn to block out the horror. They give us training on how to do our jobs and not let our emotions rule. Sometimes it works. Other times it doesn't."

She'd been trained like that, too, but it wasn't always possible to turn off her heart. "Did you ever find the person who killed that poor woman?"

"Yes, but it took a long time. The victim was a schoolteacher from Colorado visiting her folks. She was in the wrong place at the wrong time. A couple of thugs were robbing a pharmacy when she happened by. The gang member who shot her said he did it in order to know what it felt like to kill."

Zoey dealt with a lot of sick people but none that bad. She shook her head. This wasn't helping her day. "Is that why you wanted to go after gang members? For this woman?"

He leaned back and blew out a breath. She didn't want to push, but Thad was a sensitive man. Deep inside, he cared about others.

"In part, but more importantly, I wanted to understand what made a kid turn to gangs."

The teenage mind fascinated her, too. "Have you?"

"Poverty, parents who don't care. You name it. It makes me want to tell parents to love their kids."

Out of the corner of her eye, she saw Pete's fingers tightened on his glass. Talking about bad parenting was a sore subject for him. She wished he'd understand that his father's less than affectionate behavior might have nothing whatsoever to do with him. Some men spend their life battling their own demons and can never let go of the pain. Hopefully, Pete would see that at some point in his life.

Right now, she wanted to be with both of them, give them comfort, and let them bestow some loving on her. At the thought of crawling into bed with her two men and letting them hold her tight, the pain of the past few days eased.

Chapter Twenty-One

etween the stress from the funeral and eating a big meal at the restaurant, Zoey was tired. She agreed to let Pete drive because he wanted to. Tonight should be about the men's needs and what they wanted. She'd yet to make real love with Thad, and she couldn't wait to rectify that oversight. Between the murder and the funeral, the men had either been busy or perhaps not in the mood to get together.

Pete drove up her drive and Thad pulled in behind them. Pete pushed open his door and rushed to her side to open hers. A girl could get used to this treatment.

"Thank you, sir." She tugged on his sleeve, stood on her tiptoes, and kissed Pete's cheek. "And thank you for dinner. Next time I'm paying."

He grinned and excitement gushed through her. Pete Banks was one sexy man.

"That's not going to happen, sugar. You know we're not wired that way."

Before she had a chance to say it was only fair that they share the expenses, Thad jogged up next to them. "Hey, don't start without me."

"You'll just have to let me bestow a kiss on you, then." These two brought out the best in her. Zoey retrieved her key and opened the door before they could help. "Come on in." As soon as she closed the door, she punched in her code for the alarm.

Just as she turned around, Thad lifted her purse from her shoulder, placed it on the sofa, and then wrapped his arms around her waist. "Someone said something about a kiss?"

"I did indeed." When she leaned forward to meet him halfway, he pressed his lips against hers, and the pain of Gloria's death faded like bleach on black denim. Zoey blocked out every thought except for what was happening to her body. Pleasure sizzled through her veins. When she opened up to taste more of him, he brushed his thumbs against her nipples. She so needed to get naked.

"I want you to touch all of me." Her words floated out on a breath. "Which means I need to get out of these clothes."

"Now she's talking," Pete said as he took off his jacket and placed it on the living room chair. Before she had the chance to slip the sweater off her shoulders, he swooped her up into his arms. "I know a better place to get comfortable." While he didn't have a drawl, his western accent had intensified.

"That so?" This was a dream come true, and a wonderful way to end a crappy week.

His booted heels slapped against the hardwood floors, and his strong arms surrounding her gave her great comfort. Thad followed. As they neared the bedroom, he scooted ahead, opened the door, and flicked on the bedside lamp, bathing the room in soft light.

"Set her down," Thad said with an urgency she hadn't heard in a while.

Pete did. Zoey held up her palms. "Wait. Let me strip for you." She wanted to see if she could tease them into taking her hard.

Thad looked over at Pete. "We'll give you three minutes. If you're not done, we're coming after you."

She laughed. "This isn't a race. It's about seduction. Slow, easy movements that are meant to entice, titillate, and lure. I know we have to be up early tomorrow for work, but we have a few hours."

Pete's mouth opened. "You going to take that long?"

He almost sounded serious. "Perhaps. Now sit. You can both take off your shoes if you want, but nothing else. Once I get naked, I'm going to peel the clothes from your body, one piece at a time."

Pete looked as if she'd handed him the winning lottery ticket, but Thad acted like he'd combust before she finished. He kicked off his shoes then adjusted himself. She almost took pity on him by letting him help her speed her progress, but then she changed her mind. Because shoes weren't sexy, she discarded them quickly The relief was immediate and she let out a groan.

Pete leaned back on his elbows, looking delicious. "None of that moaning and groaning stuff until we're all naked."

She was tempted to go faster, but once more decided against it. After she removed her other shoe, she placed them by the side of the bed. Now for the fun part. She slid her sweater down her arms inch by inch then tossed the garment in the air to see what the men would do. Pete snagged it in mid-air.

"Wahoo." She smiled when Pete brought the garment to his face and inhaled.

Now she wished she'd worn more than a simple black dress because her seduction might end too soon. Thank goodness Jamie had convinced her to buy a few sexy underwear sets while she was at Naughty Desires.

While Zoey could have reached behind her and fumbled with her zipper, she wanted to tease them. She sashayed up to

Thad. "Want to help me undo the back?"

"Happy to help." Thad jumped up and slid the zipper down her back one sprocket at a time. With each click, her body heated. The man was control wrapped up in a selfless package. That was the definition of sex appeal.

When the tab reached the bottom, he slid his hands over her shoulders and lowered the material. Instead of him sitting back down, he kissed her bare shoulder, and she jumped as his warm lips pressed against her sensitive skin.

"Easy there. It's just a kiss."

There was nothing "just" about the way he caressed her body. So as not to give in and rip off his clothes, she stepped forward and inhaled to compose herself. She faced Thad, and his hazel eyes darkened with desire. She yearned to throw herself in his arms, but that would come later.

Thad didn't take his gaze from her face as he sat. "You are so fucking hot, Zoey."

Her need to torment the men evaporated. She wanted them now. With less fanfare than she'd intended, she slipped out of the dress and let it pool at her feet.

"Holy shit, sugar." Pete stood. "We can't take it any longer."

As if he and Thad had the same idea, they both charged. Elation at what was to come sizzled through her body. Pete stepped behind her and unhooked her bra then slid the straps down her arms while Thad dropped to his knees.

"It's been too long." Thad whispered his words as he placed his face against her belly.

"Yes." Too long. She planted her hands on his head and let the bristles of his short hair brush against her palms. She loved everything about this man—his clean scent that reminded her of the outdoors to his dark stubble and smoldering eyes.

Using his teeth as well as his hands, he lowered her panties past her knees. His lips were so close to her folds that his breath skated across her naked flesh. Anticipation sent sparks rippling up her body.

Suck on me! Lick me!

Pete slid his hands to her breasts and lifted them in his palms. "I love these," he said, and then leaned his cheek against hers. He dragged his thumbs across her distended nipples, and pleasure soared through her veins while her inner walls clenched with unmitigated need. Through Pete's thin dress slacks, his hard cock pressed against her rear.

"Would you like it if I helped you both undress?" She needed to rub her hands on their rippled flesh.

"No," they said in unison.

Because they were being ridiculous, she felt no obligation to obey. With her panties around her knees, she flipped around. As soon as her fingers touched Pete's belt buckle, he stopped her.

"Our woman might need some discipline," Pete said with a chuckle. In a blink of an eye, he ducked his shoulder and hoisted her in the air.

"Pe-te!" She laughed.

A second later he dropped her onto the bed. Both men stepped back and unbuttoned and unzipped their trousers. They'd already taken off their shoes. Seeing their sleek bodies revealed inch by delicious inch was incredible. She yearned to touch them. As if they were a synchronized team, they jammed their hands in their pants pockets, extracted their wallets then retrieved condoms. This was going to be some night.

Zoey considered helping them take off their shirts, but watching might be more fun. Pete unbuttoned his white shirt and tossed it on the floor. His thumbs hovered over his briefs as if he was debating whether to tease her.

"I thought you didn't wear underwear."

"Only when I'm in jeans. There's too much room in these slacks. One look at you, and everyone in the funeral home would have known what I wanted to do."

Zoey chuckled. Thad slipped off his shirt, folded it, and placed it on the side table. Not taking his gaze off her face, he lowered his briefs. Her heart nearly burst seeing him so hard, so erect.

"Over here, sugar." She looked at Pete who flipped around, bent over, and lowered his underwear.

She laughed. "Hurry."

"Yes, ma'am." Seconds later, Pete, too, was naked. "Now for our reward." He picked up the condom and tossed it onto the end of the bed. "Bottoms."

"You had bottoms last time," Thad said.

Please don't fight. "How about you take turns?" Her voice had an unwanted edge to it, but she couldn't handle any bickering, especially today.

Thad sat next to her and stroked her cheek. "We're not arguing. We're just trying to relax you. It's our way of being playful."

She hoped that was true. "All right, but I want my fill of both of you." She meant it, too.

Thad grinned and she drew him down for a kiss. Zoey rolled onto her side, and his muscular body pressed against hers in all the right spots. Those damned panties were annoying. She reached to take them off when Pete's hands brushed hers away.

"Let me."

He slid them down to her ankles and then they were gone. As Pete nestled between her thighs, he lifted her top leg and placed it on his shoulder. Which would come first? The lick or Thad's kiss? When Thad leaned close, she opened her mouth to greet him. Their breaths mingled, and they each acted as if they weren't able to explore every crevice this instant they'd expire. He clasped her shoulders and pressed his hard-as-granite chest against her breasts.

Pete's tongue swiped her opening, and then darted in and out. Her breath lodged in her throat. The dual thrusts had her reeling. Shutting her eyes in the hopes of concentrating, she cupped her exposed hand on Thad's cheek, loving his masculine stubble. He was all male.

When he moaned, she abandoned herself to the erotic pleasure dousing her body. She broke the kiss only to draw his lower lip between her teeth. Just then Pete slipped a finger into her pussy and sucked on her tiny bud. The exquisite ache nearly toppled her. She opened her mouth to draw in a deeper breath, and indulged in the wonderment of it all.

Thad rolled her onto her back and Pete let her leg slip off his shoulder. She was going to complain about the lack of contact when Thad nabbed one nipple between his teeth and drew the taut tip into his mouth. Electric sparks shimmied over her body, and she dragged a hand over his back. Pete slid her feet onto the mattress, opening her wide.

"Thad," Pete said, his voice strangled. "You first, man. Go quick. I'm about to lose it."

Thad kissed her quick then changed places with Pete, whose gaze zeroed in on her face. "You are so beautiful," Pete said, the golden flecks in his eyes brightening.

His words warmed her from the inside out. "Ditto."

Pete's mouth descended on hers with an intensity he hadn't shown before. Her pussy throbbed at the thought of making love with Thad. Pete's tongue begged for entrance as he slightly pinched the wet nipple Thad had just sucked. The quick shot of pain darted right down to her clit.

"Flip her over, Pete. I need her pussy something bad. Let her mouth give you a ride."

Chapter Twenty-Two

A second later, Zoey was on her elbows and knees. She hadn't expected Thad's chest to press against her back, but she loved his rippled muscles on her skin. His covered cock sat at her opening while his fingers slid along her waist, easing over her belly then capturing her breasts.

"What you do to me, Zoey. I want to touch, taste, lick, and make love to every inch of your body. My insides are throbbing with need for you."

Thad's poetic words overwhelmed her. She half expected Pete to toss back some sassy comment, but he just knelt in front of her, his hands threaded through her hair. He fingered the strands then grabbed a handful and tugged. The yank drew her attention back to his throbbing cock whose tip glistened with pre-cum.

Not waiting for an invitation, she drew his stiff dick toward her and cupped his drawn-up sac. He hissed and she smiled. As she leaned over to take him far into her mouth, Thad pressed the head of his cock into her. She squeezed her eyes shut, and stars burst on the back of her lids.

"Zoey?" Pete said, as he tightened his grip on her hair.

Reality returned, and she sucked on his dick, enjoying his rippled texture. As she swirled her tongue around his length, he grunted and moaned as if he were in heaven or very close to it. She found her own slice of heaven when Thad rubbed her breasts and slid into her deep and hard. Her pussy embraced him as his dick stretched her wide. On the next thrust, her juices exploded and slickened her walls.

Zoey pumped her fist up and down Pete's cock, matching Thad's rhythm. It was as if they all were one. Her heart beat hard, making her ears ring. Thad twirled, pinched, and soothed her nipples as he drove his cock into her. With each plunge, her climax neared. Heat swamped her and her vision blurred.

"God, Zoey," Thad's breath rushed out of him.

Just when she thought he'd take her over the edge he pulled out. *What?* Bereft, she let go of Pete's cock. He leaned back on his heels and changed places with Thad.

"I didn't come!" That sounded selfish, but she was so close to Nirvana that her impeding climax would have taken her to a place she'd never been before. Didn't they know she wanted more?

Pete donned a condom, and Thad cupped her face. He rubbed a thumb across her lips. "That was the hardest thing I've ever done. Jesus, Zoey, what you do to me."

Pete rubbed her ass. "Amazing." He hissed then rubbed a finger over her swollen, sensitive clit so many times she nearly burst.

"You have three seconds to fuck me hard, Pete Banks, or you'll be sorry."

"I love a woman who knows what she wants."

"You want this, Zoey?" Thad pressed his uncovered cock to her lips. She didn't need any more encouragement and engulfed his shaft. From everyone's heavy breaths, they were all on edge. Pete let go of her tiny pearl and guided his cock straight into her hot core, her cream dripping down her leg.

All it took was one bold thrust for her to teeter on the brink of orgasm. She clasped Thad's cock and pumped as hard as she could while she swallowed him whole.

"God." Thad's cry spurred her on.

Pete grasped her waist and fucked her hard and fast, just the way she liked it. Zoey pressed her hips back to take in more of him and rejoiced when he pounded her inner walls. She yelled. Pete grunted. Thad moaned. They might have sounded like an off-key orchestra, but the glory that consumed her robbed her of thought. When she cupped Thad's hard sac, his hot cum blasted her mouth, forcing her to swallow quickly to keep up with his pumping. As soon as Thad finished, he pulled away, his throaty groans filling her with a deep thrill.

Pete slid his hand down her belly and nabbed her clit again, rubbing it in circles until her body burst. The climax she'd tried so hard to keep at bay descended with full force. With a final thrust, ecstasy claimed her, and she floated away on a sea of unexpected glory. His cock pulsed and throbbed as his jism shot deep into the condom.

After that, her sensory overload prevented all thought. Sounds dimmed and her vision saw only white. Hands rubbed her shoulders, touched her breasts, and stroked her cheek, but she couldn't be any happier if she tried.

Then she was on her back. When she finally opened her eyes, both men were kneeling besides her grinning. Thad had a wet towel and was cleaning her.

"You okay?" Thad asked.

She smiled, but her lids fluttered closed. She forced them open, wanting to watch the range of emotions crossing their handsome faces. "More than okay."

Pete got off the bed and extracted his phone from his pocket. "Reality always intrudes. What time do you need to get up?"

"Seven."

Thad nodded. "You said Fridays are light days for you, right?"

"Thankfully. I'm not sure we'll get much sleep in a queen-sized bed though."

Pete leaned over and kissed her. "It's not the size of the bed that will keep you awake."

She laughed. "Don't tell me you're insatiable."

"Oh, sugar. When it comes to you, I can't get enough."

"How about showing me?"

When the alarm sounded at seven the next morning, Zoey groaned. Her body throbbed from all the loving, but she wouldn't trade the feeling for the world. After the three of them made love, and then rested for an hour, Thad and Pete wanted to see who was better at exciting her, so they played with her breasts. They'd teased her to a point of utter delirium and competed for her attention. Zoey finally had to plead off after her fifth climax. A woman could only take so much. With a little prodding on her part, they let her reciprocate. Touching their glorious bodies had helped return her to the land of ecstasy.

Keeping her eyes mostly shut, Zoey turned off the beeping then reached for her men. She found only cool sheets. What the—? Someone was here, as the shower was running. But which man?

Only one way to find out. Naked, she slipped out of bed and pranced into the bathroom. It was Pete. He was gloriously wet. At the sight of his muscular body, more lust tripped up her spine. "May I join you?"

He rinsed his hair. "You bet, but I'm running late, so I can't take my time with you as much as I'd like."

She only wanted to get clean. "That's okay. I think I need to rest for a day or two anyway."

Zoey stepped in and turned on her showerhead. If she could get through today, she could spend two days with her men. By the time the water warmed and she'd soaped up, Pete had finished.

"Need help?" he asked.

Zoey laughed. "I thought you said you needed to leave. I know you. You can't stop with one touch."

"Damn, you're right."

"Where's Thad?"

"Guess you didn't wake when he got a call a few hours ago. Some gang thing happened. He didn't give any details and I didn't ask." Pete turned off his shower then moved toward her with the gaze of a predator. "How about one little kiss to keep me going for the day?"

She laughed. He might be able to do one kiss, but she wasn't so sure that his touch wouldn't make her yearn for more all day. "Sure."

She wrapped her soapy hands under his arms and around his back before pulling him close. His lips descended on hers like a starving animal, and all thought of a quick goodbye kiss disappeared. His hard cock pressed against her belly, causing her pussy to clench and throb. Their tongues dueled and sparred, and they danced to a rhythm only they seemed to share.

Pete broke it off. His lids were half-closed and his lips slightly swollen from the kiss. "I want so much more, but we need to pace ourselves."

As much as she wanted to spend the day with him in bed, she did have clients. There were also physical limitations. "Rain check then."

He grinned. "Rain check." His gaze shot down to her nipples. "They a bit tender?"

If she said yes, would he respect that she needed time? "Yes."

He cupped her face. "Did we overdo it?" He winced and her heart ached.

"No. I stopped before they became too tender."

Once more, the shine returned to his eyes. This time the kiss was quick. "I promised my parents I'd stop over tonight. They've been having some issues with water leakage in their kitchen, but Saturday night for sure the three of us should plan something special."

"I'd like that." So much for being with her men the whole weekend.

Pete stepped from the shower and towel dried before she finished washing.

"Be good," he said as he stepped from the bathroom.

Zoey showered quickly and dried even faster. By the time she entered the bedroom, Pete was dressed in his suit. That meant he'd have to drive home and change before going to the construction site.

The need to give him another hug stunned her. She'd spent all evening with him, made mad passionate love with both of them, yet yearned for more. She dropped the towel and then kissed him on the cheek.

"You are a tease, girl. If I didn't have to go, you know I'd stay."

She turned him around by his shoulders. "Go."

He grinned. "Later."

Boy, did she have it bad.

234

Zoey placed the napkin on her lap and sipped her coffee, studying Thad. He looked good. Real good. "I'm glad you weren't too tired to meet for dinner. The idea of eating alone doesn't appeal to me." She leaned forward and lowered her voice. "Especially after how amazing it was last night." She hoped for a repeat performance tonight, assuming Thad could keep his eyes open.

A small smile claimed his lips. "Me, too. Knowing I'd see you for dinner helped me get through the day." Thad rotated his coffee in his hands.

Zoey wanted to know more about his job. "Can you talk about the case?"

Tension riddled his face. Damn. "Afraid not. It's an ongoing investigation." From the strain in his voice, having to keep things to himself bothered him.

"I can relate."

Thad nodded then brought the steaming cup to his lips. "How was your day?"

She chuckled. "Busy and a bit stressful. I used to look forward to going to work, but you and Pete have spoiled me."

He cocked a brow. "How so?"

"You make me want to spend time with you both instead of studying my cases."

His smiled broadened. "Ditto." He then hesitated, looking like he wanted to say more.

When he didn't, she continued. "Have you checked on Garrett McDonald?" She hadn't wanted to bring up the past, but she needed closure.

A small tic pulsed around his eye. "He's recovering nicely."

She bet Thad was glad the man hadn't died. The guilt over killing a person, no matter the reason, would have been hard to get over. "What will happen to him?"

"I spoke with his physician who said sometime next week he'll be transported to a more secure facility. When he's able, he'll stand trial."

"Good. And your ex-wife?" Zoey was curious the extent of Thad's involvement with the case.

"I stopped in a few days ago like I'd promised. Peggy's still recovering. Now that Garrett can't ever harm her again, she'll be able to go home, and hopefully get her life back on track." There seemed to be a sense of peace about him.

"I'm glad."

"Me, too. No one deserves to be in an abusive relationship, whether it's physical or verbal."

"I agree."

Thad sipped his drink. "Did Pete tell you the wallboard is finally up in the new apartments he's building for Harmony House?"

She was happy for him. "No."

"Better still, one of the local lumberyards is picking up the cost of the drywall."

"That's fantastic." Pete wouldn't have to bear the cost of the entire project.

Thad then told her about the playground plans that were being drawn up, and that Pete seemed happy with the progress. As much as she enjoyed their dinner tonight, she wished Pete had been able to come. She'd gotten used to thinking of them as a threesome. The more time they spent together, the more it was like adding another brick to their foundation.

Thad paid for the meal even though Zoey had offered. "Ready?"

"Yes." She stood and he helped her on with her sweater.

During the drive home, Thad was rather quiet. Something was on his mind, but she suspected it had to do with the case, which he couldn't share. After parking in her drive, he escorted her to the door. Not wanting the evening to end, she opened up and ushered him in. "You want some coffee?" Thad had yawned a few times during the meal, but she hoped that with some fortification, he'd perk up.

As if he was just waiting to get her alone, his eyes suddenly sparkled. It was like her offer had uncapped some internal reservoir of energy. Thad drew her close, spun her around so that her back was to the front door and leaned in. "What I want is to delve into the recesses of your body and love you so hard you'll scream my name."

"Ooh." Like a gigantic wave crashing to the shore, his intensity had surprised her, causing needlepoints of lust to prick her from head to toe.

Chapter Twenty-Three

Thad's lips edged closer. "I can picture it now. Your mouth will open to gulp in air, your eyes will flutter closed in total ecstasy, and your tight pussy will clamp down on my cock while your climax drives you so high you can't think."

Her heartbeat sped up at the promise. "When do we start?"

Thad lifted her hands over her head and pinned them against the door. The kiss that followed had bolts of electricity shooting up her spine and igniting her body. Their intimate exploration alternated between sweet and urgent, but no matter the speed, she wanted more. When he leaned back, she didn't want to open her eyes, but finally did.

He kissed her fingertips. "I need to get some shuteye or I'll be useless tomorrow when the three of us are together."

"Are you kidding me?" She was amped up with desire. He released her hands and she wrapped her arms around him, not wanting him to go. "You don't want to spend the night? It'll make Pete jealous." That wasn't nice to pit them against each other, but desperation had made her come up with that lame excuse. Pete couldn't help that his parents needed him to fix the leak in their house.

Thad kissed her forehead, her nose, and then her mouth

again. While the contact was light, it was totally sensual. "You know very well what would happen if I get anywhere near your naked body."

Yes. They'd make love. Oh, hell. It probably was for the best since she was still sore. "Okay, but tomorrow I won't take no for an answer."

He delivered another mind-altering kiss. "I'm counting on it."

As soon as Thad left, gravity tugged hard on her body. How could he get her hopes up like that, and then dash them all in a matter of seconds? Tomorrow she'd make certain he gave her what she desired.

To reduce her raging libido, she decided to take a hot bath and indulge in a nice glass of white wine. Zoey had no doubt that she'd be dreaming about the reunion with her two men. She understood that focusing on what the future might hold would only cause her to obsess, but she couldn't help it.

Zoey filled the tub with water and doused it with sweet smelling bath salts. With her glass in hand, she stepped in and moaned at the warmth. One by one, her muscles gave up their tightness, and after a half hour, her lids turned heavy. She rinsed, emptied the tub, and dried off.

Zoey then climbed into bed and inhaled the men's scent still clinging to her cool sheets. She sighed at the wonder of it all and snuggled under the blankets. Whether from the wine, the warm bath, or sheer exhaustion, Zoey fell asleep in total contentment.

She dreamed of her men. In one of them, she, Thad, and Pete were standing on top of a ridge overlooking a rugged mountain range, much like the vista at Pete's father's ranch, except the colors were all wrong. A yellow mountain stood at the end of a pink range. Then what sounded like an F-15 fighter jet came out of nowhere and buzzed close to the ground. The female figure in her dream squatted, covered her ears, and visibly shook. When her dream person opened her eyes, the men were gone.

That had been so scary, Zoey forced herself awake, expecting to be in her nice quiet bedroom—only she wasn't. She might be in her bed, but the noise was still there. A moment later she realized what it was. Holy fuck. Her house alarm was going off. Someone must have broken in. Shit. Shit. Shit.

Her heart dropped to her stomach then crawled up her throat. *Move!* She ripped off the covers and turned on the bedside lamp, despite the glowing computer screen illuminating the far half of the room.

Even though the alarm company would send someone, she didn't dare leave the confines of her bedroom before they got here. She locked the bedroom door and searched for anything she could use as a weapon. A letter opener sat on top of her desk. As she stepped across the room to get it, a sharp pain stabbed her foot. "What the hell?"

Zoey lifted her leg to check out the source of the strong ache. Blood pooled out of a cut, and her stomach clenched. Cold air poured in from the window and the source finally registered. Someone had smashed her window. "Damn it."

Adrenaline helped blunt the pain in her foot, but the blood continued to drip. She hopped the two feet to her desk chair, sat down, and pulled out the glass shard. She then pressed a hand over the wound to help stop the bleeding, but that only worked for a few seconds. From her desk drawer, she extracted a couple of tissues from a travel-sized packet and pressed them to her wound.

When the tissue filled with blood, Zoey had to do something else. On tiptoe, she crossed to the bathroom. After a

VELLA DAY

quick bandage job, she located a pair of socks from her dresser. It was then that she spotted her phone. Relief poured through her. She needed to call Thad.

Her breathing slowed as she punched in his number. It was in the middle of the night, but cops were used to receiving calls at all hours. While she waited for him to answer, Zoey kept her gaze on the broken window, not sure if the person was still outside or was hidden in her house. Given the window was locked, the odds were the person had run off after the alarm sounded. Christ, but the wailing was loud.

"Zoey?" The moment Thad answered, her blood pressure lowered, but her steely resolve to remain calm broke.

A sob escaped. "Someone...someone tried to break into my house."

"What? Are you okay?"

"Yes." Kind of.

"What is that sound?"

"The alarm," she shouted. "Hold on." Now that he was on the phone she dared to go into the living room. "I need to turn it off."

Moving as fast as the pain allowed, she hobbled down the hallway, keeping an eye out for the intruder just in case he'd been able to get inside. She punched in the code, and the ear-splitting sound stopped. Thank God. She had no idea how long it had been going off, but it must have been a while. Her ears still rang.

"Zoey. Tell me what happened." What sounded like an engine starting filtered into her brain.

She flicked off the lights and peered out the window. Red taillights exited her street. Shit. Was that the intruder running away?

"I don't know." She told him about how the alarm had

242

woken her up, that the window had been smashed, and then how she'd cut her foot.

"Where are you now?"

"In the living room." Flashing lights filled the room, casting eerie shadows on the walls. Now that the danger was gone, she made her way to the sofa and collapsed. "The cops are here. The security company must have alerted them."

"Pete and I should arrive in a few minutes. Hang in there."

Inconveniencing them sucked, but she wanted the comfort only they could bring. "Hurry."

A knock sounded on her door. With caution, she eased it open. When the cold air blasted her, Zoey realized she had on a thin nightgown and crossed her arms.

"Are you all right, ma'am?"

The cut foot she could handle. "I think so." She motioned them to come inside and explained about the window.

"Can you show us?" the beefier of the two asked.

Walking on the side of her injured foot, she brought the men into her bedroom and pointed to the window. "I didn't touch anything. Be careful. There's glass everywhere." While the men studied the scene, she drew on a warmer robe.

The thinner one faced her. "I'd advise you against staying here until the window is fixed. Do you have some place you can go?"

"Yes." Her men would probably insist she stay with them until this was resolved.

One of the cops called in the break-in, but if they planned to fingerprint the area, she bet it would take an hour or more before they finished processing the scene.

"I'm going to wait in the living room. Thad Dalton is on his way here." The beefy man's brow rose. "He's my boyfriend."

"That's fine, ma'am." He nodded to his partner. "Joe will

keep you company."

She didn't need him to, but between her headache and the spiking pain from her foot, she wasn't in the mood to argue. Taking her time, Zoey limped back to the front of the house. Standing on one foot, she watched for Thad and Pete from the window. In no time, another set of headlights pulled into her drive. The pounding at her temples subsided and the knot between her shoulder blades loosened.

Thad and Pete raced up her walkway, and she yanked open the door. They ran in and both hugged her. "Are you sure you're okay?" Pete smoothed the hair from her face.

"I cut my foot." She hadn't wanted to worry them, but Pete's concerned look made her relent.

In a flash, she was in his arms and tears of joy balanced on her lashes. Gently, he placed her on the sofa then knelt in front of her.

"Hey, Joe," Thad said. "Pete, I'm going to check in the bedroom." He then headed down the hallway.

Pete lifted a hand, indicating he'd heard. "Which foot?"

She had socks on both. "Right."

He carefully peeled it off, the bottom of which was spotted with blood. "Jesus, Zoey. We need to take you to the emergency room to get stitches."

"No, please. If it doesn't look better by tomorrow, I'll go."

"Where are your first aid supplies?" Pete's firmed lips told her he wasn't going to let her rest until he took care of her.

"In the bathroom cabinet next to the sink. Second drawer."

When Thad came back, Pete stood. "I'll get the supplies."

Thad sat next to her and picked up her hand. "Looks like the intruder broke the window with the intent of undoing the latch, but I'm betting the alarm scared him off."

"I thought that's what happened. What's confusing is why

come in the bedroom? Wouldn't that alert me?"

"Thieves target the back of the house so as not to be seen. I remember how your computer screen lit up part of the room. The person could have believed it was your office."

That made sense. "Then my intruder has never been in my house."

"Probably not."

She shrugged. "Doesn't help much. Most people haven't been inside."

"You never bring patients here?"

"No." Pete returned with an absurd amount of first aid supplies, which brought a small smile to her lips. "I wasn't shot."

He shrugged. "I don't want you to bleed all over my truck when we take you out of here." Heaven forbid if a drop of blood mixed with the paint, wallboard mud or other construction material. "Tomorrow, I'll see that the window gets fixed. Don't worry."

"Thank you." Everything was bombarding her at once. Had the person wanted to rob her or harm her?

Thad picked up her hand again. "We want you to come back to the house with us."

If he expected resistance, he wouldn't get it. "I appreciate that. Not that I expect a repeat, but do you think someone on duty could drive by the house?"

"I'll make that request."

Gertrude, the old lady across the street, was probably sitting by her window right now and would keep an eye out for her, too. Her neighbor probably hadn't had this much excitement in years.

Pete redid the bandage with such care that she barely realized he'd finished until he stood. "How about I carry you into the bedroom so you can pack?"

"I can walk."

Pete pulled her to a stand then picked her up anyway. "Your determination is admirable, but there's no need to reopen the wound." He kissed her forehead. "If anything happened to you..." He shook his head as if he couldn't finish the thought.

Hope rushed through her veins. He cared. Really cared. As they entered the room, both cops were still taking measurements and shooting photos.

Thad looked up then turned to the other officers. "Can you give us a minute, guys? Zoey needs to change and pack."

"Sure."

Pete set her down and she hopped to the dresser. "My suitcase is in the closet." Pete was right. The pressure from walking might reopen the wound.

Packing took less than ten minutes. After directing Pete where to find her clothes, she dressed while Thad stood guard at the door to make sure the cops didn't inadvertently return. She put on her most comfortable boots to give her injured foot room, and Pete carried her back to the living room.

Thad nodded to the men, indicating they were free to go return to the scene. Thad faced Pete. "How about you take Zoey's car home, and I'll drive the truck back?"

"You're staying?" Zoey wanted to be surrounded by both men.

"Someone needs to make sure the place is secure."

He was a cop through and through. She ran a hand down his arm. "I don't deserve either of you." She nodded to the alarm. "Do you need my code to arm the system when you leave?"

"That would be great." Thad pulled out his phone, and Zoey dictated the sequence of numbers to him. "Now go. I'll be home when I can."

As if Pete couldn't wait to get her away from here, Pete lifted her up and traipsed down the stairs. He set her down by the passenger side. "Need the keys."

With her foot injured, pressing on the pedal would be hard, so she relinquished them. Before running around to the driver's side, Pete made sure she was in the seat with her seatbelt securely fastened.

He started the engine and backed out. "You have any ideas who might have done this?"

Chapter Twenty-Four

Zoey leaned back against the truck seat. "I wish I had a clue who broke into my house. Thad would have a better idea if robbery were the motive. If the goal was to harm me, I might be able to come up with a few names." No suspect jumped out at her, though.

Pete glanced at her. "Name one."

"You playing cop tonight?"

He glanced over at her, but it was too dark to see his expression. "I know your mind must be going a million miles an hour. I'm hoping to quell some of your anxiety by asking questions. If you can bounce ideas off me, it might help."

Zoey reached out and squeezed his thigh. "Thank you. You're right. Talking always helps." If she didn't believe that, she wouldn't be a therapist. "At the funeral, Dr. Avery Carson was rather upset at me for mentioning his indiscretion to the police, but do I think he'd break into my house? No. He's a professional. I don't even see him hiring someone to scare me. There'd be no point without a warning." Carson had been too distraught over losing that little boy to do something like this.

"If you think this is related to Mrs. Sanchez's murder, how about her husband?"

"Why would Dr. Sanchez harm me? If he knows I saw

Carson with his wife and blabbed to the police already, he'd be happy I turned in the cheater."

"Your actions might put the hospital in a bad light. Could he fear you'll go public?"

Zoey tried to don her therapist mindset instead of that of a victim. "Why not ask me to keep it hushed up?"

Pete turned left onto Amber Way. "Embarrassed perhaps? If not him, what about one of your clients?"

She looked over at him, but his gaze was focused on the road. "It's always possible, but without proof, it would be against the rules to even give you a name."

Pete nodded. "We need to hope the burglar left a piece of physical evidence that will lead to his identity."

"That would be nice."

Before she knew it, they were back at Thad and Pete's house. He edged into the garage and closed the door. She couldn't wait to get inside and into bed. Pete helped her out.

"I can walk."

"You sure? I can carry you."

While it would be nice to be in his arms, she wanted to test her pain level. "I'll go slow." The bottom of her foot throbbed, but she managed.

With an arm around her waist, he escorted her into the kitchen and then flicked on the overhead bank of lights. "Make yourself at home. I'll get your bags."

The house was quiet—almost too quiet. She hadn't realized how the small amount of street noise at her place helped calm her. Within seconds, Pete returned with the purse she'd inadvertently left on the floor, along with her two suitcases.

"You want a cup of coffee or something?" he asked.

"Thanks, but if I have any caffeine, I won't sleep."

"I have decaf."

She gave that some thought. "I'm good. I'd probably fall asleep before it's finished brewing."

He nodded. "Where do you want to stay? Guest room? My room? Thad's room?"

That was a tough call. Being with her men would be fantastic, but the inevitable touching would occur, followed by glorious sex. Rest was what she needed. "How about the guest room for tonight?"

"That's probably smart, but if you don't mind, I'd like to hold you until you fall asleep. Then I'll sneak out. How does that sound?"

Pete must have read her mind. "You are the best."

Because she had to navigate the stairs, Pete insisted on carrying her again. Tomorrow, she hoped her cut would have healed enough that walking wouldn't be a big deal.

Pete set her down in the guest room then drew back the spread. "Take off your clothes, sugar, and I'll bring up your things so you can change."

Even though Zoey was tired, her body remained wired. Before she'd even taken off her one boot, Pete had returned. He placed the case on the bed and opened it for her.

"Need help undressing?" he asked, with a suggestive shine in his eye.

Pete was a fun man. "You know that wouldn't be a good idea."

"Suit yourself, but think about what you're missing."

She chuckled. With his arms crossed, he watched her strip. His smile warmed her heart. Once she drew on warm pajamas, she crawled under the blankets and waited for Pete to get ready. When he tucked her in and placed a light kiss on her forehead, disappointment bubbled inside her. "You said you'd hold me."

He laughed. "I was wondering when my platonic actions

would get to you."

"You did that on purpose, you sly dog. Now strip."

Her command brought another smile. Pete kicked off his boots, stepped out of his pants, and yanked off his sweater. Without socks or briefs, it hadn't take him long to get naked. She scooted over. As promised, he gathered her into his arms and kissed her. Boy, what a kiss that was.

"We can't start," she said, her body coming alive to his touch.

"I know. I won't take advantage of you, but I wanted you to know how much I need to feel you underneath me, to know you're alive."

She stroked his cheek. "Trust me, I'm very much alive, but I won't be of use to anyone unless I sleep."

Pete winked. "Have it your way."

He rolled her over so that her back was pressed against his rock hard chest. His presence soothed her until his thick shaft poked her back, reminding of the ecstasy she could have for the asking. She waffled between keeping her hands to herself and touching him, but before she could decide, she fell asleep.

When Zoey opened her eyes, light was streaming in the window, and the bed around her was cold. Damn. She'd lost the opportunity to enjoy Pete. It was Saturday, but she wasn't sure if he had to go in to work or not. Thad's schedule was equally a mystery.

A bit blurry eyed, Zoey sat, stretched, and then eased out of bed. *Get coffee or change clothes? Hmm.* Coffee won. After testing her foot to make sure she could walk, she limped across the hall and slowly went down the stairs, careful not to put too much weight on the injury. Halfway there, the aroma of strong coffee and eggs met her, and her stomach grumbled. She found Pete at the stove.

"Good morning," she said as she slipped onto the stool at the kitchen's center island. Thad must be either asleep or at work.

Pete looked over his shoulder. "Morning. Coffee's just finished brewing. Help yourself."

She pushed back her chair. While she prepared her cup, the garage door opened and she stilled.

"It's just Thad," Pete said. "He texted that he'd been called in right as he was leaving your house."

An ache raced up her spine. "Oh, my God. The poor man."

She poured her coffee then made another one for Thad and one for Pete. No sooner had she set all three cups on the counter than Thad dragged in, his eyes bloodshot, looking in need of a shave. She hobbled over to him and gave him a hug. "How are you?" Concern rushed through her.

"Tired." He kissed the top of her head. "Let me take off my jacket, and I'll tell you everything."

Everything? She stepped back. "Coffee's on the counter."

"I can sure use some." He nodded to her foot. "How's the injury?"

"Improved."

"No stitches needed?"

"I'll be fine in a few days." Zoey wanted to discuss what had caused him to be out all night.

Pete dumped the scrambled eggs onto a large platter and placed it on the island. The bacon sizzled in the pan on the other burner. "So, what happened?" Pete asked.

Thad tossed his jacket on the back of his chair and then faced Pete. "I was on my way home from Zoey's when I get a call from Max Gruden."

"The fire inspector?"

"Yes. Seems a fire broke out shortly after your break-in, and Max had photos he wanted me to look at."

"In the middle of the night?"

He nodded. "Max believed it was gang related, which I confirmed. The sooner we jumped on the case, the quicker the cops could catch the guy with the evidence. Long story short, I identified the markings on the building as that of the Blood Rights gang. I dragged Jeremy's ass out of bed and went in search of our informant who told us that this kid, who I shall call *Bob* was quite verbal about wanting revenge for some cops shooting his brother and then arresting him."

"Was that the kid Jeremy shot?" Pete asked, sliding onto the chair across from them.

"Yes. Along with the evidence Max had, I was able to get a search warrant for Bob's house. By the time we got there, though, the guy had gotten rid of any gas cans, but he failed to toss his clothes and burned shoes."

Pete waved his fork. "Committing a crime isn't as easy as it looks on TV."

Zoey sipped the hot brew, not sure if she should be privy to this information, but she was happy Thad was willing to share. "Seems like he wanted to be caught."

"That was my guess."

"What did he hope to gain by burning down a building? Did he want to be incarcerated so he could be with his brother?" After one of her teenage patients had committed suicide, Zoey decided to refer other teens to a different therapist who specialized in that age group because she realized she might never understand the teenage mind.

Thad picked up his coffee and held it in his hands as if he needed the warmth more than the caffeine. "Apparently, Bob wanted to get *my* attention, because I collared his brother." He faced her. "When we picked him up, we also found a map to your house."

It took a minute for the information to make sense. "Bob broke into my house?"

"Seems so. He said he wanted all cops to know that if we come after any of his people that we'd be sorry."

"Why me?"

Thad placed his hand over hers. "It was a way to give me the most pain."

Her fogged brain was having a hard time connecting the dots. Unease crawled up her body at the idea someone would want to harm her to get to Thad. Her mind still hadn't fully processed the break-in. "I'm not clear on this. Did he set the fire because he failed to get into my house?"

"Yes. Kids like him want recognition. Apparently, he thinks he'll be out in no time. His message, however, was clear. There will be a price to pay if we mess with his gang."

Zoey brought her coffee to her lips in the hope of stopping her heart from banging against her chest, but it didn't help. "I'm not sure landing in jail is the smartest choice."

"I've tried for years to get into the head of the typical gang member. Sometimes I can figure them out. Sometimes I can't. Here's one thing that never changes. Gang members, for all their faults and screwed-up ideals, are loyal to one another."

Her mind raced through the ramifications. "Are you saying that even with this kid in jail, others could come after me?"

Thad looked over at Pete, whose face had paled. "I don't want to scare you, but it's possible. Gangs don't play nice."

She didn't want to believe what he said was true, but it made sense. Now, every kid she passed on the sidewalk could be a possible attacker. She looked back at Pete. Zoey was surprised he hadn't offered his advice. "What do you think?"

Pete picked up his mug and brought it to his face, almost like he wanted to hide. "I don't like it."

"Neither do I." In this case, she had little control over what others did.

Thad faced her. "Pete's men will replace your bedroom window today, but I don't want you in the house alone. Alarm or not. If Bob wants to get back at me, he'll find someone else to do the deed."

"Way to keep me calm."

Guilt flashed across his face. "Sorry. It's possible he believes his message has been delivered, but I want to be careful. What I'm doing a bad job of saying is that I'd like you to move in here until we're positive the danger has passed."

Would it ever be gone? "I'd like that." Too bad it wasn't under better circumstances—like they wanted to be with her. The fact was, they hadn't known each other long enough. Relationships took time to build.

"I think Zoey should learn to shoot a gun," Pete said, with a seriousness she hadn't heard from him before.

"Guns scare me. Violence solves nothing."

"I'll be happy to teach her," Thad offered, "but if she takes the weapon out of her house, she'll still need to go through a series of courses to get a concealed weapons permit. Even then, it can't be issued for sixty days."

Pete rapped on the island. "Not good enough. What about a stun gun?"

Zoey held up her hands. "Guys. A stun gun? By the time I find my purse in my house and then fish it out, it'll be too late."

Thad's lips thinned. "While you're with us you'll be safe, but what about when you're in your office? I didn't like the way Dr. Carson looked at you."

She'd been through that discussion with Pete. From their firm tones, they wanted her to take more precautions. While she never could actually use a stun gun, it was better than if they wanted her to carry a gun. "I'll buy a stun gun, and I'll leave it at my office."

"Perfect," Pete said.

With that settled, they all dug in. After finishing, Zoey wanted to feel useful, and insisted on cleaning up.

"I'm going to crash for a few hours," Thad said in between yawns. "Maybe we can all do something fun together tonight."

"I'd like that." She could only hope it involved some hot sex.

Chapter Twenty-Five

"We're here!" Pete said.

His enthusiasm sounded forced, but Zoey was pleased he'd stopped fretting about her safety. After spending part of the day packing her things, and then moving into Pete and Thad's guest room, Zoey wanted to forget about gang members and killers.

Pete had driven the three of them about thirty minutes out of town into the National Forest. After taking a long winding road uphill, he pulled off to the side. She was a bit confused what "here" actually was, but it sure was pretty. "Don't tell me this is where you take your women to make out." The sun had set about half an hour ago and darkness was quickly inking in the sky. In the far distance, the lights of the city glowed.

Thad laughed. "That's not a bad idea." His upbeat chuckle almost sounded sincere.

"Before you even think it, it's too cold to have sex outside. I might be up for kissing, but that's all."

"Damn. Not even sex in the backseat?" Pete asked.

"Definitely not back there. It's too cramped."

Pete snapped his fingers. "Then we'll have to go to plan B."

Thad pushed open his door and guided her out. "You going to be warm enough in that coat?" He moved behind and wrapped his arms around her.

"I'll be fine." The truck's tailgate squeaked open. "What's he doing?" she asked Thad.

Thad nibbled her ear and all concerns disappeared. "Don't you worry about a thing. Pete has a surprise for you."

Zoey twisted around and wrapped her arms around Thad's neck, pressing her jacketed body against him. She kissed him hard and deep. Thad's demanding touch set her skin on fire and heated her to the core. She loved his passion and decisiveness.

Thad's callused hands cupped her cheeks, and when they kissed again, they seemed to draw life from each other. Time stood still. He emitted a throaty groan, and she had to break the kiss. "We shouldn't get started. It'll only frustrate me more."

Pete smacked his palm on his thigh. "Enough of that, you two. Come on. I have a surprise."

"Spoil sport. Just so you know, I like it when you guys kiss, nibble, and suck on my naked body, but I also like to stay warm. Next summer, I might agree to even suggest an outdoor adventure."

Damn. As soon as the words left her mouth, she realized her comment had been presumptuous. For being a psychologist, she kind of sucked at guessing their intentions. At times, the three of them were so close that she believed they'd never be apart. At other moments, she wondered if she was just the woman of the moment. It didn't help that the three of them had been thrown together by circumstances instead of by their mutual interests.

"Deal," Thad answered.

Pete carried a telescope and set it down on a flat surface about fifteen feet away. He extended the legs then cleared his throat. "Ready to see the magic of the sky?" Using his teeth to hold the flashlight, he moved some knobs and rotated some dials. The light clicked off. "Give me a sec to find something of interest."

As Zoey watched what he was doing, excitement sped through her. "I haven't been stargazing since high school, but I've always been fascinated by the universe. Pete, you never mentioned you were into astronomy."

Thad wrapped his arms around her waist again and leaned his cheek against her face. His closeness altered something inside her, and Zoey's insecurities regarding her place with these men melted.

"Pete is quite the superstar," he said. "He just likes to pretend to be low key, but he's not."

"That doesn't surprise me. All right, professor Banks. Show me what you got." A cool breeze kicked up and she shivered. Thad hugged her tighter.

The sweet scent of pine and sage rose on the wind in waves and she inhaled deeply. The clean scent helped clear her head.

"Step over here, sugar, and see our wonderful quarter moon." Pete guided her to the telescope, and then placed her hand on the focusing knob.

Zoey leaned over. "That's incredible. I didn't realize how bright it is."

"Actually it isn't much brighter than an asphalt road on a sunny day, but compared to the black sky it appears quite light." Pete leaned close and his presence made her lose focus for a minute. "Can you see both the light and the dark in the viewfinder?" he asked.

"Yes."

"That's called the terminator. If you watch closely, you'll see shadows move as the sun rises."

Thad stepped next to her and placed his hands on her waist again as if to steady her. She had a hard time not thinking about what those hands could do to her if she were underneath him right now. *Concentrate.* "Yes. Oh, wait. Something just changed."

"Let me replace the eye piece. Hold on." Without turning on the flashlight, he quickly made the exchange. "Try it now. What do you see?" Pete asked.

She looked and adjusted the knob. "This is incredible. I see mountains, craters, plains." Zoey stepped back. "Thad, take a look." Why hadn't she done this sooner? She faced Pete. "Have you always had this interest in astronomy?" He hadn't commented before when she'd mentioned his talent.

"Not until prep school. I had an amazing physics teacher who was into this stuff. A couple of times a quarter, when the weather permitted, he'd have these demonstrations where he'd invite the class to check out the constellations and our moon. His love of astronomy got me excited." His voice trailed off as if the memory was a good one, but one that could never be captured again.

"I'm glad you had the chance to meet such a man."

"Me, too. You ever have anyone profoundly influenced you?"

There were so many teachers she could honor. "The ones who left a lasting impression were the ones who challenged me. A few told me I didn't work hard enough and that I'd never succeed if I didn't change my ways. I had an advisor who wanted me to take this advanced writing class my senior year. It wasn't required, but he said it would make me a better person."

"What did you do?" Pete leaned closer, and Thad was no longer hunched over the telescope, as if he wanted to hear what she had to say, too. Their determination to learn about her boggled her mind.

"I took the class. Remember, I like to please."

Thad tugged her to his chest. "That's one of the many reasons why we like you. You're a good girl." His tone implied anything but.

"I am, which means I intend to have Pete show me some constellations, like he said he would."

Pete chuckled then pointed them out to her. But after a few sightings, his enthusiasm seemed to wane. She didn't want him to stay when he wasn't into it. Besides, the temperature had dropped significantly, and snuggling in front of the fire appealed to her.

"I'm getting a little cold. Would you all mind if we call it quits for tonight?"

"Sure, sugar." Pete folded the telescope and carried it back to the truck.

When he was out of earshot, she leaned close to Thad. "Is something wrong with Pete?"

Thad shrugged. "Seems like it. Not sure what his problem is. Don't worry. Once we're locked in the house, he'll be good. I think the aborted assault has him worried."

Pete's sudden strange mood was a downer, but hopefully with a nice glass of wine in front of a roaring fire, all would be well. She could picture the three of them engaging in a very steamy and passionate lovemaking experience.

Pete climbed in the front seat of the truck and started the engine to get it warm for Zoey. He'd never experienced this combination of angst and joy before. When Zoey had called and said someone had tried to get in her house, he'd lost it. What if that person had succeeded in harming her? Nothing had happened, thank God, but what if it had? What if another gang member came back and succeeded the next time? Pete would never be able to handle it.

Thad pulled open the passenger door. Zoey climbed in, clicked on her seatbelt, and then Thad jumped in after her.

She placed a hand on Pete's thigh and squeezed. "Thank you, again."

Her touch almost burned him. Pete wanted her so bad he could taste it, but he needed time to think.

"All set?" he asked in as cheery a voice as he could muster.

"Yup," she answered. "The stars were amazing."

"I agree." He loved her enthusiasm. Pete had done quite well keeping people at arm's length his whole life. The one time he'd actually opened his soul to a person, look what happened. He fell in love. *There*. He'd said it. He, Pete Banks, loved Zoey Donovan. Only he wasn't ready to tell her. He feared it might ruin things between them.

Every time they'd been together, their interactions had been intense. When he first met her, she'd bared her soul about being held captive. Then at his dad's place, when he'd let her see what his life was like, she seemed to understand. Too bad he'd end up disappointing her just like he'd disappointed his dad. Her rejection, though, would be worse.

"—movie?" Thad asked.

Fuck. He had no idea what Thad just suggested. "Whatever." That seemed to be an appropriate answer.

The roads were dark and deserted, which required Pete to pay attention driving and not on Zoey's delicious scent or how her leg was pressed against his.

"Eager to see the movie?" Thad said. Pete let up on the accelerator.

Thad was crazy for Zoey, too. Maybe Pete should just lay low for a while, figure out what he wanted, and let Thad and Zoey bond. Then if she were still willing, Pete could step back into her life.

As he neared the entrance to their street, he took the turn a little too fast and half the contents in the back shifted. She clenched his thigh and he slowed. When the house came into view, he decided what had to be done.

Once Pete parked, he looked over at Thad. "Why don't you take Zoey inside and start the fire? I want to make sure the telescope survived the drive."

Thad let out an audible breath. "Drive slower next time."

Fuck you. Pete waited until the door to the kitchen closed before he removed the telescope. He hadn't looked at the stars in forever. Showing Zoey one of his passions and hearing her squeal was almost too much to bear. He'd actually felt the deep connection in his gut. While he yearned to go to her, he was scared to death.

After Pete stayed in the garage for as long as he could without causing Thad to become suspicious, he walked in, acting like he was ready to delve into her hot body. The thought had his blood boiling, but if he touched her, he'd be lost for good.

"Anyone need some wine?" he asked.

"Yes, please," Zoey answered, sounding so content. Pete could get used to having her here—and that was the problem.

Thad knelt in front of the den fireplace, crumpled the newspaper, and stuffed the wad under the grate. "Hey Pete, grab the matches in the top drawer, will ya?"

"Sure."

"I'll get them," Zoey said. She came toward Pete with a determined look, and his heart nearly cracked for wanting her so much.

Pete located the matches. "Here ya go."

She smiled and pranced back to Thad. Pete's cock turned rigid. Not good.

It's time.

He poured the three glasses and carried them over to Thad and Zoey. He set his drink on the coffee table behind them. "I'll be right back."

Pete trotted into the bedroom, waited a minute, and then returned with his phone to his ear, praying this ruse would work. He didn't want to hurt Zoey, but it was for the best.

Chapter Twenty-Six

T had lit the fire and tried to act as if nothing was going on with his roommate, but he knew the signs. Jesus Christ. Pete had pulled this shit often enough, and Thad's gut couldn't stop churning.

His fellow stargazer sauntered back into the kitchen with his cell to his ear. "I just checked it, Mom. How can it be leaking again?" Pete blew out a breath and shifted his weight to one leg. The guy didn't glance their way.

Maybe Thad had been wrong, and something else was bothering Pete. He had mentioned his folks had a leak, but that he'd fixed it. Zoey placed a hand on his leg and furrowed her brows. Thad held up a finger. He didn't want to accuse his roommate of something without being certain.

Pete shook his head slightly. "Can't you call a plumber?" He walked toward them and picked up his glass of wine he'd set on the coffee table. He pounded back a mouthful. "Sure. I'll be right there."

When Pete stuffed the cell back in his pocket, the front wasn't lit. Shit. He hadn't even been connected. What the fuck was going on? Dumb question. Thad knew, but he didn't want Zoey to witness the exchange.

Drawing on his cop persona, Thad blanked his face. "Problem?" he asked.

Pete dragged a hand down his jaw and shook his head. "There's a new leak flooding the kitchen. Dad shut off the water, but my folks have guests. I need to go over there."

Zoey jumped up before Thad could stop her. "Do you want Thad and me to come with you? We could keep you company."

She stood in front of him with such hope in her eyes that Thad's heart nearly cracked. Pete cupped her face. The flash of indecision was so quick Thad doubted even Miss Therapist saw it, or if she had, she wasn't able to decipher it.

"That's so nice of you, but it won't be any fun. You stay nice and warm by the fire and take care of Thad."

"You sure?" She wrapped her arms around Pete's neck.

Would he crack and say he'd lied? Or would he run away? Thad could almost feel the foundation beneath them divide in two. If Pete walked now, Zoey would never forgive him.

Pete kissed her like it might be his last taste. Fuck.

Don't do this, man.

Pete pulled back. "Gotta go. It might be a few hours before I'm back." His roommate looked over at him. "Take good care of her."

With that, Pete grabbed his jacket off the back of the sofa and rushed through the kitchen to the garage. As soon as the door clicked close, Thad could no longer contain himself.

He kissed Zoey quick. "Hold that thought. I need to tell Pete something."

Not wanting Zoey to sense how pissed he was, he tried to keep his strides even. As he stepped into the garage, Pete was about to leave.

"Hey."

Pete stilled. "What's up?" His tone almost seemed carefree.

"That's what I want to know. What was with the fake call?"

Pete's chin tucked inward. "What are you talking about?"

"Cut the bullshit. The phone wasn't even on."

Pete drew a hand down his chin, a telltale sign he needed time to come up with some excuse. His lips skewed to the side. "I see how you look at Zoey. You're falling in love with her, and that's just not for me."

Thad had dealt with a lot of lying thugs in his life, but Pete's excuse was beyond pathetic. Thad's cool demeanor not only cracked, it burst. He grabbed Pete's jacket and slammed him against the side of his truck. "You walking out? Huh? You're going to use that lame ass excuse that you're not ready?" Thad let go of Pete's lapels.

"I need time."

"You fucking lied to her. Don't you know that a good relationship is built on trust? Even if you decide to crawl back, it'll be too late. You can't repair that kind of damage." When Pete didn't blink, Thad's disgust and disappointment reached the limit. "You know what? You can go fuck yourself. Just leave, but know that I'm staying with Zoey."

If Thad remained in the garage another minute, he'd have smashed Pete's face in. Anger roiling inside him, he stomped back to the kitchen door. He couldn't let Pete's immature attitude fuck this up with the woman he cared so much for. Thad wanted her, and he wanted her bad. He inhaled, pasted on a smile, and drew open the door.

As soon as he stepped inside, she looked up from the fire, looking content and happy. His body ached for her. If he said anything about what Pete was planning, he wasn't sure he could watch her heartache. The only way he was going to make it through the next few minutes was to lose himself in her. In her goodness. In her loving ways.

With his gaze on Zoey's beautiful face, he flicked off the

kitchen light and eased his way over to her. The fire bathed her in a warm glow and lit her auburn hair. She looked like an angel, and his heart soared. He was still reeling from Pete's rejection, but before he told Zoey anything, he wanted to show her how much he needed her. It might be the only way to make Pete's rejection less painful.

Thad grabbed the sofa seat cushions and brought them over to where she'd sprawled out. "I thought we'd be more comfortable on these."

She moved both her glass and his off to the side and sat up. "I like it."

He knelt, lifted her up a few inches and placed her on the cushions. "You are so beautiful, and I'd take a hundred more bullets if it meant I could be with you."

She reached up and placed a finger on his lips. "Don't ever say something like that."

"It's true." His life had been so empty before he'd met Zoey. "You've made me see what I've been missing." He popped open his jeans and unzipped his pants. "I want you, Zoey, in the worst way."

Her grin sent his heart in overdrive. "Me, too."

"Race ya." He unlaced his shoes and toed them off. As much as he wanted to strip off her clothes, inch by delicious inch, he needed her too much to take his time. He finished undressing just as she was about to remove her bra and panties. He stayed her hand. "Let me." Climbing on top of her, he supported himself on his elbows then brushed a lock of hair from her delicate face. The second their lips touched, his balls drew up painfully tight. Zoey was all his, and he wanted her to understand what that meant to him.

When her tongue delved into his mouth, his blood caught on fire, and Thad couldn't get enough of her. His fingers found the straps of her bra and lowered them. Then with a quick pinch, he undid the back clasp. Anticipation soared through him.

Needing some air to quell his rapid pulse, he trailed his lips down her chin, across her smooth neck, and over Zoey's soft skin. What she did to him should be outlawed. He wanted to slowly explore every inch of her body but his need was too great.

"You smell so good." It was a hint of citrus mixed with something flowery. Soft. Feminine. Sexy as hell.

Her fingers dug into his shoulders. "I need you." Her throaty groan undid him.

Quicker than the next flame could flicker, he straddled her and discarded the pretty black bra. What was underneath was ten times better. "A feast for me." His lips found one succulent nipple, and his fingers grasped her other full breast. His imagination went wild as his tongue suckled on the pert tip. "So sweet."

"I'm not food." Her giggle soothed his soul.

He loved toying with her. "So you say. When I eat you, you might come around to my way of thinking."

Zoey lifted her hips. The pressure of her body against his cock caused all hell to break loose. He dragged a hand from her breast down her waist and slipped his fingers under her panties and along her hipbone. He tightened his hold on her supple skin and inhaled her essence. "What you do to me."

She closed her eyes and dropped back her head. "Show me."

Needing no more encouragement, he slid between her legs. He loved how the light from the fire caused shadows to dance across her perfectly proportioned face and over her round breasts. Dragging a palm across her belly, he grinned when she inhaled and then let out a little mewling sound.

It was hard not to sink his cock deep inside her, but Zoey deserved more. The urge to rush slammed into him, but he needed her to see they were meant to be together.

"Lick me," she said. Her groan nearly undid his resolve not to rush.

With care, he slipped her panties to her knees, and then down her silky smooth legs. Once they were off, he lifted both ankles and placed her feet on the floor. She was open. Vulnerable. His. His cock nearly detonated. Holding her thighs wide, he licked his way up her inner thigh toward his reward.

"Thad, please."

Nothing was better than to hear a woman beg, but what he wanted more was for her to come so hard she had to gasp for breath.

"Patience."

She squeezed her butt cheeks and lifted her ass, offering him her pussy. Wanting to satisfy her, he worked a finger into her silky opening. When her walls caressed and warmed his skin, he was unable to hold out. From the way Zoey was moaning and wiggling, she was on edge, too.

From a pocket in his pants, he found a condom, tore it open with one rip, and rolled the rubber down his length. Before he slaked his own lust, he wanted to bring her higher. He swiped his tongue between her naked pussy lips, and the taste of her delicious honey altered him. He flicked her swollen nub and she bucked.

"Now, Thad." Her plea broke him.

He hooked her knees over his shoulder. This was where he needed to be. Her breasts and lips both called to him, but he captured her mouth first. The second the tip of his cock pressed against her slick opening, her fingers clamped on his hips and tugged him close. His world spun.

Using every ounce of control, Thad edged into her. Zoey opened her mouth and he kissed her hard. Their tongues touched, and his cock almost exploded. He wanted it all. They dueled, danced, played, and loved. With each new position, he came closer to release.

Zoey's heels dug into his back, drawing him near. "Zoey!"

"I'm so close." Each word came on a breath, forcing him to give in.

With one long thrust, he filled her to the hilt. Her heated walls encased his cock, pulsing and throbbing around him. Nothing mattered but her release. He broke the kiss and buried his face against her neck, pounding his cock down her tight channel. With each trip, he lost a little more of his heart and soul to the woman beneath him.

Her mouth opened and a strangled cry erupted right as her pussy strained and gripped his dick. His hot cum blasted out of him and he held her tight, never wanting to let her go.

Thad kissed her, and then hugged her some more. When the beating of their hearts finally slowed, he eased out of her.

"Be right back."

In the kitchen, he grabbed a towel and wet it. As soon as he wiped her clean, he slid next to her on the pillow and dragged her on top of him. He wanted to promise her that he'd keep her safe, and that he wanted to spend the rest of his life loving her, but the image of Pete surfaced. Thad feared she'd withdraw when she found out the threesome had crumbled.

Pete had no idea where he was headed, but as he drove down Fourth Street a spot opened up in front of Banner's Bar. It was as good a place as any to stop. He kept telling himself he was doing Zoey a favor by bowing out so early in the relationship. Sure, she responded to him in bed and seemed to enjoy the star show, but she also adored Thad. The two of them would do well together. Pete pushed aside the ache that stabbed his gut. He wanted Zoey—too much in fact—but this was for the best. A man whose own father didn't love him wasn't good for someone as amazing as Zoey Donovan.

Pete never doubted himself when it came to building homes or seducing women, but he couldn't bring himself to cause Zoey any more distress. Hadn't she mentioned that her old ménage relationship hadn't worked out? She might be happier with just one man.

He parked and headed inside. For a Saturday, the place wasn't as packed as he'd expected. Each of the four televisions was set to a different college football game. With no room at the bar, he maneuvered his way to the back to see if any of his buddies were shooting pool.

Well, what do you know? Alex was there with someone Pete didn't recognize. With intense concentration, Alex banked a striped ball, which collided with another one that ran straight into the pocket. He looked up at opponent and grinned. After Alex sank two more, he missed his next shot. His opponent took his turn, and when he failed to clear the table, Alex called the pocket and dropped the eight ball right where it needed to go.

The two shook hands and Pete slapped his coins on the edge to indicate he was challenging in. Nothing like a game of pool to take his mind off his troubles.

Christie, a pretty young thing, came by for his drink order. "I'm in a Jack Daniels frame of mind. And make it a double, honey."

Alex racked the balls. "While it's none of my business,

where's the fair lady tonight?"

"You're right. It's not your business, but I'll tell you anyway. She and Thad are enjoying a nice warm fire."

"Good for them. I can see why you'd come here. My company is much more exciting." Alex's lips pressed together like they always did when he was in his "you're-an-idiot" mode.

Well, fuck him. Pete didn't need to hear Alex's bullshit. He might try to claim Alex didn't get where he was coming from, but of all the people on earth, Alex understood him the best. It was actually unfortunate his good friend was here.

"You break," Pete said, not caring if he won or lost the game.

"Fine, but if I win, you have to answer a question for me truthfully."

"What are we? Fifteen?"

Alex centered the triangle on the table then carefully removed the rack. "You afraid?"

"I'm afraid of listening to you blabber and distracting me from my game."

Christie waltzed back over with his drink. "You want a tab, Pete?"

"Definitely."

"You got it." She set his drink on the table a few feet away, winked, and sashayed off.

"Now that's a hot chick," Alex said with fake interest.

Pete decided on the truth this time. "Christie's nice, but she's pushed my buttons on too many issues." Like only wanting sex one way.

"But Zoey doesn't?"

Before he answered, he slammed back half his drink, and set it down with a thud. "You going to shoot or what?"

Alex bent over the table with his cue in hand. "You in a

hurry to get back to your honey?"

Now the guy was pissing him off. "I like Zoey just fine. She prefers Thad." Or would prefer him if she thought about it. He and Thad hadn't given her much of a choice about which one she wanted. She was almost shot, and both he and Thad happened to be there to pick up the pieces. He'd never asked what she wanted.

Alex punched his stick into the stack of balls, and they went flying. The sound brought Pete back to the present. One of the striped balls dropped in the pocket. "Nice shot," Pete said.

"Thanks."

Two couples wandered into the back room. One went to the dartboard, while the other surrounded the Foosball table. With more people around, Alex might not discuss Pete's personal life. Before he took his turn, he polished off his whiskey, wishing he'd at least get a buzz to blot out his thoughts. Alex drove in two more balls then nicked the pocket. The ball rolled on by.

Pete walked around the table to decide on the best shot. He aimed and sank the first ball. Alex nodded approvingly at the accomplishment. Pete sank another one, but missed the third. When he stepped back to give Alex room, another Jack Daniels replaced the one he'd just finished. He liked the service around here.

"Thad okay with you going rogue on him?" Alex's voice sounded so unconcerned, it was as if he'd asked what Pete thought of the new paint color on the wall.

"He didn't say much. Now can we get on with the game?"

Alex laughed. "You know what your problem is?"

Chapter Twenty-Seven

Pete wasn't in the mood to listen to Alex's shit. "No. Tell me what my problem is."

Pete's former partner swallowed a smile, lined up the cue stick, and ran the table. "I win. Now, bring your drink. Let's see if we can find someplace quiet to talk."

No way Pete would agree to that. He didn't need to be answering questions, especially from Alex. "Rematch, then maybe."

"Didn't realize the guilt ran so deep. What the hell did you do? Sleep with someone else?"

The accusation hurt worse coming from Alex. Pete never cheated and Alex knew that. "Fuck no." Pete retrieved the balls from the side pockets and organized them in the rack. It was his turn to break.

"Then you found someone else." His statement made the irritation scrape Pete's insides raw.

He was tired of this game and considered tossing down his cue and walking out. "Wrong again. I'm not a womanizer." He hadn't had time to even date someone else. Didn't want to.

"By whose definition? Brenda's? Lisa's? Jane's?" Alex counted on his fingers. "Shall I go on?"

"You little shit." Pete leaned his stick against the table and tossed back his drink.

Alex laughed. "You're so in denial. Every time you called when I was with Dad, all you'd talk about was how the lady you were with was 'the one.' Then after a month or two, you'd pull away. Find some excuse why it wasn't right."

That was what Thad said, but they didn't know the truth. Didn't understand. "Might look like that, but this is different."

"How is it different?"

Pete didn't know why Alex had to press so hard. "It just is." With more force than was required, Pete broke. Balls flew but none dropped. In fact, he wasn't left with much of a shot. If he studied the table long enough, Alex might lose interest in his line of questioning. Or better yet, leave. Pete bent over, moved the stick back and forth then stood. "Don't have many options here."

"I know what you're doing, Pete. But go on. Stick your head in the sand."

Sometimes Alex could be such a dick. Pete tried the shot again. It went wide.

Alex moved into position. "You're just like your dad, you know."

Pete's lips firmed and his fist clenched. "That's a low blow."

Alex shrugged. "You both think very little of yourself."

"I'm not an ass to the hired help."

"No, but you both don't think enough of yourself to let another person in."

Pete wasn't quite sure what Alex was referring to, but the pain stabbed him in places he didn't know could be hurt. "You're saying because my dad regrets his past that he's afraid to love anyone?" That was what Zoey had said.

Alex glanced to the ceiling then laughed. "Sometimes I wonder how you ended up running and owning your own business. For someone who seems to get what the client wants, you can be such a fucking moron when it comes to people."

Alex was pissing him off royally. Pete needed another drink and waved to the waitress for a refill. "You saying I don't understand people?" Alex must be doing drugs or something.

Alex waved a hand as if to dismiss his question. "It shouldn't matter what your dad has done or is doing. You're almost forty fucking years old yet act like you're nine. You, Pete Banks, need to grow up and be a man. If you're not happy with the way your *daddy* has treated you, get over it." His friend stepped closer and got up in his face. The scent of beer was strong. "Why do you have to depend on his goddamn actions? Ask Zoey what that makes you. Codependent? Juvenile? Doesn't matter the term. You're a child and a whiner." Alex tossed the cue stick on the table. "I'm finished. Clear the table yourself." With that, he stormed off.

"Fuck you, buddy."

No way he was going to let Alex dismiss him like that. Pete charged, collared his friend and spun him around. He expected Alex to hold up his hands, but his friend punched him in the gut instead, sending him backward. Having downed those three Jack Daniels caused Pete to lose his balance. His butt hit the edge of a chair and sent it sprawling. A girl cried out from near the dartboard.

"You want to fight?" Alex motioned with his fingers. "I'll give you a fucking fight."

Pete got up and dusted himself off. Alex dipped his shoulder and rammed it into Pete's belly, pushing him into a table. As it upended, glass shattered. The momentum caused them both to land on the ground, and Pete's back took the brunt of the impact, but his brain was too numb to feel much. Instinct took over. They wrestled, twisting and turning, until Alex slammed

Pete's head into a chair leg, which unceremoniously went flying. Alex's fist then connected with Pete's face. Shit. Pain streaked across his jaw, possibly loosening a tooth. The next blow connected with his nose. That did it. Pete thrust his leg up and flipped the two over. He delivered a punch to Alex's face. Damn, that felt good, but his knuckles stung from the impact. His friend grunted, shook off the daze and did a quick and complicated maneuver that resulted in Alex on his knees behind Pete. In seconds, Alex had an arm wrapped around Pete's throat. The bastard held on tight, too. Try as he might, Pete couldn't get loose. Alex yanked inward, nearly crushing his windpipe. Christ.

Using what strength he had left, Pete grabbed Alex's wrists and tugged hard, but the brute wouldn't give in. Pete had spent his entire life lifting wallboard, developing muscles on top of muscles, and a few shots of whiskey had weakened every one of them.

"Break it up." The gruff voice came from one of the bouncers.

Alex was pulled off him, allowing a liter of air to rush down his windpipe.

Someone helped Pete to his feet. He swayed as he stumbled over to the chair. "Sit and don't move. I'll get you some ice." It was Christie. Bless her heart.

Reality finally entered his brain. His lungs hurt and his eye was beginning to swell shut.

The bouncer returned. "We've called the cops."

Fuck.

✧   ✧   ✧

Making love with Thad had been magical. The intensity. The passion. Thad's caring touch convinced her that these men were right for her. Everything had been absolutely perfect, except for Pete's poorly timed phone call. If he'd had been there to make love with them, she'd have marked this day down on a calendar as a time she never wanted to forget. Zoey totally got that they had busy lives. Hopefully, only something as important as a call from his folks would cause Pete to leave again.

She'd wanted to contact him to see how things were going with the plumbing issue at his parents' house, but Thad kept saying they shouldn't disturb him. From the way he kept changing the subject every time she brought up Pete's name, she got the sense something was wrong.

Thad was snuggled against her back, his arms holding her tightly as if he never wanted to let her go. "I'm not sure if Pete mentioned it, but one of his workers let him know that your window is fixed." Thad kissed her neck and shivers of delight raced up her spine.

"When do you think I can go home?"

"Not until I'm convinced it's safe. I need time to find out about the threat from our burglar turned arsonist."

Zoey was fine with that. Staying with the men gave her a warm feeling of comfort. She tried to doze, but every time she fell asleep, she'd wake, thinking her house alarm was going off. Perhaps she needed Pete in bed to make the night complete.

The clock on the nightstand next to the bed read 2:13 a.m. Had Pete decided to stay the night at his parents' house to make sure his repair held? He should have called or texted. She rolled over, and Thad woke.

He cupped her face. "Can't sleep?" he asked. From the slight moan in his voice, he'd been dreaming.

"I'm worried about Pete. He's not home."

"Mmm."

So much for Thad being concerned. "Did he text you?" *And*

you forgot to tell me?

"I'm sure he had a good reason. Go back to sleep."

That was a shitty answer. "How do you know he's not lying in a ditch somewhere bleeding to death?" She hadn't meant for her voice to escalate. "Maybe the gangs decided to hurt you by harming him instead."

Thad blew out a breath, sat up, and turned on the bedside lamp. "All right. I was planning to wait until tomorrow to tell you." He yawned. "I should amend that. I was hoping I wouldn't have to tell you tomorrow, that Pete would come to his senses."

"What are you talking about?" Her skin turned clammy.

"I don't even know how to break this to you."

His evasive comments caused acid to burn a big fat hole in her belly. "Just tell me."

"Pete wants out."

She must not have heard him right. "Out of what?"

Thad dropped back onto the bed and dragged his forearm over his face, the ugly red scar a bad reminder of how he could have been killed. "Pete's running scared, that's all."

The words finally began to make sense. She wanted to see Thad's eyes and lowered his arm to his stomach. He groaned. "Thad. Look at me." He cracked open an eye. "Are you saying Pete doesn't want to be with me anymore? When did he tell you this? You must have misunderstood." On top of the mountain, Pete had been wonderful, patient, fantastic.

"His parents never called him. He made that up."

She needed a moment to put the facts in order. "There was no water leak?" The deception slammed into her. "He lied?"

"Yes."

Her pulse pounded. "I can't believe he'd do that to me."

Thad rubbed her arm. "This isn't the first time he's pulled

this trick. As soon as he falls for a woman, he runs scared. I'm finished with him. He's acting like a fucking child, and I don't think he'll ever change."

Her mind reeled. "I need to talk with him." Desperation clawed at her belly. As angry as she was, she needed confirmation that Thad had interpreted Pete's actions correctly.

"Zoey." Thad clasped her hand. "It's two o'clock in the morning. You're tired. Pete's probably drunk. Get some sleep. We'll figure something out in the morning."

Easy for him to say. Just when she thought she'd found the two perfect men, this had to happen. Now what was she going to do? She wanted to get out of bed and pace, but Thad held her tight. As their girlfriend, what she wanted to do was throw something, pound a wall, yell. As a therapist, she needed to think. Did Pete realize what this would do to his relationship with Thad? She found it hard to believe Pete would throw away that friendship. She pounded her pillow and grunted.

Thad nuzzled her neck. "I'm pissed too, babe, but we'll work it out."

She hoped he meant the three of them would figure something out. Her gut told her he was only talking about the two of them.

Chapter Twenty-Eight

Zoey hadn't slept at all last night. Once Thad told her about Pete's lie, and that he wanted out of the relationship, she was too devastated to rest. She went back over everything Pete had said or did, even replaying the conversation about how he'd befriended Alex, and the incident where he and Joe had stolen the car, but the puzzle pieces didn't quite fit.

The "Pete is running scared" argument had a few holes in it. When they'd last spoken, Pete seemed to want a permanent relationship and even a family. He was confident of his goals. He wasn't the type to run away. After much thought last night, Zoey developed a different theory about Pete's defection, but the result was the same. Pete was gone. The three of them could never be together until he understood that no matter what he did, he couldn't make his dad love him. Pete had to stop blaming himself for something that wasn't his fault. As a therapist, Zoey was well aware the battle would be long. Pete might never reach the top of that tricky mountain. Had he been wrong to lie to her and Thad? Hell yeah. Could she forgive him? That remained to be seen.

"Can you toss what's in those dresser drawers in this suit-case while I tackle the closet?" Thad asked. Gone was any tenderness. In its place was bitterness and disappointment.

"Sure." She gathered the clothes and neatly placed them in the case. Thad was hurting. Hell, she was, too. While it was in her nature to console him, she feared that in his present state, anything she said to excuse Pete's behavior would only piss Thad off even more, so she tried a different tactic. "Don't you think it would be better if we waited until Pete returns? Walking out without any kind of discussion never solves anything."

"Pete's in jail."

Every part of her body froze. "In jail?" Her throat tightened. "Why didn't you tell me?" Thad's deception hurt. What else didn't she know? "It's bad enough that Pete lied to me, but you, too?"

His jaw tightened. "I just got a text from one of the guys on the force. It said Pete and Alex had been in a bar fight. Smashed a few chairs and tables before the bouncer broke up the struggle."

Zoey tried to make sense of the news. "He likes Alex. Why would they fight?"

His hands stopped. "Alex probably taunted him, and Pete went crazy."

"Something bad is going on with him. I should go see him."

Thad shook his head then walked over to her, his gaze never leaving her face. He dragged his hands down her arms and guided her to the bed. "Come sit with me." The dejection in his tone cut her.

"What is it?" she asked.

"Here's my real take. Pete won't cop to this, but I believe he thinks he's not good enough for you."

That was what she thought. "Pete's wrong. His degree of worthiness should be my decision. Not his."

"I know you're a shrink, but it's hard to ignore rejection."

"True, but it's Mr. Banks who has the issue. His insensitive actions have nothing to do with Pete."

"Try telling Pete that." Thad brought her fingers to his lips and kissed the tips. "If this was the first time he'd pulled this running away shit, I'd understand, but it's not. However, he's never gone off the deep end like this before."

"Has he ever been arrested?"

"No." Thad looked at the clock on the side table. "For disturbing the peace, he'll need to stay in jail twenty-four hours, which means we need to get out of here by dinner time."

His thin lips and rigid posture implied a man fighting for control. Pete had done this to him. *Damn you, Pete Banks.*

Thad stood and continued jamming his clothes in his suitcase. She'd already gathered her few possessions. "Let me get this straight," Zoey said. "You think that by moving out, you'll be making a statement?"

More stuffing occurred. Thad nodded. "He has to hit rock bottom or he won't change."

Wow. That was what she always professed to parents who enabled their children. Zoey stood and moved closer. "You're right, but it still hurts. Pete needs to realize there are severe consequences for his actions. He walked out without discussing things with us. That worries me."

"So what are you saying?"

Pete felt like twenty sledge hammers, ten nail guns, and an electric drill were going off in his head. His body ached from attempting to sleep on the pathetic excuse for a jail cot, and the strong odor of dried piss hadn't helped. The final blow was being forced to remain in jail for twenty-four hours. That hurt.

Pete glanced to the end of the row of jail cells at Alex, who was asking the guard for some water. Pete wanted to apologize to his friend, but given the number of drunks and other misfits housed between them, now wasn't the time.

About an hour ago, Pete had been given his one phone call. Because he was convinced Thad would hang up on him, Pete had called his dad. He would come to his son's rescue only because Russell Banks wouldn't want the embarrassment. Pete loathed himself right now. Once he'd sobered and thought about his actions, he'd realized how much he'd fucked up. Not only would Thad probably have nothing to do with him, the woman he loved might spurn him, too.

One of the deputies rapped on the bars then jangled the keys to unlock the cell door. "Bail's been paid, Banks. You're free to go."

Even though the place smelled of urine and mold, he wasn't sure facing his father would be any more pleasant. "What about Alex?"

"Don't worry about him. Someone's paid his bail, too." Pete wondered who.

Shit. He'd never sunk this low before. What had he been thinking? He'd been reckless, careless, and above all stupid. Sometime last night he'd finally understood what Alex had been trying to tell him. Pete saw it so clearly now. He'd spent his whole life trying to earn his father's affection, and mistakenly believed that his dad never reached out to him because Pete didn't deserve his father's love. Jesus. His dad was the fucked-up one, not him. How Pete had missed that concept, he didn't know. The question was, could he repair the damage he'd done?

When the deputy escorted him out, his wallet and phone were returned to him. His father stood with the police chief, probably discussing the details of Pete's poor behavior. Could this get any worse?

Just thank him and move on.

With shoulders squared, Pete strode up to his dad. His father faced him, the glare of disapproval all too familiar. "Thanks for posting bail, Dad. I'll write you a check as soon as I get home." He didn't want to owe his father anything.

His dad glanced at him before turning back to the chief and shaking his hand. The dismissal made Pete feel like a ten-year-old again. "Stan. Let's get together soon."

"Sure, Russell. Any time."

His dad turned and headed toward the entrance. Pete kept up with him, stride for stride. "You didn't have to post bail."

Dad said nothing until he was out of earshot of his friend. "I didn't need my son rotting in jail another minute. You've embarrassed me enough." His father ground out his words.

His dad's comment should have hurt, but surprisingly it didn't. His father was all about appearances, what was important to him. It was rather sad. "My truck's at Banner's. I'd appreciate a lift."

In silence, he followed his dad to the car. "Get in."

If Pete's head didn't pound so much, he might have had a heart-to-heart with dear old Dad. Perhaps later. Pete climbed in the front seat. While spending a day in the less than pleasant jail sucked, it had helped clarify his perspective on his bad choices.

All across town, his dad remained silent. Pete didn't mind. Let his dad stew. Was his father even questioning if he'd failed as a parent? Or didn't he think any of this was his fault? It didn't matter. His father never did see reality clearly, and that wasn't going to change.

Out of habit Pete checked his phone. He swiped the keypad, and when he typed in the code, his heart sank once more. It was a message from Thad that read: *Moved out. Staying with Zoey. She's devastated.*

If Pete thought the pain at the base of his skull had been bad before, he'd been wrong. This hurt worse. His gut and heart nearly shut down. He'd never wanted to hurt Zoey and now he had.

His dad stopped at the corner of Fourth and Nugget Road right next to his truck. "I hope you'll think the next time you get in a fight."

Unable to respond in a civil manner, Pete shook his head and pushed open the door. "I'll mail you the check. Thanks again for the ride."

He closed the door with care, though he'd been tempted to slam it. His dad had saved his butt, so Pete would be respectful. Didn't matter the man's motivation sucked. If Pete ever had kids, he'd let them know every hour of every day how proud he was of them and how much he loved them.

As soon as he lost sight of his dad's car, Pete slid into the cab, his stomach churning. If he thought staying in jail for a day was hard, apologizing to Thad and Zoey was going to be worse.

Once he pulled into his garage, he eased out of the truck. Man, did he need a shower bad. Unlocking the door to the kitchen, he stepped inside and halted. Thad's coffee maker was no longer on the counter. Pete's stomach tumbled again. Sure, Thad said he was leaving, but Pete didn't think his former roommate meant he'd leave for good. With the gang issue still unresolved, Pete didn't like his friend's decision to let Zoey be at her house.

None of the furniture appeared to be missing, but Thad might be planning on coming back later and picking up a few pieces. To make sure Pete understood the extent of Thad's intent, he pushed open his friend's bedroom door, flicked on the light, and checked out the space. Empty. Empty. Empty. Shit.

What have I done?

✧   ✧   ✧

Zoey was nervous, and she'd be the first to admit it. When Pete had called the next day and asked if he could meet her after work, it had taken all of her control not to tell him he was an idiot for ever thinking he wasn't good enough for her. Because the men hadn't settled their issues, she asked Thad if he didn't mind remaining at work until she called him and gave him the all clear. She wanted to speak with Pete alone, and Thad was fine with that

Her biggest challenge would be to keep from hugging Pete the moment she saw him. A normal woman would have been pissed he'd broken the trust the three of them had built, but she understood why he'd acted the way he had. Did that mean she should say all was well and move on? Hell, no. She didn't need a PhD in psychology to know that for Pete to heal, he had to grovel for her forgiveness. It was the only way to earn respect. Most of the psychological theories claimed that only by believing all options had expired could Pete get better.

At 5:30 p.m. on the dot, her doorbell rang. Zoey ran her hands down her skirt and hoped she was strong enough to pull this off. She'd held hundreds of sessions counseling people against expecting others to be the ones to make them whole. Now that she was faced with the most difficult and important talk of her life, she was a mess.

I have to do this. For Pete. For me. For Thad.

Inhaling, she drew open the door, but she wasn't prepared for Pete to look so lost. Her heart nearly cracked. His clothes appeared clean and, given his damp hair, he'd showered, but the black eye and slightly swollen jaw, coupled with his bloodshot eyes tore at her soul. "Hey. Come in."

Pete didn't look her in the eye, and that might have hurt worse than his lie. For some crazy reason, she believed he'd come here to apologize. Fear ran up her body like tiny paper cuts. God, she hoped she wasn't wrong about his motives.

"Thanks for seeing me." He looked toward the kitchen then down the hall. "Where's Thad?"

"Still at work. He phoned a bit ago and said he'd been called out on another gang-related robbery." That was the truth. Zoey was glad she didn't have to lie. "Can I get you some coffee?"

"Sure." From behind his back, he produced a bouquet of pink roses and a small box of chocolate. Her heart melted. "It's kind of corny, I know, but I wanted to show you how sorry I am."

There it was. The apology. Step one complete. She took the proffered gifts. "Thank you. Pink's my favorite color."

A smile flashed across his lips. "I know."

"I guess I had come rather unglued over the beige candles. Come sit in the kitchen while I put these in water." Kisses and touches would let her know the depths of his regret, but she appreciated the gesture of the gifts. She lifted them to her nose and inhaled their flowery scent. Finding roses this time of year must not have been easy.

"Want me to start the coffee?" Pete asked, sounding like he wanted to help—or rather needed to help.

"Sure." Both Thad's coffeemaker and hers sat side by side. She wondered if Pete had noticed it was missing.

In silence they worked together—she with the flowers, he with the drinks. When she looked over at his slumped shoulders, part of her wanted to hug and kiss him until every inch of hurt disappeared from the lines in his face. But Pete needed to put his recent actions and decision into words. Only by saying them out loud would he truly be able to extinguish the demons that had been plaguing him for so long.

She set out the cream and sugar while he retrieved the mugs from the cupboard. From the way he was working his mouth, he was finding it hard to know where to begin. Sympathy for him finally won.

"Tell me about the fight."

He briefly looked up at her. "Heard about that, did you?"

"Rock Hard isn't a tiny town, but people care about one another. Word gets out."

The coffee finished brewing, and he brought over the pot and poured the rich drink. They sat across from each other, reminiscent of the first time they'd met. Did he remember their conversation as vividly as she did?

He brought his cup to his lips and blew the steam across the liquid. His knuckles were almost white. "It was easier when you were pouring your soul out to me."

She appreciated his honesty. "I bet it was, but if you have any interest in us being together, I need to understand what went on in your head."

"It's complicated." He drank his coffee, either for the fortification or to keep from having to speak.

"It always is. Maybe you should start by telling me about the night you went over to your parents' house."

"I'm sure Thad told you that was an excuse to get away."

She leaned forward. "I don't get it. When you were showing me the stars, I thought we'd connected." *I thought you might even love me.*

He cleared his throat. "We did. Zoey. Ah. Okay, here it is. When we were on top of that mountain, sharing something as powerful as the universe, I realized how much I loved you."

Her heart pounded in her chest so hard, it was close to being painful. "And the problem would be?" Her words jammed in her throat as adrenaline rushed through her veins so fast she almost became lightheaded.

"I cared too much to let you be with me."

Without conscious thought, she slammed her palm on the table. "I'm furious that you didn't consider talking to me about it. Did you think I'd judge you?" She didn't wait for him to answer. "That pisses me off. You are such an amazing man, and I wish you'd have given me the chance to tell you."

He leaned his head back and blew out a breath. "I was wrong. I fucked up."

"Yes, you did, and I'd like to hear your take on it."

"After I left you and Thad, I was feeling sorry for myself. I'm not proud of that. I went to Banner's, where I ran into Alex."

"Which turned sour. What did he do? Hold your feet to the fire?" It was what Pete wanted her to do with his dad.

"Yeah. Alex told me I was just like my father, that I pushed people away whenever I feared they'd get too close." His jaw hardened. "I never realized I did that."

He seemed to get it. "We often don't want to look in the mirror. It's hard."

"You got that right. After Alex basically told me to go fuck myself—sorry for the language—and grow up, I lost it." He set his cup down. "I know now that he was right, but I wasn't willing to admit it at the time. I just reacted." He stabbed a hand through his hair.

"When you punched him, were you actually hitting what you hated most about yourself?"

His head jerked up. "Maybe. Alex's words cut me deep."

"Alex was wrong about one thing."

Pete's chin dipped. "What was that?"

"Your father has never connected deeply with anyone, but

294

you have. I've seen the inside of Pete Banks, and I like the man you are. Very much."

That brought out the smile she loved. "Zoey Donovan, you are a wonderful woman." His brows rose. "It would have been nice if you'd shared that wisdom before I self-destructed."

"I believe I did mention something to that effect, but sometimes we don't listen when we know it will hurt." She leaned forward on her elbows. "Tell me what happens now."

"Now? Today starts the first day of my new life." He pushed back his chair and walked around to her side of the island. His eyes seemed much clearer, more focused, and certainly more determined. "I want you, sugar, and I want to show you that I belong in your life."

As much as she wanted to make him beg for her forgiveness, his words of repentance pierced her heart so deep, she had to let him in. "I'm willing to give you a chance, but you need to make it good. Real good. So good, in fact, that I can't live without you."

"That's music to my ears."

Chapter Twenty-Nine

Pete leaned in so close that their breaths mixed, pounding excitement through her veins at what was to come. He pulled Zoey to a stand and shoved back her chair. The kiss that followed made her knees weaken. Twisting her back to the counter, he planted his hands on either side of her.

"I can't tell you how I drowned in regret when I realize I might have lost you, that my self-pity might have cost me the one thing I wanted in life—you. You make me want to be my best."

His words set her skin on fire. Gone was the desire to make him suffer a wee bit more. "I need you. Now."

Zoey's fingers found the waistband of his jeans and popped open the button. The zipper followed. To her delight, he'd gone commando.

Pete broke the intense kiss. "I want to love you like you've never been loved before, but I'm so on edge, I can't seem to control myself."

He stepped back and tore off his boots. He was sockless, as if he'd planned the seduction. That warmed her heart. Zoey wanted to help him undress, but she enjoyed his frantic pace too much to interfere. When he stood before her in all his glory, her mouth turned dry.

"It's been a long time for us," she said as she lifted her hands to the hem of her shirt.

"Please. Let me. I want to remember every revealing inch."

Zoey let go. "Have at me."

Her heart soared as he stepped near and slid his warm hands under her shirt. His rough fingers did a delightful dance on her waist.

"I love watching how your eyes change colors the closer I get to touching your breasts." Pete was back to his old teasing self, only this time he didn't have a catch in his voice. He was telling the truth.

"Don't keep me waiting."

"No worries." His lips found hers, and their tongues plunged into each other's mouths.

She wasn't able to kiss him fast enough. Her fingers latched onto his shoulders and her nails dug into his skin. All she could think of was having more of him. He wiggled his fingers under her bra and nabbed her nipples. The sharp pinch blasted a spike of lust straight to her clit.

Zoey pulled back. "I need to get naked. I want to feel your skin on me."

"Crap. I promised I'd help, but then you distracted me." Pete dropped to his haunches, lifted her foot and tore off her shoe in a flash. He repeated the process on the other side. Because her skirt was long and stretchy, one tug had the material pooling at her feet. He pressed his lips together as if he couldn't decide where he wanted to begin. "Jesus, Zoey. You get better every time I look at you. Turn around." He stood.

With one quick lift, he took off her top then pinched open her bra. From behind, he cupped her breasts, and the pressure and heat almost undid her. She loved it when his thumb brushed across her nipples, but she wanted his lips on the tips more.

"Harder."

"You like a bit of pain?" With her hair back in a ponytail, her neck was exposed, giving him access to her ear. Shivers of delight raced through her with each touch and nibble.

She still wore her panties. Damn. To encourage him, she pushed back her hips and reached behind her. When she grabbed his cock and rubbed her thumb across a wet slit, he groaned.

"You'll pay for that, girl." Off came her bra. He spun her around. Her panties were then unceremoniously removed from her body. He slid a finger into her wet opening as he devoured her lips. Dear God in heaven. Her moans matched his groans. She wrapped her arms around Pete's neck to draw him near, and pressed her breasts against his solid chest. The man melted every part of her body. As he swirled his finger inside her, his thumb pressed against her sensitive nub, making it harder and harder to breathe.

"I want you, Pete Banks. Now." So much for making him grovel.

He dragged his hands to her waist and lifted her onto the counter. "Lean back. No, wait." He raced over to the drawer next to the sink, grabbed a few dishtowels, and placed the soft cloth under each elbow. "There."

As soon as she was in position, he lifted her heels and placed them on the counter. She didn't see how this would accomplish her goal of having his cock, but from the purposeful way he was moving, he had a plan. When he leaned over and swiped his tongue across her slit, she let out a loud wail. This was a dream. When she thought Pete didn't want to be with her, it had been one of the worst moments of her life. Now he was back, and she wanted to embrace every second with him.

She scooted closer to the edge. He shifted his focus to her clit and twisted one nipple between his fingers. Her climax threatened to take her down. *Stay strong.* She shut her eyes and let his touch transport her higher and higher.

"I can't wait." Pete's voice came out strangled.

Next came the scraping of material across the floor. She opened her eyes. Pete had extracted a condom, torn it open, and slipped it on in seconds. "You are magnificent," she whispered.

"I'm glad you like it." He grinned, gently slid her off the counter, and then turned her around. "Keep a good grip on the edge, sugar." After he pulled her hips back, he spread her legs wide.

Her body sizzled with excitement. "Hurry."

"Shh."

Why should she keep quiet? Would talking distract him? His hands tightened on her waist as the tip of his cock pressed against her pussy. He edged in, acting as if she'd break in two if he went any faster. Taking the lead, she stepped back and half impaled herself on his cock. Bad idea. His dick was too thick and stretched her wide. What came out of her mouth sounded unintelligible.

"Aw, shit, Zoey. You've done it now."

As if she'd opened the floodgates of love, Pete drove into her hard, and she melted. Her fingers gripped the counter tight and she met him thrust for thrust. Her walls slickened and heated with each pass, but Zoey couldn't get enough of him. He twisted her nipples. Each rub and touch took her higher until she couldn't stop her climax any more.

"Ah, ah, ah." She held her breath and let the intense orgasm swoop in.

Pete wrapped his arms around her waist and planted his

face on her shoulder as he yelled her name. His release was hard and powerful. When stars burst behind her lids, she lowered her head.

Breathless, she didn't move until Pete finally pulled out. He grabbed one of the towels on the counter and wiped her clean before gathering her into his arms. He then placed kisses from her lips, to her chin, to her neck. "I'm sorry I was an ass."

Using the rest of her energy, she drew in a breath to add oxygen to her brain. "Let's get this straight. I don't ever want to hear another word about how you are not a wonderful man. We all have issues, but get over them. From now on, I decide if you deserve me, okay?" That hadn't come out the way she'd intended, but she needed to make it clear that she adored him.

"Yes, ma'am. Not another word." He tapped her nose. "Do you think Thad will be so easy?"

She punched him in the chest. "I was not easy."

"Keep telling yourself that, girl. But seriously, how pissed was Thad?"

"Pissed is a mild word. He did move out, in case you didn't notice."

He nodded. "What do you suggest?"

"Be truthful then move on." Guys weren't into gushy talk anyway.

"Good idea. Since Thad is working, what do you say we dress and head to The River Wok for dinner?"

She groaned. "You sure you want to do Asian? We can have a pizza if you'd like."

"I'm positive." He slipped into his jeans and she watched as the material covered his perfect body. He stepped over to the counter next to the fridge and picked up her new pink purchase. "You got a stun gun!"

He didn't have to act surprised. "You suggested I get one."

"I did, didn't I?"

"I plan to keep it on my desk at work. That should intimidate anyone from messing with me."

"I can tell you're going to be a heap of trouble, Dr. Donovan, but I'm just the one to keep you in line."

Pete Banks had so much to learn.

✧   ✧   ✧

After dinner, Pete said he should get back. "I need some time to think about what I'm going to say to Thad." He dreaded the conversation. Eating crow never tasted good.

Zoey nodded. "If Thad asks what we talked about, I'll tell him I made you crawl at my feet and bark like a dog before I let you make love to me."

He cupped her soft cheek. "You aren't going to make this easy for me, are you?"

"Hell no."

Zoey was full of strength and wonder. He pulled her into his arms. "You sincerely think if I'm honest that Thad will forgive me?"

"I was easy. I don't think Thad will be. You betrayed his trust."

"I know. Then grovel it will be." He didn't want to leave her, but he and Thad needed to clear the air. "I'll call you tomorrow. I'm sure Thad will give you all the details tonight." He leaned over and kissed her. "Wish me luck."

"Luck."

Using all of his willpower, he slipped out. On the drive home, his mind spun as he considered different ways to approach the uncomfortable topic. When he parked and entered the house, every square foot screamed of loneliness. He almost hated this place with Thad gone. What had he been thinking walking out like that?

He inhaled to slow his racing heart and pulled out his phone to call Thad. No surprise, he didn't answer. Leaving a message wasn't his preferred choice of how to handle this, but he needed Thad to stop by after work. It didn't matter the time.

"After the beep, please leave your message."

Pete blew out a breath, praying he didn't fuck this up, too. "It's me. Look, man, I owe you an apology bigger than the whole town. I've messed up and I know it. Zoey and I have patched things, so if you can see past my stupidity, will you swing by the house before heading over to Zoey's?" He disconnected before he said something to make things worse.

Now came the wait. He walked over to the wine rack and pulled out a bottle. "You're fucking stupid." He pushed it back in and drew water from the fridge. Without a coffee maker, he couldn't even have the caffeine kick.

The only thing to do was watch some television, and wait.

An hour later, the doorbell rang. Thad had a key, so why not use it? "I get it." As Zoey would say, his roommate was being passive aggressive. Pete didn't care as long as Thad would wait around long enough to listen to his apology.

Pete opened up. Thad's skin appeared sallow and his face drawn. He didn't look like he'd gotten any more sleep than Pete had. "Come in. Thanks for stopping over."

Thad glared at him then punched him hard in the shoulder, managing to hit the exact spot Alex had. Shit. Pete swallowed the wince.

"You suck, you know that? You also look like crap."

Pete straightened his shoulders. "I fucked up."

Thad strode past him into the family room, and dropped into his favorite chair. "Fucked up? No." He blew out a breath. "That doesn't come even close. The words to describe what you did haven't been invented yet."

In a way, Pete was glad Thad was willing to vent. Pete could only hope his friend would be his usual patient self and listen to his explanation. "So stupid, juvenile, selfish, and irresponsible won't cut it?" Pete tossed in some levity only because his gut was churning so hard.

"Not even close. You're a real shit. I don't care if Zoey says everything is good between you. It's not okay between you and me."

Shit, shit, shit. "I'd like a chance to change your mind."

Thad jumped up. "Oh, yeah? Doesn't matter what you say. You're still a fucking ass." He strode up to Pete and poked him in the chest. "You might have been able to sweet talk Zoey into believing you've changed, but I don't buy it."

Jesus. This was not going down as he'd hoped. "What's it going to take to convince you this will never happen again?" He'd do just about anything.

"I don't know." Thad turned his back, paced a few times, then faced him. "Do you even understand what a ménage relationship means?"

Was that a trick question? "We both love Zoey equally, or at least I do. For the three of us to build any kind of life, we need to take care of her and see to her needs?" Damn. Why did that have to sound like a question? He'd known the answer.

Thad's lips pressed together, shifted, and twisted. "And you went to private school?" Thad shook his head. "You didn't learn common sense, that's for fuck sure. Listen. There's so much more. There may come a time when I need to do undercover work, or I might land in the hospital because some punk stabbed me, or I just have to work late. I have to be positive that you'll be there for both of us."

"You don't have to insult me."

"Don't I? From what I've seen in the last two years, every time the going gets tough, you crap out."

What he said was true. "That was the old me."

"Is it?"

While Pete deserved the put-down, there had to be some faith here. He wasn't going to let Thad walk all over him. "I'm committed. What more do you want me to say? Alex finally knocked some sense into me. I get that my dad is the way he is because of things he's done in his life. I never should have expected anything else from him."

Thad chewed on his the inside of his cheek. "Really?"

"Yes."

"How committed are you?"

"I'm all in."

The lines around his mouth softened. "All right then. Let's discuss exactly what that means."

Chapter Thirty

T had had come to bed around two in the morning, climbed under the covers, and kissed her forehead. When Zoey asked how things had gone between him and Pete, Thad said he'd tell her everything tomorrow. That he needed time to process what had gone down. From the lack of anger in his voice, she could only hope things went well.

At seven, when Zoey got up, Thad was already gone. He left a note saying he'd been called into work early, but that he'd make it up to her. She swore he was trying to drive her crazy. As much as she was tempted to call Pete and ask about his "I'm a shit" apology, it might be best to give him time. For now, she'd go with the concept that no news was good news.

At work, Zoey tried to keep her focus, but her sessions seemed more stressful than usual. She prayed she'd been able to help her clients.

When the last person finally left, she leaned back in her seat and closed her eyes for a moment. As much as she wished she were in the men's arms right now, not rushing into things would be wise.

"Get moving, Zoey," she told herself.

Before she took off, she checked her calendar to see who she'd be meeting with tomorrow, as she liked to read the files

VELLA DAY

beforehand to make sure she wasn't missing anything. Just as she stood, her cell rang. It was Pete. Pleasure mixed with a bit of trepidation.

"Hey," she said, fingers literally crossed. That action was a carryover from something her grandmother always did. "So?"

"Thad didn't say?" Apprehension laced his voice.

"No. He had to leave before I got up."

"Oh." That didn't sound good.

Just ask him. "How did the talk go?"

"As well as could be expected, I guess." Pete detailed their rather rocky reunion, but Zoey got the sense Pete was keeping something from her.

She wanted to make sure she understood. "So he was angry, but he listened."

"I guess that's a fair assessment."

Zoey could picture Thad pacing and working hard not to yell. He honored commitment and loyalty above all else, and Pete hadn't been committed or loyal. "Do you think he understood how the clarity about your father's issues has changed you?"

"I hope so, sugar."

The relief in Pete's voice helped lower her blood pressure. "So are you two good?" She wasn't at the point to ask if the three of them had a chance of being in a relationship.

"Yes, but I had to promise that for the next twenty years of my life, I'd serve Master Thad."

The tension finally released and she let out a laugh. "I love it." From the lightness in his voice, he was kidding—or mostly kidding.

"We can talk more later," Pete said. "How about you change into something sexy and casual, and I'll pick you up at your house for dinner at five thirty? We're going to meet Thad

308

at Italiano's."

Excitement caught in her throat. "You already spoke with him today?"

"A few minutes ago. He just finished what he was dealing with and said he could get away."

"Fantastic. I'll be ready." She loved how the men made it a top priority to find time to be with her. Zoey gathered the files she wanted to read and left. She was cautious as she headed toward the elevator. Until Gloria's killer was behind bars, she wouldn't take the stairs.

As Zoey crossed the parking lot, the cold air slipped through the heavy weave of her sweater and she hugged her folders to her chest. She loved Montana with its beautiful scenery, but she wasn't sure she'd ever get used to the biting cold.

Once home, she only had a few minutes before Pete arrived. Italiano's was casual dining, so jeans and boots were called for, but she made sure to put on a sexy top and great undergarments. Another shopping trip with Jamie was definitely in order.

Just as she finished applying her makeup the doorbell rang, and a thrill raced up her spine. She pulled open the door to find Pete wearing a hot-as-hell smile. The black eye, bruised jaw, and cut lip didn't even detract from his good looks. From seeing his joy, every bit of fear she'd had that tonight wouldn't go well evaporated. Without a word, she led him inside. A second later, she was in his arms, his chest pressed against hers.

"I've missed you, sugar."

She chuckled. "It's only been a day."

"A day is too long."

Ever since Pete banished his need to prove himself to his dad, he'd been relaxed and more fun. The kiss caused ribbons of lust to weave through her body so strong that her hand automatically slid to his crotch. His hardness made her moan, and Pete pulled back.

"We can't start," he said as he clasped her hand and squeezed. "Come on. Thad texted and said he was on his way to the restaurant already."

"Really?" She'd worried that Thad might change his mind if they didn't show up on time. Once she closed up, they rushed down the stairs. "You left the car running?"

"I wanted you to stay warm."

"Aw. You are too good to me."

"I have a lot of making up to do."

As he headed downtown, she admired the lush trees that would soon be dropping their leaves when another winter descended. For now, she'd enjoy the scenery. Once in town, Pete had to drive around the block twice before snagging a spot close to the restaurant. She loved this part of town because the old buildings had been here for decades. Italiano's in particular was as homey inside as it was out.

When they walked in, Thad was speaking with someone she didn't recognize. He waved and pointed to a booth in the corner where three waters had already been poured. She slid in and Pete joined her on the same side.

Thad trotted over and eased in across from her. "Hey." He smiled, though she didn't miss the layer of concern.

She nodded to the solitary man. "Who's that?"

Thad motioned his head in the man's direction. "That's Max Gruden, the man I've been working with."

"You mean, the man who keeps you out at all hours of the night."

Thad nodded. "I think it's the gang members who are responsible for that."

Max Gruden was facing the street, looking lonely. "Do you want to invite him over?"

Thad placed a hand on hers. "Already asked, but he declined. The man is as tight-lipped as it comes, except when trying to solve a crime. He's focused, I'll give him that."

"Sounds like someone else I know."

Thad tucked in his chin. "Don't tell me you aren't as focused. If I recall, you were so absorbed in your work that you didn't know a particular man was in a standoff in a hospital corridor."

"I might be guilty of that offense, but what's Max's excuse?" Zoey didn't know why she was drawn to the sad man. Her job, she supposed. His body appeared strong, but his face was a bit gaunt as if he never indulged in wonderful foods, like sweets. "I bet he drinks his coffee black."

Both of her men laughed. They'd had discussions about her excessive use of sugar and cream in her drink.

"Max used to be a cop until a bust went bad. A few days later, his wife and child were trapped in a house fire and died. The arsonist was never caught."

"How horrible." A strong ache sliced through her. She couldn't imagine what it would be like to lose a spouse, let alone a child. She'd counseled people about picking up the pieces after a death and moving on with their lives, but she wondered if she'd ever have that kind of strength.

A man with a broad smile and confident stride came toward them. He wiped his hands on his moderately clean apron and held out his hand to Thad. "Detective." He then nodded to Pete. "Mr. Banks." His eyes sparkled as his gaze roamed over to her. "And who do we have here?"

"Zoey Donovan." Instead of a shake, the friendly man captured her hand with both of his and brought the back to his lips.

"Delighted. I'm Giuseppe Buscemi. The owner. Italiano's has been in the family for fifty-three years next month." He returned her hand. "What can I get you three to drink besides your water?"

Pete spoke up. "How about a bottle of your finest Chianti?"

"Of course."

That wasn't what they usually drank. "Is this a special occasion?" she asked after the owner slipped into the kitchen.

Pete leaned back and stretched an arm behind her. "Since my rebirth, as I'll call it, I've redefined my priorities, and I wanted to make more changes in my life, besides wanting to be with you, sugar." His look of love warmed her heart.

"Care to elaborate?" Zoey leaned close, their lips within kissing distance.

"Just tell her, for Pete's sake." Thad grinned, obviously enjoying his use of the expression.

Pete placed a hand on her thigh, and tingles shot up her back. "I asked Alex to be my partner again."

"That's a nice surprise." She was happy the tiff between them was settled. Zoey thought it interesting that Pete didn't say Alex wanted to buy his half of the partnership, since Pete had bought him out when Alex needed to take care of his ill dad. "How does that work?"

"I'm giving him thirty percent of the profit in return for his total commitment."

"How can he do that?" From what Pete had told her, Alex was already working too much.

Pete shrugged. "He's a very talented man. He'll figure it out. Actually, I suggested he hire another construction manager, and manage him."

She liked where this was going. "Will this mean more time

for the three of us?"

He tapped her nose. "That's exactly what it means."

The owner delivered the bottle of Chianti, along with three glasses. "Enjoy, my friends."

As soon as the owner left, Zoey held up her glass. "To us!"

They clinked their glasses. Tonight was going to be quite special.

Chapter Thirty-One

Zoey had never been as happy as she had been in the last two days, in large part because her men had been considerate and amazing lovers. Just knowing Pete had found contentment had made their bond stronger. The problem was that Zoey wanted to dream about them and be with them instead of working. For the first time ever, her job was no longer her top priority. At some point in the future, she hoped she'd get her verve back. Helping others always had been and always would be in her blood.

When the men sprang the weekend getaway on her, each day became increasingly more difficult to get through. Pete told her they'd be flying out at 7:55 p.m. this Friday to someplace warm. Having them all to herself for two days was going to be fantastic.

Ever since Zoey had found out about the trip, she'd made some subtle and not so subtle hints about her desire to be tied up, but neither man would say whether they were into that kind of kink. She suspected Pete was, but Thad remained an unknown.

"Knock, knock." Her office door opened and Jamie poked her head in. "Rachel said your last client was gone. I wanted to make sure you're coming to happy hour."

Zoey hadn't been to the weekly get-togethers since before her first date with Pete, and she needed some serious girl time. "I am."

"You want to go a little early? I'm off work."

"Absolutely. Give me a sec to collect my things."

Jamie's gaze latched onto the pink stun gun. She stepped closer and picked it up with her forefinger and thumb. "What are you doing with one of these? Do you know what that can do to a body?"

The horror lacing her voice had Zoey smiling. "Don't worry. I have no plans to ever use it. Pete suggested I get one after the break-in."

Jamie set the gun back down on the edge of the desk and raised her hand to the wound where Ben had shot her. "Weapons in general scare me."

"Me, too." Jamie seemed like she needed to talk, and while Zoey could suggest they stay here and have a session, from the way her friend was rubbing her arm, if might be better if they talked outside of the hospital setting. "You up for a quick detour on our way to Banner's?"

Jamie's face brightened, but in Zoey's opinion, her friend's skin was a bit sallow. "Where?" Jamie asked.

"Naughty Desires. I need some lingerie for my big weekend away."

Jamie pumped her fist in the air, looking like her old self. "My favorite store. Or at least it used to be."

Her friend didn't need to say the words "before Ben," but Zoey bet that was what she was thinking. Once Zoey grabbed her purse, coat, and some files, they left. They'd driven separately. "Meet you at Naughty Desires?"

"Yup."

The lingerie shop and Banner's were on Fourth Street, but

they were eight blocks apart, so Zoey parked halfway between. Because she'd snagged a parking place before Jamie, Zoey headed to the back of the store where a few items had caught her attention the last time she was there. She passed the whips and floggers, and went straight to the section that held the fur-lined cuffs. Nothing like this little restraint to get the men in the mood.

The bell rang above the door, and Jamie came in. "Well, well. What do we have here? Have you been keeping something from me?"

They'd never discussed Zoey's sex life. It was sometimes hard separating being Jamie's friend from her therapist. "I thought I'd spice things up a little." One of the reasons Jamie had become disillusioned with Ben was because he never wanted to experiment. "You ought to pick up something." Zoey was close to stepping on some of Jamie's major issues, but since Zoey had kept her voice light, she hoped Jamie wouldn't mind.

Her friend planted a hand on her hip. "Not my thing to self-stimulate."

Zoey grabbed a sleep mask and some soft ties. "That's a man's job, right?"

Jamie looked down for a second. "Yeah."

Zoey was about to point out that if Jamie would give some of the men who'd asked her out a chance, she might find Mr. Right—the real Mr. Right this time. Zoey understood that just because she was deliriously happy, it didn't mean everyone else would be so lucky.

"How about helping me pick out some indecent under-wear?" Zoey set her fun toys on the checkout counter and headed to the lingerie section. Whatever Jamie picked for her, Zoey would buy.

By the time they walked out of the store, Zoey must have spent half a week's wages, but she loved everything. The men were going to go crazy.

"Where did you park?" Jamie asked.

"Between here and Banner's." They walked side by side. When Zoey reached her car, she dumped her purchases in the trunk, and then they made their way to the bar.

Inside, the canned music was playing at a decent decibel level, and the place wasn't yet crowded. Amber and Melissa were already there and waved to them. She and Jamie were a bit late, so she guessed Becky wouldn't be coming.

After hugs all around, the tension slowly seeped out of Zoey's bones. The place might have that distinct odor of beer and wood, but it was a smell that reminded her of good times.

As soon as they were seated, Jamie clasped Amber's hand. "I know your mom came to visit this past weekend, but we haven't had a chance to talk. What suggestions did she have for your wedding?"

Amber already had her glass of wine and Zoey motioned to the waitress for her usual. Zoey wanted to hear what Mrs. Delacroix had suggested before showing Amber some of the pictures she'd taken of Nana's barn. Zoey had uploaded them to the Cloud so that she could share her experience with the girls.

"Mom exhausted me. We went to every church in Rock Hard. While ménage weddings are common, not all places embrace them." Amber pursed her lips. "Then we had to drive to Billings, where we met with similar disappointment."

Poor Amber. Zoey reached over to her and clasped her hand. "What do you and the men want?"

"Yes! It does matter what the bride desires. Why can't my mom see that?"

Zoey smiled. "Well, she is a bit self-centered."

That seemed to cheer up Amber. "Yes, but she's trying to be a mother, so I'm attempting to be a good daughter."

Zoey pulled out her cell phone and clicked on the app that brought up the photos of Nana's barn. "I have a place I think you might like, though I'm pretty sure your mom won't."

The glint in her eyes returned. "Let me see."

Zoey explained about Thad's grandmother's place. "Thad's cousin, Erin, sent me some photos of her wedding that had been held there. The place is quite magical and homey and awesome."

Jamie leaned closer. "Nice, but see how the light leaks between the wooden slats? I bet it'll be cold in there."

Zoey agreed. "Have you three set a wedding date?"

Amber shook her head. "We're thinking sometime in the spring."

"That will work weather wise." Zoey handed her the phone. "There are about fifteen photos. Just scroll through them."

With each swipe, Amber's face grew brighter. "These are amazing. Can you send them to me? I want Stone and Cade to see these."

"Will do."

The server came with their drinks and Zoey finally relaxed. The only thing on her agenda for the rest of the day was to pack for someplace warm, get through tomorrow, and be free for a love-filled weekend.

✧　✧　✧

Phone in hand, Thad leaned back in his office chair. "I'll be out of town all weekend," he told Max. "If you need any help with a gang insignia, call Jeremy. He's almost as good as I am."

"Will do."

Thad had expected at least a chuckle, but Max apparently wasn't much of a jokester. Thad had logged off his computer, ready to pick Zoey up for their trip to the airport, when Cade made a beeline to Thad's desk. The pinched brows and stiff shoulders weren't a good sign. Shit.

Cade tossed down a piece of paper. "Take a look at this." Cade had drawn yellow highlights through about fifty or so phone numbers.

It was someone's phone bill. "Who does this belong to?"

"Dr. Avery Carson. And those multiple calls? They're from a Kara Molloy, his assistant."

Both were at Gloria Sanchez's funeral. "So?" Thad was having a hard time pushing his own cases aside. Cade worked burglaries, domestic violence, and on occasion, murder, and rarely asked for or needed Thad's expertise.

Cade dragged a chair from an empty desk and placed it next to Thad's. "What do we know about Gloria Sanchez's murder?"

"Why are you asking me? I only know what Zoey told us."

Cade nodded, but from his stern expression, he was hoping for some additional information. "Carson admitted that he was with Gloria not long before her death. Remember, Zoey said Carson mentioned how he'd tried to get Kara to stop calling him, but she wouldn't."

The conversation came back to him. "Didn't Carson also mention that Kara had complained to HR about him?"

"Yes. Something didn't fit, so I spoke with HR." Cade detailed how Kara claimed Carson was hitting on her. "Apparently, it was the other way around."

None of this was making much sense. Did Cade just need someone to bounce an idea off of? "Even if Kara lied, what does that prove?"

He held up a finger. "I investigated Ms. Molloy's whereabouts the night of the murder. Several nurses can place her in the hospital."

The puzzle pieces clicked into place. "Are you thinking she killed Gloria Sanchez? That she was mad at Carson for paying attention to another woman?"

"Thinking it. Yes. Do I have proof? No."

Thad still hadn't figured out why Cade was coming to him. "What can I do?"

"Did Zoey ever mention that Kara was her client?"

His mind spun. "No." If Zoey suspected Kara of misconduct, would she tell him? "We don't discuss our pending cases."

"Did she tell you what she talked to Carson or Kara Molloy about at the funeral?"

He had to think back to last week. "Carson warned her not to tell Sanchez about the affair. As for Zoey and Kara's conversation, no. From my standpoint, Zoey appeared to be comforting her."

Cade stood. "We need to speak with Zoey."

From Cade's firm tone, he knew more, but from the urgency in his tone, now wasn't the time to question him. "I was on my way to the hospital now anyway. I'll text Pete and tell him to meet us there. We're taking Zoey on a weekend getaway."

"Let's go."

"I doubt Zoey will give you much information about one of her clients."

"Don't need it. I want to warn her that Kara might be dangerous."

Thad's heart nearly stopped. "I'll call her." As they rushed out, Thad dialed her number. "Voicemail. Fuck. She must be with a client. Usually, her secretary picks up." Shit.

✧   ✧   ✧

Zoey's secretary, Rachel, knocked on her door. "You all packed for your big weekend trip?"

Disbelief that the time was near had her more jittery than ten cups of coffee. "Yes."

"Excited?"

Zoey lowered her chin. That was an understatement. "What do you think?"

Rachel grinned. "I'm glad. Just a reminder, I'm leaving early today."

Zoey glanced to the ceiling trying to remember when her secretary had told her. "You are?" Not that it was a problem.

"It's my mom's birthday, remember?"

"Oh, yeah, I do."

"Kara's in the waiting room. I'll send her in on my way out."

"Thanks. And tell your mom 'happy birthday.'"

"I will."

Zoey sat back in her chair and waited for her last appointment. Kara walked in, looking a bit nervous, which of late had been her normal state.

"Hello, Kara. Have a seat."

She sat and placed her purse next to her. Her chin lifted. "What did you and Dr. Carson talk about at the funeral?" While her voice appeared in control, her darting eyes told a different story.

Kara had never walked in and asked a question before—especially one that was personal to Zoey. "I beg your pardon?" Zoey didn't conduct her business that way. Perhaps she misunderstood.

"Did you talk about me?" An edge had crept into Kara's tone, setting off alarm signals in Zoey's head.

Remaining cool, Zoey studied her client. Her eyes were

clear, and her speech wasn't slurred or noticeably different, implying Kara wasn't on drugs. "No." That was the truth. Zoey tried to figure out where Kara was going with this line of questioning.

Her jaw trembled. "I saw you stop at his table in the cafeteria. Did you discuss me then?"

Zoey searched her mind, trying to remember when she'd last seen Dr. Carson, other than at the funeral. She'd seen him when Carson and Thompson were chatting about the death of the little boy, but Zoey had merely passed by to get out the door.

"I've never shared anything about our sessions with anyone. I've taken an oath."

"Are you seeing Avery now? Do you want him for yourself?"

The idea was so preposterous that Zoey almost let out a nervous laugh, but she refrained. Kara seemed to think her question was perfectly logical.

Zoey set down her tablet she'd planned to take notes on, and came around her desk, hoping to intimidate Kara—shocking her to return to her normally rational self. It wasn't a tactic Zoey liked to use, but given the speed of her heart, she had to do something. Kara's behavior was way off. Her subsequent questions didn't even follow from Zoey's answers.

"No. Why would you think that?" Zoey asked.

Kara's face looked hard, as if chiseled from stone. When she jumped up from her seat, Zoey stopped in her tracks.

Kara gritted her teeth. "You royal bitch." The words came out slow and even.

Zoey held up a hand. "Kara. Please sit down. What has you so upset?"

Kara's mouth opened. "How could you ask me that? You

know I love Avery Carson, and yet you convinced him to seek out Gloria."

Zoey's breath stopped halfway up her throat. Kara was irrational. Zoey mostly counseled people who grieved, and those whose relationships were floundering. Dealing with someone this unstable wasn't her specialty. Zoey had to draw on every ounce of control. "Why would I do that?" Denying the allegation might upset Kara more. If Zoey could get Kara to calm down, Zoey might be able to defuse the situation. Later, she'd address the whole concept of Kara loving Avery Carson when she had claimed the opposite.

"Because you knew I wanted him."

Was there anything Zoey could say to make Kara see reason? Before Zoey could come up with another plan, light from the window glinted off the object in Kara's hand. It was a scalpel. No. No. No. Silver dots exploded in Zoey's eyes as she tried to wrap her mind around what was happening.

"Kara. You don't want to do this." It took all of Zoey's training for the words to come out even. Whether Kara planned to slice open Zoey's throat or put fear into her heart, nothing good would come from this interaction. "If you feel I've broken my oath to you, I can recommend someone else. Dr. Claire Daniels is an outstanding therapist with people who've been through a trauma."

"You know for a shrink, you're really stupid." Kara planted one hand on her hip and waved the medical instrument in a circle with the other.

At least they were having a discussion. That was good. "Why do you say that?" Zoey's heart lodged in her throat.

Kara's lips thinned. "You actually believed that Avery was the bad man I made him out to be, didn't you?"

Something awful twisted inside Zoey and her breaths came

out too fast. *Keep calm. Stall.* "You did an excellent job convincing me."

Kara lifted her chin. "Did you know that he loved me, but to protect anyone else from finding out about us, he pretended not to like me? He was the one who suggested I go to HR. He also thought it would look good if I went to counseling."

The image of Avery Carson impaling Gloria Sanchez came to mind. "No. I was unaware of his feelings. How could I have known?" Zoey inhaled to steady her beating heart so that her words would come out sounding confident and calm. "Were you and he intimate?" Zoey regretted the words as soon as she spoke them. She prayed that question didn't trigger any violent reaction.

Kara drew in her bottom lip and bit down on it, her telltale sign that her veneer was cracking. Zoey slipped her right foot back six inches. If she made small enough movements, Kara might not notice that Zoey was edging toward the desk—the desk that held the pretty pink stun gun.

Kara stepped toward her and Zoey's blood turned to sludge. She held out a hand. "Kara. Please don't come any closer."

"I saw the way Avery looked at you." Kara waved the scalpel again. "It was bad enough that you flirted with him at the funeral, but at the hospital, he's mine."

Think, think. As a therapist Zoey should be able to talk her down. Her internal thoughts seemed to mock her. "Would you believe me if I said I wasn't flirting? Why should I? I have a cop for a boyfriend." Guilt trickled over her for not mentioning Pete, but this wasn't about being truthful. It was about staying alive.

Kara's lip curled. "Like that would stop you? You're no better than that whore Gloria."

Air refused to go from her lungs to her brain. "Gloria?"

"I killed that bitch because Avery loved her, or so he said."
Kara tapped her chest and a bit of spit dribbled out of the
corner of her mouth.

She'd killed Gloria? Shit. The ramification of Kara telling
her that she'd murdered someone sunk in. "I can see why you
did. I walked in on them fornicating. It was disgusting." A few
wisps of oxygen actually seeped into her brain.

"Which is why with you out of the way, I'll have him all to
myself."

Faster than Zoey could take her next breath, Kara raised her
hand and charged.

Chapter Thirty-Two

The knife slashing through the air triggered Zoey's survival instinct. She twisted to the side, reached behind her, her fingers landing squarely on the stun gun Pete had shown her how to turn in on, but right now her mind wasn't working. With clutched fingers that held the gun painfully tight, Zoey brandished it. "Stay away."

For a split second, Kara hesitated. That was all it took for Zoey to go on the offensive. Kara's arm sliced downward, but Zoey managed to jump out of the way as she jammed the prongs against Kara's neck and depressed the button. Kara stiffened and her eyes went wide.

Adrenaline, sludge, and bile filled Zoey's body, and her mind ceased to function for a moment. Then the need for safety took over. Zoey pushed Kara backward, rotated to the side, and ran for the door. The knife clattered to the ground and the loud thud stopped Zoey in her tracks. She spun around and her breath caught. Sprawled on the hard floor was Kara, her eyes wide. Her chest heaved and then her eyes shut.

The temptation to help her nearly won, but common sense made Zoey seek safety. She yanked open the door, gulped in air, and sprinted through the empty waiting room. She dashed into the hallway. Empty again. This was supposed to be a busy hospital. Where the hell was everyone? She tried to yell, but her throat had closed up. Forcing her body to move, she stumbled down the hall. Fear had jacked up her pulse and her heart squeezed tight. As she neared the nurses' station, the far doors opened and Thad and Cade rushed in.

Zoey nearly dropped to her knees in relief. Her chest constricted and she palmed the wall to steady herself. Thad was by her side in a flash.

"Jesus, Zoey. What happened?"

She swallowed past the lump in her throat. "Call 911. Kara attacked me."

Thad checked her out. "Where are you hurt?"

"Not me." Why couldn't she put the words together? "Kara's down in my office. Stun gun. She tried to kill me."

With his phone to his ear, Cade made a call and took off running toward her office. Just then Pete called her name and sprinted toward her. "Zoey? Are you okay?"

"Yes. Just shaken."

Pete and Thad led her over to a bench at the end of the hallway where the light streamed in. Pete held her while Thad knelt in front of her. "Start from the beginning," Thad said.

Confusion fogged her brain, but in bits and pieces she was able to explain how Kara was her patient, that she'd accused Dr. Avery Carson of sexual harassment, but then admitted she'd basically stalked him.

"Cade got Carson's phone records confirming that. Cade pieced it together that Kara was dangerous. We were coming to warn you."

She sniffled. "Kara said she killed Gloria Sanchez."

"Jesus, Zoey." Pete hugged her, and the reality finally slammed into her. She couldn't stop trembling.

A few minutes later, two uniformed policemen strode down

the corridor. She was about to tell them the location of her office when Cade appeared in her doorway and motioned them in.

Zoey slumped against her seat. "Now what's going to happen? I was looking forward to having a vacation this weekend."

"Me, too." Thad pulled out his phone and did a search. "There's a flight out of Billings at nine tomorrow morning that arrives at noon. How does that sound?"

"I just want to get out of here, assuming Cade will let me," Zoey said.

Thad squeezed her hand. "If I can convince him to let me take your statement and send it to him, he might let us go."

"That would be awesome," she said.

Pete nodded. "I say we spend the night near the airport. That way, we'll be more relaxed when we get on the plane."

"I like that plan." Zoey closed her eyes for a moment while the terror twisted and churned in her stomach. Her hands still shook at having to use the stun gun. Never did she think she'd ever have to resort to such violence. If she hadn't, though, she'd be as dead as Gloria Sanchez.

Thad got up and slipped next to her on the other side. In silence, he held her. "You're lucky, you know."

"I know. If Pete hadn't made me buy that stun gun, I'd be dead."

Thad kissed the top of her head. "I meant something else, though you have an excellent point."

She glanced up at him. "What other point?"

"When I saw you run down the hallway, my heart stopped. I wasn't sure I could live through another attack. That makes you lucky that I'm still alive."

She chuckled at his drama. He'd wanted her to laugh, and he'd succeeded. "You would have survived. You're a strong man."

Chatter drew her attention in the direction of her office. The two policemen who'd entered a few minutes earlier escorted Kara in cuffs out of the room. Zoey jumped up and a wave of dizziness assaulted her, forcing her to sit back down.

"You okay?" Pete asked.

"I think I forgot to breathe."

Cade came over to them. "We have the knife, but I'll need to take your statement."

Thad stood and mentioned that he could fill out the report tonight and email it to him tomorrow.

"Works for me, but when you get back, stop in and see me, Zoey."

"I will."

Right now, all Zoey wanted to do was leave Rock Hard, and for two days pretend none of this happened.

✧   ✧   ✧

Never in a million years had Zoey imagined Pete and Thad would fly her to Las Vegas. She'd never even been before, and she'd always wanted to visit the city of lights. As soon as the taxi cab driver opened the door for them, the noise and warmth of the Vegas strip met her. Thad helped her out, and her gaze shot upward, first to the mockup of the Statue of Liberty and then to the New York skyline behind it.

"Are you kidding me?" Zoey was aware that Las Vegas had mimicked many of the great places in the world from the Eiffel Tower to the streets of Venice, but to see it in person over-whelmed her senses. To share this wonderful experience with her men was beyond her wildest dreams.

Thad tugged her close. "We figured New York City might be a bit cold this time of year, so we decided to offer you this.

Besides, it might be more fun."

Her pulse soared. She couldn't believe Thad remembered her speaking about the city. "It's fantastic."

"We'd both like you to show us New York someday," Thad said.

His sentiment spoke of a future, and a deep-seated joy raced through her. "I'd love to."

"Let's get settled, and then we can explore." Pete took the suitcase from her hand.

While she and Thad waited in the lobby for Pete to check them in, she tried to take in the grandeur of the place. Above the long lobby desk stretched an enormous mural of the New York skyline, rimmed in pink fluorescent lights. If she had to guess, she'd say the lobby was almost as large as Grand Central station.

The idea of spending two nights here was highly appealing, but not if the men coddled her. Last night had been frustrating. All three of them had been cuddled in bed at the Billings hotel, but no matter what she said, Pete and Thad were adamant that she wasn't ready for mind-blowing sex—not after all that had happened. They were right, of course, but their denial only made her want them more.

Zoey needed time to process everything, but dammit, she wasn't a fragile flower. Tonight she wanted to show them just how strong she was.

"All set." Pete flashed the key card and grinned. "Ready?"

Zoey couldn't wait to use this weekend to indulge in her fantasies and put reality at bay. Her body still vibrated from the rather bumpy flight, but that could be a combination of jitters and high expectations.

After a short elevator ride, Pete slid the keycard into the door lock and motioned she enter first. They were in the mockup of the Chrysler building. She rushed to the window and took in the expansive vista. "I feel like I'm in the city." The view from the hotel across from them probably afforded an even better view.

Thad stepped behind her and hugged her tight. "I can't wait for our adventure. No phone calls, no disturbances."

She doubted there'd be no texts between Thad and Cade. After all, Kara had attempted murder. During the flight, she'd answered all of Thad's questions about what happened. When they landed, he sent the information to Cade.

"Anyone up for a gondola ride?" Thad said.

She spun around. "Seriously?"

He laughed. "Have you ever been to Venice?"

"Years ago. My parents brought me to Europe as a high school graduation present."

Thad laughed. "I got a hunting rifle. Then Nana told me to go 'git her a deer.'"

All three of them laughed.

She ran a finger down Thad's chest. "Or we could enjoy the room for a bit." She wanted to try out those presents she'd brought.

Pete moved over to them and angled behind her. Her body heated. Lifting the hair off her neck, he inhaled. "You always smell so good."

"Oh, yeah?" Zoey pressed her hips back, thrilled when Pete groaned.

He palmed her tits then stepped into view. "As much as I'd like to ravish you right here, we have a reservation with a certain Italian gondolier."

Only because she might never get a chance to ride on a gondola with two such glorious men again did she give in. To think, her life had been turned upside down less than two weeks

ago. So much had happened that it was difficult to comprehend. Zoey had counseled enough couples to know that the initial dating period was the best, and that real life would intrude. For now, she'd enjoy every wonderful second.

"I'm ready for my adventure."

As soon as they stepped outside the hotel lobby, the balmy weather, colorful billboards, and noisy bustle invigorated her. Wide-eyed, Zoey tried to absorb all the sights and sounds. People milled about everywhere. If Zoey didn't like the mountain views so much, this would have been a fun place to live.

Even though it was daylight, she swore every light on the strip was lit. They passed through the Flamingo, where they stopped for a bit to watch the pink birds flaunt their long legs.

Zoey shook her head. "I can't imagine being an attraction and trying to compete here."

"It's tough, but each hotel seems to have something unique to offer," Pete said. "Come on. It would take a week to see everything."

She loved to watch people, but a date was a date. The noise reminded her of New York City with its cars, people, and amazing energy. When they arrived at the Venetian, her memories transported her back to her travels.

"This is incredible. The water is more like a pool than the actual waters of Venice, but the details are fantastic."

Pete spoke with a woman gondolier and then motioned Zoey and Thad to get in the boat that had two opposing benches. Thad helped her onto the seat. "How about you sit across from us so we can see you?"

She liked the idea of keeping an eye on both men, but she would miss their comfort, their touch. Once seated, the guide pushed off and then began to sing. Zoey giggled at the wonder of it all. Pete pointed out the Bridge of Sighs and several other

Venice sights. As much as she liked reminiscing, she was fascinated by Thad's expression of awe. The fancy signs, the expensive shops, and the massive amount of stone seemed to have drawn him into a world he never thought he'd experience. She would give anything to drag him off to Europe and show him the real cities.

They were probably halfway around the lagoon when Pete asked the gondola driver to stop. She pulled next to a pole and steadied the boat.

"Why are we stopping?"

They both grinned and dropped to one knee in front her. Zoey's heart nearly exploded. Her chest squeezed.

Pete nudged Thad, who kept staring at her. Thad pulled out a blue velvet case from his pocket. His mouth opened then shut.

Pete glanced to the sky then back at her. "I guess it's my turn anyway since I'm the oldest." He leaned closer. Out of the corner of her eyes, a few spectators on shore watched, but the men didn't seem to notice. "I can't even begin to tell you how my life has changed since you've walked into it, sugar."

"Me, too." She never thought she'd fall in love with two men. She'd been the woman who'd sworn off any kind of ménage relationship. Boy, had she learned a few things since then.

Thad's chest expanded and his color seemed to return. "While I wasn't the total ass-turned-good-guy, I, too, have found what I've been looking for in my life. I love you, Zoey, and I want to spend the rest of my life with you." He glanced over at Pete. "This lug comes with the package."

Tears welled in her eyes, and she was totally overwhelmed.

Pete clasped her hand. "Will you marry us?"

Her brain almost imploded. "Yes! But on one condition."

Chapter Thirty-Three

Pete's shoulders curled into what looked like defeat. "Condition? I thought you loved us," he said. Each word sliced through her.

Zoey swallowed the intense pain. "I love you both. Very much, but we've only known each other a few weeks." Didn't he see that to jump into something like this too quickly might damage their relationship?

Thad looked at Pete then back at her. "Are you saying our timing sucks?"

She leaned back against the seat. The disappointment on their faces sickened her. Hurting them was the last thing she wanted to do, but she knew better. "I've spent my life talking to people with marriage issues. I see what couples go through. We need to be more cautious."

"I'm not understanding what you're saying, sugar. We know you're the woman for us." The plea in Pete's voice tore her up.

She wet her lips needing time to figure out how to explain her reasoning. "What Thad said was true. The timing sucks. I want to marry you both. I just think we need to wait a bit. That was what I meant by a condition."

The curl of Pete's mouth grew more pronounced. "What are we talking here? A month, two months, a year?"

His enthusiasm allowed her to draw in more oxygen, and the blood finally returned to her heart and lungs. "Can we play it by ear?" The devil in her made her want to tease them a bit. She lifted her chin. "If you two can show me how incredible you are I might fold sooner."

"Hot damn!" Pete shouted as he slapped his thigh, lifted off his knee, and sat back on the padded bench. He glanced up at the driver and motioned she continue their tour. "We're going to prove to you that we are the perfect men for you."

"I can't wait."

Pete and Thad's willingness to give the three of them time to figure out the ins and outs of this relationship pleased Zoey to no end, giving her hope that tonight would be even more spectacular than the sights of Las Vegas.

They ate at a fabulous Asian restaurant and she had to laugh when Thad seemed unable to keep from making faces at the raw tuna. For their next meal, she'd insist on a place that served cooked beef.

After the gondola ride, they must have walked for over an hour, and fatigue was beginning to take its toll. "Anyone interested in going back to the room for a little R&R?" She was holding both of their hands and gave each a squeeze, hoping they'd get the hint.

They both shrugged, acting like they had no interest in making love to her. Two could play at this game. She yawned. "I could sleep for hours. I think the whole incident with Kara is finally hitting me."

Their expressions instantly changed from disinterest to concern. "Take all the time you need. We don't want to exhaust you." Thad winked. "We have big plans."

Yes! "That right? On second thought, sleep can wait." She had so much to make up to them, and she wanted to start now.

Thad held open the door to the hotel, and they made their way up to the room. Once inside, the bed looked so inviting that Zoey plopped down on the soft spread and toed off her shoes. She hadn't been kidding when she said she was tired. She reached down and rubbed her insteps. "My feet ache." She wasn't used to all this walking in her boots.

All of a sudden, two sets of hands clasped their warm palms around her feet and massaged the insteps. She moaned. "That feels amazing."

After a minute of intense rubbing, both men climbed onto the bed next to her. If the past was any indication, they'd strip her first, leaving her breathless and wanting.

It was time to turn the tables. "I have a request," she said.

Pete clasped her hand. "Anything."

"Wait here."

Before they could stop her, she slipped off the bed and rushed over to her suitcase. From the inside top pocket, she withdrew the velvet cuffs, blindfold, and two soft ropes. Her body heated from the anticipation of doing something so unorthodox. At least for her—a conservative New Englander with a PhD in psychology. Imagining the thrill about to take place, her lower body clenched with delight. She inwardly giggled. Mark and Dave never would have considered doing something so "vulgar."

Zoey whipped around, jutted out one hip, and dangled her new purchases from her open palm. "What do you think?" Her heartbeat soared, praying she hadn't misjudged them.

"Are you kidding me?" Pete's eyes were wider than saucers, and Thad's jaw lowered.

When neither man moved, indecision nearly splintered her.

Laugh and play it off as a joke or show them what she wanted? The latter won.

Zoey squatted, placed the items on the floor then stood, going for her sexiest look. "Do what I say and I might let you use these on me." Breath held, she slinked toward them.

Thad shook his head. "Handcuffs? Ropes? I don't think I could."

From the way his hand clenched then unclenched, he wanted to, but some macho thing was stopping him. She blew out a breath. "They're real soft and won't hurt me if that's what's worrying you."

Thad's cheek sucked in. "You sure?" He came off the bed, bent down, and examined her new toys. "Why haven't you mentioned you wanted to do this before?" His hesitation sounded like he didn't believe her.

"I've hinted at it, but I wasn't sure I was ready. I've never done anything like this before."

Thad turned back to Pete before facing her again. "Why now?" His shoulders squared and his eyes flickered with uncertainty.

This wasn't going to be easy to explain. She inhaled and ran her hands down his muscular arms. His fresh scent teased her nostrils. "Letting you tie me up is all about trust. I want to experience both of you in many ways. Sometimes I like it hard, other times tender."

"Me, too." Thad stroked her face. He looked like he wanted to say more, but wasn't sure how to begin.

A dreadful thought pierced her brain. "Please don't think I'm in any way dissatisfied with our lovemaking. God, no. You both are amazing and beyond my wildest dreams." Oh, shit. She hoped she hadn't blown this. "I was thinking this might be a good way to learn more about each other."

Pete got off the bed and moved toward her in a lazy fashion. "I'm up for experimentin'." The man always knew how to lighten any mood.

"Thank you, Pete. Thad?"

"Let's give it a try."

Relief almost made her knees weak. "Okay then. How about we start our little *experiment* by you two taking off your boots?"

They both got that cheeky grin she adored, and did as she asked. Being in control was a heady feeling.

"What's next?" Pete asked, clearly enjoying their little game.

"I'm going to strip you boys naked, and once I'm finished, I'll decide if I let you take off my clothes."

Thad cocked a brow. "For someone from the east, you're acting like you know your way around a cowboy or two."

She laughed, loving that Thad was willing to sign onto this adventure. "We'll just have to see, won't we?" Her fingers hooked under his waistband and flicked open the button. She pulled back the material and looked inside. "Ooh. Someone is excited." She grinned.

He clamped her wrist. "If you don't hurry, you'll be experiencing some of that excitement before you'd planned."

She tossed him her best pout. "It's all about the seduction. Now shush, and let me do my thing."

Pete stepped closer. "Yeah, Thad, let the lady take her time." He dragged a hand over her hair. "You go right ahead and go as slow as you want, sugar."

Pete always knew how to soothe her. "Thank you." She faced Thad. "For that, you'll have to wait. And no undressing yourself this time."

Thad bent down, picked up the pink cuffs, and examined them. They were fur, built like a hair tie with a metal clasp. "What good will these do? Won't keep a dead animal still."

There was lawman disdain in his voice. She laughed, shook her head, and returned her attention back to Pete.

Because she loved his chest so much, she lifted off his shirt and tossed it on the ground. "These are pecs worthy of a Calvin Klein billboard."

Thad bumped her from behind. "I got a good chest, too."

She glanced over her shoulder. "Never said you didn't, but I won't be rubbing my tits down your body if you don't simmer down." She was enticing him, but Thad seemed blind to her wily ways.

As she unbuckled Pete's belt, she rubbed her chest against his rippled body. Suddenly she was airborne and then dropped onto the bed.

Thad crawled on top of her. "Now, you get this straight, missy. When I want you, I'm gonna git you. I'm not a patient man. Pete, come help me get this little lady nikkid." Thad's hazel eyes darkened and her insides melted.

This was just where she wanted to be. Pete slipped off her pants while Thad pulled off her top rather unceremoniously. "You don't want my hands all over you?" She planned to touch them plenty, but it was fun to act hurt.

"Sure I do, which is why I'm changing the rules. I can't take this 'I'm in control, boys' attitude. We aren't play toys." He unhooked her bra, removed it, and sent it flying somewhere off to the side. "We *men* take what we want." He wagged a finger at her, but the glint in his eyes told her Thad was enjoying this as much as she was. "And I want you."

Now he was talking. "How are you going to do that?"

"You hear that sass, Pete? Strip her now."

Not much to strip as all she had left was her panties, but they were gone in a heartbeat. So much for shopping at a high-end shop. "Maybe I shouldn't have even bothered with undies if you aren't going to admire them."

Thad grinned. "Now you're talking sense." He got off the bed and undressed.

Perhaps she'd pushed him too far. One of these days she'd take her time and make him beg for mercy. *Nah.* Not going to happen with these two. That was what she loved so much about them.

Once they were both gloriously naked, Pete picked up the rope. Zoey looked around. Damn. The bed didn't have anything to attach it to. So much for her plan to be tied down and ravished.

Pete pulled over both heavy chairs and turned them upside down.

"What are you doing?"

He glanced at Thad. "How about blindfolding this little filly? She doesn't need to see how smart we are."

Another smile crossed Thad's face and dimpled one cheek. He was such a handsome man. She loved when he grinned, but his serious side spoke deeply to her, too. He nabbed the sleep mask off the floor.

"You sure about this?" he asked.

"I'm not exactly worried that you'll pull out a knife and carve me up."

He dropped back his head and laughed. "Don't have a knife. Couldn't get it past airport security."

He dealt with gangs, and she bet he was quite competent wielding one. "Good to know."

"Now lie back and let the masters take you so high you won't be able to breathe."

"Okay, but when I suck on your cocks, I would like the blindfold off. I adore seeing you squirm and pant and claw the sheets to keep from climaxing too soon."

Thad planted a palm on his chest. "You saying I'm weak?"

She raised her brows. "Hmm. Blindfold, please."

He grinned and then placed the black mask over her eyes. As soon as she lifted her hands above her head, prickles of anticipation skipped across her skin.

Thad pressed on one nipple. Or at least she assumed it was Thad since the bed hadn't dipped. That one press had been light, but heat seeped straight to her core. Maybe the blindfold was a bad idea. The bed dipped again, indicating Thad had moved.

"Still think this isn't going to work," he said as he lifted her arms from behind her head and slid the spongy cuffs around her wrists.

It didn't matter that it would be easy to get out of them. The idea of being restrained excited her. She returned her arms to above her head and straightened them to elevate her breasts.

"Ah," Thad said. "I see the light."

A second later a hand descended on her left breast and a mouth claimed her right. Instant sizzle danced across her body as he pulled and nipped at the tiny buds. Zoey arched her back for more contact, but he moved his hand down to her belly to keep her still. That only caused more hormones to race through her veins.

"You ready, sugar?" Pete was the one at the end of the bed.

It was bad enough that her pussy was already damp, but then Pete clamped his meaty palm onto her calf.

"I am."

Pete wrapped the soft rope around her ankle. When the knot he'd tied pulled taut, the image of the upside-down chair surfaced. When he repeated the procedure on the other leg, her vulnerability became clear.

"Shit, sugar. Why didn't we do this sooner?"

"I don't know." *Now lick me.*

Once she was tied open, Pete slid between her legs. The men must have signaled each other because Pete flicked his tongue across her wet slit at the same time Thad sucked hard on her nipple. Bolts of desire lit her up. She bunched the sheets above her and gulped in more air. As she tried to slide closer to Pete's delicious tongue, Thad placed a hand on her hip to stop her.

"Stay right there," Thad said. "I got plans."

Being constrained ratcheted her desire but added a ton of frustration at the same time. Her wrists might be secured, but her arms were free to move. Needing to touch one of them, she lowered her arms and ran her fingers over Thad's head. That partially helped satisfy her raging need.

Thad moved to the other nipple, twisting and twirling the sensitive nub until her body was bathed in a light sheen of sweat. Pete added to her neediness by dragging a thumb over her opening while his mouth went to town on her clit. It already felt swollen to twice its original size.

"Please, I need you both."

As if they'd been waiting for her to beg, Pete removed the ropes from around her ankles and then tilted her up on her side. Thad took off her blindfold.

Pete knelt at the end of the bed and lifted her top leg over his shoulder. His covered cock slid up her inner thigh, but stopped short of penetrating her. Damn him. The bed dipped behind her and Thad leaned over her, his warm, moist mouth once more latching onto her nipple. The tension increased as Thad pinched the other tip. A sharp stab of pain lasted only a second before shooting a shard of pleasure right between her legs.

"I'm ready, guys." She gulped in more air.

They didn't answer, damn them, but continued to take her to a new plateau. Pete rubbed her rear with one hand as he stroked her clit with his thumb. Her body caught fire a second before he breached her opening. He then lifted her leg higher and drove into her. The stretching nearly tipped her over the edge.

She grabbed the sheets in front of her for support.

"Thad, if you want some, get in there quick because I'm not sure how long I can last." Pete's words came out in small bursts.

They were supposed to last. She was the weak one.

The bed moved. Footsteps sounded. Thad slipped off the pink cuffs. "Want a little taste?"

To her delight, he placed his large cock a half-inch from her lips. "Yes, please."

Thad slid a hand under her head to give her room to suck on him. With her hands now free, she was able to grab his long shaft and draw it into her mouth. Zoey tried to seductively drag her tongue up his length, but as she neared the top, Pete plowed into her again and multicolor dots flashed before her eyes. His fingers dug into her thighs as she captured Thad's cock in her mouth. The faster Pete thrust into her, the harder she sucked.

Zoey knew the routine. Right before either man came, they'd withdraw and change places, but tonight, she was in control—or so she wanted to believe. Tightening her grip on Thad's hard dick, she drew him deeper into her throat than she ever had before, and wrapped her tongue around his hard dick. Having both men deep inside her was the ultimate joy. They were one, united, together.

Thad twirled her nipple until the pleasure and pain blurred into the ultimate high. Her breaths came out faster and faster, and the men's grunts and groans accelerated. Had Pete not rubbed his thumb over her clit again, she might have been able to stop her orgasm, but a quick pinch tossed her off the cliff.

As her climax claimed her, she opened her mouth and let out a yell that might have every hotel staff member running to her rescue, but she didn't care. Waves of delicious bliss ran up and down her body until she became dizzy.

In a flash, the men disappeared off the bed, but returned ten seconds later. Her pussy throbbed and her breasts pulsated to the beat of her heart. She was in heaven. Thad returned, having donned a condom. Given the size of his swollen dick, she bet that took work to get on.

"Get on your elbows and knees and be prepared for some real loving."

Chapter Thirty-Four

Thad was at the point where he was ready to burst. Having Zoey's mouth around his cock, taking him deep, then sucking on him hard had been the most amazing experience. Now he was ready to drive into her and make them one.

He moved behind her and clasped onto her delicate waist. The scent of her sex made his balls bullet hard. He itched to tease her without mercy for what she'd done to him, and nudged open her folds with his cock.

Don't rush. Go slow. Make her lose her mind.

Pete moved into position in front of her and cupped her face. When he closed his eyes, Thad smiled. Pete had always been cavalier about sex, but Zoey had turned him into a serious lover. He seemed to be quite tender, caring, and yes, even sensitive to her needs.

Zoey's soft, dewy skin altered something inside him. No matter how long it took, Thad would make sure Dr. Zoey Donovan knew without a doubt that he and Pete were the men for her.

When he brushed his palms against her distended nipples, his cock pulsed. He had to have her. Pete was on his own. When Thad drove into her, her honey-coated walls welcomed him. All was good until she gasped, and when she clamped down on his dick, he almost lost it. Where the hell was his control? He slid out of her creamy channel and palmed her heavy tits.

Her head bobbed on Pete's cock. His roommate's grunts quickened, implying he'd explode soon. Zoey was pushing her hips back, trying to take in more of Thad's cock. Then Pete let out a feral scream, signaling his climax was both powerful and earth-shattering.

Damn it, Pete. Thad had wanted them to come together. He stopped all movement in the hopes he'd garner a bit more control, but it didn't help. Her nipples brushing against his palms turned him into a mass of need.

As soon as she lifted her head, Pete dropped onto his haunches and Thad withdrew, ready to go back in a moment. Needing her heat, he lowered his chest to her back and wrapped his arms around her, inhaling her hair's sweet peachy scent. Everything about this woman tantalized him, and drove him crazy with need.

Thad wanted to take these last few minutes slow, but she lowered her head to her hands, raising her ass. The change in angle caught him off guard and signaled the beginning of the end for him.

He reached between her thighs and rubbed her tiny pearl. That always set her off.

"Ah, ah, ah. Yes!"

Her plea was all it took to catapult him over the edge. His vision blurred and his heart pressed in on his lungs. With renewed vigor he lost himself in her sweet body. As his cum jettisoned out, he held her with all his might, promising to love her for the rest of his life.

Minutes later, Pete tapped his shoulder. Thad needed to let

her go. He pulled out and let Pete clean her up. Once he finished, Thad stretched out next to her then pulled her on top of him, loving the feel of her body pressed against his.

Pete slipped onto the other side. "I have an idea," Pete said.

Zoey's eyes only half lifted. "I'm listening."

"What do you say you move in with us?"

✧   ✧   ✧

This time Zoey answered without hesitation. "I think that's a fantastic idea." She slipped off Thad and rolled onto her back, and then lifted up on her elbows so she could see both men.

"Really?" Pete's voice held more surprise than she'd hoped.

"Yes, really. Make no mistake. I love both of you more than you can know. I said I didn't think marrying you right away was a good idea only because I wanted you to be sure you wanted to be with me." She tapped her chest. "I have a tendency to analyze things too much, and I don't always express my emotions like I should." Thad ran his hand over her breasts and down her belly. She immediately grabbed his wrist. "No fair playing with me. We need to have a discussion without our hormones interfering with our thought process."

He tapped her nose. "Did you know that the first thing that attracted me to you was your amazing ability to be logical in the face of adversity?"

She laughed at his assessment. "I think better when I'm logical."

Pete waved his hand. "Let's stop *analyzing* this anymore. Our woman has agreed to move in with us. Let's leave it at that. I suggest we all take a long shower with lots of touching then go eat. We have a surprise for you."

"Another one? I thought the gondola ride was the high-light."

Pete shook his head. "What would you say to seeing a Cirque Du Soleil show tonight?"

Her breath caught. "Seriously? I've always wanted to see one."

"If you can control yourself in the shower, we just might make it in time."

She punched him. Life with these two was going to be amazing.

✧ ✧ ✧

Six months later

"Let me make the sash tighter." Zoey couldn't believe how much weight Jamie had lost in this past half year. Even though Zoey understood the reason, she didn't like it. After retying the bridesmaid bow, Jamie still swam in the dress. They'd bought the outfits three months ago and Jamie had been on a downward spiral ever since. Her boyfriend's betrayal, coupled with the fact Jamie no longer had someone to take care of, had taken a once vibrant woman down a dangerous path. The only ones who'd benefitted had been her patients. Fortunately, Amber had intervened and convinced Jamie to leave the hospital for a job at the free clinic. So far, the new job seemed to be working out, but Jamie was still working too many hours.

Today was Amber Delacroix's wedding to Cade Carter and Stone Benson, and Zoey didn't want anything to ruin it. "Remember to act happy and be nice to Max Gruden. He's quite a catch." Amber had paired Jamie up with that groomsman because he'd experienced something terrible in his life, too, and had emerged from the depths of despair. He'd even seemed willing to help Jamie.

Jamie faced her. "I am happy. See?" She gave her an award-winning smile. "But if you're trying to match me up, no thanks. Didn't you see him at the bar when I met Thad and Pete? He didn't say a word. I swear my hospice patients had more life inside them than he did."

"Thad worked with him on an arson case, and he never said anything to that effect. Besides, that was before he found the arsonist who killed his family. Give him a chance." Since then, he'd gotten his life together. Jamie would benefit from a man like him.

"I'd rather eat a live fish."

The image made Zoey laugh, but she knew when to push and when to pull back. "You only have to dance with him once. That's all. Let's go back to the living room. I can hear everyone talking." They left the spare bedroom and assembled with the rest the wedding party outside Nana's kitchen.

Amber was beaming, Becky seemed to be in a mental fairyland, no doubt dreaming of the day she'd be walking down the aisle, and Melissa just smiled and giggled at something Amber had said. Amber's boss, Tammy White, stood off to the side, looking sophisticated and regal.

The wedding planner finished fussing with Amber's dress. "Looking good, ladies. Let's get this show on the road."

Nana was watching from the side. "Carrie Sue, pick up Amber's train. Won't do no good to get that white dress dirty."

When everyone was assembled in order, they all traipsed outside toward the barn. Stone's father was waiting next to the door to escort Amber down the aisle. She'd tried to contact her dad, but he made some excuse why he couldn't make it to her wedding. That had to hurt.

Someone had laid down wide white paper, and secured it with rocks on both sides so their heels wouldn't sink into the dirt or soil Amber's dress. Maybe getting married in a barn wasn't the best idea, but it sure would be fun.

Two of Erin's sons pulled open the barn door, and the music piped up. The boom box sat next the makeshift altar and sounded rather tinny in the cavernous place, but it brought a smile to Amber's face, which was all that mattered.

Two rows of folding chairs were on either side of the aisle. Big pink bows adorned the chairs for the bride's side and navy blue ones for friends of the grooms. The ceiling rafters had been decked out in white Christmas lights, while gas heaters stood guard along the walls. Tables clustered near the back of the room were filled with food and interspersed with vases of fresh cut flowers. While Nana claimed no animals had been in here in years, the scent of hay still floated above the rich aroma of the floral arrangements. The large ornate crystal chandelier seemed out of place in the rustic setting, but it was probably Amber's mom's way of bringing a bit of elegance to the old place.

Reverend James, who often officiated weddings for multiple partners, stood on the podium next to Stone, Cade, Thad, Dan Hartwick, Ethan Harper, Max Gruden, and three other groomsmen.

Finally, the entourage had assembled on the raised platform, and Zoey looked over at Pete, who was in the third row on the left. He was such a handsome man. As soon as the ceremony began, her mind wandered. Zoey could be the one standing on this stage getting married to Pete and Thad, but Ms. Logical had yet to set a date. What was stopping her?

Pete often talked about kids. In fact, he volunteered his time playing with the children at the shelter, and Zoey knew Thad wanted a big family.

"You may now kiss the bride," the minister said, pride lacing his voice, "but keep it short, you three." The congregation laughed and Zoey smiled. Stone's kiss was soft, sweet, and oh, so romantic. Cade gently tugged the beautiful bride away, dipped her into a deep backbend and planted a dramatic kiss on her lips. The crowd cheered and the music once more boomed.

The threesome marched back down the aisle. By the time they were halfway to the back door, the crowd abandoned their seats and surrounded the loving couple. Pete worked his way through the crowd toward her.

"Hey, beautiful," Pete said.

They hugged. "Ready to eat?" she asked. "I'm starving."

"Sure, but in a minute," Pete said.

Thad took her hand. "We want to speak with you outside for a minute. This won't take long." They led her past the crowd.

The serious look on their faces scared her. "What is it?"

Thad glanced over at Pete. "We don't want to wait any longer."

"For?"

Pete stepped forward. "You know what for. To set a date. I believe I've proven to both you and Thad that I'm in this for life."

Giddiness flooded her. She'd wanted to bring up the wedding for a month now, but somehow wanted to see if they meant it when they'd asked her to marry them.

"So?" Thad asked.

Her mind raced. "I was hoping you'd asked again. How about in eight weeks? It takes time to set up a wedding."

Both men beamed. "Eight weeks it is." Thad grabbed her hand. "Let's go tell the world."

She laughed at his pure joy. They rushed back inside and wove their way through all those congratulating Amber and her men. Thad brought Zoey up to the stage and tapped the microphone.

Heat raced up her face. "We shouldn't take the limelight away from Stone, Cade, and Amber."

Thad waved a hand. "Nonsense. This will make them even happier."

Thad tapped the microphone again and the crowd finally quieted. "I have an announcement. One that has been a long time coming. Dr. Zoey Donovan has agreed to marry me and Pete eight weeks from today. And you're all invited."

The crowd clapped and cheered as the men bestowed so many kisses on her that she lost track.

"Hey, don't you boys hog her. I need to be the first to congratulate her."

The men broke apart, and Nana, still dressed in her jeans and apron, welcomed her with open arms. Emotion choked her. Zoey was finally home.

The End

About the author

I love to read, write, dream, and connect with people. A book with a happily ever after is a must, as is having characters I can relate to. My men are always wonderful, dynamic, smart, strong, and the best lovers in the world.

I love hearing from readers, too!!

You can contact me at:
velladayauthor@gmail.com

Visit my website at:
www.velladay.com

Check me out on facebook, too at:
www.facebook.com/vella.day.90

Follow me on twitter at:
www.twitter.com/velladay4

I also write as Melody Snow Monroe:
www.melodymonroe.com

Want to know more? Sign up for my newsletter:
http://eepurl.com/I0OX5

OTHER BOOKS
BY THE AUTHOR

MONTANA PROMISES

GENRE: Medical Romance, Contemporary Western Romance, Erotica ménage romance, (MFM)

PROMISES OF MERCY (BOOK 1)

Killing is wrong. The reason doesn't matter.

When oncology nurse, Amber Delacroix, learns her reckless brother has been in a paralyzing motorcycle accident, sorrow fills her soul. He's murdered a few days later, and now she's utterly devastated. Adding to life's cruelty, the cowboy cop assigned to her brother's case brings her in for questioning.

Stone Benson, the paramedic who brought Amber's brother into the hospital, stays by her side throughout the tragedy. He treats her with kindness and compassion—something she hasn't experienced much in her life. Amber yearns for more than his comforting words, and they embark on a tremulous journey. Just when she feels that their relationship is at a turning point, he reveals that he likes to share his women with his good friend and roommate, Cade. That turns out to be a huge problem, because Cade is the cop who believes she's guilty of killing her brother.

As chance would have it, another murder occurs when both Cade and Amber are in the same location. Realizing she's not the mercy killer, Cade offers a heartfelt apology—one that includes dinner and a sharing of souls. When things heat up between them, she succumbs to his passionate ways. The big question that plagues her now is where does Stone fit in?

Stone knows exactly where Amber needs to be. Right between him and his best friend, Cade. He'll do whatever is necessary to convince her that she has finally met two men she can trust and build a life with.

Too bad the killer has other ideas. When he goes after Amber, what will the men need to do to save her in time to pursue a loving ménage relationship?

PUBLISHER'S NOTE: This adult contemporary romance contains explicit sexual content, graphic language, and situations that some readers may find objectionable (double penetration, ménage, violence). Not intended for those under the age of 18.

CAVEAT: But if you love medical erotica with a contemporary western setting, this book is for you.

FOUNDATION FOR THREE (BOOK 2)

You aren't free to love until you realize you can't make someone love you back.

As builder Pete Banks is finishing a remodel for psychologist Zoey Donovan, she arrives home dazed, injured, and distraught. As he calms her down, she draws him in with her halting story of how Thad Dalton, a local cop and Pete's roommate, saved her life. When Pete learns Thad was shot, he's torn between staying with a woman in need and being there for his roommate.

Zoey never intended to blurt out to a man she's never met how she almost died, but Pete's understanding nature alters something inside her. Usually, she's the one trying to figure out her clients' needs, not the other way around. While Pete Banks is one of kind, she can't tear her mind from Thad, the man who risked his life for her.

Detective Thad Dalton was never so scared in his life when a madman grabs Zoey in the hospital corridor and threatens to kill her if his demands aren't met. Thad ends up taking a bullet to save her but would do it again if it means having her in his life.

When Zoey, Thad, and Pete attend Thad's parents' anniversary party sparks fly. She realizes she wants a more personal connection to these two men. While Thad's on board, Pete doesn't think he's worthy. His self-loathing forces him to retreat and casts doubt on their future together.

Zoey and Thad are justifiably both mad and hurt. It's going to take a miracle to patch this threesome back together for their happily ever after.

PUBLISHER'S NOTE: This adult contemporary romance contains explicit sexual content, graphic language, and situations that some readers may find objectionable (double penetration, ménage, violence). Not intended for those under the age of 18.

PACK WARS

NOTE: These THREE novellas (50K each) were previously released as single titles.

GENRE: Paranormal Werewolf Romance, Paranormal Erotica, Paranormal Menage (MFM)

TRAINING THEIR MATE (BOOK 1)

She failed to stop him. Now he's coming after her.

Liz Wharton has one goal—to kill the man who raped her mother. Had she known Harvey Couch was a werewolf, she never would have tried to take him on by herself.

Determined to put an end to the pest bent on revenge, Harvey sends his goons after her. When two wolves attack her, Liz is sure she's hallucinating. Good thing Trax Field is there to stop them.

Trax and Dante Field, members of the Pack, have devoted their lives to stopping bad shifters like Harvey Couch. Saving

Liz would have been just an ordinary day, but when Trax finds her huddled in an alley, bruised and shaken, he's convinced she's his mate.

To keep her safe, Trax and Dante hold her captive in their loft apartment. When they aren't searching for Couch, Trax and his brother spend the night training their future mate in the art of bondage and sensual pleasures. How will they be able to convert her into embracing not only their lifestyle but also their animalistic side?

CLAIMING THEIR MATE (BOOK 2)

She saw the killer. Now he wants her dead.

Realtor Chelsea Wilson enters a vacant home she wants to show and comes face-to-face with a dead man—and a killer. Freaked out, she runs, but the killer nabs her.

Ricardo Mendez, a werewolf who runs a drug operation, doesn't need a witness to the murder. He viciously attacks her, but the dead man's brother, werewolf Kurt Wendlick and his Pack partner, Drake Stanton stop the final assault.

When Kurt and Drake save Chelsea, they're certain she's their mate and will do anything to keep her safe. Her loving ways puts Kurt in a tailspin. He wants to claim her, but first he needs to avenge his brother's murder.

What can Chelsea do to help the tormented man? Will the three ever explore the world of BSDM together?

RESCUING THEIR VIRGIN MATE (BOOK 3)

She's sold into slavery. Now she's on the run.

All Elena Sanchez wanted was to get on the plane to Costa Rica and visit her parents. When the authorities tell her they need to search her, she finds herself drugged and caged by a

362

sadistic bastard who plans to sell her virginity to the highest bidder.

Two Pack members, Clay Demmers and Dirk Tilton, learn that Elena, Harvey Couch's former secretary, is a victim of a human trafficking scheme. They go undercover and bid for her. As soon as they see her, they realize she's their mate. More determined than ever to save her, they buy her, but at what cost?

Elena doesn't know who to trust. They inform her they're werewolves, but is that any better than being sold into slavery to humans? With care, Clay and Dirk teach her how to embrace her submissive ways. The problem is this good Catholic girl likes it. Will the guilt from her upbringing prevent her from having the best ménage relationship possible or can she find a way to have both?

PUBLISHER'S NOTE: This adult contemporary romance contains explicit sexual content, graphic language, and situations that some readers may find objectionable (double penetration, ménage, violence). Not intended for those under the age of 18.

THE BURIED TRILOGY

NOTE: These books have been published previously under their separate titles.

GENRE: Romance, Mystery, Thriller, Suspense, Serial killer

BURIED ALIVE (BOOK 1)

When loner homicide detective, Hunter Markum, finds the skeletons of four women in a mass grave just outside Tampa, Florida, he's distraught as hell. It leaves a bitter taste in his mouth, as it's a harsh reminder of his own sister's unsolved murder.

For the first time in his career, the usually detached Hunter feels a more personal connection to this case, and agrees to team up with Dr. Kerry Herlihy, a forensic anthropologist, in the hopes she can decipher the buried bones. Her compassion for these cold case victims draws her to him.

Kerry too finds Hunter's strong family attachment appealing, as her family abandoned her as a child, but she tamps down her desires. The case must come first.

Against their will, the attraction ignites, and their quest to find the killer soon reveals the identities of the victims and the chilling fact that each woman had been abused. When Kerry's work throws her directly in the killer's path, Hunter realizes how much she's come to mean to him. In a race against the clock, Hunter must apprehend the murderer if he hopes to save the woman he loves once she's buried alive.

BURIED SECRETS (BOOK 2)

When rookie Tampa Police Officer, Jenna Holliday, goes undercover at a local occult store to investigate a rash of grave robberies, she never expects to become the victim of a black magic death spell.

Dr. Sam Bonita, a forensic anthropologist, in search of answers regarding a headless body, visits the store where Jenna works and is enchanted by her.

Believing Sam holds the key to her case, Jenna tries to get close to him. When his house is burned to the ground, with both of them inside, she's unsure if her cover has been blown or if Sam is the object of some deranged killer.

Only after a series of murders, and a few death threats, do Jenna and Sam suspect a serial killer is on the loose and after both of them.

BURIED DEEP (BOOK 3)

When forensic anthropologist, Dr. Lara Romano, first examines the exhumed skeletons of two Native American men buried in Tampa, she has no idea she's caught the eye of a serial killer who's intent on dipping her in plaster and covering her in hot wax to complete a twisted ode to his Seminole mother.

Isolated by her profound hearing loss she suffered as a child, Lara jumps at the chance to work in the field and prove she's as competent as any hearing scientist. Not even the easy-on-the-eyes cop bucking to work with her will distract her from her goal.

Missing Persons detective, Jake Kinsey, needs a high profile case to land him a job in Homicide. Though he suspects the attractive rookie scientist may hinder his success, he believes the cadavers in Lara's investigation are linked to his current case—eight missing men, all Native Americans, believed to be dead.

What Jake and Lara don't realize is that the missing bodies have been left in plain sight as part of a tableau constructed by the madman who plans to use Lara and Jake for his final scene.